THE EAGLE
OF THE
NINTH

MAR CVS

ROSEMARY SUTCLIFF

THE EAGLE

OF THE

NINTH

Illustrated by

C. WALTER HODGES

New York
HENRY Z. WALCK, INC.

First published in England by Oxford University Press in 1954
First published in the United States of America in 1954

Reprinted 1955, 1957, 1959, 1961

Printed in Great Britain by Richard Clay and Company, Ltd.,
Bungay, Suffolk

Foreword

Sometime about the year 117 A.D., the Ninth Legion, which was stationed at Eburacum where York now stands, marched north to deal with a rising among the Caledonian tribes, and was never heard of again.

During the excavations at Silchester nearly eighteen hundred years later, there was dug up under the green fields which now cover the pavements of Calleva Atrebatum, a wingless Roman Eagle, a cast of which can be seen to this day in Reading Museum. Different people have had different ideas as to how it came to be there, but no one knows, just as no one knows what happened to the Ninth Legion after it marched into the northern mists.

It is from these two mysteries, brought together, that I have made the story of ' The Eagle of the Ninth '.

R. S.

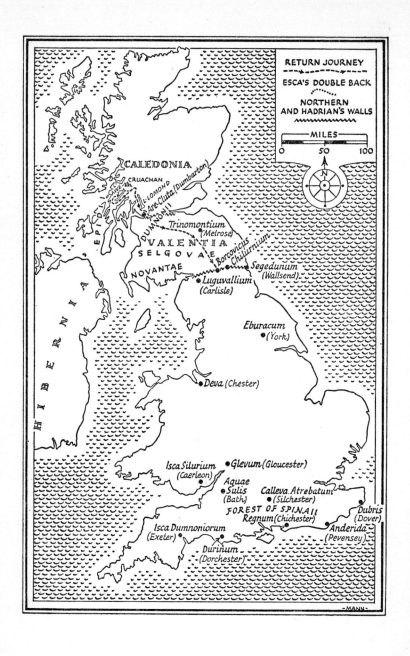

Contents

I	FRONTIER FORT	1
II	FEATHERS IN THE WIND	12
III	ATTACK	24
IV	THE LAST ROSE FALLS	37
V	SATURNALIA GAMES	46
VI	ESCA	60
VII	TWO WORLDS MEETING	72
VIII	THE HEALER WITH THE KNIFE	82
IX	TRIBUNE PLACIDUS	94
X	MARCHING ORDERS	104
XI	ACROSS THE FRONTIER	118
XII	THE WHISTLER IN THE DAWN	126
XIII	THE LOST LEGION	138
XIV	THE FEAST OF NEW SPEARS	153
XV	VENTURE INTO THE DARK	166
XVI	THE RING-BROOCH	183

CONTENTS

XVII   THE WILD HUNT 197

XVIII THE WATERS OF LETHE 208

XIX   TRADUI'S GIFT 220

XX   VALEDICTORY 231

XXI   THE OLIVE-WOOD BIRD 244

      LIST OF PLACE-NAMES 256

I

FRONTIER FORT

FROM the Fosseway westward to Isca Dumnoniorum the
road was simply a British trackway, broadened and
roughly metalled, strengthened by corduroys of logs in
the softest places, but otherwise unchanged from its old estate,
as it wound among the hills, thrusting farther and farther into
the wilderness.

It was a busy road and saw many travellers: traders with
bronze weapons and raw yellow amber in their ponies' packs;
country folk driving shaggy cattle or lean pigs from village to
village; sometimes a band of tawny-haired tribesmen from
farther west; strolling harpers and quack-oculists, too, or a
light-stepping hunter with huge wolf-hounds at his heel; and
from time to time a commissariat wagon going up and down to
supply the Roman frontier post. The road saw them all, and
the cohorts of the Eagles for whom all other travellers must
make way.

There was a cohort of leather-clad auxiliaries on the road

today, swinging along at the steady Legion's pace that had brought them down from Isca Silurium at twenty miles a day; the new garrison coming to relieve the old one at Isca Dumnoniorum. On they went, following the road that now ran out on a causeway between sodden marsh and empty sky, now plunged into deep boar-hunted forest, or lifted over bleak uplands where nothing grew save furze and thorn-scrub. On with never a halt nor a change of rhythm, marching century by century, the sun bright on the Standard at their head, and the rolling dust-cloud kicked up over the pack-train behind.

At the head of the column marched the Pilus Prior Centurion, the cohort Commander, the pride that shone from him showing clearly that this was his first command. They were, he had long since decided, a command worthy of anyone's pride; six hundred yellow-haired giants recruited from the tribes of Upper Gaul, with the natural fighting power of mountain cats, drilled and hammered into what he firmly believed to be the finest auxiliary cohort ever to serve with the Second Legion. They were a newly joined cohort; many of the men had not yet proved themselves in action, and the spear-shaft of their Standard had no honours on it, no gilded laurel wreath nor victor's crown. The honours were all to win— perhaps during his command.

The Commander was a complete contrast to his men: Roman to his arrogant finger-tips, wiry and dark as they were raw-boned and fair. The olive-skinned face under the curve of his crested helmet had not a soft line in it anywhere—a harsh face it would have been, but that it was winged with laughter lines, and between his level black brows showed a small raised scar that marked him for one who had passed the Raven Degree of Mithras.

Centurion Marcus Flavius Aquila had seen little of the Eagles until a year ago. His first ten years had been lived quietly with his mother on the family farm near Clusium, while his father soldiered in Judaea, in Egypt, and here in Britain. They had been going to join his father in Britain, but before the time came for them to do so, rebellion had flared up among the northern tribes, and the Ninth Hispana, his father's Legion, had marched north to deal with it, and never came marching back.

His mother had died soon afterwards, leaving him to be brought up in Rome by a rather foolish aunt and the plump and purse-proud official who was her husband. Marcus had loathed the official, and the official had loathed Marcus. They saw everything with different eyes. Marcus came of a line of soldiers—one of those Equestrian families who, when the rest of their kind had turned from soldiering to trade and finance, had kept to the old way of life, and remained poor but held their noses high in consequence. The official came of a line of officials, and his code of life was quite other than Marcus's. Neither of them had a shred of understanding for each other's ideas, and they had both been thankful when Marcus was eighteen and could apply for a centurion's commission.

Marcus, his eyes narrowed into the sun as he marched, smiled to himself a little wryly, as he remembered how almost pathetically thankful that plump official had been. (Tramp, tramp, tramp, said the cohort's feet behind him.)

He had asked to be sent to Britain, though it meant starting in an auxiliary cohort instead of a line-of-battle one, partly because his father's elder brother had settled there when his own years of soldiering were done, but mostly because of his father. If ever anything became known of the lost Legion, it would be known first in Britain, and it might even be that here in Britain he would find out something for himself.

Marching down the Isca Dumnoniorum road in the run-honey evening light, he found himself thinking about his father. He had very vivid memories of a slight, dark man with laughter lines at the corners of his eyes, who had come home from time to time, and taught him to fish, to play ' Flash the Fingers ', and throw a javelin. He remembered vividly that last leave of all. His father had just been appointed to command the First Cohort of the Hispana, which meant having charge of the Eagle and being something very like second-in-

command of the Legion beside; and he had been like a jubilant
boy about it. But his mother had been faintly anxious, almost
as if she knew. . . .

'If it was any *other* Legion!' she had said. 'You have told
me yourself that the Hispana has a bad name.'

And his father had replied: 'But I would not have it any
other Legion if I could. I held my first command in the
Hispana, and a man's first Legion is apt to hold chief place in
his heart ever after, be its name good or bad; and now that I go
back to it as First Cohort, we will see whether there is nothing
can be done to better its name.' He had turned to his small
son, laughing. 'Presently it will be your turn. It has fallen
on evil days, but we will make a Legion of the Hispana yet,
you and I.'

Looking back across the years, Marcus remembered that his
father's eyes had been very bright, like the eyes of a man going
into action; and the light had caught suddenly in the great
flawed emerald of the signet-ring he always wore, striking from
it a spark of clear green fire. Odd how one remembered
things like that: little things that somehow mattered.

(Tramp, tramp, tramp, came the sound of the cohort's feet
behind him.)

It would be pleasant, he thought, if Uncle Aquila was like
his father. He had not met his uncle yet; after learning his
foot-drill he had arrived in Britain in the sleety days of late
autumn, and been sent straight up to Isca; but he had a rather
vague invitation to spend his leave with him at Calleva, when
he had any leave to spend. It would be very pleasant if Uncle
Aquila was like his father.

Not of course that he and his uncle were likely to have much
to do with each other. In a few years' time he would probably
be serving in quite a different part of the Empire, since a cohort
centurion seldom moved up all the way in the same Legion.

All the way . . . from his present rank right up to his father's
rank of First Cohort; and after that? For most of the men
who got so far there was nothing after that, but for the out-
standing few who went farther—as Marcus intended to go

farther—the ways divided there. One could become a camp commandant, as Uncle Aquila had done, or one could go on, by way of the Praetorian Guard, to try for command of a Legion. Legion Commanders were almost always men of Senator's rank, with no experience of soldiering save a year's service as Military Tribune in their youth; but by long custom the two Egyptian Legions were exceptions to the rule. They were commanded by professional soldiers; and an Egyptian Legion had been Marcus's shining goal for as long as he could remember.

But one day, when he had finished with the Eagles, when he had made an honourable name and become Prefect of his Egyptian Legion, he would go home to the Etruscan hills, and perhaps even buy back the old farm, which the plump official had ruthlessly sold to defray expenses. For a moment he remembered almost painfully the sunlit courtyard flickered over with the shadow of pigeons' wings, and the wild olive-tree in the loop of the stream, on a twisted root of which he had once found a kind of gall growing, that was shaped something like a little bird. He had cut it from the root with the new knife his father had given him, and spent much loving care, all one absorbed summer evening, trimming and carving feathers on it. He had that little bird still.

The road topped a gentle rise, and suddenly Isca Dumnoniorum lay before them, with the fortress-crowned Red Mount dark with shadows against the evening sky; and Marcus came back to the present with a jerk. The farm in the Etruscan hills could wait until he was old and tired and famous; in the present was the glory of his first command.

The British town was spread below the southern scarp of the Mount; a sprawling huddle of reed-thatched roofs, every colour from the gold of honey to the black of dried peat, according to the age of the thatch; with the squared, clean lines of the Roman forum and basilica looking oddly rootless in their midst; and the faint haze of wood-smoke lying over all.

The road led straight through the town and up to the cleared slope beyond, to the Praetorian gate of the fort; here and there, crimson or saffron-cloaked men turned to look at the cohort as it swung by, a look that was reserved rather than hostile. Dogs sat scratching in odd corners, lean pigs rooted among the garbage piles, and women with bracelets of gold or copper on very white arms sat in hut doorways, spinning or grinding corn. The blue smoke of many cooking-fires curled up into the quiet air, and the savoury smell of many evening meals mingled with the blue reek of wood-smoke and the sharper tang of horse-droppings, which Marcus had by now come to associate with all British towns. Little that was Roman was here as yet, despite the stone-built forum. One day there would be straight streets, he supposed, and temples and bath-houses and a Roman way of life. But as yet it was a place where two worlds met without mingling: a British town huddled under the dominion of the turf ramparts where once the tribe had had its stronghold and now the Roman sentries paced up and down. He looked about him under the curve of his helmet as he marched, knowing that this place would be part of his life for the next year; then looked up to the turf ramparts, and saw a Roman banner drooping in the still air, and the tall crest of a sentry burning in the sunset, and heard a trumpet-call ring out, as it seemed, from the fiery sky.

.   .   .   .   .

'You have brought clear skies with you,' said Centurion Quintus Hilarion, lounging in the window of the Commander's quarters, and peering into the night. 'But Hercle! you need not expect it to last.'

'As bad as that?' said Centurion Marcus Aquila, who was seated on the table.

'Quite as bad as that! It rains always, here in the west, save when Typhon, the father of all ills, brews up a mist to come between a man and his own feet. By the time you have served your year here you will have toadstools sprouting out of your ears, the same as me, *and* not from the damp alone!'

'From what beside?' inquired Marcus with interest.

'Oh, lack of company, for one thing. I am a sociable soul

myself; I like my friends around me.' He turned from the window, and folded up on to a low cushioned bench, hugging his knees. 'Ah well, I am off to rub away the blue mould as soon as I have marched the troops back to Isca.'

'Going on leave?'

The other nodded. 'Long leave, lovely leave, among the fleshpots of Durinum.'

'Durinum—that is your home?' asked Marcus.

'Yes. My father retired and settled there a few years ago. There is a surprisingly good circus, and plenty of people— pretty girls too. A pleasant enough place to get back to, out of the wilds.' An idea seemed to strike him. 'What shall you do when *your* leave falls due? I suppose, coming out from home, you have no one here to go to?'

'I have an uncle at Calleva, though I have not yet met him,' Marcus said, 'and certainly there is no one at home I should want to spend my leave with.'

'Father and mother both dead?' inquired Hilarion with friendly interest.

'Yes. My father went with the Ninth Legion.'

'Pericol! You mean when they——'

'Disappeared. Yes.'

'So. That is bad!' said Hilarion, wagging his head. 'A deal of ugly stories, there were—still are, for that matter; and of course, they did lose the Eagle.'

Instantly Marcus was up in arms to defend his father and his father's Legion. 'Since not a man of the Legion came back, it is scarcely a matter for wonder that neither did the Eagle,' he flashed.

'Surely not,' agreed Hilarion amicably. 'I was not blowing on your father's honour, so you can keep your feathers on, my Marcus.' He looked up at the other with a wide, friendly grin, and suddenly Marcus, who had been ready to quarrel with him the instant before, found himself grinning back.

It was several hours since Marcus had marched his cohort across the hollow-ringing bridge, answering the sentry's challenge, 'Fourth Gaulish Auxiliaries of the Second Legion, come to relieve this garrison.' Dinner was over, in the officers' mess, with the Quartermaster, the Surgeon, and the double complement of ranker centurions. Marcus had taken charge of the pay-chest keys—in a garrison as small as this there was no paymaster; and for the past hour, here in the Commander's quarters in the Praetorium, he and Hilarion had been going through the office work of the frontier fort. Now, crested helmets and embossed breastplates laid aside, the two of them were taking their ease.

Through the doorless opening Marcus could see almost the whole of the sleeping-cell, the narrow cot piled with gay native rugs, the polished oaken chest, the lamp-bracket high on the bare wall, and nothing more. The outer room held the battered writing-table on which Marcus was sitting, a cross-legged camp-stool, the cushioned bench to represent comfort, another chest for the record rolls, and a bronze pedestal lamp of peculiarly hideous design.

In the little silence that had fallen between them, Marcus looked round him at the austere room in the yellow flood of lamplight, and to him it seemed beautiful. But though it would be his tomorrow, for this one night he was a guest here, and he looked back to his host with a quick smile of apology for having looked too soon at his surroundings with the eye of mastery.

Hilarion grinned. 'You will not be feeling like that this day next year.'

'I wonder,' said Marcus, swinging one sandalled foot and idly watching the swing of it. 'What does one do here, beside growing toadstools? Is there good hunting?'

'Good enough; it is the one thing to be said for this particular corner of the Empire. Boar and wolf in the winter, and the forest swarms with deer. There are several hunters below in the town, who will take you out for the price of the day's work. Unwise to go alone, of course.'

Marcus nodded. 'Have you any advice for me? I am new to this country.'

The other considered. 'No, I think not.' Then he sat up with a jerk. 'Yes, I have, if no one has warned you already. But it has nothing to do with the hunting. It is the priest-kind—the wandering Druids. If one of them appears in the district, or you get the least idea that there is one about, look to your weapons. Good advice, that is.'

'The Druids?' Marcus was surprised and puzzled. 'But surely Suetonius Paulinus dealt with them once and for all, sixty years ago?'

'As an organized priesthood, maybe; but as easily hold off these heathen mists with a palm-leaf umbrella as end the Druids by destroying their stronghold. They spring up still, from time to time, and wherever they do spring up, there is likely to be trouble for the Eagles. They were the heart and soul of British resistance in the early days, and even now, when there is any sign of unrest among the tribes, you can wager your sandals there is a holy man at the bottom of it.'

'Go on,' Marcus prodded, as the other seemed to have finished. 'This becomes interesting.'

B

'Well, the thing is this. They can preach holy war, and
that is ever the most deadly kind, for it recks nothing of con-
sequences.' Hilarion spoke slowly, as though he was thinking
the thing out as he went along. 'The frontier tribes are not like
those of the south coast, who were half Romanized before ever
we landed; they are a wild lot, and superbly brave; but even
they have mostly come to think that we are not fiends of darkness, and they have enough sense to see that destroying the local
garrison will only mean a punitive expedition and their homes
and standing crops burned, and a stronger garrison with a
heavier hand thereafter. But let one of their holy men lay hold
of them, and all that goes whistling down the wind. They
cease to think whether there can be any good come of their
rising, cease to think at all. They are keeping faith with their
gods by smoking out a nest of the unbelievers, and what happens after is no concern of theirs, for they are going West of the
Sunset by the warriors' road. And when you get men into that
state there is apt to be trouble coming.'

Outside in the quiet darkness the trumpets sounded for the
second watch of the night. Hilarion uncurled himself and
stood up. 'We had best do Late Rounds together tonight,' he
said, and reached for his sword, slipping the baldrick over his
head. 'I am native born,' he added as though in explanation.
'That is how I come to have some understanding of these
matters.'

'I imagined that you must be.' Marcus tested a buckle of
his own equipment. 'You have had no holy man round here, I
suppose?'

'No, but my predecessor had a certain amount of trouble just
before I took over, and the trouble-maker slipped through his
fingers and disappeared. We lived a month or two on Vesuvius
—all the more so as the harvest was bad for the second year
running—but it never erupted.'

Footsteps sounded outside, and a red light glimmered at the
window; and they went out together to the Duty Centurion,
who stood outside with a flaring torch. The clashing Roman
salute was exchanged, and they set out on their tour of the

darkened fort, from sentry-post to sentry-post along the rampart
walk, from guard-point to guard-point, with the low exchange
of the password; lastly to the small lighted room in the Praetorium where the pay-chest was kept and the Standard stood
against the wall, and between rounds the Duty Centurion sat
with his drawn sword on the table before him, through the
night.

Marcus thought: 'After tonight it will be for me alone to
follow the centurion's torch from guard-post to guard-post,
from barrack block to horse-lines, seeing that all is well with the
frontier of the Empire.'

Next morning, after the formal take-over ceremony in the
forum, the old garrison marched out. Marcus watched them
go, out across the ditch and downhill between the crowding
hovels of the native town whose reed-thatched roofs were gold-
dusted by the morning sun. Century after Century, marching
away up the long road that led to Isca; and at their head the
glint of gold and crimson that was the cohort Standard. He
narrowed his eyes into the piercing light, and watched that
coloured glint till it disappeared into the brightness of the
morning. The last driver of the baggage-train dropped out of
sight beyond the lift of the road, the rhythmic tramp-tramp-
tramp of heavily sandalled feet ceased to pulse through the
sunlit air, and Marcus was alone with his first command.

II

FEATHERS IN THE WIND

BEFORE many days had passed, Marcus had slipped so completely into the life of the frontier fort that it seemed as though he had never known any other. The plan of all Roman forts was much the same, and the pattern of life lived in them, so that knowing one meant knowing them all, whether it was the stone-built camp of the Praetorian Guard itself, or a baked mud fort on the Upper Nile, or this one at Isca Dumnoniorum, where the ramparts were of rammed turf, and the cohort Standard and the officers were all housed together in one small square of wattle-and-daub buildings round a colonnaded courtyard. But after a few days Marcus began to know the individualities that made every camp different, after all, from every other; and it was these differences, rather than the samenesses, that made him feel at home in Isca. An artist of some long-departed garrison had scratched with his dagger a beautiful leaping wild cat on the bath-house wall, and someone less gifted had scratched a very rude picture of a centurion he had not liked; you could tell that it was a centurion, by the vine staff and the centurion's mark > scored beneath it. There was a martin's nest under the eaves of the shrine where the Standard was housed, and an odd and untraceable smell behind Number Two storehouse. And in one corner of the officers' courtyard, some past commander, homesick for the warmth and colour of the South, had planted a rose-bush in a great stone wine-jar, and already the buds were showing crimson among the dark leaves. That rose-bush gave Marcus a sense of continuance; it was a link between him and those who had been before him, here on the frontier, and the others who would come after. It must have been there a long time, and it was becoming pot-bound; he thought that in the

autumn he would see about having a proper bed made
for it.

It took him a little while to settle down with his officers.
The Surgeon, who appeared, like the Quartermaster, to be a
fixture, was a gentle soul, content enough in his backwater so
long as it contained sufficient of the fiery native spirit; but the
Quartermaster himself was something of a trial, a little red
angry man who had missed promotion and grown overfull of his
own importance in consequence. Lutorius, who commanded
the fort's one squadron of Dacian Horse, spent all his friendliness on his horses and was reserved to the point of sullenness
with all men, even his own. Marcus's five ranker centurions
were all so much older and more experienced than he was that
at first he was uncertain how to deal with them. It was not
easy, with less than a year with the Eagles behind him, to tell
Centurion Paulus that he was overfond of using his vine-staff
on his men's backs; or make Centurion Galba understand that,
whatever might be the custom in other cohorts, the centurions
of the Fourth Gaulish were not going to take bribes from their
men for letting them off fatigues, while he was in command.
But he managed it somehow, and the odd thing was that though
both Galba and Paulus raged inwardly at the time, and even
talked to each other about puppies, there was a better understanding between them and the Cohort Commander afterwards.
And between Marcus and his second-in-command there was a
good working understanding from the first, which grew to
a warm liking as time went by. Centurion Drusillus, like
most of his kind, was promoted from the ranks; he was a
veteran of many campaigns, full of odd wisdom and hard
counsel; and Marcus had need of such, that summer. Day
started with the trumpets sounding Cockcrow from the ramparts, and ended with Late Rounds; and between came all the
complicated pattern of parades and fatigues, patrols out and in,
stables, arms drill. He had to be his own magistrate too; he
had to deal with the situation when one of his men claimed that
a tribesman had sold him a worthless dog; or a tribesman com-
plained that someone from the fort had stolen his poultry; or

when the Dacians and the Gauls fell out over some obscure question of a tribal god whom he had never heard of before.

It was hard work, especially in the earliest days, and he was thankful for Centurion Drusillus; but the work was in his blood, just as farming was, and it was work that he loved. And it was not all work: there was the occasional day's hunting too—good hunting, even as Hilarion had said.

His usual guide and companion on the trail was a Briton not many years older than himself, a hunter and horse-dealer, Cradoc by name. And on a morning of late summer he went down from the fort, carrying his hunting-spears, to pick up Cradoc according to custom. It was very early, the sun not yet up, and the mist lying like a white sea between the hills. Scent would lie low and heavy on such a morning, and he sniffed the dawn chill like a hound. And yet he could not find his usual pleasure in the fine hunting morning, for he was worried. Not very worried, but enough to take the keen edge off the blade of his enjoyment; turning over in his mind the rumour that had been drifting through the fort for the past day or two—the rumour of a wandering Druid having been seen in the district. Oh, no one had actually seen him themselves; it was much more vague than that. None the less, remembering Hilarion's warning, he had checked up as best he could, without of course the least result. But even if there *were* something in the wind, there would be no result—nothing to be got even from the few men who held official positions from Rome; if their first loyalty was to Rome they would know nothing; if it was to their Tribe they would tell nothing. Probably there was not a scrap of truth in the story; it was just one of those floating rumours that blew up from time to time, like a wind out of nowhere. But he would keep his eyes and ears open, all the same, especially as once again, for the third year running, the harvest was going to be a poor one. You could tell that from the faces of the men and women, as well as you could from their little fields, where the corn stood thin and shrivelled in the ear. A bad harvest was always the time to look for trouble.

As he threaded his way among the crowding huts beyond the forum, it struck Marcus again how untouched this place was by Rome.   The tribe found the forum and basilica useful to hold their markets in.   One or two men had laid aside their hunting-spears to become Roman officials, occasionally one even saw a Roman tunic.   There were wine-shops everywhere, the craftsmen of the town made things to please the garrison, and everybody else sold them dogs, skins, vegetables, and fighting-cocks, while the children scrambled after the auxiliaries for denarii.   But all the same, here in Isca Dumnoniorum, Rome was a new slip grafted on to an old stock—and the graft had not yet taken.

He reached the cluster of huts that were Cradoc's, and turned aside at the house-place door, whistling a few bars of the latest tune running in the Legions, with which he was used to announce his arrival.   The leather apron over the doorway was drawn aside at once, but instead of the hunter, there appeared a girl with a solemn sunburned baby on her hip. She was tall, as were most British women, and carried herself like a queen; but the thing that Marcus noticed about her was the look on her face: a queer, guarded look, as though she had drawn a veil behind her eyes so that he should not see in.

'My man is out behind with his chariot team. If the Commander goes to look, he will find him,' she said, and stepped back, letting the leather apron fall between them.

Marcus went to look.   The sound of the hunter's voice and a horse's soft whinny gave him his direction, and making his way between the wood-pile and a tethered cock whose feathers shone with metallic colours among the duller hens, he reached the doorway of a stable hut, and looked in. Cradoc turned to the doorway as he appeared, and gave him a courteous greeting.

Marcus returned it—by this time he spoke the Celtic tongue fluently, though with an appalling accent—but he was staring into the shadows behind the other man.   ' I did not know you drove the Royal Fours in these parts,' he said.

'We are not above learning some lessons from Rome. Have you never chanced to see my team before?'

Marcus shook his head. 'I did not even know you for a charioteer, though I suppose I might have guessed. The British are all charioteers.'

'The Commander is mistaken,' Cradoc said, drawing his hand down a glossy neck. 'The British can all drive after a fashion; not everyone is a charioteer.'

'You, I take it, are a charioteer?'

'I am accounted among the best of my tribe,' Cradoc said with quiet dignity.

Marcus had moved in from the doorway. 'May I see your team?' he asked, and the other stood aside for him without a word.

The four were loose in their stable, and they came to him almost like dogs to sniff inquiringly at his breast and out-stretched hands; four superbly matched black chariot ponies. He thought of the Arab team he had sometimes driven in Rome. These were smaller—under fourteen hands, he judged —thicker coated, and for their size a little more heavily built, but in their way they seemed to him without match; the heads

16

that turned to him gentle and intelligent, the ears pricked and delicate as flower petals, the quivering nostrils lined with vivid red, the breasts and haunches deep and powerful. He turned from one to another, moving among them, fondling them, running a practised hand over their lithe bodies from proud crest to sweeping tail.

Before he left Rome, Marcus had been in a fair way to becoming a charioteer, in Cradoc's sense of the word, and now desire woke in him, not to possess this team, for he was not one of those who must be able to say ' Mine ' before they can truly enjoy a thing, but to have them out and harnessed; to feel the vibrating chariot floor under him, and the spread reins quick with life in his hands, and these lovely, fiery little creatures in the traces, his will and theirs at one.

Turning, with a soft muzzle against his shoulder, he said, ' Will you let me try your team? '

' They are not for sale.'

' If they were, I could not afford to buy them. I asked that I might try them.'

' The Commander also is a charioteer? ' Cradoc said.

At the Saturnalia Games last year, Marcus had been put up to race a borrowed team against a staff officer, reputed to be the finest driver in the Legion; and he had won. ' I am accounted the best in my Legion,' he said.

Cradoc did not seem to think his question answered. ' I doubt if you could handle these black jewels of mine.'

' Will you take a wager on it? ' Marcus asked, his eyes suddenly cool and bright, and his mouth smiling.

' A wager? '

' That I will handle your team to your satisfaction, over ground of your own choosing.' Marcus slipped a brooch from the shoulder of his rough cloak, and held it out, the red cornelian with which it was set gleaming faintly in the shadows. ' This fibula against—against one of your hunting-spears. Or if that does not suit you, name your own stakes.'

Cradoc did not look at the fibula. He was looking at Marcus, rather as though the young Roman was a horse whose mettle he wished to gauge, and Marcus, facing the cool stocktaking, felt himself flushing. The hunter noticed the angry colour, and the arrogantly raised head, and a queer little twisted smile lifted one side of his mouth. Then, as though satisfied by his scrutiny, he said: 'I will take the wager.'

'When do we put the matter to the test?' asked Marcus, returning the brooch to the shoulder of his cloak.

'I am taking a draft of horses up to Durinum tomorrow; but in eight days I shall be back. We will hold the trial on my return. And now, it is time that we were away.'

'So be it,' said Marcus; and with a final pat to a glossy neck, he turned and followed Cradoc from the stable. They whistled the waiting hounds to heel, collected hunting-spears from the house-place wall where they had been propped, and disappeared into the wilderness.

.   .   .   .   .

Cradoc was away longer than he expected, and the harvest, such as it was (there would be many hungry in Isca Dumnoniorum that winter), was gathered in by the time the trial took place. Marcus was turning over in his mind the question of getting in extra grain supplies when he arrived at the appointed meeting ground, a wide stretch of level land in the curve of the river, to find the other waiting for him. Cradoc flung up an arm in greeting as he appeared from the woodshore, and springing into the chariot, turned the team and came thundering towards him through the swaying fern at a gallop. The sun flashed back in spars of light from the bronze ornaments on the breasts and foreheads of the team, and the long hair of the charioteer was flying like his ponies' manes. Marcus stood his ground, though with an uncomfortable tightening of his stomach, until at the last moment the ponies were brought to a rearing halt almost on top of him and the charioteer ran out along the yoke-pole and stood poised against the sky.

'A pretty trick,' said Marcus, grinning up at him. 'I have heard of it before, but never seen it until today.'

The other laughed and stepped back into the chariot, and as he brought the team round, Marcus side-stepped and sprang in beside him. The reins and the many-folded lash changed hands, and Cradoc drew back into the spearman's place, with a hand on the wickerwork side of the chariot. 'Take them across to the dead ash-tree yonder, for a start.'

'All in good time,' said Marcus. 'I am not yet ready.'

The ponies were harnessed Roman fashion, the two inner to the yoke-pole, the two outer by traces to the axles. So far, so good; but the chariot was another matter. Until now his driving had all been done in a Roman racing chariot, a mere cockle-shell with room for no one but the driver; this thing was twice as big, though fairly light, and the open front gave one a sense of being on top of the team which was new to him. To get the best out of chariot and team, certain allowances must be made. Holding the carefully separated reins high, in the approved Colosseum manner, his feet wide planted on the interlaced straps of the chariot bed, he set the fidgeting team in motion; easily at first, getting the feel of them, then steadying them from a trot into a canter, as he headed for the silvery target of the dead ash-tree. Just before it, he wheeled them, obedient to Cradoc's direction, and sent them weaving delicately down the curved row of javelins that the other had stuck upright in the turf before his arrival, in the same way that he had woven the white Arabs between the practice posts on Mars Field, his speed quickening to a gallop, but with never a grazed wheel-hub to disgrace him. He took the team through every trick and test that their master ordered, until the moment came for a final burst of speed, and they were sweeping at full gallop round the mile-wide curve of the wood-shore.

To Marcus that moment was always like being born from one kind of life into another. So must an arrow feel when it leaves the bow! It had been hot and sultry in the old life, but in this one the cool wind flowed against him like water, pressing his thin scarlet tunic into his body, singing past his ears above the soft thunder of the ponies' flying hooves. He crouched lower, feeling the chariot floor buoyant and vibrating under his wide-set feet, feeling the reins quick with life in his hands, his will flowing out along them to the flying team, and their response flowing back to him, so that they were one.   He called to them in the Celtic tongue, urging them on.

'On, brave hearts!   On, bold and beautiful!   Thy mares shall be proud of thee, the tribe shall sing thy praises to their children's children!   Sweff!   Sweff, my brothers!'

For the first time he loosed the lash, letting it fly out and flicker like dark lightning above their ears without ever touching them.   The forest verge spun by, the fern streaked away beneath flying hooves and whirling wheels.   He and his team were a comet shooting down the bright ways of the sky; a falcon stooping against the sun. . . .

Then, on a word from Cradoc, he was backed on the reins, harder, bringing the team to a rearing halt, drawn back in full gallop on to their haunches.   The wind of his going died, and the heavy heat closed round him again.   It was very still, and the shimmering, sunlit scene seemed to pulse on his sight. Before the wheels had ceased to turn, Cradoc had sprung down and gone to the ponies' heads.   After the first plunging moment, they stood quite quiet, their flanks heaving a little, but not over-much.

'Well?' demanded Marcus, rubbing the back of his hand across his wet forehead.

Cradoc looked up at him, unsmiling. 'The Commander begins to be a charioteer,' he said.

Marcus laid by reins and lash, and stepped down to join him. 'I have not driven a team to better these,' he said, and curved his arm over an arched neck. 'Do I win my spear?'

'Come and choose it for yourself, before you go back to the fort,' said the other. He had brought sweet crusts with him in the breast of his tunic, and he held them out on his open palms to the soft questing lips of the ponies. 'These four are the jewels of my heart. They are descended out of the Royal Stables of the Iceni, and there are few could handle them better than the Commander.' And there was a queer note of regret in his voice, for which there seemed no reason; but Marcus was to remember it afterwards.

They drove back slowly, walking the ponies through the summer evening.

'It will not harm them to stand for a little, now that they have cooled off,' Cradoc said, as, after threading their way through the confused huddle of the town, he pulled up before his own house-place. He drew the reins over the ponies' heads and turned to the dark doorway, calling, 'Guinhumara, bring out to me my spears.'

The leather apron had been drawn back to let in what air there was, and the red fire glowed in the centre of the house-place. Marcus saw the tall girl rise without a word—she had been turning wheat cakes among the hot ash for her man's supper—and melt into the darkness of some inner place. Several dogs which had been lying in the piled fern, with the small brown baby sleeping in their midst, came out with waving tails to fawn around their master, but the baby slept on, sucking its thumb. In a few moments the girl came back and joined them in the doorway, carrying a sheaf of spears whose polished blades caught the evening light like so many tongues of flame.

'The Commander and I have laid a wager,' said Cradoc. 'His brooch against one of my hunting-spears. He has won, and now he is come to choose his spear.' As he spoke, he took one from the sheaf and stood leaning on it with a gesture that said quite plainly, 'But not this one.'

Those that were left were fine weapons, beautiful as were all the weapons of the Celts, perfectly balanced and deadly; some light for throwing, some broad-bladed for close work, some for war, some for hunting. The girl handed them to Marcus one by one, and he tested and examined them, finally picking one with a slender, barbed blade and a cross-piece just below the neck. 'This one,' he said. 'It shall be this one, for when I hunt boar with your husband this winter.' He smiled at her, but she did not smile back; her face had the same veiled look that he remembered on it before. She stepped back without a word, and carried the remaining spears with her into the house-place. But Marcus had already turned to the hunter, for that other spear had caught his interest, and been in his mind even while he made his choice. It was to the rest of the sheaf what a king is to his bodyguard; the shaft darkened with much handling, the iron blade perfect in shape as a laurel leaf, engraved with a strange and potent design that swirled like the eddies in running water. The weight of the head was counterbalanced by a ball of enamelled bronze on the butt, and about its neck was a collar of blue-grey heron's feathers.

'I have not seen the like of this before,' Marcus said. 'It is a war spear, is it not?'

Cradoc's hand caressed the smooth shaft. 'It was my father's war spear,' he said. 'It was in his hand when he died—up yonder under our old ramparts where the fortress walls stand now. See, the mark is still upon it . . . his own blood, and the blood of his enemy.' He parted the heron's feathers to show the neck of the shaft blackened by an old stain.

A little while afterwards, carrying his newly-won boar spear, Marcus made his way back towards the Praetorian gate. Children and hounds were playing together in the low sunshine, and here and there a woman in a hut doorway called the evening greeting to him as he passed. It all seemed very peaceful, and yet he was filled with an uneasy feeling that the peace was only a film—a veil like that which the girl Guinhumara had drawn behind her eyes—and that underneath, something very different was stirring. Again he remembered Hilarion's warning.

For the collar of the old war spear had been lately renewed, and the heron's feathers were still bright with the lustre of a living bird.

In all likelihood that spear had been refurbished many times, kept bright by a son in memory of his father; and yet, he wondered suddenly, in how many of these thatched homesteads had an old spear been put in fighting trim? Then he shook his shoulders impatiently, and strode on at a quickened pace up the steep way to the gate. He was simply growing toadstools, even as Hilarion had prophesied. All this because of a few feathers. Yet even a feather might show which way the wind blew.

If only they could have had a good harvest!

III

ATTACK!

Iɴ the dark hour before the dawn, two nights later, Marcus was roused out of his sleep by the Duty Centurion. A pilot lamp always burned in his sleeping-cell against just such an emergency, and he was fully awake on the instant.

'What is it, Centurion?'

'The sentries on the south rampart report sounds of movement between us and the town, sir.'

Marcus was out of bed and had swung his heavy military cloak over his sleeping-tunic. 'You have been up yourself?'

The centurion stood aside for him to pass out into the darkness. 'I have, sir,' he said with grim patience.

'Anything to be seen?'

'No, sir, but there is something stirring down there, for all that.'

Quickly they crossed the main street of the fort, and turned down beside a row of silent workshops. Then they were mounting the steps to the rampart walk. The shape of a sentry's helmet rose dark against the lesser darkness above the breastwork, and there was a rustle and thud as he grounded his pilum in salute.

Marcus went to the breast-high parapet. The sky had clouded over so that not a star was to be seen, and all below was a formless blackness with nothing visible save the faint pallor of the river looping through it. Not a breath of air stirred in the stillness, and Marcus, listening, heard no sound in all the world save the whisper of the blood in his own ears, far fainter than the sea in a conch-shell.

He waited, breath in check; then from somewhere below came the kee-wick, kee-wick, wick-wick, of a hunting owl, and a moment later a faint and formless sound of movement that was gone almost before he could be sure that he had not imagined it. He felt the Duty Centurion grow tense as a strung bow beside him. The moments crawled by, the silence became a physical pressure on his eardrums. Then the sounds came again, and with the sounds, blurred forms moved suddenly on the darkness of the open turf below the ramparts.

Marcus could almost hear the twang of breaking tension. The sentry swore softly under his breath, and the centurion laughed.

'Somebody will be spending a busy day looking for his strayed cattle!'

Strayed cattle; that was all. And yet for Marcus the tension had not snapped into relief. Perhaps if he had never seen the new heron's feathers on an old war spear it might have done, but he had seen them, and somewhere deep beneath his thinking mind the instinct for danger had remained with him ever since. Abruptly he drew back from the breastwork, speaking quickly to his officer. 'All the same, a break-out of cattle might make good cover for something else. Centurion, this is my first command: if I am being a fool, that must excuse me. I am going back to get some more clothes on. Turn out the cohort to action stations as quietly as may be.'

And not waiting for a reply, he turned, and dropping from the rampart walk, strode off towards his own quarters.

In a short while he was back, complete from studded sandals to crested helmet, and knotting the crimson scarf about the waist of his breastplate as he came. From the faintly lit

c

doorways of the barrack rows, men were tumbling out, buckling sword-belts or helmet-straps as they ran, and heading away into the darkness. 'Am I being every kind of fool?' Marcus wondered. 'Am I going to be laughed at so long as my name is remembered in the Legion, as the man who doubled the guard for two days because of a bunch of feathers, and then turned out his cohort to repel a herd of milch-cows?' But it was too late to worry about that now. He went back to the ramparts, finding them already lined with men, the reserves massing below. Centurion Drusillus was waiting for him, and he spoke to the older man in a quick, miserable undertone. 'I think I must have gone mad, Centurion; I shall never live this down.'

'Better to be a laughing-stock than lose the fort for fear of being one,' returned the centurion. 'It does not pay to take chances on the Frontier—and there was a new moon last night.'

Marcus had no need to ask his meaning. In his world the gods showed themselves in new moons, in seed-time and harvest, summer and winter solstice; and if an attack were to come, the new moon would be the time for it. Holy War. Hilarion had understood all about that. He turned aside to give an order. The waiting moments lengthened; the palms of his hands were sticky, and his mouth uncomfortably dry.

The attack came with a silent uprush of shadows that swarmed in from every side, flowing up to the turf ramparts with a speed, an impetus that, ditch or no ditch, must have carried them over into the camp if there had been only the sentries to bar the way. They were flinging brushwood bundles into the ditch to form causeways; swarming over, they had poles to scale the ramparts, but in the dark nothing of that could be seen, only a flowing up and over, like a wave of ghosts. For a few moments the utter silence gave sheer goose-flesh horror to the attack; then the auxiliaries rose as one man to meet the attackers, and the silence splintered, not into uproar, but into a light smother of sound that rippled along the ramparts: the sound of men fiercely engaged, but without giving

tongue. For a moment it endured; and then from the darkness came the strident braying of a British war-horn. From the
ramparts a Roman trumpet answered the challenge, as fresh
waves of shadows came pouring in to the attack; and then
it seemed as if all Tartarus had broken loose. The time for
silence was past, and men fought yelling now; red flame
sprang up into the night above the Praetorian gate, and was
instantly quenched. Every yard of the ramparts was a reeling,
roaring battle-line as the tribesmen swarmed across the breastwork to be met by the grim defenders within.

How long it lasted Marcus never knew, but when the attack
drew off, the first cobweb light of a grey and drizzling dawn
was creeping over the fort. Marcus and his second-in-command
looked at each other, and Marcus asked very softly, 'How long
can we hold out?'

'For several days, with luck,' muttered Drusillus, pretending
to adjust the strap of his shield.

'Reinforcements could get to us in three—maybe two—
from Durinum,' Marcus said. 'But there was no reply to our
signal.'

'Little to wonder in that, sir. To destroy the nearest signal
station is an obvious precaution; and no cresset could carry the
double distance in this murk.'

'Mithras grant it clears enough to give the smoke column a
chance to rise.'

But there was no sign of anxiety in the face of either of
them when they turned from each other an instant later, the
older man to go clanging off along the stained and littered
rampart walk, Marcus to spring down the steps into the
crowded space below. He was a gay figure, his scarlet cloak
swirling behind him; he laughed, and made the 'thumbs up'
to his troops, calling 'Well done, lads! We will have breakfast
before they come on again!'

The 'thumbs up' was returned to him. Men grinned, and
here and there a voice called cheerfully in reply, as he disappeared with Centurion Paulus in the direction of the
Praetorium.

No one knew how long the breathing space might last; but at the least it meant time to get the wounded under cover, and an issue of raisins and hard bread to the troops. Marcus himself had no breakfast, he had too many other things to do, too many to think about; amongst them the fate of a half Century under Centurion Galba, now out on patrol, and due back before noon. Of course the tribesmen might have dealt with them already, in which case they were beyond help or the need of it, but it was quite as likely that they would merely be left to walk into the trap on their return, and cut to pieces under the very walls of the fort.

Marcus gave orders that the cresset was to be kept alight on the signal roof; that at least would warn them that something was wrong as soon as they sighted it. He ordered a watch to be kept for them, and sent for Lutorius of the Cavalry and put the situation to him. ' If they win back here, we shall of course make a sortie and bring them in. Muster the squadron and hold them in readiness from now on. That is all.'

' Sir,' said Lutorius. His sulks were forgotten, and he looked almost gay as he went off to carry out the order.

There was nothing more that Marcus could do about his threatened patrol, and he turned to the score of other things that must be seen to.

It was full daylight before the next attack came. Somewhere, a war-horn brayed, and before the wild note died, the tribesmen broke from cover, yelling like fiends out of Tartarus as they swarmed up through the bracken; heading for the gates this time, with tree-trunks to serve as rams, with firebrands that gilded the falling mizzle and flashed on the blade of sword and heron-tufted war spear. On they stormed, heedless of the Roman arrows that thinned their ranks as they came. Marcus, standing in the shooting turret beside the Praetorian gate, saw a figure in their van, a wild figure in streaming robes that marked him out from the half-naked warriors who charged behind him. Sparks flew from the firebrand that he whirled aloft, and in its light the horns of the young moon, rising from his forehead, seemed to shine with a fitful radiance of its own. Marcus said quietly to the archer beside him, ' Shoot me that maniac.'

The man nocked another arrow to his bow, bent and loosed in one swift movement. The Gaulish Auxiliaries were fine bowmen, as fine as the British; but the arrow sped out only to pass through the wild hair of the leaping fanatic. There was no time to loose again. The attack was thundering on the gates, pouring in over the dead in the ditch with a mad courage that took no heed of losses. In the gate towers the archers stood loosing steadily into the heart of the press below them. The acrid reek of smoke and smitch drifted across the fort from the Dexter Gate, which the tribesmen had attempted to fire. There was a constant two-way traffic of reserves and armament going up to the ramparts and wounded coming back from them. No time to carry away the dead; one toppled them from the rampart walk that they might not hamper the feet of the living, and left them, though they had been one's best friend, to be dealt with at a fitter season.

The second attack drew off at last, leaving their dead lying twisted among the trampled fern. Once more there was breathing space for the desperate garrison. The morning dragged on; the British archers crouched behind the dark masses of uprooted blackthorn that they had set up under cover of the first assault, and loosed an arrow at any movement on the ramparts; the next rush might come at any moment. The garrison had lost upward of fourscore men, killed or wounded: two days would bring them reinforcements from Durinum, if only the mizzle which obscured the visibility would clear, just for a little while, long enough for them to send up the smoke signal, and for it to be received.

But the mizzle showed no signs of lifting, when Marcus went up to the flat signal-roof of the Praetorium. It blew in his face, soft and chill-smelling, and faintly salt on his lips. Faint grey swathes of it drifted across the nearer hills, and those beyond were no more than a spreading stain that blurred into nothingness.

'It is no use, sir,' said the auxiliary who squatted against the parapet, keeping the great charcoal brazier glowing.

Marcus shook his head. Had it been like this when the Ninth Legion ceased to be? he wondered. Had his father and all those others watched, as he was watching now, for the far hills to clear so that a signal might go through? Suddenly he found that he was praying, praying as he had never prayed before, flinging his appeal for help up through the grey to the clear skies that were beyond. 'Great God Mithras, Slayer of the Bull, Lord of the Ages, let the mists part and thy glory shine through! Draw back the mists and grant us clear air for a space, that we go not down into the darkness. O God of the Legions, hear the cry of thy sons. Send down thy light upon us, even upon us, thy sons of the Fourth Gaulish Cohort of the Second Legion.'

He turned to the auxiliary, who knew only that the Commander had stood beside him in silence for a few moments, with his head tipped back as though he was looking for something in the soft and weeping sky. 'All we can do is wait,' he said. 'Be ready to start your smother at any moment.' And swinging on his heel, he rounded the great pile of fresh grass and fern that lay ready near the brazier, and went clattering down the narrow stairway.

Centurion Fulvius was waiting for him at the foot with some urgent question that must be settled, and it was some while before he snatched another glance over the ramparts; but when he did, it seemed to him that he could see a little farther than before. He touched Drusillus, who was beside him, on the shoulder. 'Is it my imagining, or are the hills growing clearer?'

Drusillus was silent a moment, his grim face turned towards the east. Then he nodded. 'If it is your imagining, it is also mine.' Their eyes met quickly, with hope that they dared not put into any more words; then they went each about their separate affairs.

But soon others of the garrison were pointing, straining their eyes eastward in painful hope. Little by little the light grew:

the mizzle was lifting, lifting . . . and ridge behind wild ridge of hills coming into sight.

High on the Praetorium roof a column of black smoke sprang upward, billowed sideways and spread into a drooping veil that trailed across the northern rampart, making the men there cough and splutter; then rose again, straight and dark and urgent, into the upper air. In the pause that followed, eyes and hearts were strained with a sickening intensity toward those distant hills. A long, long pause it seemed; and then a shout went up from the watchers, as, a day's march to the east, a faint dark thread of smoke rose into the air.

The call for help had gone through. In two days, three at the most, relief would be here; and the uprush of confidence touched every man of the garrison.

Barely an hour later, word came back to Marcus from the northern rampart that the missing patrol had been sighted on the track that led to the Sinister Gate. He was in the Praetorium when the word reached him, and he covered the distance to the gate as if his heels were winged; he waved up the Cavalry waiting beside their saddled horses, and found Centurion Drusillus once again by his side.

'The tribesmen have broken cover, sir,' said the centurion.

Marcus nodded. 'I must have half a Century of the reserves. We can spare no more A trumpeter with them and every available man on the gate, in case they try a rush when it opens.'

The centurion gave the order, and turned back to him. 'Better let me take them, sir.'

Marcus had already unclasped the fibula at the shoulder of his cloak, and flung off the heavy folds that might hamper him. 'We went into that before. You can lend me your shield, though.'

The other slipped it from his shoulder without a word, and Marcus took it and swung round on the half Century who were already falling in abreast of the gate. 'Get ready to form testudo,' he ordered. 'And you can leave room for me. This tortoise is not going into action with its head stuck out!'

It was a poor joke, but a laugh ran through the desperate little band, and as he stepped into his place in the column head, Marcus knew that they were with him in every sense of the word; he could take those lads through the fires of Tophet if need be.

The great bars were drawn, and men stood ready to swing wide the heavy valves; and behind and on every side he had a confused impression of grim ranks massed to hold the gate, and draw them in again if ever they won back to it.

'Open up!' he ordered; and as the valves began to swing outward on their iron-shod posts, 'Form testudo.' His arm went up as he spoke, and through the whole column behind him he felt the movement echoed, heard the light kiss and click of metal on metal, as every man linked shield with his neighbour, to form the shield-roof which gave the formation its name. 'Now!'

The gates were wide; and like a strange many-legged beast, a gigantic woodlouse rather than a tortoise, the testudo was out across the causeway and heading straight downhill, its small, valiant cavalry wings spread on either side. The gates closed behind it, and from rampart and gate-tower anxious eyes watched it go. It had all been done so quickly that at the foot of the slope battle had only just joined, as the tribesmen hurled themselves yelling on the swiftly formed Roman square.

The testudo was not a fighting formation; but for rushing a position, for a break through, it had no equal. Also it had a strange and terrifying aspect that could be very useful. Its sudden appearance now, swinging down upon them with the whole weight of the hill behind it, struck a brief confusion into the swarming tribesmen. Only for a moment their wild ranks wavered and lost purpose; but in that moment the hard-pressed patrol saw it too, and with a hoarse shout came charging to join their comrades.

Down swept Marcus and his half Century, down and forward into the raging battle-mass of the enemy. They were slowed almost to a standstill, but never quite halted; once they were broken, but re-formed. A mailed wedge cleaving into the wild ranks of the tribesmen, until the moment came when the tortoise could serve them no longer; and above the turmoil Marcus shouted to the trumpeter beside him: 'Sound me " Break testudo ".'

The clear notes of the trumpet rang through the uproar. The men lowered their shields, springing sideways to gain fighting space; and a flight of pilums hurtled into the swaying horde of tribesmen, spreading death and confusion wherever the iron heads struck. Then it was ' Out swords ', and the charge driven home with a shout of ' Caesar! Caesar! ' Behind them the valiant handful of cavalry were struggling to keep clear the line of retreat; in front, the patrol came grimly battling up to join them. But between them was still a living rampart of yelling, battle-frenzied warriors, amongst whom Marcus glimpsed again that figure with the horned moon on its forehead. He laughed, and sprang against them, his men storming behind him.

Patrol and relief force joined, and became one.

Instantly they began to fall back, forming as they did so a roughly diamond formation that faced outward on all sides and was as difficult to hold as a wet pebble pressed between the fingers. The tribesmen thrust in on them from every side, but slowly, steadily, their short blades like a hedge of living, leaping steel, the cavalry breaking the way for them in wild rushes, they were drawing back towards the fortress gate—those that were left of them.

Back, and back. And suddenly the press was thinning, and Marcus, on the flank, snatched one glance over his shoulder, and saw the gate-towers very near, the swarming ranks of the defenders ready to draw them in. And in that instant there came a warning yelp of trumpets and a swelling thunder of hooves and wheels, as round the curve of the hill towards them, out of cover of the woodshore, swept a curved column of chariots.

Small wonder that the press had thinned.

The great battle-wains had long been forbidden to the tribes, and these were light chariots such as the one Marcus had driven two days ago, each carrying only a spearman beside the driver; but one horrified glance, as they hurtled nearer behind their thundering teams, was enough to show the wicked, whirling scythe-blades on the war-hubs of the wheels.

Close formation—now that their pilums were spent—was useless in the face of such a charge; again the trumpets yelped an order, and the ranks broke and scattered, running for the gateway, not in any hope of reaching it before the chariots were upon them, but straining heart and soul to gain the advantage of the high ground.

To Marcus, running with the rest, it seemed suddenly that there was no weight in his body, none at all. He was filled through and through with a piercing awareness of life and the sweetness of life held in his hollowed hand, to be tossed away like the shining balls that the children played with in the gardens of Rome. At the last instant, when the charge was almost upon them, he swerved aside from his men, out and back on his tracks, and flinging aside his sword, stood tensed to spring, full in the path of the oncoming chariots. In the breath of time that remained, his brain felt very cold and clear, and he seemed to have space to do quite a lot of thinking. If he sprang for the heads of the leading team, the odds were that he would merely be flung down and driven over without any check to the wild gallop. His best chance was to go for the charioteer. If he could bring him down, the whole team would be flung into confusion, and on that steep scarp the chariots coming behind would have difficulty in clearing the wreck. It was a slim chance, but if it came off it would gain for his men those few extra moments that might mean life or death. For himself, it was death. He was quite clear about that.

They were right upon him, a thunder of hooves that seemed to fill the universe; black manes streaming against the sky; the team that he had called his brothers, only two days ago. He hurled his shield clanging among them, and side-stepped, looking up into the grey face of Cradoc, the charioteer. For one splinter of time their eyes met in something that was almost a salute, a parting salute between two who might have been

friends; then Marcus leapt in under the spearman's descending thrust, upward and sideways across the chariot bow. His weight crashed on to the reins, whose ends, after the British fashion, were wrapped about the charioteer's waist, throwing the team into instant chaos; his arms were round Cradoc, and they went half down together. His ears were full of the sound of rending timber and the hideous scream of a horse. Then sky and earth changed places, and with his hold still unbroken, he was flung down under the trampling hooves, under the scythe-bladed wheels and the collapsing welter of the overset chariot; and the jagged darkness closed over him.

IV

THE LAST ROSE FALLS

O N the other side of the darkness was pain. For a long time that was the only thing Marcus knew. At first it was white, and quite blinding; but presently it dulled to red, and he began to be dimly aware of the other things through the redness of it. People moving near him, lamplight, daylight, hands that touched him; a bitter taste in his mouth which always brought back the darkness. But it was all muddled and unreal, like a dissolving dream.

And then one morning he heard the trumpets sounding Cockcrow. And the familiar trumpet-call, piercing through the unreality like a sword-blade through tangled wool, brought with it other real and familiar things: the dawn chill on his face and an uncovered shoulder, the far-off crowing of a real cock, the smell of lamp-smitch. He opened his eyes, and found that he was lying flat on his back on the narrow cot in his own sleeping-cell. Close above him the window was a square of palest aquamarine in the dusky gold of the lamplit wall, and on the dark roof-ridge of the officers' mess opposite was a sleeping pigeon, so clearly and exquisitely outlined against the morning sky that it seemed to Marcus as though he could make out the tip of every fluffed-out feather. But of course that was natural, because he had carved them himself, sitting between the roots of the wild olive-tree in the bend of the stream. And then he remembered that that had been a different bird; and the last shreds of his confusion fell away from him.

So he was not dead, after all. He was faintly surprised, but not very interested. He was not dead, but he was hurt. The pain, which had been first white and then red, was still there, no longer filling the whole universe, but reaching all up and down his right leg: a dull, grinding throb with little sparks of

sharper pain that came and went in the dullness of it.   It was
the worst pain that he had ever known, save for the few blinding
moments when the brand of Mithras pressed down between his
brows; but he was not much more interested in it than in the
fact that he was still alive.   He remembered exactly what had
happened; but it had all happened so long ago, at the other
side of the blackness; and he was not even anxious, because
Roman trumpets sounding from the ramparts could only mean
that the fort was still safely in Roman hands.

Somebody moved in the outer room and, a moment later,
loomed into the doorway.   Marcus turned his head slowly—it
seemed very heavy—and saw the garrison Surgeon, clad in a
filthy tunic, and with red-rimmed eyes and several days'
growth of beard.

'Ah, Aulus,' Marcus said, and found that even his tongue felt
heavy.   'You look—as if you had not been to bed for a month.'

'Not quite so long as that,' said the Surgeon, who had come
forward quickly at the sound of Marcus's voice, and was bending
over him.   'Good!   Very good!' he added, nodding his vague
encouragement.

'How long?' began Marcus, stumblingly.

'Six days; yes, yes—or it might be seven.'

'It seems—like years.'

Aulus had turned back the striped native rugs, and laid a
fumbling hand over Marcus's heart.   He seemed to be counting, and answered only with a nod.

But suddenly everything grew near and urgent again to
Marcus.   'The relief force?—They got through to us, then?'

Aulus finished his counting with maddening deliberateness,
and drew the rugs up again.   'Yes, yes.   The best part of a
cohort of the Legion, from Durinum.'

'I must see Centurion Drusillus—and the—the relief force
Commander.'

'Maybe presently, if you lie still,' said Aulus, turning to deal
with the smoking lamp.

'No, not presently.   Now!   Aulus, it is an order: I am still
in command of this——'

He tried to crane up on his elbow, and his rush of words ended in a choking gasp. For a few moments he lay very still, staring at the other man, and there were little beads of sweat on his forehead.

'Tch! Now you have made it worse!' scolded Aulus in a slight fluster. 'That is because you did not lie still, as I bade you.' He picked up a red Samian bowl from the chest top, and slipped an arm under Marcus's head to raise him. 'Best drink this. Tch! tch! It will do you good.'

Too weak to argue, and with the rim of the bowl jolting against his teeth, Marcus drank. It was milk, but with the bitter taste in it which always brought back the darkness.

'There,' said Aulus, when the bowl was empty. 'Now go to sleep. Good boy; now go to sleep.' And he laid Marcus's head back on the folded rug.

Centurion Drusillus came next day, and sitting with his hands on his knees and the shadow of his crested helmet blue on the sunlit wall behind him, gave his Commander a broad outline of all that had happened since he was wounded. Marcus listened very carefully; he found that he had to listen very carefully indeed, because if he did not, his attention wandered: to the crack in a roof-beam, to the flight of a bird across the window, to the pain of his wounds or the black hairs growing out of the centurion's nostrils. But when the centurion had finished, there were still things that Marcus needed to know.

'Drusillus, what became of the holy man?'

'Gone to meet his own gods, sir. Caught between the relief force and ourselves. There was a-many of the tribe went with him.'

'And the charioteer?—my charioteer?'

Centurion Drusillus made the 'thumbs down'. 'Dead as we thought you were when we pulled you from the wreck.'

After a moment's silence, Marcus asked, 'Who brought me in?'

'Why, now, that is hard to say, sir. Most of us had our hand in it.'

'I had hoped to gain time for the rest.' Marcus rubbed the back of one hand across his forehead. 'What happened?'

'Nay now, sir, it was all so quick. . . . Galba doubled back to you, and the rest with him, and it was a time for desperate measures; so we took down the reserves—'twas not much more than a javelin throw—and brought you off.'

'And got cut to pieces by the chariots in doing it?' Marcus asked quickly.

'Not so badly as we might have been. Your wreck broke the weight of the charge.'

'I want to see Galba.'

'Galba is in the sick-block, with his sword arm laid open,' Drusillus said.

'How bad is the damage?'

'A clean wound. It is healing.'

Marcus nodded. 'You will be seeing him, I suppose? Salute him for me, Centurion. Tell him I shall come and compare scars with him if I am on my feet before he is. And tell the troops I always *have* said the Fourth Gaulish was the finest cohort with the Eagles.'

'I will, sir,' said Drusillus. 'Very anxiously inquiring, the troops have been.' He got up, raised an arm heavy with silver good-conduct bracelets in salute, and tramped off back to duty.

Marcus lay for a long time with his forearm across his eyes, seeing against the blackness of his closed lids picture after picture that Drusillus had left behind him. He saw the relief force coming up the road, tramp-tramp-tramp, and the dust rising behind them. He saw the last stand of the tribesmen crumble and the moon-crested fanatic go down. The British town a smoking ruin and the little fields salted by order of the relief force Commander. (Wattle-and-daub huts were easily rebuilt, and salted fields would bear again in three years, but not all the years in eternity would bring back the young men of the tribe, he thought, and was surprised to find that he cared.) He saw dead men, Lutorius among them; he hoped that there would be horses for Lutorius in the Elysian Fields. Most clearly of all, again and again, he saw Cradoc, lying broken among the trampled bracken of the hillside. He had felt very bitter towards Cradoc; he had liked the hunter and thought that his liking was returned; and yet Cradoc had betrayed him. But that was all over. It was not that Cradoc had broken faith; simply that there had been another and stronger faith that he must keep. Marcus understood that now.

Later, the Commander of the relief force came to see him, but the interview was not a happy one. Centurion Clodius Maximus was a fine soldier, but a chilly mannered, bleak-faced man. He stood aloofly in the doorway, and announced that since everything was under control, he intended to continue his interrupted northward march tomorrow. He had been taking troops up to Isca when the Frontier fort's distress signal had reached Durinum and he had been deflected to answer it. He would leave two Centuries to bring the garrison temporarily up to strength, and Centurion Herpinius, who would take command of the fort until Marcus's relief could be sent from Isca, when no doubt fresh drafts of auxiliaries would be sent with him.

Marcus realized that it was all perfectly reasonable. The Relief Force were Legionaries, line-of-battle troops, and in the nature of things a Legionary Centurion ranked above an auxiliary one; and if he, Marcus, was going to be laid by for a while, a relief would of course have to be sent down to take his place until he was once more fit for duty. But all the same, he was annoyed by the man's high-handed manner, annoyed on Drusillus's account, and on his own. Also, quite suddenly, he began to be afraid. So he became very stiff, and very proud, and for the rest of the short and formal interview treated the stranger with an icy politeness that was almost insulting.

Day followed day, each marked off in its passing by lamplight and daylight, food that he did not want, and the changing shadows that moved across the courtyard outside his window. These, and the visits of Aulus and a medical orderly to dress the spear-gash in his shoulder (he had never felt the blade bite, as he sprang in under the spearman's thrust), and the ugly mass of wounds that seared his right thigh.

D

There was some delay about the arrival of his relief from Isca, for several cohort centurions were down with marsh fever; and the moon, which had been new when the tribe rose, waxed and waned into the dark, and the pale feather of another new moon hung in the evening sky; and all save the deepest and most ragged of Marcus's wounds were healed.   That was when they told him that his service with the Eagles was over.

Let him only be patient, and the leg would carry him well enough, one day, Aulus assured him, but not for a long time; no, he could not say how long.   Marcus must understand, he pointed out with plaintive reasonableness, that one could not smash a thigh-bone and tear the muscles to shreds and then expect all to be as it had been before.

It was the thing that Marcus had been afraid of ever since his interview with Centurion Maximus.   No need to be afraid now, not any more.   He took it very quietly; but it meant the loss of almost everything he cared about.   Life with the Eagles was the only kind of life he had ever thought of, the only kind that he had any training for; and now it was over.   He would never be Prefect of an Egyptian Legion, he would never be able to buy back the farm in the Etruscan hills, or gather to himself another like it.   The Legion was lost to him and, with the Legion, it seemed that his own land was lost to him too; and the future, with a lame leg and no money and no prospects, seemed at first sight rather bleak and terrifying.

Maybe Centurion Drusillus guessed something of all this, though Marcus never told him.   At all events he seemed to find the Commander's quarters a good place to spend every off-duty moment, just then; and though Marcus, longing to be alone like a sick animal, often wished him at the other side of the Empire, afterwards he remembered and was grateful for his centurion's fellowship in a bad time.

.   .   .   .   .

A few days later, Marcus lay listening to the distant sounds of the new Commander's arrival.   He was still in his old quarters, for when he had suggested that he should go across to the sick-block, and leave the two rooms in the Praetorium free for their rightful owner, he was told that other quarters had been made ready for the new Commander, and he was to stay where he was until he was fit to travel—until he could go to Uncle Aquila. He was lucky, he supposed rather drearily, to have Uncle Aquila to go to. At all events he would know quite soon now whether the unknown uncle was like his father.

Now that he could sit up, he could look out into the courtyard, and see the rose-bush in its wine-jar, just outside his window. There was still one crimson rose among the dark leaves, but even as he watched, a petal fell from it like a great slow drop of blood. Soon the rest would follow. He had held his first and only command for just as long as the rose-bush had been in flower. . . . It was certainly pot-bound, he thought; maybe his successor would do something about it.

His successor: whoever that might be. He could not see the entrance to the courtyard, but quick footsteps sounded along the colonnade and then in the outer room, and a moment later the new Commander stood in the doorway; an elegant and very dusty young man with his crested helmet under one arm. It was the owner of the chariot team which Marcus had driven in the Saturnalia Games.

'Cassius!' Marcus greeted him. 'I wondered if it would be anyone I knew.'

Cassius crossed to his side. 'My dear Marcus; how does the leg?'

'It mends, in its fashion.'

'So. I am glad of that, at all events.'

'What have you done with your bays?' Marcus asked quickly. 'You are not having them brought down here, are you?'

Cassius collapsed on to the clothes-chest and wilted elegantly. 'Jupiter! No! I have lent them to Dexion, with my groom to keep an eye on them, and him.'

'They will do well enough with Dexion. What troops have you brought down with you?'

'Two Centuries of the Third: Gauls, like the rest. They are good lads, seasoned troops; been up on the wall laying stone courses and exchanging the odd arrow now and then with the Painted People.' He cocked a languid eyebrow. 'But if they can give as good an account of themselves in action as your raw Fourth have done, they will have no need to feel themselves disgraced.'

'I think there will be no more trouble in these parts,' Marcus said. 'Centurion Maximus took good care of that.'

'Ah, you mean the burned villages and salted fields? A punitive expedition is never pretty. But I gather from your embittered tone that you did not take warmly to Centurion Maximus?'

'I did not.'

'A most efficient officer,' pronounced Cassius, with the air of a grey-headed Legate.

'To say nothing of officious,' snapped Marcus.

'Maybe if you saw the report he sent in when he got back to Headquarters, you might find yourself feeling more friendlily disposed towards him.'

'It was good?' asked Marcus, surprised. Centurion Maximus had not struck him as the type who sent in enthusiastic reports.

Cassius nodded. 'Rather more than good. Indeed, before I marched south there was beginning to be talk of some trifle— say a gilded laurel wreath—to make the standard of the Gaulish Fourth look pretty when it goes on parade.'

There was a short silence, and then Marcus said, 'It is no more than we—than they deserve! Look, Cassius, if anything more than talking comes of it, send me word. I will give you the direction to write to. I should like to know that the cohort won its first honours under my command.'

'Possibly the cohort would like to know it too,' said Cassius gruffly, and lounged to his feet. 'I am for the bath-house. I am gritty from head to foot!' He paused a moment, looking down at Marcus, with his air of weary elegance quite forgotten. 'Do not worry. I shall not let your cohort go to ruin.'

Marcus laughed, with a sudden aching in his throat. ' See that you do not, or I swear I shall find means to poison your wine! They are a fine cohort, the best with the Legion: and—good luck to you with them.'

Outside in the courtyard, the last crimson petals fell in a little bright flurry from the rose-bush in the old wine-jar.

V

SATURNALIA GAMES

UNCLE AQUILA lived on the extreme edge of Calleva. One reached his house down a narrow side street that turned off not far from the East Gate, leaving behind the forum and the temples, and coming to a quiet angle of the old British earthworks—for Calleva had been a British Dun before it was a Roman city—where hawthorn and hazel still grew and the shyer woodland birds sometimes came. It was much like the other houses of Calleva, timbered and red-roofed and comfortable, built round three sides of a tiny courtyard that was smoothly turfed and set about with imported roses and gum-cistus growing in tall stone jars. But it had one peculiarity: a squat, square, flat-roofed tower rising from one corner; for Uncle Aquila, having lived most of his life in the shadow of watch-towers from Memphis to Segedunum, could not be comfortable without one.

Here, in the shadow of his own watch-tower, which he used as a study, he was very comfortable indeed, with his elderly wolf-hound Procyon, and the History of Siege Warfare which he had been writing for ten years, for company.

By the dark end of October, Marcus had been added to the

46

household. He was given a sleeping-cell opening on to the courtyard colonnade; a lime-washed cell with a narrow cot piled with striped native blankets, a polished citron-wood chest, a lamp on a bracket high against the wall. Save that the door was differently placed, it might have been his old quarters in the Frontier fort, seven days' march away. But most of his days were spent in the long atrium, the central room of the house, occasionally with Uncle Aquila, but for the most part alone, save when Stephanos or Sassticca looked in on him. He did not mind Stephanos, his uncle's old Greek body-slave, who now looked after him as well as his master, but Sassticca the cook was another matter. She was a tall and gaunt old woman who could hit like a man, and frequently did when either of her fellow slaves annoyed her; but she treated Marcus as though he were a small sick child. She brought him little hot cakes when she had been baking, and warm milk because she said he was too thin, and fussed and tyrannized over him, until—for he was very afraid of kindness just then—he came near to hating her.

That autumn was a bad time for Marcus, feeling wretchedly ill for the first time in his life, almost always in pain, and face to face with the wreckage of everything he knew and cared about. He would wake in the dark mornings to hear the distant notes of Cockcrow sounding from the transit camp just outside the city walls, and that did not make it any easier. He was homesick for the Legions; he was desperately homesick for his own land; for now that they seemed lost to him, his own hills grew achingly dear, every detail of sight and scent and sound jewel-vivid on his memory. The shivering silver of the olive-woods when the mistral blew, the summer scent of thyme and rosemary and little white cyclamen among the sun-warmed grass, the songs that the girls sang at vintage.

And here in Britain the wind moaned through the desolate woods, the skies wept, and wet gale-blown leaves pattered against the windows and stuck there, making little pathetic shadows against the steamy glass. There had been wild weather often enough in his own country, but that had been the wild weather of home: here was the wind and rain and wet leaves of exile.

It would have gone less hardly with him if he had had a companion of his own age; but he was the only young thing in the house, for even Procyon had grey hairs in his muzzle, and so he was shut in on himself, and though he did not know it, he was bitterly lonely.

There was just one gleam of light for him in the darkness of that autumn. Not long after he came to Calleva, he had word from Cassius that henceforth the Standard of the Gaulish Fourth would have its gilded laurel wreath to carry on parade; and a little later there came to Marcus himself the award of a military bracelet, which was a thing that he had never for an instant expected. This was not, as the various crowns were, purely a gallantry award; rather it was given for the same qualities which had earned for the Second Legion its titles ' Pia Fidelis '; those titles which were cut deep upon the heavy gold bracelet under the Capricorn badge of the Legion. From the day that it came to him, it was never off Marcus's wrist; and yet it meant rather less to him than the knowledge that his old cohort had won its first laurels.

The days grew shorter and the nights longer, and presently it was the night of the winter solstice. A fitting night for the dark turn of the year, Marcus thought. The inevitable wind was roaring up through the forest of Spinaii below the old British ramparts, driving with it squalls of sleet that spattered against the windows. In the atrium it was warm, for whatever the peculiarities of Uncle Aquila's house, the hypercaust worked perfectly, and for the pleasant look of it rather than for need, a fire of wild-cherry logs on charcoal burned in the brazier hearth, filling the long room with faint, aromatic scent. The light from the single bronze lamp, falling in a golden pool over the group before the hearth, scarcely touched the lime-washed walls, and left the far end of the room in crowding shadows, save for the glim of light that always burned before the shrine of the household gods. Marcus lay propped on one elbow on his usual couch, Uncle Aquila sat opposite to him in his great cross-legged chair; and beside them, outstretched on the warm tessellated floor, Procyon the wolf-hound.

Uncle Aquila was huge; that had been the first thing Marcus noticed about him, and he noticed it still. His joints appeared to be loosely strung together as if with wet leather; his head with its bald freckled top and his bony beautiful hands were big even in proportion to the rest of him, and Authority seemed to hang on him in easy and accustomed folds, like his toga. Even allowing for their twenty years of difference in age, he was not in the least like Marcus's father; but Marcus had long ago ceased to think of him as like, or unlike, anyone. He was simply Uncle Aquila.

The evening meal was over, and old Stephanos had set out a draughts-board on the table between Marcus and his uncle, and gone his way. In the lamplight the ivory and ebony squares shone vividly white and black; Uncle Aquila's men were already in place, but Marcus had been slower, because he was thinking of something else. He set down his last ivory man with a little click, and said: 'Ulpius was here this morning.'

'Ah, our fat physician,' said Uncle Aquila, his hand, which had been poised for an opening move, returning to the arm of his chair. 'Had he anything to say worth the listening to?'

'Only the usual things. That I must wait and wait.' Suddenly Marcus exploded between misery and laughter. 'He said I must have a little patience and called me his dear young man and wagged a scented fat finger under my nose. Fach! He is like the white pulpy things one finds under stones!'

'So,' agreed Uncle Aquila. 'None the less, you *must* wait—there being no help for it.'

Marcus looked up from the board. 'There's the rub. How long can I wait?'

'Hmph?' said Uncle Aquila.

'I have been here two months now, and we have never spoken of the future. I have put it off from one visit of that pot-bellied leech to the next because—I suppose because I have never thought of any life but following the Eagles, and I do not

quite know how to begin.' He smiled at his uncle apolo-
getically. 'But we must discuss it sometime.'

'Sometime, yes: but not now. No need to trouble about the
future until that leg will carry you.'

'But Mithras knows how long that will be. Do you not see,
sir, I cannot go on foisting myself on you indefinitely.'

'Oh, my good lad, do try not to be such a fool!' snapped
Uncle Aquila; but his eyes under their jut of brow were
unexpectedly kindly. 'I am not a rich man, but neither am I
so poor that I cannot afford to add a kinsman to my household. You do not get in my way; to be perfectly honest, I
forget your existence rather more than half the time; you play
a reasonably good game of draughts. Naturally you will stay
here, unless of course '—he leaned forward abruptly—' is it that
you would rather go home?'

'Home?' Marcus echoed.

'Yes. I suppose you still have a home with that peculiarly
foolish sister of mine?'

'And with Uncle-by-Marriage Tullus Lepidus?' Marcus's
head went up, his black brows twitched almost to meeting point
above a nose which looked suddenly as though there was a very
bad smell under it. 'I'd sooner sit on Tiber-side and beg my
bread from the slum women when they come to fill their water-
pots!'

'So?' Uncle Aquila nodded his huge head. 'And now,
that being settled, shall we play?'

He made the opening move, and Marcus answered it. For a
while they played in silence. The lamplit room was a shell of
quiet amid the wild sea-roaring of the wind; the small saffron
flames whispered in the brazier, and a burned cherry log collapsed with a tinselly rustle into the red hollow of the charcoal.
Every few moments there would be a little clear click as Marcus
or his uncle moved a piece on the board. But Marcus did not
really hear the small peaceful sounds, nor see the man opposite,
for he was thinking of things that he had been trying not to
think of all day.

It was the twenty-fourth evening of December, the eve of the winter solstice—the eve of the birth of Mithras; and quite soon now, in camps and forts wherever the Eagles flew, men would be gathering to his worship. In the outposts and the little frontier forts the gatherings would be mere handfuls, but in the great Legionary Stations there would be full caves of a hundred men. Last year, at Isca, he had been one of them, newly initiated at the Bull-slaying, the brand of the Raven Degree still raw between his brows. He ached with longing for last year to be given back to him, for the old life and the comradeship to be given back to him. He moved an ivory man a little blindly, seeing, not the black-and-white dazzle of the board before his eyes, but that gathering of a year ago, filing out by the Praetorian gate and downhill to the cave. He could see the crest of the centurion in front of him up-reared blackly against the pulsing fires of Orion. He remembered the waiting darkness of the cave; then, as the trumpets sounded from the distant ramparts for the third watch of the night, the sudden glory of candles, that sank and turned blue, and sprang up again; the reborn light of Mithras in the dark of the year. . . .

A great gust of wind swooped against the house like a wild thing striving to batter its way in; the lamplight jumped and fluttered, sending shadows racing across the chequered board— and the ghosts of last year were once more a year away. Marcus looked up, and said, as much for the sake of shutting out his own thoughts as for anything else, ' I wonder what possessed you to settle here in Britain, Uncle Aquila, when you could have gone home? '

Uncle Aquila moved his piece with meticulous care before he answered with another question. ' It seems very odd to you, that anyone free to go home should choose to strike his roots in this barbarous country? '

' On a night like this,' said Marcus, ' it seems odd almost past believing.'

' I had nothing to take me back,' said the other, simply. ' Most of my service years were spent here, though it was in Judaea that my time fell due for parting with the Eagles. What have I to do with the South? A few memories, very few.

I was a young man when first I saw the white cliffs of Dubris above the transport galley's prow. Far more memories in the North. Your move. . . .'

Marcus moved an ivory man to the next square, and his uncle shifted his own piece. 'If I settled in the South, I should miss the skies. Ever noticed how changeful British skies are? I have made friends here—a few. The only woman I ever cared a denarius for lies buried at Glevum.'

Marcus looked up quickly. 'I never knew—— '

'Why should you? But I was not always old Uncle Aquila with a bald head.'

'No, of course not. What was—she like? '

'Very pretty. She was the daughter of my old Camp Commandant, who had a face like a camel, but she was very pretty, with a lot of soft brown hair. Eighteen when she died. I was twenty-two.'

Marcus said nothing. There seemed nothing to say. But Uncle Aquila, seeing the look on his face, gave a deep chuckle. 'No, you have it all quite wrong. I am a very selfish old man, perfectly well content with things as they are.' And then, after a pause, he harked back to an earlier point in their discussion. 'I killed my first boar in Silurian territory; I have sworn the blood brotherhood with a painted tribesman up beyond where Hadrian's Wall stands now; I've a dog buried at Lugu-vallium—her name was Margarita; I have loved a girl at Glevum; I have marched the Eagles from end to end of Britain in worse weather than this. Those are the things apt to strike a man's roots for him.'

Marcus said after a moment, 'I think I begin to understand.'

'Good. Your move.'

But after they had played a few more moves in silence, Uncle Aquila looked up again, the fine wrinkles deepening at the corners of his eyes. 'What an autumnal mood we have wandered into! We need livening up, you and I.'

'What do you suggest? ' Marcus returned the smile.

'I suggest the Saturnalia Games tomorrow. We may not be able to compete quite on equal terms with the Colosseum, here at Calleva; but a wild-beast show, a sham fight with perhaps a little blood-letting—we will certainly go.'

And they went, Marcus travelling in a litter, for all the world, as he remarked disgustedly, like a Magistrate or a fine lady. They arrived early, but by the time they were settled on one of the cushioned benches reserved for the Magistrates and their families (Uncle Aquila was a Magistrate, though he had not come in a litter), the amphitheatre just outside the East Gate was already filling up with eager spectators. The wind had died down, but the air struck cold, with a clear, chill tang to it that Marcus sniffed eagerly while he pulled the folds of his old military cloak more closely round him. After being so long within four walls, the sanded space of the arena seemed very wide; a great emptiness within the encircling banks up which the crowded benches rose tier on tier.

Whatever else of Rome the British had not taken to, they seemed to have taken to the Games with a vengeance, Marcus thought, looking about him at the crowded benches where townsfolk and tribesmen with their womenfolk and children jostled and shoved and shouted after the best places. There was a fair sprinkling of Legionaries from the transit camp, and Marcus's quick glance picked out a bored young tribune sitting with several British lads all pretending to be equally Roman and equally bored. He remembered Colosseum crowds, chattering, shouting, quarrelling, laying bets and eating sticky sweets. The British took their pleasures a little less loudly, to be sure, but on almost every face was the same eager, almost greedy look that the faces of the Colosseum crowds had worn.

A small disturbance near him drew Marcus's attention to the arrival of a family who were just entering their places on the Magistrates' benches a little to his right. A British family of the ultra-Roman kind, a large, good-natured-looking man, running to fat as men do who have been bred to a hard life and take to living soft instead; a woman with a fair and rather foolish face, prinked out in what had been the height of fashion in Rome two years ago—and very cold she must be, Marcus thought, in that thin mantle; and a girl of perhaps twelve or thirteen, with a sharply pointed face that seemed all golden eyes in the shadow of her dark hood. The stout man and Uncle Aquila saluted each other across the heads between, and the woman bowed. All Rome was in that bow; but the girl's eyes were fixed on the arena with a kind of horrified expectancy.

When the new-comers were settled in their places, Marcus touched his uncle's wrist, and cocked an inquiring eyebrow.

'A fellow Magistrate of mine, Kaeso by name, and his wife Valaria,' Uncle Aquila said. 'Incidentally, they are our next-door neighbours.'

'Are they so? But the little maiden; she is no bud of their branch, surely?'

But he got no answer to his question then, for at that moment a great crashing of cymbals and a fanfare of trumpets announced that the Games were about to begin. All round the crowded circus there was a sudden quietness and a craning forward. Again the trumpets sounded. The double doors at the far side were flung open, and out from their underground lodgements a double file of gladiators came marching into the arena, each carrying the weapons he would use later in the show. Shout on shout greeted their appearance. For a small colonial circus they seemed rather a good lot, Marcus thought, watching them as they paraded round the arena; too good, maybe, though probably they were all slaves. Marcus was something of a heretic where the Games were concerned; he liked well enough to see a wild-beast show, or a sham fight if it were well done, but to put up men—even slaves—to fight to the death for a crowd's amusement, seemed to him a waste.

The men had halted now, before the Magistrates' benches; and in the few moments that they stood there, Marcus's whole attention was caught by one of them: a sword-and-buckler man of about his own age. He was rather short for a Briton, but powerful. His russet-brown hair, flung back by the savage pride with which he carried his head, showed the clipped ear that branded him for a slave. Seemingly he had been taken in war, for his breast and shoulders—he was stripped to the waist—were tattooed with blue warrior patterns. But it was none of these things that Marcus saw, only the look in the wide-set grey eyes that strained back at him out of the gladiator's young sullen face.

'This man is afraid,' said something deep in Marcus. 'Afraid—afraid,' and his own stomach cringed within him.

A score of weapons flashed in the wintry light as they were tossed up with a shout and caught again, and the gladiators wheeled and strode on down the wide curve that led back to their starting point. But the look that he had seen in the young swordsman's eyes remained with Marcus.

The first item on the programme was a fight between wolves and a brown bear. The bear did not want to fight, and was driven into battle by the long curling whip-lashes of the attendants. Presently, amid a great shouting from the on-lookers, it was killed. Its body was dragged away, and with it the bodies of two wolves it had slain; the others were decoyed back into their wheeled cage for another time, and attendants spread fresh sand over the blood in the arena. Marcus glanced, without quite knowing why, at the girl in the dark hood, and saw her sitting as though frozen, her eyes wide and blank with horror in an ashy face. Still oddly shaken by that queer moment of contact with the young gladiator who was so very much afraid, he was filled with a sudden unreasoning anger against Kaeso and his wife for bringing the little maiden to see a thing like this, against all Games and all mobs who came to watch them with their tongues hanging out for horrors, even against the bear for being killed.

The next item was a sham fight, with little damage done save a few flesh wounds. (In the back of beyond, circus masters could not afford to be wasteful with their gladiators.) Then a boxing match in which the heavy cestus round the fighters' hands drew considerably more blood than the swords had done. A pause came, in which the arena was once again cleaned up and freshly sanded; and then a long gasp of expectancy ran through the crowd, and even the bored young tribune sat up and began to take some notice, as, with another blare of trumpets, the double doors swung wide once more, and two figures stepped out side by side into the huge emptiness of the arena. Here was the real thing: a fight to the death.

At first sight the two would seem to be unequally armed, for while one carried sword and buckler, the other, a slight dark man with something of the Greek in his face and build, carried only a three-pronged spear, and had over his shoulder a many-folded net, weighted with small discs of lead. But in truth, as Marcus knew only too well, the odds were all in favour of the man with the net, the Fisher, as he was called, and he saw with an odd sinking of the heart that the other was the young swordsman who was afraid.

'Never did like the net,' Uncle Aquila was grumbling. 'Not a clean fight, no!' A few moments earlier, Marcus had known that his damaged leg was beginning to cramp horribly; he had been shifting, and shifting again, trying to ease the pain without catching his uncle's notice, but now, as the two men crossed to the centre of the arena, he had forgotten about it.

The roar which greeted the pair of fighters had fallen to a breathless hush. In the centre of the arena the two men were being placed by the captain of the gladiators; placed with exquisite care, ten paces apart, with no advantage of light or wind allowed to either. The thing was quickly and competently done, and the captain stepped back to the barriers. For what seemed a long time, neither of the two moved. Moment followed moment, and still they remained motionless, the centre of all that great circle of staring faces. Then, very slowly, the swordsman began to move. Never taking his eyes from his adversary, he slipped one foot in front of the other; crouching a little, covering his body with the round buckler, inch by inch he crept forward, every muscle tensed to spring when the time came.

The Fisher stood as still as ever, poised on the balls of his feet, the trident in his left hand, his right lost in the folds of the net. Just beyond reach of the net, the swordsman checked for a long, agonizing moment, and then sprang in. His attack was so swift that the flung net flew harmlessly over his head, and the Fisher leapt back and sideways to avoid his thrust, then whirled about and ran for his life, gathering his net for another cast as he ran, with the young swordsman hard behind him. Half round the arena they sped, running low; the swordsman had not the other's length and lightness of build, but he ran as a hunter runs—perhaps he had run down deer on the hunting trail, before ever his ear was clipped—and he was gaining on his quarry now. The two came flying round the curve of the barrier towards the Magistrates' benches, and just abreast of them the Fisher whirled about and flung once more. The net whipped out like a dark flame; it licked round the running swordsman, so intent on his chase that he had forgotten to guard for it; the weight carried the deadly folds across and across again, and a howl burst from the crowd as he crashed headlong and rolled over, helplessly meshed as a fly in a spider's web.

Marcus wrenched forward, his breath caught in his throat. The swordsman was lying just below him, so near that they could have spoken to each other in an undertone. The Fisher was standing over his fallen antagonist, with the trident poised to strike, a little smile on his face, though his breath whistled through widened nostrils, as he looked about him for the bidding of the crowd. The fallen man made as though to raise his hampered arm in the signal by which a vanquished gladiator might appeal to the crowd for mercy; then let it drop back, proudly, to his side. Through the fold of the net across his face, he looked up straight into Marcus's eyes, a look as direct and intimate as though they had been the only two people in all that great amphitheatre.

Marcus was up and standing with one hand on the barrier rail to steady himself, while with the other he made the sign for mercy. Again and again he made it, with a blazing vehemence, with every atom of will-power that was in him, his glance thrusting like a challenge along the crowded tiers of benches where already the thumbs were beginning to turn down. This mob, this unutterably stupid, blood-greedy mob that must somehow be swung over into forgoing the blood it wanted! His gorge

E

rose against them, and there was an extraordinary sense of
battle in him that could not have been more vivid had he been
standing over the fallen gladiator, sword in hand.   Thumbs up!
Thumbs up! you fools! . . . He had been aware from the first
of Uncle Aquila's great thumb pointing skyward beside him;
suddenly he was aware of a few others echoing the gesture, and
then a few more.   For a long, long moment the swordsman's
fate still hung in the balance, and then as thumb after thumb
went up, the Fisher slowly lowered his trident and with a little
mocking bow, stepped back.

Marcus drew a shuddering breath, and relaxed into a flood of
pain from his cramped leg, as an attendant came forward to
disentangle the swordsman and aid him to his feet.   He did
not look at the young gladiator again.   This moment was
shame for him, and Marcus felt that he had no right to witness it.

.   .   .   .   .

That evening, over the usual game of draughts, Marcus asked
his uncle: 'What will become of that lad now?'

Uncle Aquila moved an ebony piece after due consideration.
'The young fool of a swordsman?   He will be sold in all likelihood.   The crowd do not pay to see a man fight, when once
he has been down and at their mercy.'

'That is what I have been thinking,' Marcus said.   He looked
up from making his own move.   'How do prices run in these
parts?   Would fifteen hundred sesterces buy him?'

'Very probably.   Why?'

'Because I have that much left of my pay and a parting
thank-offering that I had from Tullus Lepidus.   There was not
much to spend it on in Isca Dumnoniorum.'

Uncle Aquila's brows cocked inquiringly.   'Are you sug-
gesting buying him yourself?'

'Would you give him house-room?'

'I expect so,' said Uncle Aquila.   'Though I am somewhat
at a loss to understand why you should wish to keep a tame
gladiator.   Why not try a wolf instead?'

Marcus laughed.   'It is not so much a tame gladiator as a

body-slave that I need. I cannot go on overworking poor old Stephanos for ever.'

Uncle Aquila leaned across the chequered board. 'And what makes you think that an ex-gladiator would make you a suitable body-slave?'

'To speak the truth, I had not thought about it,' Marcus said. 'How do you advise me to set about buying him?'

'Send down to the circus slave-master, and offer half of what you expect to pay. And sleep with a knife under your pillow thereafter,' said Uncle Aquila.

VI

ESCA

THE purchase was arranged next day, without much difficulty, for although the price that Marcus could afford was not large, Beppo, the master of the circus slaves, knew well enough that he was not likely to get a better one for a beaten gladiator. So, after a little haggling, the bargain was struck, and that evening after dinner Stephanos went to fetch home the new slave.

Marcus waited for their return alone in the atrium, for Uncle Aquila had retired to his watch-tower study to work out a particularly absorbing problem in siege warfare. He had been trying to read his uncle's copy of the Georgics, but his thoughts kept wandering from Virgil on bee-keeping to the encounter before him. He was wondering for the first time —he had not thought to wonder before—why the fate of a slave gladiator he had never before set eyes on should matter to him so nearly. But it did matter. Maybe it was like calling to like; and yet it was hard to see quite what he had in common with a barbarian slave.

Presently his listening ear caught the sound of an arrival in the slaves' quarters, and he laid down the papyrus roll and turned towards the doorway. Steps came along the colonnade, and two figures appeared on the threshold. 'Centurion Marcus, I have brought the new slave,' said Stephanos, and stepped discreetly back into the night; and the new slave walked forward to the foot of Marcus's couch, and stood there.

For a long moment the two young men looked at each other, alone in the empty lamplit atrium as yesterday they had been alone in the crowded amphitheatre, while the scuff-scuffling of Stephanos's sandals died away down the colonnade.

'So it is you,' the slave said at last.

'Yes, it is I.'

The silence began again, and again the slave broke it. 'Why did you turn the purpose of the crowd yesterday? I did not ask for mercy.'

'Possibly that was why.'

The slave hesitated, and then said defiantly, 'I was afraid yesterday; I, who have been a warrior. I am afraid to choke out my life in the Fisher's net.'

'I know,' Marcus said. 'But still, you did not ask for mercy.'

The other's eyes were fixed on his face, a little puzzled. 'Why have you bought me?'

'I have need of a body-slave.'

'Surely the arena is an unusual place to pick one.'

'But then, I wished for an unusual body-slave.' Marcus looked up with the merest quirk of a smile into the sullen grey eyes fixed so unswervingly on his own. 'Not one like Stephanos, that has been a slave all his life, and is therefore—nothing more.'

It was an odd conversation between master and slave, but neither of them was thinking of that.

'I have been but two years a slave,' said the other quietly.

'And before that you were a warrior—and your name?'

'I am Esca, son of Cunoval, of the tribe of Brigantes, the bearers of the blue war-shield.'

'And I am—I was, a centurion of auxiliaries with the Second Legion,' Marcus said, not knowing quite why he made the reply, knowing only that it had to be made. Roman and Briton faced each other in the lamplight, while the two statements seemed to hang like a challenge in the air between them.

Then Esca put out a hand unconsciously and touched the edge of the couch. 'That I know, for the goaty one, Stephanos, told me; and also that my Master has been wounded. I am sorry for that.'

'Thank you,' Marcus said.

Esca looked down at his own hand on the edge of the couch,

and then up again. ' It would have been easy to escape on my
way here,' he said slowly. ' The old goaty one could not have
held me back if I had chosen to break for freedom. But I chose
to go with him because it was in my heart that it might be you
that we went to.'

' And if it had been another, after all? '

' Then I should have escaped later, to the wilds where my
clipped ear would not betray me. There are still free tribes
beyond the Frontiers.' As he spoke, he drew from the breast
of his rough tunic, where it had lain against his skin, a slender
knife, which he handled as tenderly as if it had been a thing
living and beloved. ' I had this, to my release.'

' And now? ' Marcus said, not giving a glance to the narrow,
deadly thing.

For a moment the sullenness lifted from Esca's face. He
leaned forward and let the dagger fall with a little clatter on
to the inlaid table at Marcus's side. ' I am the Centurion's
hound, to lie at the Centurion's feet,' he said.

.   .   .   .   .

So Esca joined the household and, carrying the spear that
marked him for a personal slave and superior to mere household slaves, stood behind Marcus's couch at meals to pour wine
for him, fetched and carried and saw to his belongings, and
slept on a mattress across his door at night. He made a very
good body-slave, so good that Marcus guessed him to have been
somebody's armour-bearer in the days before his ear was
clipped; a father's, or an elder brother's, perhaps, after the
custom of the tribes. He never asked about those days, nor
how Esca had come into the Calleva arena, because something
about his slave, some inner reserve, warned him that to ask
would be an intrusion, a walking in without leave. One day,
perhaps, Esca would tell him freely, but not yet.

The weeks went by, and suddenly the rose-bushes in the
courtyard were gemmed with swelling leaf-buds, and the air
had a sense of quickening that was the first distant promise of
spring. Slowly, very slowly, Marcus's leg was mending. It

no longer woke him with a stab of pain every time he turned in the night, and he could hobble round the house more and more easily.

As time passed, he got into the way of leaving his stick behind him and walking with a hand on Esca's shoulder instead. It seemed natural to do that, for without quite realizing it, he was slipping more and more often from the master to the friend in his dealings with Esca; though, after that first night, Esca never for an instant forgot the slave in his dealings with Marcus.

That winter there was a lot of trouble with wolves in the district. Driven out from their fastnesses by hunger, they hunted under the very walls of Calleva; and often Marcus would hear their long-drawn cry in the night, setting every dog in the town baying in that frenzy that was half hate and half longing, half enemy hurling defiance at enemy, half kin calling to kin. In the outlying farms of the forest clearings, lambing pens were attacked, and anxious men kept the wolf-guard every night. At a village a few miles away a pony was killed, at another a baby was taken.

Then one day, Esca, going into the town on an errand for Marcus, returned with news of a country-wide wolf hunt planned for next day. It had started simply among the outlying farms, desperate to save their lambing ewes, then gathered to itself professional hunters, and a couple of young officers from the transit camp out for a day's sport; and now it seemed that half the countryside was out to end the menace. He poured it all out to Marcus. The hunters were to meet at such a place, two hours before sunrise; at such another place they were going to drive the thickets with dogs and torches; and Marcus laid aside the belt he was mending, and listened to him as eager to hear as his slave was to tell.

Listening, he longed to be off on that wolf hunt and run the spring fret out of his bones; and he knew that the same longing was hot in his slave. For him, it did not seem likely that there would be any more hunting, but that was no reason why there should be none for Esca. 'Esca,' he said abruptly, when the other had told all that there was to tell. 'It would surely be a good thing if you joined this wolf hunt.'

Esca's whole face lit with eagerness, but after a moment he said, 'It would mean maybe a night and a day that the Centurion must do without his slave.'

'I shall do well enough,' Marcus told him. 'I shall borrow half of Stephanos from my uncle. But what will you do for spears? I left my own for the man who came after me at Isca, else you could have had those.'

'If my Master is sure, really sure, I know where I can borrow spears.'

'Good. Do you go and borrow them now.'

So Esca borrowed the spears he needed, and in the pitch dark of that night, Marcus heard him get up and collect them from the corner where they had been stacked. He turned on his elbow and spoke into the darkness. 'You are going now?'

A light footfall and a sense of movement told him that Esca was standing at his side. 'Yes, if the Centurion is still sure—quite sure?'

'Perfectly sure. Go and spear your wolf.'

'It is in my heart that I wish the Centurion came too,' Esca said in a rush.

'Maybe I'll come another year,' Marcus said sleepily. 'Good hunting, Esca.'

For an instant a dark shape showed in the lesser darkness of the doorway, and then it was gone, and he lay listening, not at all sleepily now, to the quick, light footfall dying away along the colonnade.

In the grey of the next dawn, he heard the footfall returning, a little heavier than at the setting out, and the dark shape loomed again into the cobweb pallor of the doorway.

'Esca!—How went the hunting?'

'The hunting was good,' Esca said. He stacked the spears with a slight clatter against the wall, and came and bent over the cot; and Marcus saw that there was something curled in the crook of his arm, under the rough cloak. 'I have brought

back the fruits of my hunting for the Centurion,' he said, and
set the thing down on the blanket. It was alive, and being
disturbed, it whimpered: and Marcus's gently exploring hand
discovered that it was warm and harshly furry.

'Esca! A wolf cub?' he said, feeling a scrabble of paws
and a thrusting muzzle.

Esca had turned away to strike flint and steel and kindle the
lamp. The tiny flame sank and then sprang up and steadied;
and in the dazzle of yellow light he saw a very small grey cub,
who staggered to uncertain paws, sneezing at the sudden light,
and pushed in under his hand with the nuzzling thrust of all
very young things. Esca came back to the cot and dropped
on one knee beside it. And as he did so Marcus noticed that
there was a hot look in his eyes, a brightness that he had not
seen there before, and wondered with an odd sense of hurt if his
return to bondage from a day and night of freedom was the
cause.

'In my tribe, when a she-wolf with whelps is killed, we
sometimes take the young ones to run with the dog-pack,'
Esca said. 'If they are like this one, little, little, so that they
remember nothing before; so that their first meat comes from
their master's hand.'

'Is he hungry now?' Marcus asked, as the cub's muzzle
poked and snuggled into his palm.

'No, he is full of milk—and scraps. Sassticca will not miss
them. See, he is half asleep already; that is why he is so
gentle.'

The two of them looked at each other, half laughing; but
the queer hot look was still in Esca's eyes; while the cub
crawled whimpering into the warm hollow of Marcus's shoulder,
and settled there. His breath smelled of onions, like a puppy.

'How did you get him?'

'We killed a she-wolf in milk, so I and two others went to
look for the whelps. They killed the rest of the litter, those
fools of the South; but this one, I saved. His sire came. They
are good fathers, the wolf kind, fierce to protect their young.
It was a fight: aie ! a good fight.'

'It was taking a hideous risk,' Marcus said. 'You should not have done it, Esca!' He was half angry, half humbled, that Esca should have taken such a deadly risk to bring him the cub, for he was enough of a hunter himself to know what the hazard was in robbing a wolf's lair while the sire still lived.

Esca seemed to draw back into himself on the instant. 'I forgot it was my Master's property that I risked,' he said, his voice suddenly hard and heavy as stone.

'Don't be a fool,' Marcus said quickly. 'I didn't mean that, and you know it.'

There was a long silence. The two young men looked at each other, and there was no trace of laughter now in their faces.

'Esca,' Marcus said at last, 'what has happened?'

'Nothing.'

'That is a lie,' Marcus said. 'Someone has been working mischief.'

The other remained stubbornly silent.

'Esca, I want an answer.'

The other moved a little, and some of the defiance went out of him. 'It was my own fault,' he began at last, speaking as though every word was dragged out of him. 'There was a young Tribune; one of those from the transit camp, who I think is taking troops up to Eboracum—a very splendid young Tribune, smooth as a girl, but a skilled hunter. He was one of us who went into the lair; and after the old dog-wolf was dead, and we had come away, and I was cleaning my spear, he laughed and said to me, "So, that was a noble thrust!" And then he saw my clipped ear, and he said, "for a slave". I was angry, and I let my tongue run away from me. I said: "I am body-slave to the Centurion Marcus Flavius Aquila; does the Tribune Placidus (that was his name) see any cause therein that I should be a worse hunter than himself?"' Esca broke off for a moment, drawing a harsh breath. 'He said: "None in the world; but at least the Tribune Placidus's life is his own to hazard as he wills. Your Master, having paid good money for his slave, will not thank you for leaving him with a carcass that he cannot even sell to the knacker's yard. Remember that when next you thrust your head into a wolf's lair." And then he smiled, and his smile is a sickness in my belly, still.'

Esca had been speaking in a dull, hopeless monotone, as though he had the bitter lesson by heart; and as he listened, Marcus was filled with a cold anger against the unknown Tribune; and the light of his rage suddenly made clear to him certain things that he had never thought of before.

Abruptly he reached out his free hand and grasped the other's wrist. 'Esca, have I ever, by word or deed, given you to believe that I think of you as that six-month soldier evidently thinks of his slaves?'

Esca shook his head. His defiance was all gone from him, and his face in the paling lamplight was no longer set and sullen, but only wretched. 'The Centurion is not such a one as the Tribune Placidus, to show the whip-lash without need to his hound,' he said drearily.

Marcus, baffled, hurt, and angry, suddenly lost his temper. 'Oh, curse Tribune Placidus!' he burst out, his grasp tightening fiercely on the other's wrist. 'Does his word strike so much deeper with you than mine, that because of it you must needs talk to me of hounds and whip-lashes? Name of Light! Do I have to tell you in so many words that I really do not imagine a clipped ear to be the dividing-line between men and beasts? Have I not shown you clearly enough all this while? I have not thought of equal or unequal, slave or free in my dealings with you, though you were too proud to do the same for me! Too *proud*! Do you hear me? And now'—forgetful for the moment of the sleeping cub, he made a sudden movement to get on to his elbow, and collapsed again, exasperated but half laughing, his fury gone like a pricked bubble, holding up a bleeding thumb. 'And now your gift has bitten me! Mithras! His mouth is full of daggers!'

'Then you had best pay me a sesterce for the lot of them,' said Esca, and suddenly they were both laughing, the quick light laughter of breaking strain that has very little to do with whether or not there is anything to laugh at, while between them on the striped native blanket the small grey wolf-cub crouched, savage, bewildered, but very sleepy.

The household varied a good deal in their reactions to the sudden appearance of a wolf-cub in their midst. Procyon was doubtful at their first meeting; the new-comer had the wolf smell, the outland smell, and the great hound walked round him on stiff legs, the hair on his neck rising a little, while the cub squatted like a hairy malignant toad on the atrium floor, ears laid back and muzzle wrinkled in his first attempt at a snarl. Uncle Aquila scarcely noticed his arrival, being at the moment too deeply absorbed in the siege of Jerusalem; and Marcipor, the house slave, and Stephanos looked on him rather askance—a wolf-cub that would one day be a wolf, roaming at large about the house. But Sassticca was unexpectedly an ally. Sassticca, her hands on her hips, told them roundly that they should be ashamed of themselves. Who were they, she demanded shrilly, with two sound legs apiece, to begrudge the young Master a pack of wolf-cubs if he wanted them? And she finished her baking in a state of high indignation, and presently brought Marcus three brown honey-cakes in a napkin, and a chipped bowl of castor ware with a hunting scene on it, which she said he might have for the little cub's feeding-bowl.

Marcus, who had overheard her championship—she had a loud voice—accepted both gifts with becoming gratitude, and when she had gone, he and Esca shared the cakes between them. He no longer minded Sassticca quite so desperately as he had done at first.

A few days later, Esca told Marcus about the days before his ear was clipped.

They were in the bath-house when it happened, drying themselves after a cold plunge. The time that he spent in the plunge-bath each day was one of Marcus's greatest pleasures, for it was big enough to splash about in and swim a few strokes; and while he was in the water, unless he was very careless, he could forget about his lame leg. It was a little like his old sense of being born from one kind of life into another, that he had been used to know in his charioteering days. But the likeness was the kind that a shadow bears to the real thing, and this morning as he sat up on the bronze couch, drying himself, he was suddenly sick with longing for the old splendour. Once more, just once more, to know that burst of speed as the team sprang forward, the swoop and the strength of it, and wind of his going singing by.

And at that moment, as though called up by the intensity of his longing, a swiftly driven chariot came whirling up the street beyond the bath-house wall.

Marcus reached out and took his tunic from Esca, saying as he did so, ' Not often that we hear anything but a vegetable cart in this street.'

' It will be Lucius Urbanus, the contractor's son,' Esca said. ' There is a back way from his stables which comes through behind the temple of Sull-Minerva.' The chariot was passing the house now, and evidently the driver was having trouble, for the crack of a whip and the loud burst of swearing reached them through the bath-house wall, and Esca added with disgust, ' It should be a vegetable cart and drawn by an ox. Listen to him! He is not worthy to handle horses! '

Marcus pulled the folds of fine wool over his head and reached for his belt. ' So Esca also is a charioteer,' he said, fastening it.

' I was my father's charioteer,' Esca said. ' But that was a long time ago.'

And suddenly Marcus realized that he could ask Esca, now, about the time before his ear was clipped. It would no longer be walking in without leave. He shifted a little, making a quick gesture towards the foot of the couch, and as the other sat down, he said: ' Esca, how did your father's charioteer come to be a gladiator in the Calleva arena? '

Esca was buckling his own belt; he finished the task very deliberately, and then, locking his hands round one updrawn knee, sat silent for a moment, staring down at them. ' My father was a Clan Chieftain of the Brigantes, lord of five hundred spears,' he said at last. ' I was his armour-bearer

until such time as I became a warrior in my own right—with
the men of my tribe that happens after the sixteenth summer.
When I had been a year or more a man among men and my
father's charioteer, the Clan rose against our overlords, for the
lust for freedom that was in us. We have been a thorn in the
flesh of the Legions since first they marched north; we, the
bearers of the blue war-shield. We rose, and we were beaten
back. We made our last stand in our strong place, and we
were overwhelmed. Those of the men's side who were left—
there were not many—were sold as slaves.' He broke off,
jerking up his head to look at Marcus. ' But I swear before the
gods of my people, before Lugh the Light of the Sun, that I was
lying for dead in a ditch when they took me. They would not
have taken me, else. They sold me to a trader from the South,
who sold me to Beppo, here in Calleva; and you know the
rest.'

' You alone of all your kin? ' Marcus asked after a moment.

' My father and two brothers died,' Esca said. ' My mother
also. My father killed her before the Legionaries broke
through. She wished it so.'

There was a long silence, and then Marcus said softly:
' Mithras! What a story! '

' It is a common enough story, still. Was it so very different
at Isca Dumnoniorum, do you suppose? ' But before Marcus
could answer, he added quickly, ' None the less, it is not good
to remember too closely. The time before—all the time
before—that is the good time to remember.'

And sitting there in the thin March sunshine that slanted
down through the high window, without either of them quite
knowing how it happened, he began to tell Marcus about the
time before. He told of a warrior's training; of river-bathing
on hot summer days when the midges danced in the shimmering air; of his father's great white bull garlanded with
poppies and moon flowers for a festival; of his first hunt, and
the tame otter he had shared with his elder brother. . . . One
thing led to another, and presently he told how, ten years before,
when the whole country was in revolt, he had lain behind a

boulder to watch a Legion marching north, that never came marching back.

'I had never seen such a sight before,' he said. 'Like a shining serpent of men winding across the hills; a grey serpent, hackled with the scarlet cloaks and crests of the officers. There were queer tales about that Legion; men said that it was accursed, but it looked stronger than any curse, stronger and more deadly. And I remember how the Eagle flashed in the sun as it came by—a great golden Eagle with its wings arched back as I have seen them often stoop on a screaming hare among the heather. But the mist was creeping down from the high moors, and the Legion marched into it, straight into it, and it licked them up and flowed together behind them, and they were gone as though they had marched from one world into—another.' Esca made a quick gesture with his right hand, the first two fingers spread like horns. 'Queer tales there were, about that Legion.'

'Yes, I have heard those tales,' Marcus said. 'Esca, that was my father's Legion. His crest will have been the scarlet hackle next after the Eagle.'

VII

TWO WORLDS MEETING

ROM the open end of Uncle Aquila's courtyard, two
shallow steps flanked by a bush of rosemary and a slender
bay-tree led down into the garden. It was a rather wild
garden, for Uncle Aquila did not keep a full-time garden slave,
but a very pleasant one, running down to the crumbling
earthworks of British Calleva. In some places the fine stone-
faced city walls were already rising. One day they would
rise here too, but as yet there was only the curved wave-break
of old quiet turf, glimpsed between the branches of wild fruit-
trees; and where the bank dipped, stray glimpses over mile
upon mile of forest country rolling away into the smoke-
blue distance where the Forest of Spinaii became the Forest of
Anderida, and the Forest of Anderida dropped to the marshes
and the sea.

To Marcus, after being cooped within doors all winter long,
it seemed a wonderfully wide and shining place when he
reached it for the first time some days later; and when Esca
had left him to go off on some errand, he stretched himself
out on the bench of grey Purbeck marble, under the wild
fruit-trees, his arms behind his head, gazing upwards with eyes
narrowed against the brightness, into the blown blue heights
of heaven, which seemed so incredibly tall after roof-beams.
Somewhere in the forest below him, birds were singing, with
that note of clear-washed surprise that belongs to the early
spring; and for a while Marcus simply lay letting it all soak into
him, the wideness and the shine and the bird-song.

Close beside him, Cub lay curled into a compact ball.
Looking at him now, it was hard to believe what a small fury
he could be, crouched over his food-bowl with laid-back ears
and bared milk-teeth, Marcus thought. Then he took up the

task that he had brought out with him. He was one of those people who need something to do with their hands at all times, even if it is only a stick to whittle; and something of the craftsman in him demanded always to have an outlet. If he had not been wounded, he would have turned that craftsmanship to the making of a happy and efficient cohort; things being as they were, he had turned it this spring to overhauling and renovating the Celtic weapons which were the only ornament Uncle Aquila allowed on his walls. Today he had brought out the gem of the small collection, a light cavalry buckler of bull's hide faced with bronze, the central boss exquisitely worked with red enamel; but the straps must have been in a poor state when Uncle Aquila came by it, and now they were ready to tear like papyrus. Laying out his tools and the leather for the fresh straps beside him on the broad seat, he set to work to cut away the old ones. It was a delicate task, needing all his attention, and he did not look up again until he had finished it, and turned to lay the outworn straps aside.

And then he saw that he was no longer alone with Cub. A girl was standing among the wild fruit-trees where the hedge ran up into the slope of the old earthwork, and looking down at him. A British girl, in a pale saffron tunic, straight and shining as a candle-flame; one hand raised to thrust back heavy masses of hair the colour of red baltic amber, which the light wind had blown across her face.

They looked at each other in silence for a moment. Then the girl said in clear, very careful Latin, ' I have waited a long time for you to look up.'

' I am sorry,' Marcus said stiffly. ' I was busy on this shield.'

She came a step nearer. ' May I see the wolf-cub? I have not seen a tame wolf-cub before.'

And Marcus smiled suddenly, and laid aside his defences with the shield he had been working on. ' Surely. Here he is.' And swinging his feet to the ground, he reached down and grabbed the sleeping cub by the scruff of his neck, just as the girl joined him. The wolfling was not fiercer than most hound puppies,

F

save when annoyed, but being bigger and stronger for his age, he could be very rough, and Marcus was taking no chances. He set Cub on his feet, keeping a restraining hand under his small chest. 'Be careful; he is not used to strangers.'

The girl gave him a smile, and sat down on her heels, holding out her hands slowly to Cub. 'I will not startle him,' she said. And Cub, who at first had crouched back against Marcus, ears flattened and hairs bristling, seemed very slowly to change his mind. Warily, ready to flinch back or snap at any sign of danger, he began to smell at her fingers; and she held her hands quite still, to let him. 'What is his name?' she asked.

'Just Cub.'

'Cub,' she said crooningly. 'Cub.' And as he whimpered and made a little darting thrust towards her, against Marcus's guarding hand, she began to caress the warm hollow under his chin with one finger. ' See, we be friends, you and I.'

She was about thirteen, Marcus imagined, watching her as she played with Cub. A tall, thin girl, with a pointed face wide at the temples and narrow at the chin; and the shape of her face and the colour of her eyes and hair gave her a little the look of a young vixen. If she were angry, he thought, she would probably look very like a vixen indeed. He had the glimmering of an idea that he had seen her before, but he could not remember where.

' How did you know about Cub? ' he asked at last.

She looked up. ' Narcissa, my nurse, told me—oh, about a moon ago. And at first I did not believe it, because Nissa so often gets her stories wrong. But yesterday I heard a slave on this side of the hedge call to another, " Oh worthless one, thy Master's wolf-whelp has bitten my toe ! " And the other called back, " Then the gods grant that the taste of it will not make him sick ! " So I knew that it was true.'

Her imitation of Esca and Marcipor the house slave was unmistakable, and Marcus flung up his head with a crow of laughter. ' And it did !—at all events, something did.'

The girl laughed too, joyously, showing little pointed teeth as white and sharp as Cub's. And as though their laughter had unlocked a door, Marcus suddenly remembered where he had seen her before. He had not been interested enough in Kaeso and Valaria to remember that they lived next door, and although he had noticed her so vividly at the time, he had not remembered the girl he had seen with them, because Esca, coming immediately afterwards, had been so much more important; but he remembered her now.

' I saw you at the Saturnalia Games,' he said. ' But your hair was hidden under your mantle, and that was why I did not remember you.'

' But I remember you ! ' said the girl. Cub had wandered off after a beetle by that time, and she let him go, sitting back and folding her hands in her lap. ' Nissa says you bought that gladiator. I wish you could have bought the bear too.'

' You minded very badly about that bear, didn't you? ' said Marcus.

' It was cruel! To kill on the hunting trail, that is one thing; but they took away his freedom! They kept him in a cage, and then they killed him.'

' It was the cage, then, more than the killing? '

' I do not like cages,' said the girl in a small hard voice. ' Or nets. I am glad you bought that gladiator.'

A little chill wind came soughing across the garden, silvering the long grass and tossing the budding sprays of the wild pear- and cherry-trees. The girl shivered, and Marcus realized that her yellow tunic was of very thin wool, and even here in the shelter of the old earthworks it was still very early spring.

' You are cold,' he said, and gathered up his old military cloak which had been flung across the bench. ' Put this on.'

' Do you not want it? '

' No. I have a thicker tunic than that flimsy thing you are wearing. So. Now, come and sit here on the bench.'

She obeyed him instantly, drawing the cloak around her. In the act of doing so, she checked, looking down at the bright folds, then up again at Marcus. ' This is your soldier's cloak,' she said. ' Like the cloaks the centurions from the transit camp wear.'

Marcus made her a quick mocking salute. ' You behold in me Marcus Aquila, ex-Cohort Centurion of Gaulish Auxiliaries with the Second Legion.'

The girl looked at him in silence for a moment. Then she said, ' I know. Does the wound hurt you still? '

' Sometimes,' Marcus said. ' Did Nissa tell you that too? ' She nodded.

' She seems to have told you a deal of things.'

' Slaves! ' She made a quick, contemptuous gesture. ' They stand in doorways and chatter like starlings; but Nissa is the worst of them all! '

Marcus laughed, and a small silence fell between them; but after a little while he said: ' I have told you my name. What is yours? '

'My aunt and uncle call me Camilla, but my real name is Cottia,' said the girl. 'They like everything to be very Roman, you see.'

So he had been right in thinking she was not Kaeso's daughter. 'And you do not?' he said.

'I? I am of the Iceni! So is my Aunt Valaria, though she likes to forget it.'

'I once knew a black chariot team who were descended out of the Royal Stables of the Iceni,' Marcus said, feeling that perhaps Aunt Valaria was not a very safe subject.

'Did you? Were they yours? Which strain?' Her face was alight with interest.

Marcus shook his head. 'They were not mine, and I only had the joy of driving them once; it was a joy too. And I never knew their strain.'

'My father's big stallion was descended from Prydfirth, the beloved of King Prasutogus,' said Cottia. 'We are all horse-breeders, we of the Iceni, from the King downward—when we had a king.' She hesitated, and her voice lost its eager ring. 'My father was killed, breaking a young horse, and that is why I live with my Aunt Valaria now.'

'I am sorry. And your mother?'

'I expect that all is well with my mother,' Cottia said, matter-of-factly. 'There was a hunter who had wanted her always, but her parents gave her to my father. And when my father went West of the Sunset, she went to the hunter, and there was no room in his house for me. It was different with my brother, of course. It is always different with boys. So my mother gave me to Aunt Valaria, who has no children of her own.'

'Poor Cottia,' Marcus said softly.

'Oh no. I did not wish to live in that hunter's house; he was not *my* father. Only . . .' Her voice trailed into silence.

'Only?'

Cottia's changeable face was suddenly as vixenish as he had guessed it could be. 'Only I hate living with my Aunt; I hate living in a town full of straight lines, and being shut up

inside brick walls, and being called Camilla; and I hate—
hate—*hate* it when they try to make me pretend to be a Roman
maiden and forget my own tribe and my own father!'

Marcus was quickly coming to the conclusion that he did not
like Aunt Valaria. 'If it is any consolation to you, they seem
to have succeeded very ill so far,' he said.

'No! I will not let them! I pretend, outside my tunic. I
answer when they call me Camilla, and I speak to them in
Latin: but underneath my tunic I am of the Iceni, and when I
take off my tunic at night, I say, "There! That rids me of
Rome until the morning!" And I lie on my bed and think—
and think—about my home, and the marsh birds flighting
down from the north in the Fall of the Leaf, and the brood
mares with their foals in my father's runs. I remember all
the things that I am not supposed to remember, and talk to
myself inside my head in my own tongue——' She broke off,
looking at him in quick surprise. 'We are talking in my
tongue now! How long have we been doing that?'

'Since you told me about your real name being Cottia.'

Cottia nodded. It did not seem to strike her that the
hearer to whom she was pouring out all this was himself a
Roman: and it did not strike Marcus either. For the moment
all he knew was that Cottia also was in exile, and his fellowship
reached out to her, delicately, rather shyly. And as though
feeling the touch of it, she drew a little nearer, huddling the
scarlet folds more closely round her.

'I like being inside your cloak,' she said contentedly. 'It
feels warm and safe, as a bird must feel inside its own feathers.'

From beyond the hedge at that moment there arose a voice,
shrill as a peahen before rain. 'Camilla! Ladybird! Oh,
my Lady Camilla!'

Cottia sighed in exasperation. 'That is Nissa,' she said.
'I must go.' But she did not move.

'*Camilla!*' called the voice, nearer this time.

'That is Nissa again,' said Marcus.

'Yes, I—must go.' She got up reluctantly, and slipped off
the heavy cloak. But still she lingered, while the screeching

voice drew nearer. Then with a rush, ' Let me come again !
Please let me ! You need not talk to me, nor even notice that
I am here.'

' Oh, my Lady! Where are you, child of Typhon? ' wailed
the voice, very near now.

' Come when it pleases you—and I shall be glad of your
coming,' Marcus said quickly.

' I will come tomorrow,' Cottia told him, and turned to the
old rampart slope, carrying herself like a queen. Most British
women seemed to carry themselves like that, Marcus thought,
watching her drop out of sight round the hedge; and he
remembered Guinhumara in the hut doorway at Isca Dumnoniorum. What had happened to her and the brown baby,
after Cradoc lay dead and the huts were burned and the fields
salted? He would never know.

The shrill voice was raised in fond scolding on the far side
of the hedge; and footsteps came across the grass, and Marcus
turned his head to see Esca coming towards him.

' My Master has had company,' Esca said, laying spear-blade
to forehead in salute, as he halted beside him.

' Yes, and it sounds as though she is getting a sharp
scolding from her nurse on my account,' Marcus said a little
anxiously, as he listened to the shrill voice fading.

' If all I hear be true, scolding will not touch that one,'
Esca said. ' As well scold a flung spear.'

Marcus leaned back, his hands behind his neck, and looked
up at his slave. The thought of Guinhumara and her baby
was still with him, standing behind the thought of Cottia.
' Esca, why do all the Frontier tribes resent our coming so
bitterly? ' he asked on a sudden impulse. ' The tribes of the
south have taken to our ways easily enough.'

' We have ways of our own,' said Esca. He squatted on one
heel beside the bench. ' The tribes of the south had lost their
birthright before ever the Eagles came in war. They sold it
for the things that Rome could give. They were fat with
Roman merchandise and their souls had grown lazy within them.'

' But these things that Rome had to give, are they not good

things?' Marcus demanded. 'Justice, and order, and good roads; worth having, surely?'

'These be all good things,' Esca agreed. 'But the price is too high.'

'The price? Freedom?'

'Yes—and other things than freedom.'

'What other things? Tell me, Esca; I want to know. I want to understand.'

Esca thought for a while, staring straight before him. 'Look at the pattern embossed here on your dagger-sheath,' he said at last. 'See, here is a tight curve, and here is another facing the other way to balance it, and here between them is a little round stiff flower; and then it is all repeated here, and here, and here again. It is beautiful, yes, but to me it is as meaningless as an unlit lamp.'

Marcus nodded as the other glanced up at him. 'Go on.'

Esca took up the shield which had been laid aside at Cottia's coming. 'Look now at this shield-boss. See the bulging curves that flow from each other as water flows from water and wind from wind, as the stars turn in the heaven and blown sand drifts into dunes. These are the curves of life; and the man who traced them had in him knowledge of things that your people have lost the key to—if they ever had it.' He looked up at Marcus again very earnestly. 'You cannot expect the man who made this shield to live easily under the rule of the man who worked the sheath of this dagger.'

'The sheath was made by a British craftsman,' Marcus said stubbornly. 'I bought it at Anderida when I first landed.'

'By a British craftsman, yes, making a Roman pattern. One who had lived so long under the wings of Rome—he and his fathers before him—that he had forgotten the ways and the spirit of his own people.' He laid the shield down again. 'You are the builders of coursed stone walls, the makers of straight roads and ordered justice and disciplined troops. We know that, we know it all too well. We know that your justice is more sure than ours, and when we rise against you, we see our hosts break against the discipline of your troops, as the sea breaks against a rock. And we do not understand, because all these things are of the ordered pattern, and only the free curves of the shield-boss are real to us. We do not understand. And when the time comes that we begin to understand your world, too often we lose the understanding of our own.'

For a while they were silent, watching Cub at his beetle-hunting. Then Marcus said, 'When I came out from home, a year and a half ago, it all seemed so simple.' His gaze dropped again to the buckler on the bench beside him, seeing the strange, swelling curves of the boss with new eyes. Esca had chosen his symbol well, he thought: between the formal pattern on his dagger-sheath and the formless yet potent beauty of the shield-boss lay all the distance that could lie between two worlds. And yet between individual people, people like Esca, and Marcus, and Cottia, the distance narrowed so that you could reach across it, one to another, so that it ceased to matter.

VIII

THE HEALER WITH THE KNIFE

MARCUS had said 'Come when you like,' and Cottia had said, 'I will come tomorrow.' But it was not so simple as that, after all. Kaeso would have made no particular difficulty, for he was an easy-going and kindly man, very eager to stand well with his Roman fellow-Magistrate. But Aunt Valaria, always so careful to follow the custom of what she called 'civilized Society', was very sure that it was not the custom for gently nurtured Roman maidens to take themselves into other people's gardens and make friends with the total strangers they found there. It was not as though Aquila had ever shown himself in the least friendly.

Marcus of course knew nothing of this; he only knew that Cottia did not come tomorrow, nor the day after. And he told himself that there was no reason why she should. It had been to see Cub that she came in the first place, and having seen him, why should she come again? He had thought that perhaps she wanted to be friends, but it seemed that that had been a mistake, and it did not much matter.

And then on the third day, when he had sworn to himself that he would not look for her coming any more, he heard her calling his name, softly and urgently, and when he looked up from the spear-blade that he had been burnishing, there she was, standing where he had first seen her, among the wild fruit-trees.

'Marcus! Marcus, I could not get free of Nissa before,' she began breathlessly. 'They say that I must not come again.'

Marcus laid down the spear, and demanded, 'Why?'

She glanced quickly over her shoulder into her own garden. 'Aunt Valaria says it is not seemly for a Roman maiden to do as

82

I have done. But I am not a Roman maiden; and oh, Marcus, you must make her let me come! You *must*!'

She was hovering on the edge of flight, even while she spoke, and clearly it was no time for needless talk or long explanations. ' She *shall* let you come,' Marcus said quickly, ' but it may take time. Now go, before they catch you.' He made her a swift half-laughing obeisance, palm to forehead, and she turned and dropped out of sight.

Marcus returned to his burnishing. The whole incident had come and gone as quickly as the flight of a bird across the garden, but behind it he was suddenly happier that he had been for three days.

That evening, after talking it over with Esca, he laid the whole problem before Uncle Aquila.

' And what,' inquired Uncle Aquila when he had finished, ' do you suggest that I should do about it? '

' If you could make a few neighbourly remarks to the Lady Valaria the next time you cross her path, I think it would help.'

' But Jupiter! I scarce know the woman, save to bow to her as Kaeso's wife.'

' Which is exactly why a few neighbourly remarks seem indicated.'

' And what if she becomes neighbourly in return? ' demanded Uncle Aquila in blighting tones.

' She cannot invade you here in your stronghold, at all events, since there are no womenfolk to receive her,' Marcus pointed out, quite unblighted.

' There is truth in that, admittedly. Why do you want the chit to come? '

' Oh—because she and Cub understand each other.'

' And so I am to be thrown to the lions in order that Cub may have his playmate? '

Marcus laughed. ' It is only one lion, or rather lioness.' And then the laughter left him. ' Uncle Aquila, we do need your help. I would contrive to play Perseus for myself, but at this stage nothing I could do would in the least avail to rescue Andromeda. It is a job for the head of the household.'

'It was peaceful in this house before you came,' said Uncle Aquila with resignation. 'You are an unutterable nuisance, but I suppose you must have your own way.'

Marcus was never quite sure how it was brought about. Certainly Uncle Aquila never appeared to bestir himself at all in the matter, but from that time forward there began to be more of surface friendliness between the two houses, and before the woods below the old ramparts had thickened into full leaf, Cottia had become a part of life in the Aquila household, and came and went as it pleased her, and as it pleased Marcus.

Esca, who was by nature silent and withdrawn with anyone save the young Roman, was somewhat prone at first to stand on his dignity as a slave, where she was concerned; but he lowered his barriers to her little by little, so far as it was in him to lower them to anyone who was not Marcus. And Marcus tyrannized over and laughed at her, and was content in her company; he taught her to play 'Flash the Fingers', a game beloved of Legionaries and gladiators; and told her long stories about his old home in the Etruscan hills. Telling Cottia about it, conjuring up for her the sights and sounds and smells, seemed somehow to bring it all nearer and ease the ache of exile; and as he told about it, he would catch again that first glimpse of the farmstead from the corner of the hill track where the wild cherry-trees grew. 'There were always a lot of pigeons strutting and fluttering about the courtyards and the roofs, and their necks would catch the sunlight and shine iridescent green and purple; little white stock-doves, too, with coral-pink feet. And when you came into the courtyard they would all burst upwards with a great deal of fuss, and then come circling down again round your feet. And then old Argos would come out of his kennel and bark and wag his tail at the same time; and there would be a wonderful smell of whatever was for supper—grilled river trout, perhaps, or fried chicken if it was a special occasion. And when I came home in the evening, after being out all day, my mother would come to the door when she heard Argos barking. . . .'

Cottia never tired of hearing about the farm in the Etruscan hills, and Marcus, homesick as he was, never tired of telling her.   One day he even showed her his olive-wood bird.

But towards the summer's end he began to have more and more trouble with the old wound.   He had grown so used to the dull ache of it that often he could forget about it altogether, but now there was a jangling sharpness in the old ache, that could not be forgotten, and sometimes the scars were hot to touch and reddened and angry to the sight.

Matters came to a head on a hot August evening, when Marcus and his uncle had just played out their usual game of draughts.   It had been a blazing day, and even out here in the courtyard there seemed no air.   The evening sky was drained of all colour by the day's heat, a bleached and weary sky, and the scent of the roses and cistus in the courtyard jars hung heavy in the air, as smoke hangs in misty weather.

Marcus had been feeling sick with pain all day, and the heavy sweetness of the flowers seemed to stick in his throat. He had played a thoroughly bad game, and he knew it.   He could not lie still.   He shifted a little in search of an easier position, and then shifted again, pretending that he had only moved to look at Cub—half grown now, and superbly handsome lying sprawled on the cooling turf beside Procyon, with whom he had long ago made friends.

Uncle Aquila was watching a yellow wagtail on the bath-house roof, and Marcus shifted yet again, hoping that he would not notice.

'Wound troublesome tonight?' inquired Uncle Aquila, his eye still following the yellow wagtail as it scuttled after flies on the warm tiles.

Marcus said, 'No, sir.   Why?'

'Oh, I merely wondered.   You are quite sure?'

'Perfectly.'

Uncle Aquila brought his eye down from the yellow wagtail, and fixed it on Marcus.   'What a liar you are,' he remarked conversationally.   Then, as Marcus's mouth tightened, he leaned forward, crashing a huge hand on the draughts-board and scattering the pieces broadcast.   'This has been going on long enough! If that fat fool Ulpius does not know his craft, I have an old friend in practice at Durinum who does. Rufrius Galarius. He was one of our field surgeons. He shall come and take a look at that leg.'

' I should not think for a moment that he will,' Marcus said. ' It is a long way from Durinum.'

' He will come,' said Uncle Aquila. ' He and I used to hunt boar together. Oh yes, he will come.'

And come he did.

Rufrius Galarius, one-time field surgeon of the Second Legion, was a blue-jowled Spaniard with a merry eye, close curling black hair scarcely touched with grey, and a chest like a barrel. But his blunt wrestler's hands were very sure and gentle, Marcus found, a few evenings later, when he lay on his narrow cot while his uncle's friend examined the old wounds.

It seemed a long time before he had finished; and when he had, he replaced the rug, straightened his back and strode swearing up and down the little cell. 'Who in the name of Typhon searched this wound?' he demanded at last, swinging round on him.

' The camp surgeon at Isca Dumnoniorum,' Marcus said.

' Been there twenty years, and drunk as a mule-driver at Saturnalia, every night of them,' snapped Galarius. ' I know these passed-over camp surgeons. Butchers and assassins, every one!' He made an indescribable and very vulgar noise.

' Not every night, and he was a very hard-working soul,' said Marcus, doing his best for the shaggy and rather pathetic old man whom he remembered with liking.

' Puh!' said Galarius. Then his manner changed abruptly, and he came and sat himself down on the edge of the cot. ' The thing is that he did not finish his work,' he said.

Marcus ran the tip of his tongue over uncomfortably dry lips. ' You mean—it is all to do again?'

The other nodded. ' You will have no peace until the wound has been re-searched.'

'When——' Marcus began, and checked, trying desperately to steady the shameful flinching at the corner of his mouth.

'In the morning. Since it must be done, the sooner it were done the better.' He put a hand on Marcus's shoulder, and kept it there.

For a moment Marcus lay rigid under the blunt, kindly hand, then he drew a long, uneven breath, and relaxed, with a rather crooked attempt at a smile. 'I beg your forgiveness. I think I—am rather tired.'

'It seems possible,' agreed the surgeon. 'You have had rough marching lately. Oh yes, I know. But soon you will have it behind you and better things ahead. I promise you that.'

For a while he sat there, talking of matters that were a long way from tomorrow morning, drifting from the flavour of native oysters to the iniquities of provincial tax-gatherers, yarning about the early days on the Silurian frontier, and long-ago boar hunts with Uncle Aquila. 'We were great hunters, your uncle and I; and now we grow stiff in our joints and set in our ways. Sometimes I think I will pack up and go on my travels again, before it is too late and I am utterly rusted into my socket. But I chose the wrong branch of my calling for that. A surgeon's craft is none so easily picked up and carried about the world. An oculist's, now, that is the craft for a follower of Aesculapius with the itch to wander! Here in the north, where so many have the marsh-blindness, an oculist's stamp is a talisman to carry a man safely where a Legion could not go.' And he launched out into an account of the adventures of an acquaintance who had crossed the Western Ocean and plied his trade through the wilds of Hibernia, a few years before, while Marcus listened with about half his attention, little guessing that the time was to come when that story would be tremendously important to him.

Presently Galarius got up, stretching until the little muscles cracked behind his bull-shoulders. 'Now I go to talk hunting with Aquila until bedtime. Do you lie still, and sleep as well as may be, and I shall be back early in the morning.'

And with a brusque nod, he turned and strode out into the colonnade.

With him, most of Marcus's hard-held courage seemed to go too.   He was horrified to find that he was shivering—shivering at the smell of pain as a horse shivers at the smell of fire. Lying with his forearm pressed across his eyes, he lashed himself with his own contempt, but found no help in it.   He felt cold in his stomach and very alone.

There came a sudden pattering across the floor, and a cold muzzle was thrust against his shoulder.   He opened his eyes to see Cub's grinning head within a few inches of his own. ' Thanks, Cub,' he said, and shifted a little to catch the great head between his hands as Cub put his fore-paws on the cot and blew lovingly in his face.   It was near to sunset, and the light of the westering sun was flooding into the cell, splashing like quivering golden water on walls and ceiling.   Marcus had not seen it come, and it seemed to break singing on his sight, as a fanfare of trumpets breaks upon the ear.   The light of Mithras, springing out of the dark.

Esca, who had come hard behind Cub, appeared in the doorway, sending a great thrust of shadow up the sunlit wall as he came to Marcus's side.   ' I have spoken with Rufrius Galarius,' he said.

Marcus nodded.   ' He will need your help in the morning. You will do that for me? '

' I am the Centurion's body-slave; who but I should do it? ' Esca said, and bent to disentangle the blanket.

As he did so, sounds of a scuffle arose somewhere in the courtyard.   Stephanos's old bleating voice was raised in protest, and then a girl's, high, clear, and hard.   ' Let me pass. If you do not let me pass, I'll bite! '   The scuffle seemed to be resumed, and an instant later a howl of anguish from Stephanos told all too clearly that the threat had been carried out.   As Marcus and Esca exchanged questioning glances, flying feet came along the colonnade, and Cottia burst into the doorway, a burnished, warlike figure, with the setting sun making a nimbus round her.

Marcus raised himself on one elbow. 'You little vixen! What have you done to Stephanos?'

'I bit his hand,' said Cottia, in the same clear, hard voice. 'He tried to keep me out.'

The scuff-scuff of hurrying sandals sounded behind her even while she spoke, and Marcus said urgently, 'Esca, in the name of Light, go and keep him out of here!' He felt suddenly that he could not deal with a righteously indignant Stephanos at this moment. Then, as Esca strode out to do his bidding, he turned on Cottia. 'And what is it that you suppose you are doing here, my Lady?'

She came close, thrusting in beside Cub, and stood looking down at him accusingly. 'Why did you not tell me?' she demanded.

'Tell you what?' But he knew what.

'About the Healer with the Knife. I saw him come in a mule carriage, through the storeroom window, and Nissa told me why he came.'

'Nissa talks too much,' Marcus said. 'I did not mean that you should know until it was all over and done with.'

'You had no right not to tell me,' she said stormily. 'It was mine to know!' And then in an anxious rush, 'What will he do to you?'

Marcus hesitated an instant, but if he did not tell her, the unspeakable Nissa undoubtedly would. 'I am to have the wound cleaned up. That is all.'

Her face seemed to grow narrower and more sharply pointed while he looked at it. 'When?' she asked.

'In the morning, very early.'

'Send Esca to tell me when it is over.'

'It will be *very* early,' Marcus said firmly. 'You will scarcely be awake by then.'

'I shall be awake,' Cottia said. 'I shall be waiting at the bottom of the garden. And I shall wait there until Esca comes, whoever tries to take me away. I can bite others beside Stephanos, and if anyone tries to take me away, I will, and then I shall be beaten. You would not like to know that I had

G

been beaten because you would not send Esca, would you, Marcus?'

Marcus recognized defeat. 'Esca shall come and tell you.'

There was a long pause. Cottia stood very still, looking down at him. Then she said, 'I wish it could be me instead.'

It was a thing more easily said than meant, but Cottia did mean it. Looking at her, Marcus knew that. 'Thank you, Cottia. I shall remember that. And now you must go home.'

She drew back obediently, as Esca reappeared in the doorway. 'I will go home. When may I come again?'

'I do not know,' Marcus said. 'Esca shall come and tell you that also.'

Without another word she turned and walked out into the golden light. At a sign from Marcus, the slave fell in behind her, and their steps sounded fainter and fainter along the colonnade.

Marcus listened to them until they faded into silence, lying quiet, with the familiar rough warmth of Cub's head under his hand. He was still unpleasantly cold in the pit of his stomach, but he no longer felt alone. In some way that he did not understand, Cub and Esca and Cottia had comforted and steadied him for what was coming.

The golden light was fading, and into the quietness stole a shimmering thread of bird-song, the thin, regretful autumn song of a robin in the wild pear-tree; and he realized that summer was nearly over. Suddenly he knew, with a sense of discovery, that it had been a good summer. He had been homesick, yes, dreaming night after night of his own hills, and waking with a sore heart; but none the less, it had been a good summer. There had been the day that Cub discovered how to bark. Marcus had been almost as surprised as Cub. 'But wolves never bark,' he said to Esca; and Esca had said: 'Rear a wolf with the dog-pack and he will do as the dog-pack does in all things.' And Cub, proud of his new accomplishment, had filled the garden with his shrill puppy clamour for days. Other small sharp-edged memories sprang to meet him: twists of hot pastry brought out by Sassticca and eaten by the four of them as a feast; the hunting-bow which he and Esca had built between them; Cottia holding his olive-wood bird in her cupped hands.

A kind summer, a kingfisher summer; and suddenly he was grateful for it.

He slept that night quietly and lightly as a hunter sleeps, and woke to the call of distant trumpets sounding Cockcrow from the transit camp.

.   .   .   .   .

It was so early that the gossamer still lay thick and dew-grey over the courtyard grass and the smell of the day-spring was cold and fresh in the air when Rufrius Galarius returned; but Marcus had been waiting his coming for what seemed a long time. He returned the surgeon's greeting, and explained, ' My slave is gone to shut up the wolf-cub. He should be back at any moment.'

Galarius nodded. ' I have seen him. He is also fetching sundry things that we shall need,' he said, and opening the bronze case that he had brought with him he began to set out the tools of his trade on the chest top.

Before he had finished, Esca was back, carrying hot water and new linen, and a flask of the native barley spirit which Galarius considered better than wine, though fiercer, for cleansing a wound. ' There will be more hot water when you need it,' he said, setting the things down on the chest top beside the instrument case; and came to stand over Marcus, a little as Cub might have done.

Galarius finished his preparations, and turned. ' Now, if you are ready?'

' Quite ready,' Marcus said, tossing off the blanket, and shut his teeth for what was coming.

A long while later he drifted out of the darkness that had come roaring up over him before the work was finished, to find himself lying under warm rugs, with Rufrius Galarius standing beside him with a square hand set over his heart, as old Aulus had stood in that other waking, just a year ago. For one confused moment he thought that it was still that other waking and he had dreamed in a circle; and then, as his sight and hearing cleared somewhat, he saw Esca standing just behind the surgeon, and a huge shadow in the doorway that could only be Uncle Aquila, and heard the despairing howls of Cub shut in the storeroom: and came back to the present like a swimmer breaking surface.

The ache of the old wound was changed to a jangling throb that seemed to beat through his whole body with a sickening sense of shock, and involuntarily he gave a little moan.

The surgeon nodded. 'Aye, it strikes sharp at first,' he agreed. 'But it will ease presently.'

Marcus looked up rather hazily into the blue-jowled Spaniard's face. 'Have you done?' he mumbled.

'I have done.' Galarius drew up the blanket. There was blood on his hand. 'In a few months' time you will be a sound man again. Lie still and rest now, and this evening I will come back.'

He gave Marcus's shoulder a small brisk pat, and turned to gather up his instruments.

'I leave him in your hands. You can give him the draught now,' he said to Esca, over his shoulder as he went out. Marcus heard him speak to someone in the colonnade. 'Enough splinters to quill a porcupine; but the muscles are less damaged than one might expect. The boy should do well enough now.'

Then he found Esca beside him, holding a cup. 'Cottia— and Cub——' he stammered.

'I will see to them soon, but first you must drink this.'

Esca dropped to one knee beside the cot, and Marcus found that he was lying with his head on his slave's shoulder and the rim of the cup was cool against his mouth as he drank. He remembered the bitter taste from last year. Then, as the cup was withdrawn, he turned his head contentedly on Esca's arm. There was a pinched greyness in the other's face, he realized, an odd wryness about his mouth, like the look of a man who wishes to be sick but has nothing in his stomach to be sick with.

'Was it as bad as that?' he asked with a weak attempt at laughter.

Esca grinned. 'Go to sleep.'

IX

TRIBUNE PLACIDUS

A MILE or two south of Calleva, where the forest opened suddenly to a steep drop of bracken-clad hillside, two men were standing: a Roman and a Briton; and between them, head up and muzzle quivering into the wind, a young brindled wolf.

Abruptly, the Roman stooped to unbuckle the heavy bronze-studded collar from the wolf's neck. Cub was full grown now, though not yet come to his full strength, and the time had arrived when he must have his choice of returning to the wild. You could tame a wild thing, but never count it as truly won until, being free to return to its own kind, it chose to come back to you. Marcus had known that all along, and he and Esca had made their preparations with infinite care, bringing Cub to this spot again and again, that he might be sure of the way home if he wished to take it. If he wished to take it. With his fingers on the buckle, Marcus wondered whether he would ever feel the hairy living warmth of Cub's neck again.

The collar was off now, and he thrust it into the breast of his tunic. For a lingering moment he fondled the pricked ears. Then he stood erect. 'Go free, brother. Good hunting.' Cub looked up into his face, puzzled; then, as a fresh burst of woodland smells reached his quivering nose, trotted off down the woodshore.

The other two watched him go in silence, a brindled shadow slipping away into the undergrowth. Then Marcus turned and made for the trunk of a fallen birch-tree a little way down the slope, moving quickly but awkwardly over the rough ground with a sideways lurch of the shoulders at every step. Rufrius Galarius had done his work well, and now, some eight months later, Marcus was to all intents and purposes as sound

as ever, just as the surgeon had promised. He would carry
the scars to his dying day, and a twisted leg that would bar him
from the Legions, but that was all; indeed, after a winter
spent with Esca's help in training as though for the arena, he
was now as hard as a gladiator. He reached the fallen tree-
trunk and sat down on it, and an instant later Esca was
squatting at his feet.

This was a favourite vantage point of theirs. The tree-
trunk made a convenient seat, and the steep drop of the hillside
gave a clear view of wooded hills and the blue lift of the downs
beyond. He had seen these rolling woods in their winter
bareness, dappled like a partridge's breast. He had seen
the first outbreaking of the blackthorn foam; and now the full
green flame of spring was running through the forest and the
wild cherry-trees stood like lit candles along the woodland ways.

The two in their vantage point sat talking lazily, with long
silences between, of many things under the sun, including the
guest whom Uncle Aquila was expecting that evening; no
less a person than the Legate of the Sixth Legion on his way
down from Eburacum to Regnum, and thence to Rome.

'He is a very old friend of your uncle's?' asked Esca idly.

'Yes. I believe they served together in Judaea when my
uncle was First Cohort of the Fretensis and this man was doing
his year as a Tribune on the Staff. He must be a great deal
younger than Uncle Aquila.'

'And now he goes home, to his own place?'

'Yes, but only on some business with the Senate, Uncle
Aquila says; then back to the Eagles again.'

After a time they fell silent altogether, each busy with his
own thoughts. Marcus's were mainly concerned, as they had
been for some time past, with the question of what he was going
to do with himself and his life, now that he was well again.
The Legions were closed to him, and that left just one other way
of life that he would have turned to as a bird flies home.
Farming was in the blood of most of his race, from the Senator
with his estate in the Alban Hills to the time-expired Legionary
with his pumpkin patch; and to Marcus, born and bred as he

had been, farming and soldiering were yoke-mates, the two natural ways of life. But to start anything of that sort, one needed money. It was all right for the time-expired Legionary with his government grant of land. It would have been all right for Marcus if he had served his twenty years—even though he never became Prefect of an Egyptian Legion—and had savings from his pay and a centurion's gratuity behind him. But as it was, he had nothing. He might have turned to Uncle Aquila for help, he knew, but he would not do that. His uncle, although he had sufficient for his needs, was not a rich man, and had done enough for him already. He should have set about finding some way to earn his living before now, he supposed, but there were so few ways open to a free man, and the frightful conviction was growing on him that he would end up as somebody's secretary. There were people who preferred a free secretary to a slave, here—or even at home in Etruria. But even as that thought touched his mind, he knew that for him to drift home, rootless, and without any stake in the country that had bred him, nor any hope of such, would be only the shadow and none of the substance of homecoming. He would have carried his exile with him into his own hills and spoiled them; and that was all. No, he must look for his secretary-ship here in Britain.

Only this morning he had made up his mind to lay the secretary idea before Uncle Aquila tonight, but the Legate's message had arrived, and now of course it would have to wait until the sudden guest had gone on his way. And part of him —a part of which he was rather ashamed—caught at the delay as a breathing-space; one day's grace in which something might happen, though what was likely to happen he would have been hard put to it to say.

In their silence, the wild had drawn close in to the two in the vantage point. Presently a red glint slipping through the uncurling bracken and young foxgloves at the lower end of the clearing told them where a vixen passed. She paused an instant in full view, her pointed muzzle raised, the sun shining with almost metallic lustre on her coat; then she turned in

among the trees.   And watching the russet glint of her flicker
out of sight, Marcus found himself thinking of Cottia.

The closer friendliness between her house and his had continued.   He knew Kaeso quite well now, and even Valaria a
little; Valaria, plumpish and prettyish and foolish, floating
with pale-coloured mist-linen, clanking with bracelets, her
hair closely curled as a ram's fleece.   He was for ever meeting
her in her litter, as he came and went about Calleva, to the
baths or the gymnasium or the Golden Vine, from whose
stables he and Esca had lately hired ponies once or twice for a
trip into the outback; and always he had to stop and talk.
But of Cottia herself, he suddenly realized, he had seen less and
less as the months went by.

With life opening to him again, he had had less need of her,
and she had drawn back little by little, without a shadow of
reproach.   Yet he did not feel in the least guilty, and all at
once, realizing how very easily Cottia could have made him
feel guilty if she had chosen to, he felt a quick rush of warmth
towards her.   The odd thing was that now he came to think of
it he did need Cottia as much as ever; he often forgot her
altogether with the surface of his mind, but he knew that if he
were never to see her again he would be very unhappy, perhaps
as unhappy as he would if Cub never came back. . . .

And would Cub ever come back?   Would the call of his own
kind prove stronger than the tie that bound him to his master?
Either way, Marcus hoped that it would be quick and easy and
final; no tearing of the heart in two, for Cub.   He stirred, and
looked down at Esca.   'We have been roosting here long
enough.'

The other tipped back his head, and for a moment their eyes
met.   Then Esca got up, and reached a helping hand to Marcus.
'Let the Centurion whistle once, in case he is near; then we
will go home.'

Marcus gave the shrill, broken whistle he had always used to
summon Cub, and stood listening.   A magpie, startled by the
sound, scolded sharply from the woods behind them, and
nothing more.   After a few moments he whistled again.   Still

no answering bark, no brindled shape trotting out of the wood-shore.

'He is out of hearing,' said Esca. 'Well, he knows the way home, and there'll be no harm come to him.'

No, there would be no harm come to Cub. He was well known in and around Calleva, and since he had long since lost his wolf-smell, the dog-pack accepted him for one of them-selves, and one to be respected. No harm would come to him from his own kind, either, for save when man took a hand, there was little war between wolf-pack and dog-pack, who indeed mated together often enough to make it sometimes hard to tell which was which. Only, if he went back to his own kind, the day might come when men would hunt Cub as they had hunted his mother.

Marcus longed to look back once, as they turned in among the hazel scrub of the forest verge, in case, even now, Cub might be coming uphill at a canter. But looking back was not in the bargain, and with his slave beside him he turned resolutely homeward.

They came to the South Gate of Calleva and passed through, Esca immediately falling the usual three paces to the rear. They made their way round by the short cut behind the temple of Sull-Minerva and entered the house by the nearest door, which gave on to the slaves' quarters and the garden. Cub, if he came at all, would likely come over the old earthworks at the foot of the garden, for he was used to that road, but Marcus had had word with the City gatekeepers in case he came the other way.

They reached the courtyard without meeting anyone, and while Esca went to set out a fresh tunic for his master, Marcus turned off along the colonnade towards the atrium. As he neared the doorway, a strange voice sounded behind it. The guest had arrived already, then.

'You are sure?' said the voice, a harsh, clipped voice, but pleasant. 'It would be a simple matter to send him up to the transit camp.'

And Uncle Aquila's voice replied: 'When I have not the

space to lodge two guests at the same time, I will tell you.
You are a fool, Claudius.'

There were two strangers in the long room with Uncle
Aquila, both in uniform: one, resplendent under his coating
of dust in the gilded bronze of a Legate; the other, standing a
little behind him, evidently a Staff Officer. It seemed that
they had only just arrived, for they had done no more than lay
aside cloak and crested helmet. That much Marcus saw as he
hesitated an instant on the threshold before his uncle looked
round and saw him.

' Ah, you are back, Marcus,' said Uncle Aquila; and then, as
he came forward to join the group, ' Claudius, I present to you
my nephew Marcus. Marcus, this is my very old friend
Claudius Hieronimianus, Legate of the Sixth Legion.'

Marcus raised his hand in salute to his uncle's friend, and
found himself looking into a pair of long, jet-black eyes that
seemed to have the sun behind them. The Legate was an
Egyptian, and, he judged, of the old strain, for there was none
of the Syrian softness in his face that he had seen so often in the
faces of the men of the Nile. ' I am very much honoured to
meet the Legate of Victrix,' he said.

The Legate's face crinkled into a smile that sent a thousand
fine lines deepening about his mouth and eyes. ' And I am
very glad to meet a kinsman of my ancient friend, all the more
so because until today he might have been hatched out of a
turtle's egg in the sand, for all the kith and kin that he had
to my knowledge.' He indicated his companion. ' I make
known to you Tribune Servius Placidus, of my staff.'

Marcus turned to the young officer, and instantly became
painfully conscious of his twisted leg. Once or twice before he
had met people who made him feel like that, and he did not
find that it endeared them to him. The two greeted each other
as custom demanded, but without warmth. The Staff Officer
was about Marcus's own age, an extremely beautiful young man,
with the graceful carriage, the oval face, and clustering hair
that suggested Athenian ancestry. ' Smooth as a girl,' Marcus
thought with quick dislike; and the phrase seemed vaguely

familiar. So did the name, Placidus, for that matter; but it
was a common enough name, and anyhow, this was no time
to be trailing marsh-light memories. Marcus supposed that
until the guests went to wash off the dust of the journey, it
was for him to hold the Tribune in conversation, leaving Uncle
Aquila free to talk to his old friend.

Marcipor had brought in wine for the travellers, and when
it has been poured, the two young men turned from their elders
and drifted over to a sunlit window. For a while they made
casual small-talk to each other; but as the moments went by,
Marcus found it harder and harder to think of anything to say,
while the Tribune appeared to have been born bored. At last
Marcus, at his wits' end for another word, asked: ' You return
to Rome with the Legate, or only as far as Regnum? '

' Oh, to Rome. Praise be to Bacchus, I am done with
Britain once and for all when I board the galley in two days'
time.'

' You have not, I take it, found Britain much to your taste? '

The other shrugged, and took a gulp of his wine. ' The
girls are well enough, and the hunting. For the rest—Roma
Dea! I can bear to leave it behind me! ' A doubt seemed to
strike him. ' You are not native born to this benighted
province? '

' No,' Marcus said. ' I am not native born.' And then,
feeling that he had been over abrupt, he added: ' Indeed, I
have been out less than three years.'

' What possessed you to come out at all? You must have
found the long journey very trying.'

There was nothing so very much in the words, but the tone
in which they were spoken made Marcus, who was rather on
edge because of Cub, feel his hackles rising. ' I came out to
join my Legion,' he said coldly.

' Oh.' Placidus was slightly put out. ' A wound, then? '

' Yes.'

' I do not think that I have ever met you in the Tribune's
Club, at home? '

' It would be strange if you had. I was a mere cohort

centurion.' Marcus smiled, but all the contempt that the professional soldier could feel for the aristocrat playing at soldiers for a year was politely but thinly veiled behind his quiet words.

Placidus flushed a little. ' Really? Do you know, I should scarce have guessed it.' He returned the thrust, with the silken suggestion in his tone that really Marcus seemed almost civilized. ' Do I salute a brother of the Victrix? Or was it Capricorn or the charging boar with you? '

Before Marcus could answer, a low chuckle came from the Legate, whose back was towards them. ' For one who considers himself—I believe not without the right—a somewhat skilled hunter, you can be singularly unobservant of small things, my Placidus.' He said over his shoulder, ' I have mentioned the fact to you before. You will find the Signum of his Legion on his left wrist,' and he returned to his conversation with Uncle Aquila.

At his words, something had clicked in Marcus's mind, and as the Tribune's glance jerked down to the heavy gold bracelet that he always wore, he remembered. ' Smooth as a girl, but a skilled hunter,' Esca had said; and the name had been Placidus. His mouth felt dry with disgust, and the flicker of discomfiture—yes, and something very like envy—that showed for an instant in the other's face, gave him a quick satisfaction that was on Esca's account rather than his own.

Placidus recovered himself at once, and looked up with his faintly supercilious air. ' See what it is to serve under a Legate renowned for his appreciation of his junior officers,' he murmured. ' My dear Marcus, I do congratulate——' His eyes widened suddenly, and the soft, drawling voice sharpened into life. ' Roma Dea! A wolf! '

Before the words were out, Marcus had swung round. There in the colonnade doorway stood a brindled shape, savage head alertly raised, and eyes wary of the strangers within, whose unfamiliar scent had halted him on the threshold.

' Cub! ' Marcus called, ' Cub! ' and crouched down as, with a joyful bark, the brindled shape hurled itself upon him, fawning against his breast and singing as a crock sings on the boil. Cub's flanks were heaving with the speed that he had made to find his master, and he was frantically apologetic for having somehow lost him. And Marcus caught the great head in his hands, rubbing his thumbs into the hollows behind the pricked ears. 'So you have come back, brother,' he said. 'You have come back, Cub.'

'It is a wolf! It really *is* a wolf—and the brute behaving like a puppy!' said Placidus, in tones of disgusted unbelief above him.

'It seems that we are witnesses to a reunion. Surely we have come in a happy hour,' said the Legate.

Marcus freed himself from Cub's embraces and got to his feet. 'A reunion—yes, you could call it so,' he said.

Then Cub did a thing that he had never done before. He thrust his lowered head between Marcus's knees, as a dog will sometimes do with someone he perfectly trusts; and stood there contentedly, in the one position in which he was utterly defenceless and at his master's mercy.

And while he stood like that with slowly swinging tail, Marcus brought out the bronze-studded collar from the breast of his tunic, and bent to put it round his neck again.

'How long have you had him?' Placidus asked, watching with a gleam of interest as, his collar safely buckled on again, the young wolf shook himself violently, and sat down with lolling tongue and eyes half closed, propped against his master's leg.

'Since he was a very small cub, more than a year ago,' Marcus said, fondling a twitching ear.

'Then, if I am not mistaken, I saw him taken from the lair after his dam was killed! The painted barbarian who fetched him out claimed to be slave to a Marcus Aquila. I remember now.'

'You are not mistaken,' Marcus said quietly. 'The painted barbarian told me that story.'

Rather fortunately Stephanos appeared at that moment hovering in the doorway; and Uncle Aquila took the Legate's

empty wine-cup from him. 'You will be wishing to soak off
the dust of the road,' he said. 'We may live at the world's
end, but the bath-water could not be hotter in Rome itself.
Your own slaves will be awaiting you in your quarters, no
doubt. That is so, Stephanos? Good. I look forward to
our next meeting at dinner.'

X

MARCHING ORDERS

Presently, having bathed and changed, the four came together again in the small dining recess which opened from the atrium. This room was as austere as the rest of the house; the lime-washed walls bare of ornament save for the bronze-faced cavalry buckler with a pair of crossed javelins behind it, hanging opposite the entrance; the three couches about the table spread with beautifully dressed deerskins instead of the usual quiltings and embroideries. And, ordinarily, the meals which Marcus and his uncle ate there were as austere as the room. But tonight was an occasion, and Sassticca had bestirred herself to produce a dinner worthy of it.

To Marcus, because Cub had come back, the whole room seemed to shimmer with a faint air of festival, as he glanced about him by the soft yellow light of the palm-oil lamps on the table. The future and the question of finding a livelihood could wait for the moment; he was pleasantly tired after a long day in the open; he had had a cold plunge and changed his rough tunic for one of soft white wool; and he was prepared even to keep a truce with Placidus, since Esca had only laughed when told of his arrival.

The main part of dinner was over. Uncle Aquila had just poured the second libation to the household gods, whose little bronze statues stood with the salt-cellars at the corners of the table; and Esca and the other slaves had gone their way. The soft, uncertain lamplight cast a delicate web of radiance over the table, making the red Samian bowls glow like coral, turning the withered yellow apples of last year's harvest to the fruit of the Hesperides, casting here a bloom of light over the fluted curve of a glass cup, kindling there a pointed scarlet flame in the heart of a squat flask of Falernian wine, strangely

intensifying the faces of the men who leaned each on a left
elbow round the table.

So far the two older men had had most of the conversation
to themselves, talking over old days, old skirmishes, old frontier
camps, old friends and enemies, while Marcus and Placidus
put in a word from time to time, spoke to each other occasionally
—the truce was holding quite well—but for the most part ate
their dinner in silence.

And then, splashing water into the Falernian in his cup,
Uncle Aquila asked, ' Claudius, how long since you left the
Fretensis? '

' Eighteen years in August.'

' Jupiter ! ' said Uncle Aquila, reflectively. Suddenly he
glared at his old friend. ' Eighteen years in August since you
and I last sat at meat in the same mess; and yet you have been
in Britain almost three, and made no attempt—not the faintest
attempt—to come near me ! '

' Nor you to come near me,' said Claudius Hieronimianus,
helping himself to one of Sassticca's honey cakes and topping it
with a cluster of raisins. He looked up from his plate, his
strange face breaking into a winged, eager smile. ' Is it not
most often so, when we follow the Eagles? We make a friend
here and there, in Achaea, in Caesarea or Eburacum; and our
ways part again, and we take remarkably few pains to keep in
touch one with another. But if the gods who rule the destinies
of men bend our paths to cross again—why then . . .'

' Why then we take up the old threads very much where we
laid them down,' said Uncle Aquila. He raised his re-charged
cup. ' I drink to the old threads. No, I don't. It is only old
men who look backward all the time. I drink to the *renewing*
of old threads.'

' Do you come and renew them at Eburacum, after I return,'
said the Legate, as he set down his own cup.

' It may be that I will even do that—one day. It is all of
five-and-twenty years since I was last at Eburacum, and I
should be interested to see the place again.' Suddenly,
bethinking himself of his manners, Uncle Aquila turned to

H

include the young Tribune. ' I took a contingent of the Second up there in one of the Troubles; it was thus that I came to know the Station a little.'

' So? ' Placidus contrived to sound bored and polite at the same time. ' That would be in the Hispana's time, of course. You would scarce recognize the Station now. It is really almost habitable.'

' The new generally build in stone where the old cleared the forest and built in wood,' said Uncle Aquila.

The Legate was staring reflectively into the heart of his wine. ' Sometimes at Eburacum it seems to me that the foundations of that old building lie uneasy beneath the new,' he said.

Marcus turned on him quickly. ' You mean, sir? '

' Eburacum is still—how shall I put it?—still more than a little ghost-ridden by the Ninth Legion. Oh, I do not mean that their spirits have wandered back from the fields of Ra, but the place is haunted, none the less. By the altars to Spanish gods that they set up and worshipped at; by their names and numbers idly scratched on walls; by British women whom they loved and children with Spanish faces whom they fathered. All this lying, as it were, like a sediment under the new wine of another Legion. Also they linger strongly, almost terrifyingly, in the minds of the people.' He made a small gesture with his open hand. ' It sounds little enough, put into words, and yet it can create an atmosphere which is unpleasantly strong. I am not an imaginative man, but I tell you that there have been times, when the mist comes down from the high moors, when I have more than half expected to see the lost Legion come marching home.'

There was a long silence, and a little shiver ran through the room like a little wind through long grass. Uncle Aquila's face was unreadable. Placidus's showed clearly his opinion of such vapourings. Then Marcus said: ' Have you any idea —any theory—as to what became of the Hispana, sir? '

The Legate looked at him shrewdly. ' Their fate has some importance for you? '

'Yes. My father was their First Cohort—Uncle Aquila's brother.'

The Legate turned his head. 'Aquila, I never knew that.'

'Oh yes,' said Uncle Aquila. 'Did I never mention him to you? He never came much in my way; we were at opposite ends of the family, with twenty years between us.'

The Legate nodded, and after seeming to consider a moment, gave his attention back to Marcus. 'There is, of course, the possibility that somewhere they were cut off and annihilated so completely that no survivors were left to carry back word of the disaster.'

'Oh, but surely, sir,' put in Placidus with a great show of deference, 'in a Province the size of Valentia, even in the whole of Caledonia, upward of four thousand men could not be destroyed without trace? Is it not far more likely that having had their fill of the Eagles, they merely butchered such of their officers as would not join with them, and deserted to the Tribes?'

Marcus said nothing; the Tribune was his uncle's guest; but his mouth shut into a hard, hot line.

'No, I do not think it particularly likely,' said the Legate.

But Placidus had not yet finished planting his sting. 'I stand corrected,' he said silkily. 'I was led to think it was the only possible explanation to the mystery, by the extremely unsavoury reputation the Hispana left behind them. But I am happy to find that I was at fault.'

'I am sure you are,' said the Legate, with a glint of humour.

'But you do not find the ambush theory a very likely one, either, I think, sir?' Marcus helped himself carefully to a cluster of raisins which he did not want.

'I do not greatly care to believe that any Legion of the Empire could have fallen so low, could have become such rotten fruit, as the other explanation would prove them.' The Legate hesitated, and his face seemed to grow keener; no longer the face of a man enjoying a pleasant meal, Marcus thought, but that of a soldier. He began to speak again, abruptly. ' There has been a rumour quite lately, along the Wall—incidentally giving me cause to wish profoundly that the Senate had not chosen this moment to recall me, though I leave behind a Camp Commandant and a First Cohort both knowing more of the game than I shall ever do—a rumour which, if it were true, would suggest that the Hispana did indeed go down fighting.   Only market talk, but in such there is often a core of truth.   The story runs that the Eagle has been seen; that it is receiving divine honours in some tribal temple in the far north.'

Uncle Aquila, who had been playing with his wine-cup, set it down so sharply that a drop splashed over on to his hand. ' Go on,' he said, as the other halted.

' That is all; there is no more to add, no more to work on, which is the cursed part of it.   But you take my point? '

' Oh yes, I take your point.'

' But I am afraid that I do not, not with any clearness,' Marcus said.

' A Legion which went rogue would probably hide its Eagle or hack it to pieces, or simply topple it into the nearest river. It would be most unlikely to have either the wish or the chance to set it up in the temple of some local godling.   But an Eagle taken in war is in a very different case.   To the Outland Tribes it must seem that they have captured the god of the Legion : and so they carry it home in triumph, with many torches and perhaps the sacrifice of a black ram, and house it in the temple of their own god to make the young men strong in war and help the grain to ripen.   You see now? '

Marcus saw.   ' What do you intend doing about it, sir? ' he asked, after a moment.

' Nothing.   For all the evidence that I can gather, there may be no shred of truth in the story.'

' But if there is? '

' There is still nothing that I can do about it.'

' But, sir, it is the Eagle; the Hispana's lost *Eagle*! '   Marcus said, as though trying to drive an idea into the head of one half-witted.

'Eagle lost—honour lost; honour lost—all lost,' the Legate quoted. 'Oh yes, I know.' The regret in his voice sounded very final.

'More than that, sir.' Marcus was leaning forward, almost stammering in his sudden desperate eagerness. 'If the Eagle could be found and brought back, it—it might even mean the re-forming of the Legion.'

'That also I know,' said the Legate. 'And I know a thing which interests me even more. If trouble were to break out again in the north, a Roman Eagle in the hands of the Painted People might well become a weapon against us, owing to the power it would undoubtedly have to fire the minds and hearts of the Tribes. The fact remains that on a mere wind-blown rumour, I can take no action. To send an expeditionary force would mean open war. A whole Legion would scarcely win through, and there are but three in Britain.'

'But where a Legion could not get through, one man might; at least to find out the truth.'

'I agree, if the right man came forward. It would have to be one who knew the Northern Tribes and would be accepted by them and allowed to pass; and it would have, I think, to be one who cared very deeply for the fate of the Hispana's Eagle, else he would not be madman enough to thrust his head into such a hornet's nest.' He set down the cup that he had been turning between his fingers while he spoke. 'If I had had such a one among my young men, I would have given him his marching orders. The matter seems to me serious enough for that.'

'Send me,' Marcus said deliberately. His glance moved from one to another of the men round the table; then he turned to the curtained entrance and called, 'Esca! Hi! Esca!'

'Now by the——' began Uncle Aquila, and broke off, for once at a loss for words.

No one else spoke.

Quick footsteps came through the atrium, the curtain was drawn aside, and Esca appeared on the threshold. 'The Centurion called?'

In as few words as might be, Marcus told him what was toward. 'You will come with me, Esca?'

Esca moved forward to his master's side. His eyes were very bright in the lamplight. 'I will come,' he said.

Marcus turned back to the Legate. 'Esca was born and bred where the Wall runs now: and the Eagle was my father's. Between us we fulfil your conditions finely. Send us.'

The queer silence that had held the other men was shattered abruptly as Uncle Aquila banged an open hand on the table. 'This is lunacy! Sheer, unmitigated lunacy!'

'No, but it is not!' Marcus protested urgently. 'I have a perfectly sane and workable plan. In the name of Light, listen to me.'

Uncle Aquila drew breath for a blistering reply, but the Legate put in quietly, 'Let the boy speak, Aquila,' and he subsided with a snort.

For a long moment Marcus stared down at the raisins on his plate, trying to get the rough plan in his head into some sort of order. Trying also to remember exactly what Rufrius Galarius had told him that would help him now. Then he looked up and began to speak, eagerly, but with great care and long pauses, rather as though he were feeling his way, as indeed he was.

'Claudius Hieronimianus, you say that it would have to be one whom the Tribes would accept and allow to pass. A travelling oculist would be such a one. There are many sore eyes here in the north, and half the travellers on the roads are quack-salvers. Rufrius Galarius, who used to be a field surgeon with the Second' (he glanced at his uncle with a half smile), 'once told me of a man well known to him, who even crossed the Western Waters and plied his trade through the length and breadth of Hibernia, and came back with a whole hide to tell the tale. And if an oculist's stamp will carry a man safely through Hibernia, of a surety it will carry Esca and me through what was once, after all, a Roman Province!' He sat up on the couch, almost glaring at the two older men. Placidus he had forgotten. 'It may be that we shall not be able to

bring back the Eagle; but the gods willing, we will at least find
out the truth or untruth of your rumour for you.'

There was a long pause. The Legate was looking at Marcus
searchingly. Uncle Aquila broke the silence. ' An enter-
prising plan, but with one trifling objection to it, which you
would appear to have overlooked.'

' And what is that? '

" You know rather less than an addled egg about the
doctoring of sore eyes.'

' The same could be said for three out of four quack-salvers
on the roads; but I shall go on a visit to Rufrius Galarius.
Oh yes, he is a surgeon and not an oculist, I have not forgotten
that; but he will know enough of the craft to put me in the way
of getting a few needful salves, and give me some idea how to
use them.'

Uncle Aquila nodded, as conceding the point.

And then, after a moment, the Legate asked abruptly, ' How
serviceable is that leg of yours? '

Marcus had been expecting the question. ' Save that it
would not do for the parade ground, very near as serviceable
as ever it was,' he said. ' If we should have to run for it, it
would load the dice against us, I grant you, but in strange
country we should not stand a dog's chance on the run, anyway.'

Again the silence settled. And he sat with his head up,
gazing from the Legate to his uncle and back again. They were
summing up his chances, and he knew it: his chances of
coming through, his chances of doing the thing that he went
out to do. Moment by lengthening moment it became more
desperately urgent to him that he should win his marching
orders. The very life or death of his father's Legion was at
stake; the Legion that his father had loved. And because he
had loved his father with all the strength of his heart, the matter
was a personal quest to him and shone as a quest shines. But
beneath that shining lay the hard fact of a Roman Eagle in
hands that might one day use it as a weapon against Rome;
and Marcus had been bred a soldier. So it was in no mood of

high adventure alone, but in a soberer and more purposeful spirit that he awaited the verdict.

'Claudius Hieronimianus, you said just now that had you had the right man among your young men, you would have sent him,' he said at last, able to keep silent no longer. 'Do I get my marching orders?'

It was his uncle who answered first, speaking to the Legate as much as to Marcus. 'The gods of my fathers forbid that I should hold back any kinsman of mine from breaking his neck in a clean cause, if he has a mind to.' His tone was distinctly caustic; but Marcus, meeting the disconcertingly shrewd eyes under his fierce jut of brow, realized that Uncle Aquila knew and understood very much more of what all this was meaning to him than he would somehow have expected.

The Legate said, 'You understand the position? The Province of Valentia, whatever it once was, whatever it may be again, is not worth an outworn sandal-strap today. You will be going out alone into enemy territory, and if you run into trouble, there will be nothing that Rome can or will do to help you.'

'I understand that,' Marcus said. 'But I shall not be alone. Esca goes with me.'

Claudius Hieronimianus bent his head. 'Go then. I am not your Legate, but I give you your marching orders.'

Later, after certain details had been thrashed out round the brazier in the atrium, Placidus said an unexpected thing. 'I almost wish that there was room for a third in this insane expeditionary force! If there were, Bacchus! I would leave Rome to fend for itself awhile, and come with you!'

For the moment his face had lost its weary insolence, and as the two young men looked at each other in the lamplight Marcus was nearer to liking him than he had been since they first met.

But the faint fellowship was short-lived, and Placidus killed it with a question. 'Are you sure that you can trust that barbarian of yours in a venture of this kind?'

'Esca?' Marcus said in surprise. 'Yes, quite sure.'

The other shrugged. 'Doubtless you know best. Personally I should not care to let my life hang by so slender a thread as the loyalty of a slave.'

'Esca and I——' Marcus began, and broke off. He was not going to make a circus show of his innermost feelings and Esca's for the amusement of such as Tribune Servius Placidus. 'Esca has been with me a long time. He nursed me when I was sick; he did everything for me, all the while that I was laid by with this leg.'

'Why not? He is your slave,' said Placidus carelessly.

Sheer surprise held Marcus silent for a moment. It was a long time since he had thought of Esca as a slave. 'That was not his reason,' he said. 'It is not the reason that he comes with me now.'

'Is it not? Oh, my Marcus, what an innocent you are; slaves are all—slaves. Give him his freedom and see what happens.'

'I will,' said Marcus. 'Thanks, Placidus, I will!'

.   .   .   .   .

When Marcus, with Cub at his heels, entered his sleeping-quarters that night, Esca, who was waiting for him as usual, laid down the belt whose clasps he had been burnishing, and asked: 'When do we start?'

Marcus closed the door and stood with his back against it. 'Probably the morn's morning—that is, for myself, at least. The details can wait awhile; but first you had best take this,' and he held out a slim papyrus roll he had been carrying.

Esca took it with a puzzled glance at his face, and unrolling it, he held it to the lamplight. And watching him, Marcus remembered suddenly and piercingly the moment that afternoon when he had taken off Cub's collar. Cub had come back to him; but Esca?

Esca looked up from the papyrus, and shook his head. 'Capitals are one thing,' he said, 'but I can make nothing of this script. What is it?'

'Your manumission—your freedom,' Marcus said. 'I

made it out this evening, and Uncle Aquila and the Legate witnessed it.   Esca, I ought to have given it to you long ago; I have been a completely unthinking fool, and I am sorry.'

Esca looked down to the thing in his hands once more, and again back to Marcus, as though he was not sure that he understood.   Then he let the roll spring back on itself, and said very slowly: 'I am free?   Free to go?'

' Yes,' Marcus said.   ' Free to go, Esca.'

There was a long dragging silence.   An owl cried somewhere afar off, with a note that seemed at once desolate and mocking.   Cub looked from one to the other, and whined softly in his throat.

Then Esca said, ' Is it that you are sending me away?'

' No!   It is for you to go, or stay, as you wish.'

Esca smiled, the slow grave smile that always seemed to come a little unwillingly to his face.   ' Then I stay,' he said, and hesitated.   ' It is perhaps not only I who think foolish thoughts because of the Tribune Placidus.'

' Perhaps.'   Marcus reached out and set both hands lightly on the other's shoulders.   ' Esca, I should never have asked you to come with me into this hazard when you were not free to refuse.   It is like to prove a wild hunt, and whether or no we shall come back from it lies on the knees of the gods.   No one should ask a slave to go with him on such a hunting trail; but—he might ask a friend.'   He looked questioningly into Esca's face.

Esca tossed the slender papyrus roll on to the cot, and set his own hands over Marcus's.   ' I have not served the Centurion because I was his slave,' he said, dropping unconsciously into the speech of his own people.   ' I have served Marcus, and it was not slave-service . . . My stomach will be glad when we start on this hunting trail.'

.   .   .   .   .

Next morning, promising to pay his old friend another visit on his way north again in the autumn, the Legate departed with Placidus, escorted by half a squadron of Cavalry.   And

Marcus watched them ride away down the long road to Regnum
and the waiting galleys, without quite the heart-ache that the
sight would once have given him, before he set about his own
preparations.

Esca's freedom caused less interest, and certainly less ill-
feeling in the household than might have been expected.
Sassticca, Stephanos, and Marcipor had all been born slaves,
the children of slaves; and Esca, the freeborn son of a free
chieftain, had never been one with them, even while he ate at
their table. They were old and well content with things as
they were; they had a good master, and slavery sat easy on
them, like an old and familiar garment. Therefore they did
not greatly begrudge freedom to Esca, accepting it as something
that was likely to have happened one day or another—he
and the young master having been, as Sassticca said, the two
halves of an almond these many moons past, and only grumbled
a little among themselves, for the pleasure of grumbling.

And anyhow, with Marcus going off—as the household had
been told—about some sudden business for his uncle next day,
and Esca going with him, no one, including Esca, had much
time for raising difficulties or even for feeling them.

That evening, having made the few preparations that were
needful, Marcus went down to the foot of the garden and
whistled for Cottia. Lately she had always waited to be
whistled for; and she came out to him among the wild fruit-
trees under the old ramparts, with one end of her damson-
coloured mantle drawn over her head against the heavy
spring shower that had come with her.

He told her the whole story as briefly as might be, and she
heard him out in silence. But her face seemed to grow sharper
and more pointed in the way that he knew of old, and when he
had finished, she said, ' If they want this Eagle back; if they
fear that it may harm them, where it is, let them send someone
else for it! Why need _you_ go? '

' It was my father's Eagle,' Marcus told her, feeling instinctively that that would make sense to her as the other
reasons behind his going would never do. A personal loyalty

needed no explaining, but he knew that it was quite beyond him to make Cottia understand the queer, complicated, wider loyalties of the soldier, which were as different from those of the warrior as the wave-break curve of the shield-boss was from the ordered pattern of his dagger sheath. 'You see, with us, the Eagle is the very life of a Legion; while it is in Roman hands, even if not six men of the Legion are left alive, the Legion itself is still in being. Only if the Eagle is lost, the Legion dies. That is why the Ninth has never been re-formed. And yet there must be more than a quarter of the Ninth who never marched north that last time at all, men who were serving on other frontiers, or sick, or left on garrison duty. They will have been drafted to other Legions, but they could be brought together again to make the core of a new Ninth. The Hispana was my father's first Legion, and his last, and the one he cared for most of all the Legions he served in. So you see . . .'

'It is to keep faith with your father, then?'

'Yes,' Marcus said, 'amongst other things. It is good to hear the trumpets sounding again, Cottia.'

'I do not think that I quite understand,' Cottia said. 'But I see that you must go. When will you start?'

'Tomorrow morning. I shall go down to Rufrius Galarius first, but Calleva will not come in my way again as I go north.'

'And when will you come back?'

'I do not know. Maybe, if all goes well, before winter.'

'And Esca goes with you? And Cub?'

'Esca,' Marcus said. 'Not Cub. I leave Cub in your charge, and you must come and see him every day and talk to him about me. In that way neither of you will forget about me before I come back.'

Cottia said, 'We have good memories, Cub and I. But I will come every day.'

'Good.' Marcus smiled at her, trying to coax a smile in return. 'Oh, and Cottia, do not mention the Eagle to anyone. I am supposed to be going on business for my uncle; only—I wanted you to know the truth.'

The smile came then, but it was gone again at once. 'Yes, Marcus.'

'That is better. Cottia, I cannot stay any longer, but before I go, there is one thing else that I want you to do for me.' As he spoke he pulled off the heavy gold bracelet with its engraved signum. The skin showed almond white where it had been, on the brown of his wrist. 'I cannot wear this where I am going; will you keep it safe for me until I come back to claim it?'

She took it from him without a word, and stood looking down at it in her hands. The light caught the Capricorn badge and the words beneath. '*Pia Fidelis*'. Very gently she wiped the rain-drops from the gold, and stowed it under her mantle. 'Yes, Marcus,' she said again. She was standing very straight and still, very forlorn, and with the darkness of her mantle covering her bright hair as it had done when he first saw her.

He tried to think of something to say; he wanted to thank her for the things that he was grateful for; but with everything that was in him reaching out to what lay ahead, somehow he could not find the right words, and he would not give Cottia words that meant nothing. At the last moment he would have liked to tell her that if he never came back, she was to keep his bracelet; but maybe it were better that he told Uncle Aquila. 'You must go now,' he said. 'The Light of the Sun be with you, Cottia.'

'And with you,' said Cottia. 'And with you, Marcus. I shall be listening for you to come back—for you to come down here to the garden foot and whistle for me again, when the leaves are falling.'

Next instant she had put aside a dripping blackthorn spray and turned from him; and he watched her walking away without a backward glance, through the sharp thin rain.

XI

ACROSS THE FRONTIER

FROM Luguvallium in the west to Segedunum in the east, the Wall ran, leaping along with the jagged contours of the land; a great gash of stone-work, still raw with newness. Eighty miles of fortresses, mile-castles, watch-towers, strung on one great curtain wall, and backed by the vallum ditch and the coast-to-coast Legionary road; and huddled along its southern side, the low sprawl of wine shops, temples, married quarters, and markets that always gathered in the wake of the Legions. A great and never-ceasing smother of noise: voices, marching feet, turning wheels, the ring of hammer on armourer's anvil, the clear calling of trumpets over all. This was the great Wall of Hadrian, shutting out the menace of the north.

On a morning in early summer, two travellers who had been lodging for some days in a dirty and dilapidated inn close under the walls of Chilurnium presented themselves at the Praetorian gate of the fortress, demanding to pass through to the north. There was not much coming and going across the frontier, save for the military patrols; but such as there was, hunters for the most part, or trappers with chained wild beasts for the arena, or a stray fortune-teller or quack-salver, had all to pass through the great fortresses of the Wall.

They were a faintly disreputable couple, mounted on small ex-cavalry mares of the Arab type which had certainly seen better days. The Legions could always find a steady market for their old mounts, cheap and well trained, and with several years of working life in them. They were to be seen everywhere along the Empire's roads, and there was nothing about these two to suggest that they had been bought, not for money, but by a few words signed by the Legate of the Sixth Legion, on a sheet of papyrus.

Esca had made very little real difference to his appearance, for he had no need; he had returned to the dress of his own people, and that was all. But with Marcus it was quite otherwise. He also had taken to British dress, and wore long bracco of saffron wool, cross-gartered to the knee, under a tunic of faded and distinctly dirty violet cloth. Bracco were comfortable in a cold climate, and many of the wandering herbalists and suchlike wore them. But the dark cloak flung back over his shoulders hung in folds that were foreign and exotic, and he wore a greasy Phrygian cap of scarlet leather stuck rakishly on the back of his head. A small silver talisman shaped like an open hand covered the brand of Mithras on his forehead, and he had grown a beard. Being little over a month old, it was not a very good beard; but such as it was, he had drenched it in scented oils. He looked much like any other wandering quack-salver, though somewhat young, despite the beard; and there was certainly no trace about him of the Centurion of the Eagles he had once been. His box of salves, provided for him by Rufrius Galarius, was stowed in the pack behind Esca's saddlepad, and with it his oculist's stamp, a slab of slate on which the hardened salves were ground, which proclaimed in engraved letters round the edge, ' The Invincible Anodyne of Demetrius of Alexandria, for all kinds of defective eyesight '.

The sentries passed them through without trouble into the fortress of Chilurnium, into the world of square-set barrack lines, and life ordered by trumpet calls that was familiar as a home-coming to Marcus. But at the Northern Gate, as they reached it, they met a squadron of the Tungrian Cavalry Cohort that formed the garrison coming up from exercise. They reined aside and sat watching while the squadron trotted by; and that was when the pull of long-familiar custom laid hold of Vipsania, Marcus's mare, and as the tail of the squadron passed she flung round with a shrill whinny, and tried to follow. Because of the old wound, Marcus had little power in his right knee, and it was a few trampling and sweating moments before he could master her and swing her back to the gate, and when he finally managed it, it was to find the decurion of the gate guard leaning against the guard-house wall, holding his sides and yelping with laughter, while his merry men stood grinning in the background.

'Never bring a stolen cavalry nag into a cavalry barracks,' said the decurion amiably, when he had had his laugh out. 'That's good advice, that is.'

Marcus, still soothing his angry and disappointed mare, demanded with a cool hauteur that Aesculapius himself could scarcely have bettered, had he been accused of being a horse-thief, 'Do you suggest that I, Demetrius of Alexandria, *the* Demetrius of Alexandria, am in the habit of stealing cavalry horses? Or that if I were, I should not have had the wisdom to steal a better one than this?'

The decurion was a cheerful soul, and the small grinning crowd that had begun to gather spurred him on to further efforts. He winked. 'You can see the brand on her shoulder, as plain as a pilum shaft.'

'If you cannot also see as plain as a pilum shaft that the brand has been cancelled,' Marcus retorted, 'then you must be in dire need of my Invincible Anodyne for all kinds of defective eyesight! I can let you have a small pot for three sesterces.'

There was a roar of laughter. 'Better have two pots, Sextus,' somebody called out. 'Remember the time you didn't see that Pict's legs sticking out from under the furze bush?'

The decurion evidently did remember the Pict's legs, and

would rather not, for though he laughed with the rest, his laughter rang a trifle hollow, and he made haste to change the subject. 'Are there not enough sore eyes for your salving in the Empire, that you must needs go jaunting beyond the Pale to look for more?'

'Maybe I am like Alexander, in search of fresh worlds to conquer,' said Marcus modestly.

The decurion shrugged. 'Every man to his own taste. The old world is good enough for me—with a whole hide to enjoy it in!'

'Lack of enterprise. That is the trouble with you.' Marcus sniffed. 'If I had been so lacking, should I now be *the* Demetrius of Alexandria, the inventor of the Invincible Anodyne, the most celebrated oculist between Caesarea and——'

'*Cave!* Here's the Commander,' somebody said. Instantly such of the group who had no business there melted away, and the rest straightened themselves on their feet and became painfully efficient. And Marcus, still discoursing loudly on his own importance and the healing powers of the Invincible Anodyne, was hustled out through the dark crowded arch of the gatehouse, with Esca, solemn-faced, in his wake.

The Frontier was behind them, and they rode out into the one-time Province of Valentia.

Chilurnium must be a pleasant place for the garrison, Marcus thought, as his quick glance took in the shallow wooded vale, the quiet river. There would be fishing and bathing here—when no trouble was brewing—and good hunting in the forest; a very different life from that of the upland fortresses farther west, where the Wall crossed bare moorland, leaping from crest to crest of the black hills. But his own mood just now was for the high hills, the tearing wind, and the curlews crying, and as soon as Chilurnium was well behind, he was glad to swing westward following the directions given them by a hunter before they set out, leaving the quiet vale for the distant lift of damson-dark uplands that showed through a break in the oakwoods.

Esca had ranged up alongside him, and they rode together in

I

companionable silence, their horses' unshod hooves almost soundless on the rough turf. No roads in the wilderness and no shoe-smiths, either. The country south of the Wall had been wild and solitary enough, but the land through which they rode that day seemed to hold no living thing save the roe-deer and the mountain fox; and though only the man-made wall shut it off from the south, the hills here seemed more desolate and the distances darker.

It was almost like seeing a friendly face in a crowd of strangers when, long after noon, they came dipping down over a shoulder of the high moors into a narrow green glen through which a thread of white water purled down over shelving stones, where the rowan-trees were in flower, filling the warm air with the scent of honey. A good place to make a halt, it seemed to them, and they off-saddled accordingly, and having watered the horses, and seen them begin to graze, they drank from their cupped hands and sprawled at their ease on the bank. There was wheaten biscuit and dried fish in the saddle-pack, but they left it there, having long since learned—Marcus on the march and Esca on the hunting trail—that morning and evening were the times for food.

Esca had stretched himself full length, with a sigh of content, under the leaning rowan-trees; but Marcus lay propped on one elbow to watch the little torrent out of sight round the shoulder of the glen. The silence of the high hills was all about them, made up of many small sounds: the purling of the water, the murmur of wild bees among the rowan blossom overhead, the contented cropping of the two mares. It was good to be up here, Marcus thought, after the long contriving of ways and means, the days of hanging along the Wall, kicking one's heels and listening for the faintest breath of a rumour that had evidently died as a stray wind dies, since it came to the Legate's ears. Up here in the silence of the hills, the strivings and impatiences of the past few weeks that had seemed to web him round all fell away, leaving him face to face with his task.

They had worked out a rough plan of campaign weeks ago, in Uncle Aquila's study, which now seemed a whole world away. It was very simple: merely to work their way north in a series of casts that would take them from coast to coast each time, in the manner of a hound cutting across a scent. In that way they must cut the trail of the Eagle—and the Legion, too, for that matter—at every cast; and surely somewhere, if they kept their eyes and ears open, they must pick it up. It had all seemed fairly simple in Uncle Aquila's study, but out here in the great emptiness beyond the Frontier it seemed a gigantic task.

And yet its seeming hopelessness was a challenge that he took up joyously. For the moment he forgot the sober facts of his search, and remembered only the personal quest. And sitting there in the little sun-warmed glen, his heart lifted suddenly and almost painfully to the crowning moment when he would carry the lost Eagle back into Eburacum, knowing that his father's Legion would live again, its name clean before the world; and surely, surely, no god worth the serving would be so unjust as not to see that his father knew that he had kept faith.

Esca broke the silence presently. 'So the contriving is done with,' he said, speaking apparently into the bee-loud rowan branches above his head, 'and the hunting is begun at last.'

'The hunting-ground is a wide one,' Marcus said, and turned to look down at his companion. 'And who knows into what strange covers the hunt may lead us? Esca, you know this sort of country better than I can do, and if the people are not of your tribe, at least they are nearer to you than to me. They are people of the shield-boss, and not of the pattern on my dagger sheath. Therefore, if you tell me to do a thing, I will do it, without clamouring to know why.'

'There may be wisdom in that,' Esca said.

Presently Marcus shifted, looking up at the sun. 'Soon we must be moving on, I suppose, lest we sleep in the woods tonight, seeing that we have not yet found this village that the man at the inn spoke of'; for even south of the Wall one did not go to a strange village after dark, unless one was tired of life.

'We shall not have far to seek,' Esca said, ' if we follow the stream downward.'

Marcus quirked an eyebrow at him.   'What tells you that?'

'Smoke.   Over the shoulder of the hill yonder; I caught the blur of it against the birch-trees, a while back.'

'It could be heath fire.'

'It was hearth fire,' Esca said with simple conviction.

Marcus relaxed again on the grass.   Then, as though on a sudden impulse, he drew his dagger and fell to cutting small square turfs from the fine burnside grass, loosening and lifting them with infinite care.   Having cut as many as he wanted, he drew the arching briars and the hemlock leaves back over the scars, and shifting farther up the bank, began to build them one a-top the other.

'What is it that you do?' Esca asked, after watching him in silence for a while.

'I build an altar,' Marcus said, ' here in the place of our first halt.'

'To what god?'

'To my own god.   To Mithras, the Light of the Sun.'

Esca was silent again.   He did not offer to help with this altar to Marcus's god, who was not his; but he drew closer and sat hugging his knees and looking down at the work.   Marcus went on trimming and shaping the sods; the crumbling soil was faintly warm under his fingers, and a low-hanging rowan branch cast ring-streaked shadows over his intent hands.   When the altar was finished and squared to his satisfaction, he cleaned and sheathed his dagger, and brushed away the scatter of loose soil from the surrounding grass with his palms.   Then with scraps of birch bark and dry sticks and sprigs of dead heather—Esca helped him gather these—he built a small fire on the altar top.   He built it very carefully, hollowing it slightly in the middle, as though to make a nest for something that he loved, and breaking a creamy curd of blossom from the rowan spray, nipped floweret from floweret, and scattered them over all.   Lastly, he took from the breast of his tunic his olive-wood bird—his olive-wood bird.   It was polished smooth and dark with years of carrying; rather a clumsy and ridiculous little bird, now that he came to look at it, but dear to him; and its dearness made it a fitting sacrifice. It had been part of his life, something that continued back from him to the wild olive-tree in the loop of the stream, and the life and places and things and people that the wild olive-tree belonged to. And suddenly, as he laid it in the hollow among the tiny stars of the rowan blossom, it seemed to him that with it—in it—he was laying the old life down too.

He held out his hand to Esca for the flint and steel which he always carried on him.

The golden sparks that he struck out dropped on to the tinder-dry scraps of birch bark, and hung there an instant like jewels; then, as he blew on them, nursing them to life, they flared up into crackling flame; a flower of flame with the olive-wood bird sitting at its heart like a dove on her nest.

He fed the fire carefully, with bits of wood from a fallen branch that Esca brought him.

XII

THE WHISTLER IN THE DAWN

ALL that summer Marcus and Esca wandered through the abandoned Province of Valentia, crossing and recrossing from coast to coast, and making steadily northward. They ran into no serious trouble, for Rufrius Galarius had spoken the truth when he said that the oculist's stamp was a talisman that would carry its owner anywhere. In Valentia, as in the rest of Britain, there were many people with marsh ophthalmia, and Marcus did his best for those who came to him for help, with the salves which the old field surgeon had shown him how to use. They were good salves, and Marcus had common sense and gentle hands and the craftsman's dislike of a job ill done, and so he succeeded better than most of

the few quack-salvers who had passed that way. The tribesmen were not exactly friendly; it was not in them to be
friendly towards men not of their own tribe, but they were
certainly not unfriendly. There was generally somebody in
each village who would give them food and shelter at the day's
end; and always, if the way was difficult to find or dangerous
to follow, a hunter from one village would act as their guide to
the next. They would have paid well, too, for Marcus's skill,
with a palmful of jet beads, a fine javelin-head or a dressed
beaver skin—things which would have fetched many times the
value of the salves, south of the Wall. But Marcus was not in
this adventure to make a fortune, nor did he wish to jingle
round the country loaded like a trader, and he shelved the
difficulty by saying to each offer, ' Keep it for me until I come
again on my way south.'

Late summer came, and the rowan-trees that had been in
new flower when Marcus built his altar in the glen of their first
halt were heavy now with flaming bosses of berries; and on an
August noon they sat side by side, looking down through the
birch-woods to the great firth which half cut Valentia from
what lay beyond. It was a day like a trumpet blast, the
wooded hills swimming in the heat, and at their backs the mares
stamped and fretted, swishing their tails against the cloud of
flies that beset them. Marcus sat with his hands locked round
his updrawn knees and stared out across the firth. The sun
was hot on the nape of his neck, scorching his shoulders
through the cloth of his tunic, and he would have dearly liked
to copy Esca, lying on his stomach beside him, who had
discarded his tunic altogether and now went stripped to the
waist like the Painted People. But to ride round the country
in his bracco would have been beneath the dignity of Demetrius of Alexandria, and he supposed that he must continue to
stew in his woollen tunic.

He heard the bees zooming among the bell-heather of the
clearing, smelled the warm aromatic scents of the sun-baked
birch-woods overlaying the cold saltiness of the sea; singled
out one among the wheeling gulls and watched it until it

became lost in a flickering cloud of sun-touched wings. But he was not really conscious of any of these things.

'We have missed the trail somehow,' he said abruptly. ' It is in my mind that we have come too far north. We are all but up to the old frontier now.'

' The Eagle is surely more likely to be found beyond the northern wall,' said Esca. ' The tribesmen would scarcely leave it in territory that was even in name a Roman province. They will have carried it away into one of their holy places.'

' I know,' Marcus said. ' But the traces should be in Valentia; and if the accounts of Caledonia that we have heard are true, we stand small chance of sighting our quarry among the mountains, unless we have some trail to follow. We shall simply wander up through Caledonia until we fall into the sea off the northernmost headland.'

' A holy place is apt to spread signs of itself abroad, for those, having eyes to see, who come even a little near,' Esca suggested.

Marcus sat silent for a moment, still hugging his knees. Then he said, ' When there is nothing, nothing at all, to guide a man in his choice, then it is time to lay the choice on the gods,' and fishing in the breast of his tunic, he brought out a small leather bag, and from the bag, a sesterce.

Esca rolled over and sat up, the blue warrior patterns moving on arms and breast as the muscles slid under his brown skin.

The disc of silver lay in Marcus's palm, showing the head of Domitian crowned with laurel; a small thing to hold their destinies. ' Heads we push on, ships we try a cast back,' Marcus said, and sent the coin spinning into the air. He caught it on the back of his hand, clapping the other over it, and for an instant their eyes met, questioningly. Then Marcus lifted the covering hand and they looked down at the winged victory on the obverse side of the coin, which had been called ' Ships ' from the days of the Republic, when the design had been the prow of a galley.

' We turn south again,' Marcus said.

Turn south they did; and a few nights later they encamped

in the old fort which Agricola had raised at Trinomontium, the Place of Three Hills.

Thirty years ago, when Valentia was a Roman province in more than name, before Agricola's work had been all undone by meddling from the Senate, Trinomontium had been a busy fort. A double cohort had drilled in the wide forum and slept in the barrack rows; there had been many horses in the stables, cavalry manoeuvres on the gentle southern slope below the ramparts, with the riders crested with tossing yellow plumes, the usual baths and wine-shops and the turf bothies of the women's quarters; and over all, the crested sentries marching to and fro. But now the wild had flowed in again; grass covered the cobbles of the streets, timber roofs had fallen in, and the red sandstone walls stood gaunt and empty to the sky. The wells were choked with the debris of thirty autumns, and an elder-tree had taken root in one corner of the roofless shrine where once had stood the cohort's standard and the altars of its gods, and had thrust a jagged gap in the wall to make room for itself. In all that desolation the only living creature that Marcus and Esca found as they wandered through it in the heavy stillness of the summer evening, was a lizard basking on a fallen block of stone, which darted off like a whip-lash at their approach. Looking down at the stone, Marcus saw roughly carved on it the charging boar of the Twentieth Legion. Somehow the sight brought the desolation home to him very sharply.

'If ever the Legions come north again, they will have a fine building job on their hands,' he said.

The hoof-beats of their led mounts sounded unnaturally loud in the silence; and when they halted at a crossways, the silence that came rushing in on them seemed almost menacing.

'It is in my heart that I wish we had pushed on to the next village,' Esca said, half under his breath. 'I do not like this place.'

'Why not?' Marcus asked. 'You did not mind it when we were here before.' For they had turned aside to look at the derelict fort on their way north, hoping against hope that it might hold some clue for them.

'That was at noon.   Now it is evening, and soon the light will go.'

'We shall do well enough with a fire,' Marcus said in surprise. 'We have slept out time and again since we started on this venture, and had no trouble while the fire burned.   And surely the only creatures likely to lair in these ruins are wild pig, and we have seen no signs of any such.'

'I have not been a hunter since first I could hold a spear, without growing used to sleeping in the wild,' Esca said, in the same suppressed voice.   'It is not the forest folk that make me cold between my shoulders.'

'What, then?'

Esca laughed, and broke off his laughter midway.   'I am a fool.   Maybe the ghosts of a lost Legion.'

Marcus, who had been gazing out over the grass-grown forum, looked round quickly.   'It was a cohort of the Twentieth that served here, never the Ninth.'

'How do we know where the Ninth served,' Esca said, 'after they marched into the mist?'

Marcus was silent for a moment.   He came of a breed that did not trouble unduly about ghosts, but he knew that with Esca it was quite otherwise.   'I do not think that they would bring us any harm, if they did come,' he said at last.   'It seemed to me that this would be a good place to sleep, especially with the curlews calling rain as they are this evening; but if you say the word, we will find a sheltered place among the hazel woods, and sleep there.'

'I should be ashamed,' Esca said simply.

Marcus said, 'Then we had best set about choosing our quarters.'

They settled finally on one end of a barrack row, where the roof had not fallen in, and the few feet of timber and rotten thatch made a shelter from the coming rain.   There they unloaded the mares, rubbed them down and turned them loose in the long building, in the British fashion; after which

Esca went off to gather a few armfuls of fodder, and bracken for bedding, while Marcus collected a stock of the rotten timber which lay about, and got a fire going, watched with close attention by Vipsania and Minna.

Later that evening the tumble-down shelter bore a much more cheerful aspect; a small fire burned brightly at its entrance, the smoke finding its own way round the bat-wing edge of the rotten thatch, into the darkening sky; and the piled bracken in the far corner spread with the sheepskins which by day were folded to serve as saddles. Marcus and Esca ate some of the food which they had brought with them from last night's village, coarse barley bannock and strips of strong part-smoked deer meat, which they broiled over the fire; and afterwards Esca lay down at once to sleep.

But Marcus sat for a while beside the fire, watching the sparks fly upward, hearing nothing but the occasional shifting of the mares in the farther shadows. From time to time he bent forward to put more wood on the fire; otherwise he sat quite unmoving, while, on the piled bracken against the wall, Esca slept the quiet, light sleep of the hunter. Looking at him, Marcus wondered whether he would have had the courage to lie quietly down to sleep on what he believed to be haunted ground. With the full dark, the rain came up, soft, heavy swathes of rain; and the swish and whisper of it on the rotten thatch seemed to deepen the utter desolation of this place that had once been living and was now dead. Marcus found himself listening with straining ears to the silence, his thoughts growing full of crowding ghosts that came and went along the rampart walls and through the forsaken forum, until it was all he could do to make himself bank the fire and lie down beside Esca.

Normally when they camped in the wild they took turns to sit up and keep the fire in while the other slept, but here, with four walls round them and a pile of thorn branches across the door to keep the horses in, there could be no need for that. For a while he lay wakeful, every nerve jumping with a queer expectancy; but he was tired, and the spread skins and the fragrant, high-piled bracken were very comfortable. And before long he fell asleep, and dreamed that he was watching Legionaries at pilum practice, quite ordinary Legionaries, save that between their chin-straps and the curves of their helmets—they had no faces.

He woke to a sense of light, steady pressure below his left ear, woke quietly and completely as people roused in that way always do, and opened his eyes to see that the fire had sunk to a few red embers and Esca was crouching beside him in the first faint pallor of the dawn. The evil taste of the dream was still in his mouth. 'What is it?' he whispered.

'Listen.'

Marcus listened and felt a small unpleasant chill trickling up his spine. His own eerie fancies of last night returned to him uncomfortably. Maybe Esca had been right about this place, after all. For somewhere in the abandoned fort, somebody—or some *thing*—was whistling the tune of a song that he knew well. He had marched to it more than once, for though an old song, it was a favourite with the Legions, and for no particular reason had outlived many and many that they picked up and marched to for a few months and then forgot.

> ' Oh when I joined the Eagles,
> (As it might be yesterday)
> I kissed a girl at Clusium
> Before I marched away.'

The familiar words joined themselves to the tune in Marcus's head, as he rose silently, and stood getting his stiffened leg into marching order. The whistling was drawing nearer, becoming every moment more clearly recognizable:

> ' A long march, a long march, and twenty years in store,
> When I left my girl at Clusium, beside the threshing-floor.'

There were many more verses, all describing girls that the maker of the song had kissed in different parts of the Empire; but as Marcus went purposefully to the doorway, and Esca stooped to drag aside the thorn branches, the whistling ceased, and a voice—a husky voice with a queer, brooding quality in it, as though the singer's thoughts were turned inward and backward—took up the song at the last verse of all:

> ' The girls of Spain were honey-sweet,
> And the golden girls of Gaul:
> And the Thracian maids were soft as birds
> To hold the heart in thrall.
>
>> ' But the girl I kissed at Clusium
>> Kissed and left at Clusium,
>> The girl I kissed at Clusium
>> I remember best of all.
>
> ' A long march, a long march, and twenty years behind,
> But the girl I kissed at Clusium comes easy to my mind.'

Rounding the end of the barrack row, they came face to face with the singer, who was standing in the Sinister Gate. Marcus had not known what he had expected to see—perhaps nothing, which would have been worst of all. But what he did see pulled him up in astonishment, for the man—it was no ghost —standing with his hand on the bridle of a rough-coated pony, was one of the Painted People, such as he had lived among all summer.

The man had checked at sight of Marcus and Esca, and stood looking at them warily, with upflung head, like a stag when it scents danger; his hunting-spear held as though for instant attack. For a moment they surveyed each other in the dawn light, then Marcus broke the silence. By now he could make himself understood without much trouble in the dialect of the Northern Tribes. ' It has been a good hunting, friend,' he said, pointing to the carcass of a half-grown roe-buck that was slung across the pony's back.

' Good enough until I can do better,' said the man. ' There is none to spare.'

' We have food of our own,' Marcus said. ' Also we have a fire, and unless it seems good to you to build your own or eat your meal raw, you are welcome to share it.'

' What do you here, in the Place of Three Hills? ' asked the man suspiciously.

' Camp for the night. Not knowing how far we might be from a village, and judging that rain was on the way, it seemed to us a better sleeping-place than the open moor. Is not the Place of Three Hills free to all, or only to the raven and the lizard—and yourself? '

For an instant the man did not answer, then slowly and deliberately he reversed the spear in his hand, so that he was carrying it with head trailing, as a man carries his spear when he comes in peace. ' I think that you will be the Healer of sore eyes, of whom I have heard? ' he said.

' I am.'

' I will come and share your fire.' He turned and whistled, and in answer to the summons, two swift brindled hunting dogs came springing up through the bracken to join him.

A few moments later they were back in their shelter, and the small, shaggy pony, free of his burden now, was hitched to a fallen beam beside the door. Esca threw a birch branch on to the red embers, and as the silver bark blackened and flared up, Marcus turned for a better look at the stranger. He was a middle-aged man, lean and powerful, his eyes wary and a little furtive under the wild hair that was coarse and grey as a badger's pelt; he wore nothing but an ochre-coloured kilt, and in the light of the fire his body and arms were covered all over with bands of tattooing, after the manner of the Painted People. Even on his cheeks and forehead and the wings of his nostrils the blue curves and spandrils showed. The dogs were nosing at the body of the deer which lay at his feet, and as their master stooped to cuff them away, the firelight fell strongly slantwise across his forehead, throwing into relief the scar of a curiously shaped brand, just between the brows.

Esca squatted down by the fire and put more strips of smoked meat to broil in the hot ash, then sat with his arms across his knees and his spear within easy reach, watching the stranger under his brows; while the stranger, kneeling over the flattened carcass of the buck—which had been gralloched already— began to skin it with the long hunting-knife which he drew from his raw-hide belt. Marcus also watched him, though less obviously. He was puzzled. The man seemed a tribesman like any other of his kind; yet he had sung ' The Girl I Kissed at Clusium ' in good Latin; and at some time, years ago to judge by the faintness of the scar, he had been initiated into the Raven Degree of Mithras.

He might of course have learned the song from the Legionaries who had served here; he was fully old enough for that. Mithra sometimes found followers in unexpected places. But taking the two things together, it was unusual, to say the least of it, and Marcus had been looking for something unusual all summer.

The hunter had laid back a large flap of hide from the flank and haunch of the buck. He cut thick collops of meat from it, and a shapeless lump with the hair still on, which he flung to the dogs who crouched beside him. And while they fought over it, snarling and worrying, he heaved up what remained of the carcass and flung it across a half-rotten tie-beam, where it hung, the dangling legs out of reach of the hounds. He put the collops that he had cut for his own eating to broil in the hot ash, rubbed his hands on his kilt, for they were juicy, and sitting back on his heels, peered from Marcus to Esca and back again with a strange intent look, as though their faces—Marcus's at all events—had some meaning for him which he could not fathom.

' I thank you for the heat of your fire,' he said, speaking less roughly than he had done before. ' It is in my heart that I might have been swifter to reverse my spear; but I had not thought to find any before me, here in the Place of Three Hills.'

' I can well believe that,' Marcus said.

' Aye, in all the years that I have come here on the hunting trail, never until now have I found any man here before me.'

' And now you have found two. And since we share the same fire,' said Marcus with a smile, ' surely we should know each other's names. I am Demetrius of Alexandria, a travelling oculist, as you seem to know, and this, my friend and spear-bearer, is Esca Mac Cunoval, of the tribe of the Brigantes.'

' The Bearers of the blue war-shield. You have heard maybe of my tribe, if not of me,' added Esca, and his teeth flashed white in his tanned face as he lifted his head and smiled.

'I have heard of your tribe—a little, yes,' said the stranger, with, as it seemed to Marcus, a hint of grim amusement in his voice, though there was no amusement in his gaunt face, as he blinked at the fire. 'For myself, I am called Guern, and I am a hunter, as you see. My rath lies upwards of a day's trail to the west, and I come here sometimes for the sake of the fat deer to be had in the hazel woods yonder.'

Silence fell between the three, while the daylight grew around them, and the dogs snarled and tussled over their lump of meat. Then Marcus, idly peeling a bit of stick, began half under his breath to whistle the tune that had so startled him an hour before. Out of the corner of his eyes he was aware that Guern had started and looked towards him. For a few moments he continued with the peeling and the whistling, and then, seeming suddenly to tire of his pastime, tossed the stick into the fire and looked up. 'Where did you learn that song, friend Guern the Hunter?'

'Where else but here?' said Guern. For an instant his face took on a look of blank stupidity, but Marcus had an idea that behind it he was thinking furiously. 'When this was a Roman fort there were many Roman songs sung here. That one I learned from a centurion who used to hunt boar with me. I was only a boy, but I have a good memory.'

'Did you pick up any Latin, other than the words of the song?' Marcus shot at him, speaking in that language.

The hunter made as if to answer, checked, and looked at him an instant slantwise, under down-twitched brows. Then he spoke in Latin, very slowly, like a man fumbling back across the years for a speech that comes half-forgotten to his tongue. 'A few words I remember still, such words as soldiers use.' Then, dropping back into the Celtic speech, 'Where did *you* learn that song?'

'I have followed my trade in fortress towns before now,' Marcus said, 'and ones that were not deserted to the wild boar, as the Place of Three Hills. I have a quick ear for a tune.'

Guern leaned forward to turn the cooking meat with his hunting-knife. 'Yet surely you can have been but a short while at this trade you practise. There are not many years under that beard of yours.'

'Maybe there are more than there seem,' Marcus said, and stroked the beard tenderly. It had grown well in the months since he came north, though it was still very clearly a young beard. 'Moreover, I began early, following my father's footsteps in the way of sons. . . . And talking of this trade of mine, are there any that have sore eyes in your village?'

Guern poked experimentally at the meat. He seemed to be making up his mind about something; and after a few moments he looked up as though he had made it. 'I am an outdweller, living to myself and my family,' he said, 'and we have no sore eyes for your healing. None the less, if you wait until my hunting is done, you are very welcome to come with me; and we will eat salt together, and later I will set you on your way to another village. That is for the place that you have given me at your fire.'

For an instant, Marcus hesitated; then, with the instinct still strong upon him that this man was not what he seemed, he said, 'All ways are alike to us. We will come, and gladly.'

'There is more flesh on my kill than I had thought,' said Guern, suddenly and shamefacedly, and stood up, knife in hand.

So the three of them ate fresh broiled buck together, in good fellowship; and a day later, when Guern's hunting was done, they set out, Marcus and Esca riding, and the hunter leading his own pony, across whose back was bound the carcass of a great red stag, and the dogs cantering ahead. Swishing through the rain-wet bracken they went, over the heathery shoulder of three-headed Eildon and away into the west, leaving the red sandstone fort deserted once again to the creatures of the wild.

K

XIII

THE LOST LEGION

GUERN's homestead, when they reached it, proved to be a bleak huddle of turf huts high among the dark moors. A small boy herding wild-eyed cattle up from the drinking-pool to the night-time shelter of the cattle-yard greeted their appearance with a kind of fascinated dismay. Evidently strangers were not in his scheme of things, and while stealing constant sly peeps at them, he took care to keep the great herd bull, which he managed with casual pokes and slaps, between him and danger, as they went on towards the rath together.

'This is my house,' said Guern the Hunter, as they reined in before the largest of the huts. 'It is yours for so long as it pleases you.'

They dismounted, while the yelling small boy and the lowing herd pelted by in the direction of the cattle-yard, and, tossing the reins over a hitching-post, turned to the doorway. A girl child of perhaps eighteen months old, wearing nothing but a red coral bead on a thong round her neck to ward off the Evil Eye, sat before the door, busily playing with three dandelions, a bone, and a striped pebble. One of the hounds poked a friendly muzzle into her face as he stalked past her into the darkness, and she made a grab at his disappearing tail, and fell over.

The doorway was so small that Marcus had to bend double under the heather thatch, as he stepped over the little sprawling figure and followed his host steeply down into the firelit gloom. The blue peat-smoke caught him by the throat and made his eyes smart, but he was used to that by now: and a woman rose from beside the central hearth.

'Murna, I have brought home the Healer of sore eyes and his

138

spear-bearer,' said Guern. ' Do you make them welcome while
I tend to their horses and the fruits of my hunting.'

' They are very welcome,' said the woman, ' though praise be
to the Horned One, there are no sore eyes here.'

' Good fortune on the house, and on the women of the house,'
Marcus said courteously.

Esca had followed their host out again, trusting no one but
himself to see to the mares, and Marcus sat down on the roe
deerskin that the woman spread for him on the piled heather
of the bed-place, and watched her as she returned to whatever
she was cooking in the bronze cauldron over the fire. As his
eyes grew used to the peat-smoke and to the faint light which
filtered down through the narrow doorway and the smoke-hole
in the roof, he saw that she was much younger than Guern:
a tall, raw-boned woman with a contented face. Her tunic
was of coarse reddish wool, such as only a poor woman would
have worn in the south; but clearly she was not a poor woman,
or rather her husband was not a poor man, for there were
bracelets of silver and copper and blue Egyptian glass on her
arms, and the mass of dull-gold hair knotted up behind her head
was held in place with amber-headed pins. Above all, she
was the proud possessor of a large bronze cauldron: Marcus
had been long enough in the wilderness to know that a bronze
cauldron, more than anything else, brought a woman the envy
of her neighbours.

After a short while footsteps sounded outside, and Esca and
Guern came ducking in, followed almost at once by the small
herdsman and an even younger boy, both very like Guern in
face, and already tattooed as he was, against the day when they
would be warriors. They watched the strangers warily under
their brows, and drew back against the far wall of the hut,
while their mother brought bowls of black pottery from some
inner place, and served the steaming stew to the three men
sitting side by side on the bed-place. She poured yellow mead
for them into the great ox-horns, and then went to eat her own
meal on the far side of the fire, the woman's side, with the small
girl child in her lap. The younger boy sat with her, but the

elder, suddenly overcoming his distrust, came edging round to examine Marcus's dagger, and finished up by sharing his bowl.

They were a pleasant small family, yet oddly isolated in a land where most people lived in groups for greater safety; and it seemed to Marcus that here was another hint of the unusual to add to the song and the brand of Mithras. . . .

It was next morning that he got the final proof of his suspicions.

That morning, Guern decided to shave. Like many of the British tribesmen, he went more or less clean shaven save for his upper lip, and he was certainly in need of a shave. As soon as he announced his intention, preparations began as though for a solemn festival. His wife brought him a pot of goose-fat to soften his beard, and the whole family gathered to watch their lord and master at his toilet; and so, amid an enthralled audience of three children and several dogs, sitting in the early light before the hut-place door, Guern the Hunter set to work, scraping away at his chin with a heart-shaped bronze razor. How little difference there was between children, all the world over, Marcus thought, looking on with amusement, or fathers, or shaving, for that matter; the small patterns of behaviour and relationship that made up family life. He remembered the fascination of watching his own father on such occasions. Guern squinted at his reflection in the polished bronze disc his patient wife was holding for him, cocked his head this way and that, and scraped away with an expression of acute agony, that made Marcus look forward with foreboding to the day when he and Esca would have to rid themselves of their own beards.

Guern had begun to shave under his chin, tipping his head far back, and as he did so, Marcus saw that just under the point of his jaw, the skin was paler than elsewhere, and had a thickened look, almost like the scar of an old gall. It was very faint, but still to be seen; the mark made by the chin-strap of a Roman helmet, through many years of wearing it. Marcus had seen that gall too often to be mistaken in it, and his last doubt was gone.

Something forbade him to tax Guern with his old life, here at the heart of the new life that he had made. And so a little later, while preparing to take the trail once more, he reminded the hunter of his promise, to set them on their way to the next village. He had a mind to go westward, he said, and Guern replied willingly enough, that since westward there were no more villages for two days' trail, if they were set on going that way, he would ride with them the first day and share their camp that night.

So presently they set out. And in the long-shadowed evening, many miles to the west, the three of them ate their evening meal in the curved lee of a rocky outcrop, and afterwards sat together round their small fire. Their three mounts, each hobbled by a rein from the head to the left foreleg to prevent them straying, cropped contentedly at the short hill-turf that spread here and there like green runnels among the bell-heather. Below them the hills rolled away north-westward, falling gradually to a blue haze of low ground, maybe forty miles away, and Marcus followed the fall of them with his eyes, knowing that somewhere in that blueness the wreck of Agricola's northern wall slashed across the land, severing Valentia from the country beyond that the Romans called Caledonia and the Celts Albu; knowing that somewhere beyond the blueness was the lost Eagle of his father's Legion.

In all the world there seemed no sound but the dry soughing of the wind through the heather, and the sharp yelp of a golden eagle circling the blue spirals of the upper air.

Esca had drawn back a little into the heather, and sat polishing his spear, and Marcus and Guern were alone by the fire, save for the hunter's favourite hound, who lay, nose on paws, with his flank against his master's thigh. Presently Marcus turned to his companion. ' Soon, very soon now, our ways part,' he said, ' but before you go your way and I go mine, there is a question that I have in my heart to ask you.'

' Ask, then,' said the other, playing with his dog's ears.

Marcus said slowly, ' How did you come to be Guern the Hunter who once served with the Eagles? '

There was a sudden flicker in the other's eyes; and then for a long moment he became very still, with a sullen stillness, peering at Marcus under his brows, in the way of the Painted People. 'Who told you such a thing?' he asked at last.

'No one. I go by a song, and the scar between your brows. But most of all by the gall-mark under your chin.'

'If I were—what you say,' Guern growled, 'what need have I to tell you of it? I am a man of my tribe, and if I was not always so, there is none among my sword-brethren who would speak of that to a stranger. What need, then, have I to tell?'

'None in the world,' said Marcus, 'save that I asked you in all courtesy.'

There was another long silence, and then his companion said, with a queer mingling of sullen defiance and a long-forgotten pride, 'I was once Sixth Centurion of the Senior Cohort of the Hispana. Now go and tell it to the nearest Commander on the Wall. I shall not stop you.'

Marcus took his time, sitting quiet and searching the fierce face of the man before him. He was looking for any trace that might be left under the painted hunter of the Roman centurion of twelve years ago; and presently he thought he had found it. 'No patrol could reach you, and you know it,' he said. 'But even if it were not so, still there is a reason that I should keep my mouth shut.'

'And that reason?'

Marcus said, 'That I bear on my forehead a mark which is brother to the mark that you bear on yours,' and with a quick movement he freed the crimson riband that bound the silver talisman in place, and jerked it off. 'Look!'

The other bent forward swiftly. 'So,' he said lingeringly. 'Never before have I known one of your trade who made his evening prayer to Mithras.' But even as he spoke, his gaze narrowed into a new intentness, became like a dagger-thrust. 'Who are you? What are you?' he demanded; and suddenly his hands were on Marcus's shoulders, wrenching him round to face the last windy gold of the sunset. For a long moment he held him so, kneeling over him and glaring into his face;

while Marcus, with his lame leg twisted under him, stared back, his black brows frowning, his mouth at its most disdainful.

The great hound crouched watchfully beside them, and Esca got quietly up, fingering his spear; both man and hound ready to kill at a word.

'I have seen you before,' said Guern in a rasping voice. 'I remember your face. In the Name of Light, who are you?'

'Maybe it is my father's face that you remember. He was your Cohort Commander.'

Slowly Guern's hands relaxed and dropped to his side. 'I should have known,' he said. 'It was the talisman—and the beard. But none the less, I should have known.' He sat rocking himself a little, almost as if he were in pain, his eyes never leaving Marcus's face. 'What is it that you do, your father's son, here in Valentia?' he said at last. 'You are no Greek of Alexandria, and I think that you are no eye doctor.'

'No, I am no eye doctor. Nevertheless, the salves that I carry are good, and I was shown how to work with them by one skilled in their use. When I told you that I had followed my father's trade, that at least was the truth. I followed it until I got me this leg and my discharge, two years ago. As to what I do, here in Valentia——' he hesitated, but only for an instant. He knew that in this one matter, at least, he could trust Guern utterly.

And so, very briefly, he told him what it was he did in Valentia, and why. 'And when it seemed to me that you were not as the other hunters of the Painted People,' he finished, 'it seemed to me also that from you I might learn the answer to my questions.'

'And could you not have asked me at the first? Because I was drawn to you, not knowing why, and because you spoke the Latin tongue that I had not heard these twelve years, I brought you to my own place, and you slept under my roof and ate of my salt; with this hidden in your heart concerning me. It would have been better that you asked me at the first!'

'Much better,' Marcus agreed. 'But all that I had in my heart concerning you was a guess, and a wild guess enough!

If I had spoken out to you without first being sure, and found too late that you were, after all, no other than you seemed, would there not have been Ahriman the Dark One to pay?'

'What is it that you want to know?' Guern said dully, after a moment.

'What became of my father's Legion. Where is the Eagle now?'

Guern looked down at his own hand, on the head of the great dog who was once more lying quiet beside him; then up again. 'I can answer the first of your questions, at least in part,' he said, 'but it is a long story, and first I will mend the fire.'

He leaned forward as he spoke, and fed the sinking flames from the pile of thorn branches and heather snarls beside him. He did it slowly, deliberately, as though holding off the moment when he must begin his story. But even when the flames sprang up again, he still squatted silent on his haunches, staring into the smoke.

Marcus's heart had begun to race, and suddenly he felt a little sick.

'You never knew your father's Legion,' Guern began at last. 'No, and if you had, you would have been too young to read the signs. Too young by many years.' He had changed his tongue to Latin, and with the change, all that was of the tribes in him seemed to have dropped away. 'The seeds of death were in the Hispana before ever it marched north that last time. They were sown sixty years ago, when men of the Legion carried out the Procurator's orders to dispossess the Queen of the Iceni. Boudicca her name was; maybe you have heard of her? She cursed them and their whole Legion, it is said, for the treatment that she had at their hands, which was hardly just, for they had their orders: if she was minded to curse anyone, it had better have been the Procurator himself. But a woman who thinks herself wronged is seldom over particular where her thrust lands, so that it draws blood. Me, I am not one to set much store by cursings, or I was not in the old days. But be that as it may, the Legion was cut to pieces in the rising that followed. When at last the rising failed, the Queen took poison, and maybe her death gave potency to her cursing.

'The Legion was re-formed and brought up to strength again, but it never prospered. Perhaps if it had been moved elsewhere it might have been saved, but for a Legion to serve year after year, generation after generation, among tribes who believe it to be accursed is not good for that Legion. Small misfortunes bloat into large ones, outbreaks of sickness are set down to the working of the curse, instead of the marsh mists; the Spaniards are a people quick to believe in such things. So it became harder to find recruits, and the standard of those taken grew lower, year by year. It was very slow at first—I have served with men no older than myself, who remembered the Ninth when it was only a little rough and run to seed. But at the last it was terribly swift, and when I joined the Legion as a centurion, two years before the end—I was promoted from the ranks of the Thirtieth, which was a proud Legion—the rind seemed sound enough, but the heart was rotten. Stinking rotten.'

Guern the Hunter spat into the fire.

' I strove to fight the rot in my own Century at first, and then —the fighting grew to be too much trouble. The last Legate was a hard and upright man without understanding—the worst man to handle such a Legion—and soon after his coming the Emperor Trajan withdrew too many troops from Britain for his everlasting campaigns; and we who were left to hold the Frontier began to feel the tribes seethe under us like an over-ripe cheese. Then Trajan died, and the tribes rose. The whole North went up in flames, and barely had we settled with the Brigantes and the Iceni when we were ordered up into Valentia to hammer the Caledonians. Two of our cohorts were serving in Germany; we had suffered heavy casualties already, and leaving a cohort to garrison Eburacum and be cut to shreds by the Brigantes if they happened to feel like it, that left well under four thousand of us to march north. And when the Legate took the omens in the usual way, the sacred chickens had gone off their feed and would not touch the pulse he threw to them. After that we gave ourselves up for doomed, which is a bad state of mind for a Legion to march in.

'It was autumn, and almost from the start the mountain country was blanketed in mist, and out of the mist the tribesmen harried us. Oh, it never came to a fight; they hung about our flanks like wolves; they made sudden raids on our rearguard and loosed their arrows into us from behind every tuft of sodden heather, and disappeared into the mist before we could come to grips with them; and the parties sent out after them never came back.

'A Legate who was also a soldier might have saved us; ours had seen no more of soldiering than a sham fight on Mars Field, and was too proud to listen to his officers who had, and by the time we reached Agricola's old headquarters on the Northern Wall, which was to be our base, upward of another thousand of us had gone, by death or desertion. The old fortifications were crumbling, the water supply had long since given out, and the whole North had gathered in strength by then. They sat round the walls and yelled, like wolves howling to the moon. We stood one attack in that place. We rolled the dead down the scarp into the river; and when the tribes drew off to lick their wounds, we chose a spokesman and went to the Legate and said: "Now we will make what terms we can with the Painted People, that they may let us march back the way we came, leaving Valentia in their hands, for it is no more than a name, and a name that tastes sour on the tongue at that." And the Legate sat in his camp chair, which *we* had had to carry for him all the way from Eburacum, and called us evil names. Doubtless we deserved the names, but they did not help. Then more than half of us mutinied, many of my own Century among them.'

Guern turned from the fire to face Marcus. 'I was not one of them. Before the Lord of the Legions I swear it. My full shame was not yet come upon me and I held the few men left to me in leash yet awhile. Then the Legate saw where his mistake had lain, and he spoke more gently to his Legion in

revolt than ever he had done before, and that was not from fear.
He bade the mutineers lay down the arms that they had taken
up against their Eagle, and swore that there should be no sum-
mary punishment, even of the ringleaders; swore that if we
did our duty from thenceforth, he would make fair report of
it, the good with the bad, on our return. As though we should
ever return! But even had the way back been clear, it was too
late for such promises. From the moment that the cohorts
mutinied it was too late. There could be no turning back for
them, knowing all too well what the word of the Senate would
be.'

'Decimation,' Marcus said quietly, as the other halted.

'Aye, decimation. It comes hard, to draw lots out of a
helmet, knowing that one in every ten means death by stoning
to the man who draws it.

'So the thing ended in fighting. That was when the Legate
was killed. He was a brave man, though a fool. He stood out
before the mob, with his hands empty, and his Eagle-bearer
and his beardless Tribunes behind him, and called on them to
remember their oath, and called them curs of Tiber-side.
Then one struck him down with a pilum, and after that there
was no more talking. . . .

'The tribesmen came swarming in over the barricades to
help the red work, and by dawn there were barely two full
cohorts left alive in the fort. The rest were not all dead, oh
no; many of them went back over the ramparts with the
tribesmen. They may be scattered about Caledonia now, for
all I know, living even as myself, with a British wife, and sons
to come after them.

'Just after dawn, your father called together the few that
were left in the open space before the Praetorium, and there,
every man with his sword ready in his hand, we took hurried
counsel, and determined to win out of the old fort, which was
become a death-trap, and carry the Eagle back to Eburacum
as best we might. It was no use by then to think of making
terms with the tribesmen, for they had no longer any cause to
fear us. And besides, I think there was the thought in all of us

that if we won through, the Senate could scarcely count us as
disgraced. That night the fools feasted—so low had we sunk
in their contempt—and while they drank, baying to the moon,
we got out, all that were left of us, by the southern scarp, and
passed them by in the darkness and the mist—the first time ever
the mist had seemed our friend—and began the forced march
back, heading for Trinomontium.

   ' The tribes picked up our trail at dawn and hunted us as
though it had been for sport. Have you ever been hunted?
All that day we struggled on, and the sorest wounded, who
dropped out, died. Sometimes we heard them die, in the mist.
Then I dropped out too.' Guern rubbed his left flank. ' I
had a wound that I could put three fingers in, and I was sick.
But I could have gone on. It was being hunted—the being—
hunted. I took my chance at dusk, when the hunters drew
off a space; I slipped into some long furze-cover, and hid.
One of the Painted People nearly trod on me presently, but
they did not find me, and after dark, when the hunt had passed
far away, I stripped off my harness and left it. I look like a
Pict, do I not? That is because I am from Northern Gaul.
Then I suppose I wandered all night. I do not know, but in
the dawn I came to a village and fell across the door-sill of the
first hut.

   ' They took me in and tended me. Murna tended me. And
when they found that I was a Roman soldier, they did not
greatly care. I was not the first of my kind to desert to the
tribes; and Murna spoke for me, like a lioness whose cub is
threatened.' For an instant, a glint of laughter sounded in
his voice, and then it grew harsh and heavy again. ' A few
nights later I saw the Eagle carried by on its way north again,
with a great triumph of torches following behind.'

   There was a long, strained silence. Then Marcus said in a
quiet, hard voice, ' Where did they make an end? '

   ' I do not know. But they never reached Trinomontium.
I have looked there again and again, and found no sign of
fighting.'

   ' And my father? '

'He was with the Eagle when I dropped out.   There were no
captives with it when they carried it north again.'

'Where is the Eagle now?'

Guern reached out and touched the dagger in the other's
belt, looking at him steadily.   'If you are minded to die, here
is the means to your hand.   Save yourself the further journey.'

'Where is the Eagle now?'   Marcus repeated his question,
as though the other had not spoken.

For a moment he held the hunter's eyes with his own; then
Guern said, 'I do not know.   But tomorrow, when there is
light to see by, I will give you what direction I can.'

And Marcus realized suddenly that he was seeing the other's
face by firelight, and all beyond him was blurred into the blue
dusk.

He did not sleep much that night, but lay rigid with his head
in his arms.   All these months he had followed a dream; in a
way, he realized now, he had followed it since he was eight years
old.   It had been bright and warm, and now it was broken,
and without it he felt very cold, and suddenly older than he had
been a few hours ago.   What a fool he had been!   What a
blind fool!   Clinging to the stubborn faith that because it had
been his father's, there had been nothing much wrong with the
Ninth Legion, after all.   He knew better now.   His father's
Legion had been putrid, a rotten apple that fell to pieces when
it was struck by a heel.   And God of the Legions! what his
father must have suffered!

Out of the ruin, one thing stood up unchanged: that the
Eagle was still to be found and brought back, lest one day it
became a menace to the Frontier.   There was something com-
forting about that.   A faith still to be kept.

Next morning when the early meal had been eaten, and the
fire quenched and scattered, Marcus stood beside his mare,
looking away north-west, along the line of Guern's pointing
finger.   The light wind whipped his face, and his morning
shadow ran away downhill as though eager to be off before
him, and he heard the wild, sweet calling of the green plover
that seemed to be the voice of the great loneliness.

' Yonder where the vale opens,' Guern was saying. ' You will know the ford by the leaning pine that grows beside it. You must cross there, and follow the right bank, or you will find yourself at the last with the whole broad Firth of Cluta between you and Caledonia. Two days' march, three at the most, will bring you to the old northern line.'

' And then? ' Marcus said, not turning his narrowed gaze from the blue hazed distance.

' I can tell you only this : that the men who carried the Eagle north were of the tribe of the Epidaii, whose territory is the deep firths and the mountains of the west coast, running from the Cluta.'

' Can you hazard any guess as to where in this territory their holy place may be? '

' None. It may be that if you find the Royal Dun, you will find the Holy Place not far off; but the Epidaii is divided into many clans, so I have heard, and the Royal Clan may not be the guardians of the Holy Place and the holy things of the tribe.'

' You mean—it might be some quite small and unimportant clan? '

' Not unimportant; it would be as powerful as the Royal Clan, maybe more so. But small, yes. There is no more help that I can give you.'

They were silent a moment until there sounded behind them the faint jink of a bridle-bit, as Esca brought up the other mare. Then Guern said hurriedly, ' Do not follow that trail; it leads into the mouth of death.'

' I must take my chance of that,' Marcus said. He turned his head. ' And you, Esca? '

' I go where you go,' said Esca, busy with a buckle.

' Why? ' Guern demanded. ' Now that you know the truth? They will not re-form the Legion. Why should you go on? Why? '

' There is still the Eagle to be brought back,' Marcus said.

Another silence, and then Guern said almost humbly, ' You have said nothing about all this that I have told you; no

more than if it had been a story told to while away an idle
evening.'

'What should I say?'

The other laughed, shortly and harshly. 'Mithras knows!
But my belly would be the lighter if you said it.'

'Last night I felt too sick in my own belly to care over much
for yours,' Marcus said wearily. 'That is passed now, but if I
cursed the Hispana with every foul Tiber-side word that I
could lay my tongue to, it would not serve my father, nor
sweeten the stink of the Legion's name.' He looked for the
first time at the man beside him. 'As for you, I have never
been hunted, and the Lord of the Legions forbid that I should
be your judge.'

The other said defiantly, 'Why did you come? I was happy
with my woman; she is a good woman to me. I am a great
man in my tribe, though an outdweller. Often I forget—
almost—that I was not born into my tribe, until once again
Trinomontium draws me back for a little while. And now I
shall be ashamed to my dying day, because I let you go north
on this trail alone.'

'No need that you should carry a new shame,' Marcus said.
'This is a trail that three can follow better than four, and two
better than three. Go back to your tribe, Guern. Thank
you for your salt and your shelter, and for answering my
questions.'

He turned away to mount his horse, and a few moments later
was heading down the stream-side with Esca close behind.

XIV

THE FEAST OF NEW SPEARS

O N an evening more than a month later, Marcus and
Esca reined in to breathe their tired horses, on the
crest of a steep ridge above the Western Ocean. It
was an evening coloured like a dove's breast; a little wind
feathered the shining water, and far out on the dreaming
brightness many scattered islands seemed to float lightly as
sleeping sea-birds. In the safe harbourage inshore, a few
trading-vessels lay at anchor, the blue sails that had brought
them from Hibernia furled as though they, too, were asleep.
And to the north, brooding over the whole scene, rose Cruachan,
sombre, cloaked in shadows, crested with mist; Cruachan,
the shield-boss of the world.

Mountain and islands and shining sea were all grown
familiar to Marcus. For a month now he had seldom been
out of sight of one or other of them, as he came and went among
the mist-haunted glens where the Epidaii had their hunting
grounds. It had been a heartbreaking month. So often, since
he crossed the northern line, it had seemed to him that he was
at last on the trail of what he sought, and always he had been
wrong. There were so many holy places along the coast.
Wherever the Ancient People, the little Dark People, had left
their long barrows, there the Epidaii, coming after, had made a

holy place at which to worship their gods; and the Ancient People had left so many barrows. Yet nowhere could Marcus hear any whisper of the lost Eagle. These people did not speak of their gods, nor of the things which had to do with their gods. And suddenly, this evening, looking out over the shining sea, Marcus was heart-sick and not far from giving up hope.

He was roused from his bleak mood by Esca's voice beside him. 'Look, we have companions on the road.' And following the direction of his friend's back-pointing thumb, he turned to look down the deer-path by which they had come, and saw a party of hunters climbing towards them. He wheeled Vipsania, and sat waiting for them to come up. Five men in all, two of them carrying the slung carcass of a black boar; and the usual pack of wolfish hounds cantering among them. How different they were from the men of Valentia: darker and more slightly built. Maybe that was because the blood of the Dark People ran more strongly in them than in the lowland tribes; less outwardly fierce than the lowlanders too, but in the long run, Marcus thought, more dangerous.

'The hunting has been good.' He saluted them as they came up at a jog-trot.

'The hunting has been good,' agreed the leader, a young man with the twisted gold torc of a chieftain round his neck. He looked inquiringly at Marcus, forbidden by courtesy to ask his business, but clearly wondering what this stranger, who was not one of the traders from the blue-sailed ships, was doing in his territory.

Almost without thinking, Marcus asked him the question which had become a habit with much asking. 'Are there any in your dun who have the eye sickness?'

The man's look grew half eager, half suspicious. 'Is it that you can cure the eye sickness?'

'Can I cure the eye sickness?—I am Demetrius of Alexandria. *The* Demetrius of Alexandria,' said Marcus, who had long since learned the value of advertisement. 'Speak my name south of the Cluta, speak it in the Royal Dun itself, and

men will tell you that I am indeed a healer of all sickness of
the eye.'

'There are several that I know of in the dun, who have the
eye sickness,' said the man. 'None of your trade ever came
this way before. You will heal them?'

'How should I know, even I, until I see them?' Marcus
turned his mare into the way. 'You are for the dun now?
Let us go on together.'

And on they went, Marcus with the Chieftain loping at his
horse's shoulder, then Esca and the rest of the hunting party
with the slung boar in their midst and the hounds weaving to
and fro among them. For a while they followed the ridge, then
turned inland, and came looping down through thin birch-
woods towards a great loch that lay, pearl-pale with evening,
among the hills. Marcus and Esca knew that loch—they
had touched its further shores more than once. The Loch of
Many Islets it was called, from the little islands scattered in it,
some of them steep and rocky, or low and willow-fringed where
the herons nested.

It was twilight when they reached the dun on its hill
shoulder above the still waters of the loch; the soft mulberry
twilight of the west coast, through which the firelit doorways
of the living-huts bloomed like yellow crocus flowers dimly
veined with red. The cluster of huts that made up the rath of
the Chieftain was at the head of the dun, in a sharp curve of
the turf ramparts, and they turned aside to it, while the other
hunters, after arranging for the sharing of the boar, scattered
to their own houses.

At the sound of their arrival, a lad who Marcus took to be
the Chieftain's brother ducked out from the firelit doorway
and came running to meet them. 'How went the hunting,
Dergdian?'

'The hunting was good,' said the Chieftain, 'for see, beside
a fine boar, I have brought home a healer of sore eyes; also his
spear-bearer. Look to their horses, Liathan.' He turned
quickly to Marcus, who was rubbing his thigh. 'You are
saddle-stiff? You have ridden over-far today?'

'No,' said Marcus.   'It is an old hurt which still cramps me sometimes.'

He followed his host into the great living-hut, ducking his head under the low lintel.   Inside it was very hot, and the usual blue peat-reek caught at his throat.   Two or three hounds lay among the warm fern.   A little, wizened woman, evidently a slave, bent over the raised hearth, stirring the evening stew in a bronze cauldron, and did not look up at their coming in; but a gaunt old man who sat beyond the fire peered at them through the eddying peat-smoke with bright, masterful eyes.   That was in the first instant;   then the curtain of beautifully worked deerskins over the entrance to the women's place was drawn aside, and a girl appeared on the threshold;   a tall girl, dark even for a woman of the Epidaii, in a straight green gown, clasped at the shoulder with a disc of red-gold as broad and massive as a shield-boss.   She had been spinning, it seemed, for she still carried spindle and distaff.

'I heard your voice,' she said.   'Supper is ready and waiting.'

'Let it wait a while longer, Fionhula my heart,' said Dergdian the Chieftain.   'I have brought home a healer of sore eyes;   therefore do you bring out to him the little cub.'

The woman's long dark eyes moved quickly, with a kind of startled hope in them, to Marcus's face, then back to the Chieftain's.   She turned without a word, letting the curtain fall behind her, and a few moments later she was back, holding a little boy of about two in her arms.   A brown pleasant infant, dressed in the usual coral bead, but as the light fell on his face, Marcus saw that his eyes were so swollen and red and crusted that they would scarcely open.

'Here is one for your healing,' said the Chieftain.

'Yours?' Marcus asked.

'Mine.'

'He will be blind,' said the old man by the fire.   'All along, I have said that he will be blind, and I am never wrong.'

Marcus ignored him.   'Give the little cub to me,' he commanded.   'I will not hurt him.'   He took the little boy from his mother with a quick reassuring smile, and slipped down awkwardly on to his sound knee beside the fire. The child whimpered, turning away from the fire; evidently the light hurt him. Not blind already, then. That was something. Very gently, he turned the little boy's face back to the firelight. 'There, cubling, it is but for a moment. Let me look. What is this you have been putting in the child's eyes?'

'Toad's fat,' said the old man. 'With my own hands I salved them, though it is women's work, for my grandson's wife is a fool.'

'Have you found it do any good?'

The old man shrugged his gaunt shoulders. 'Maybe not,' he said grudgingly.

'Then why use it?'

'It is the custom. Always our womenfolk put toad's fat on such places; but my grandson's wife——' The old man spat juicily to express his opinion of his grandson's wife. 'But all along, I have said the child will be blind,' he added, in the satisfied tone of a true prophet.

Marcus heard the girl behind him catch her breath in agonized protest, and felt his own temper flash up in him, but he had the sense to know that if he made an enemy of the old devil he might as well give up any hope of saving the child's sight. So he said peaceably enough, 'We will see. Toad's fat is doubtless good for sore eyes, but since it has failed, this time, I shall try my own salves; and it may be that they will do better.' And before the old man could get in another word he turned to Fionhula. 'Bring me warm water and linen rags,' he said, 'and light a lamp. I must have light to work by, not this flickering fire-glow. Esca, do you bring in my medicine box.'

And there and then, while the mother held the sick child in her lap, he set to work, bathing, salving, bandaging, by the light of the lamp which the slave woman deserted the stew to hold for him.

Marcus and Esca remained many days in the dun of Dergdian. Always before, Marcus had merely started the good work, left a lump of salve and instructions how to use it, and moved on. But this time it was different. The child's eyes were worse than any that he had had to tend before, and there was grandfather and his toad fat to be reckoned with. This time he would have to stay. Well, he might as soon stay here as in any other place, since he was as likely, or as unlikely, to be near finding the Eagle here as anywhere else.

So he stayed, and a weary stay it seemed. The days went very slowly, for he had long empty stretches of time on his hands, and after the first sharp battle for the little cub's sight had been won, and it was only a question of waiting, they seemed to crawl more slowly still.

Most of the time he sat in the hut-place doorway, watching the womenfolk at work, or grinding sticks of dried salves for the small leaden pots that needed replenishing, while Esca went off with the hunters, or joined the herdsmen in the steep cattle-runs. In the evening he talked with the men round the fire; exchanged travellers' tales with the dark Hibernian traders who came and went through the dun (for there was a constant trade in gold-work and weapons, slaves and hunting dogs, between Hibernia and Caledonia); listening patiently to old Tradui, the Chieftain's maternal grandfather, telling interminable stories of seal hunts when he and the world were young and men and seals stronger and fiercer than they were now.

But all the while, listen as they might, neither he nor Esca heard anything to suggest that the place and the thing they were looking for was nearby. Once or twice, during those days, Marcus glimpsed a black-cloaked figure passing through the dun, remote from the warm and crowded humanity of the tribe and seeming to brood over it as Cruachan brooded over the land. But Druids were everywhere, up here beyond the reach of Rome, just as holy places were everywhere. They did not live among the people, but withdrawn into themselves, in the misty fastnesses of the mountains, in the hidden glens, and among the forests of birch and hazel. Their influence lay heavy on the duns and villages, but no one spoke of them, any

more than they spoke of their gods and the prowling ghosts of
their forefathers.   Neither did anyone ever speak of a captured
Eagle.   But still Marcus waited, until he knew that the little
cub's sight was safe.

And then one evening, returning with Esca from a plunge in
the deep water below the dun, he found the Chieftain squatting
in his hut-place doorway with his hunting dogs around him,
lovingly burnishing a heavy war-spear with a collar of eagles'
feathers.   Marcus folded up beside him and watched, vividly
remembering another war-spear whose collar had been the
blue-grey feathers of a heron.   Esca stood leaning one
shoulder against the rowan-wood doorpost, watching also.

Presently the Chieftain looked up and caught their gaze.
' It is for the Feast of New Spears,' he said.   ' For the warrior
dancing that comes after.'

' The Feast of New Spears,' Marcus echoed.   ' That is when
your boys become men, is it not?   I have heard of such a feast,
but never seen it.'

' You will see in three nights from now; on the Night of the
Horned Moon,' Dergdian said, and returned to his burnishing.
' It is a great feast.   From all over the tribe, the boys come,
and their fathers with them.   If it were the King's son, still
he must come to us, when it is time for him to receive his
weapons.'

'Why?' Marcus asked, and then hoped that he had not
sounded too eager.

' We are the keepers of the Holy Place, we, the Seal People,'
said Dergdian, turning the spear on his knee.   ' We are the
guardians of the Life of the Tribe.'

After a long pause, Marcus said casually, ' So.   And it is
allowed to anyone to witness this mystery of the New Spears? '

' Not the mystery, no; that is between the New Spears and
the Horned One, and none save the priest-kind may see and
live; but the ceremonies of the forecourt, they are for any who
choose to be there.   They are not hidden, save from the
women's side.'

' Then with your leave I shall most assuredly choose to be

there. We Greeks—we are born asking questions,' Marcus said.

Next day began a bustle of preparation that reminded Marcus of his own Etruscan village on the eve of Saturnalia; and by evening the first inflow of the New Spears had begun; boys and their fathers from the farthest fringes of the tribal lands, riding fine small ponies, wearing their brightest clothes, and many of them with their hounds cantering along beside. Odd, he thought, watching them, odd that people so poor in many ways, hunters and herdsmen who do not till the soil, and live in mud hovels in acute discomfort, should enrich the bridles of their superbly bred ponies with silver and bronze and studs of coral, and clasp their cloaks with buckler-brooches of red Hibernian gold. There was an in-swarming of another kind too, of merchants and fortune-tellers, harpers and horse-dealers, who encamped with the tribe on the level shores of the loch until the whole stretch below the dun was dark with them. It was all warm and gay and human, a market crowd on a large scale, and nowhere any sign of the strangeness that Marcus had expected.

But there was to be strangeness enough before the Feast of New Spears was over.

It began on the second evening, when suddenly the boys who were to receive their weapons were no longer there. Marcus did not see them go; but suddenly they were gone, and behind them the dun was desolate. The men daubed their foreheads with mud; the women gathered together, wailing and rocking in ritual grief. From within the dun and from the encampment below the ramparts the wailing rose as the night drew on, and at the evening meal a place was left empty and a drinking-horn filled and left untouched for every boy who had gone, as for the ghosts of dead warriors at the feast of Samhain; and the women made the death chant through the long hours of darkness.

With morning, the wailing and the lamentation ceased, and in its place there settled on the dun a great quietness and a great sense of waiting. Towards evening the tribe gathered on the level ground beside the loch.   The men stood about in groups, each clan keeping to itself.   Wolf Clan to Wolf Clan, Salmon to Salmon, Seal to Seal; skin-clad or cloaked in purple or saffron or scarlet, with their weapons in their hands and their dogs padding in and out among them.   The women stood apart from the menfolk, many of the young ones with garlands of late summer flowers in their hair: honeysuckle, yellow loose-strife, and the wild white convolvulus.   And men and women alike turned constantly to look up into the south-western sky.

Marcus, standing with Esca and Liathan, the Chieftain's brother, on the outskirts of the throng, found himself also looking again and again to the south-west, where the sky was still golden, though the sun had slipped behind the hills.

And then, quite suddenly, there it was, the pale curved feather of the new moon, caught in the fringes of the sunset. Somewhere among the women's side a girl saw it at the same instant, and raised a strange, haunting, half-musical cry that was caught up by the other women, then by the men.   From somewhere over the hills, seaward, a horn sounded.   No braying war-horn, but a clearer, higher note that seemed per-fectly akin to the pale feather hanging remote in the evening sky.

As though the horn had been a summons, the crowd broke up, and the men moved off in the direction from which it had sounded; a long, ragged train of warriors moving quietly, steadily, leaving the dun to the women, to the very old, and the very young.   Marcus went with them, keeping close to Liathan, as he had been told, and suddenly very glad to know that Esca was walking at his shoulder in this strange multitude.

They climbed steadily to the mountain saddle, and came dropping down on the seaward side.   They traversed a steep glen and swung out along a ridge.   Down again, and another steep climb, and suddenly they were on the lip of a wide upland valley running at an angle to the sea.   It lay at their feet, already brimmed with shadows under a sky still webbed and washed with light that seemed to burst upward from the hidden sun; but at its head a great turf mound rose steeply, catching still a faint glow from the sunset on its thorn-crowned

crest and the tips of the great standing stones that ringed it
round like a bodyguard.   Marcus had seen the long barrows
of the Ancient People often enough before, but none had caught
and held his awareness as this one did, at the head of its lonely
valley, between the gold of the sunset and the silver of the new
moon.

' Yonder is the Place of Life ! ' said Liathan's voice in his ear.
' The Life of the Tribe.'

The many-coloured throng had turned northward, winding
along the valley towards the Place of Life.   The great mound
rose higher on their sight, and presently Marcus found himself
standing among the Seal People, in the shadow of one of the
great standing stones.   Before him stretched the emptiness of
a wide, roughly paved forecourt, and beyond the emptiness,
in the steep mass of the bush-grown mound, a doorway.   A doorway whose massive uprights and lintel were of age-eaten granite.
A doorway from one world into another, Marcus thought with a
chill of awe, closed seemingly by nothing but a skin apron en-
riched with bosses of dim bronze.   Was the lost Eagle of the
Hispana somewhere beyond that barbaric entrance?   Somewhere in the dark heart of this barrow that was the Place of Life?

There was a sudden hiss and flare of flame, as somebody
kindled a torch from the fire-pot they had brought with them.

The fire seemed to spread almost of its own
accord from torch to torch, and several
young warriors stepped out from the silent
waiting crowd, into the vast emptiness within the standing stones.   They carried the
flaming brands high above their heads, and
the whole scene, which had begun to blur
with the fading light, was flooded with a
flickering red-gold glare that fell most fiercely
on the threshold of that strange doorway,
showing the uprights carved with the same
curves and spirals that swirled up the standing stones, flashing on the bronze bosses of
the sealskin apron so that they became discs

of shifting fire. Sparks whirled upward on the light, sea-scented wind, and by contrast with their brightness, the hills and the dark thorn-crowned crest of the mound seemed to sink back into the sudden twilight. A man's shape showed for an instant high among the thorn-trees, and again the horn sounded its high clear note; and before the echoes had died among the hills, the sealskin curtain was flung back, its bronze discs clashing like cymbals.

A figure stooped out under the low lintel into the torchlight. The figure of a man, stark naked save for the skin of a grey dog-seal, the head drawn over his own. The Seal Clan greeted his coming with a quick, rhythmic cry that rose and fell and rose again, setting the blood jumping back to the heart. For an instant the man—Seal-priest or man-seal—stood before them, receiving their acclamation, then with the clumsy scuffling motion of a seal on dry land, moved to one side of the doorway; and another figure sprang out of the darkness, hooded with the snarling head of a wolf. One after another they came, naked as the first had been, their bodies daubed with strange designs in woad and madder, their head-dresses of animal pelts or bird-feathers, the wings of a swan, the pelt of an otter with the tail swinging behind the wearer's back, the striped hide of a badger shining black and white in the torchlight. One after another, prancing, leaping, shuffling; men who were not merely playing the part of animals, but who in some strange way, impossible of understanding, actually *were* for the moment the animals whose skins they wore.

One after another they came, until for every clan of the tribe, a totem priest had joined the grotesque dance—if dance it could be called, for it was like no dance that Marcus had ever seen before, and none that he wanted ever to see again. They had swung into a chain, into a circle, hopping, scuffling, bounding, the animal skins swinging behind them. There was no music—indeed music of any sort, however weird, however discordant, seemed worlds away from this dancing; but there seemed to be a pulse beating somewhere—perhaps a hollow log being struck with an open palm—and the dancers took their time from it. Quicker and quicker it beat, like a racing heart, like the heart of a man in fever; and the wheel of dancers spun faster and faster, until, with a wild yell, it seemed to break of its own spinning, and burst back to reveal someone —something—that must have come unnoticed into its midst from the blackness of that doorway in the barrow.

Marcus's throat tightened for an instant as he looked at the figure standing alone in the full red glare of the torches, seeming to burn with its own fierce light. An unforgettable figure of nightmare beauty, naked and superb, crested with a spreading pride of antlers that caught the torch-light on each polished tip, as though every tine bore a point of flame.

A man with the antlers of a stag set into his head-dress so that they seemed to grow from his brow—that was all. And yet it was not all; even for Marcus, it was not all. The people greeted him with a deep shout that rose and rose until it was like a wolf-pack howling to the moon; and while he stood with upraised arms, dark power seemed to flow from him as light from a lamp. 'The Horned One! The Horned One!' They were down on their faces, as a swathe of barley going down before the sickle. Without knowing that he did so, Marcus stumbled to his knee; beside him Esca was crouching with his forearm covering his eyes.

When they rose again, the priest-god had drawn back to the threshold of the Place of Life, and was standing there, his arms fallen to his sides. He burst into a spate of speech, of which Marcus could understand just enough to gather that he was telling the tribe that their sons who had died as boys were now reborn as warriors. His voice rose into pealing triumph, passing little by little into a kind of wild chant in which the tribesmen joined. Torches were springing up all along the close-packed throng, and the standing stones were reddened to their crests and seemed to pulse and quiver with the crashing rhythm of the chant.

When the triumphal chanting was at its height, the priest-god turned and called, then moved from before the doorway; and again someone stooped out from the darkness of the entrance into the glare of torches. A red-haired boy in a chequered kilt, at sight of whom the tribesmen sent up a welcoming shout. Another followed, and another, and many more, each greeted with a shout that seemed to burst upward and break in a wave of sound against the standing stones, until fifty or more New Spears were ranged in the great forecourt. They had a little the look of sleep-walkers, and they blinked dazzled eyes in the sudden blaze of torches. The boy next to Marcus kept running his tongue over dry lips, and Marcus could see the quick panting of his breast, as though he had been running—or very much afraid. What had happened to them in the dark, he wondered, remembering his own hour, and the smell of bull's blood in the darkened cave of Mithra.

After the last boy, came one last priest, not a totem priest, as the others had been. His head-dress was made of the burnished feathers of a golden eagle, and a long roar burst from the crowd, as the curtain dropped clashing into place behind him. But to Marcus everything seemed for the moment to have grown very still. For the last comer was carrying something that had once been a Roman Eagle.

XV

VENTURE INTO THE DARK

A MAN stepped out from the ranks of the tribe, stripped and painted as for war, and carrying shield and spear; and at the same instant a boy started forward. The two—they were clearly father and son—came together in the centre of the open space, and the boy stood with shining pride to take shield and spear from his father's hand. Then he turned slowly on his heel, showing himself to the tribe for their acceptance; turned to the place where Cruachan was hidden by the darkness; turned last of all to the new moon, which had strengthened from a pale feather to a sickle of shining silver in a deep-green sky; and brought his spear crashing down across his shield in salute, before following his father, to stand for the first time among the warriors of his tribe.

Another boy stepped out, and another, and another; but Marcus was aware of them only as moving shadows, for his eyes were on the Eagle; the wreck of the Ninth's lost Eagle. The gilded wreaths and crowns that the Legion had won in the days of its honour were gone from the crimson-bound staff; the furious talons still clutched the crossed thunderbolts, but where the great silver wings should have arched back in savage pride, were only empty socket-holes in the flanks of gilded bronze. The Eagle had lost its honours, and lost its wings; and without them, to Demetrius of Alexandria it might have seemed as commonplace as a dunghill cock; but to Marcus it was the Eagle still, in whose shadow his father had died; the lost Eagle of his father's Legion.

He saw very little of the long-drawn ritual that followed, until at last the Eagle had been carried back into the dark, and he found himself part of a triumphal procession led by the New Spears, heading back for the dun: a comet-tail of tossing

166

torches, a shouting like a victorious army on the homeward march. As they came down the last slope they were met by the smell of roasting meat, for the cooking-pits had been opened. Great fires burned on the open turf below the dun, flowering fiercely red and gold against the remote, sheeny pallor of the loch below, and the women linked hands and came running to join their returning menfolk and draw them home.

Only a few men who were not of the tribe had cared to go with the warriors to the Place of Life. But now the ceremonies were over and it was time for feasting; and traders and soothsayers and harpers had thronged in from the encampment, a party of seal-hunters from another tribe, even the crews of two or three Hibernian ships; they crowded with the warriors of the Epidaii around the fire and feasted nobly on roast meat, while the women, who did not eat with their lords, moved among them with great jars of fiery yellow metheglin, to keep the drinking-horns brimming.

Marcus, sitting between Esca and Liathan at the Chieftain's fire, began to wonder if the whole night was going to be spent like this, in eating and drinking and shouting. If it was, he should go raving mad. He wanted quiet; he wanted to think; and the joyous uproar seemed to beat inside his head, driving all thought out of it. Also he wanted no more metheglin.

Then quite suddenly the feasting was over. The noise and the vast eating and deep drinking had been, maybe, only a shield raised against the too-potent magic that had gone before. Men and women began to draw back, leaving a wide space of empty turf amid the fires; dogs and children were gathered in. Again torches flared up, casting their fierce light on to the empty space. Again there came that sense of waiting. Marcus, finding himself beside the Chieftain's grandfather, turned to the old man, asking under his breath, 'What now?'

'Dancing now,' said the other without looking round. 'See. . . .'

Even as he spoke, the flaming brands were whirled aloft,

and a band of young warriors sprang into the torch-lit circle and began to stamp and whirl in the swift rhythm of a war-dance. And this time, strange and barbaric as it might be, Marcus found this was dancing as he understood the word. Dance followed dance, blending into each other so that it was hard to tell where one ended and another began. Sometimes it would seem that the whole men's side was dancing, and the ground would tremble under their stamping heels. Some-times it would be only a chosen few who leapt and whirled and crouched in mimic hunting or warfare, while the rest raised the terrifying music of the British before battle by droning across their shield-rims. Only the women never danced at all, for the Feast of New Spears had nothing to do with womenkind.

The moon had long since set, and only the fierce light of fire and torches lit the wild scene, the twisting bodies and brandished weapons, when at last two rows of warriors stepped out on to the trampled turf and stood facing each other. They were stripped to the waist like the rest of the men's side, and carried shield and feathered war spear; and Marcus saw that one rank was made up of the boys who had become men that day, and the other of their fathers who had armed them.

'It is the Dance of the New Spears,' Esca told him as the two lines swept together with upraised shields. 'So, we dance it, too, we the Brigantes, on the night our boys become men.'

On his other side Tradui leaned towards him, asking, 'Do not your people hold the Feast of New Spears?'

'We hold a feast,' Marcus said, 'but it is not like this. All this is strange to me, and I have seen many things tonight that make me wonder.'

'So?—and these things?' The old man, having got over his first annoyance with Marcus over the toad's fat, had gradually become more friendly as the days went by; and tonight, warmed still further by the feasting and the metheglin, he was eager to enlighten the stranger within his gates. 'I will explain them to you, these things at which you wonder; for you are young and doubtless wish to know, and I am old and by far the wisest man in my tribe.'

M

If he went warily, Marcus realized, here might be a chance to gather certain information that he needed. 'Truly,' he said, ' wisdom shines from Tradui the Chieftain's grandsire, and my ears are open.' And he settled himself, with a most flattering show of interest, to ask and listen. It was slow work, but little by little, drawing the old man on with all the skill he possessed, listening patiently to a great deal that was of no use to him whatever, he gathered the scraps of knowledge that he needed. He learned that the priest-kind had their living-place in the birchwoods below the Place of Life, and that no guard was kept over the holy place, no watch of attendant priests.

'What need?' said the old man when Marcus showed surprise at this. ' The Place of Life has guardians of its own, and who would dare to meddle with that which is of the Horned One?' He broke off, abruptly, as though catching himself in the act of speaking of forbidden things, and stretched out an old thick-veined hand with the fingers spread horn-wise.

But presently he began to talk again. Under the influence of the metheglin and the torch-light and the dancing, he, too, was remembering his own night: the long-ago night when he had been a New Spear, and danced for the first time the warrior dances of the tribe. Never taking his eyes from the whirling figures, he told of old fights, old cattle-raids, long-dead heroes who had been his sword-brothers when the world was young and the sun hotter than it was now. Pleased at finding an attentive listener who had not heard the story before, he told of a great hosting of the tribes, no more than ten or twelve autumns ago; and how he had gone south with the rest— though some fools had said that he was too old for the war-trail, even then—to stamp out a great army of the Red Crests. And how, having given them to the wolf and to the raven, they had brought back the Eagle-god that the Red Crests carried before them, and given it to the gods of his own people in the Place of Life. The Healer of sore eyes must have seen it tonight when it was carried out and shown to the men's side?

Marcus sat very still, his hands linked round his updrawn knees, and watched the sparks fly upward from the whirling torches.

'I saw it,' he said. 'I have seen such Eagle gods before, and I wondered to see it here. We are always curious, we Greeks; also we have small cause to love Rome. Tell me more of how you took this Eagle-god from the Red Crests; I should like to hear that story.'

It was the story that he had heard once already, from Guern the Hunter; but told from the opposite side; and where Guern's story had ended, this one went on.

Much as he might tell of a bygone hunting that had been good, the old warrior told how he and his sword-brethren had hunted down the last remnants of the Ninth Legion, closing round them as a wolf-pack closes round its prey. The old man told it without a shadow of pity, without a shadow of understanding for the agony of his quarry; but with a fierce admiration that lit his face and sounded in every word.

'I was an old man even then, and it was my last fight, but *what* a fight! Ayee! Worthy to be the last fight of Tradui the Warrior! Many a night when the fire sinks low, and even the battles of my youth grow thin and cold, I have kept warm thinking of that fight! We brought them to bay at last in the bog country a day north of the place they call the Three Hills; and they turned like a boar at bay. We were flushed with easy triumph, for until that day it had been very easy. They crumbled at a prick, but that day it was not so. Those others had been but the flakings of the flint, and these were the core; a small core, so small. . . . They faced outward all ways, with the winged god upreared in their midst; and when we broke their shield-wall, one would step over his fallen brother, and lo, the shield-wall would be whole as before. We pulled them down at last—aye, but they took a goodly escort of our warriors with them. We pulled them down until there were left but a knot—as many as there are fingers on my two hands—and the winged god still in their midst. I, Tradui, I slew with my last throw-spear the priest in the spotted hide who held the

staff; but another caught it from him as he fell, and held it so
that the winged god did not go down, and rallied the few who
were left, yet again.   He was a chieftain among the rest, he
had a taller crest, and his cloak was of the warrior scarlet.
I wish that it had been I who killed him, but one was before
me. . . .

'Well, we made an end.   There will be no more Red Crests
going to and fro in our hunting grounds.   We left them to the
raven and the wolf, and also to the bog.   Bog country is swift
to swallow the traces of fighting.   Yes, and we brought back the
winged god; we, the Epidaii, claiming it as our right because
it was the warriors of the Epidaii who were First Spear at the
killing.   But there was heavy rain later, and the rivers coming
down in spate; and at a ford the warrior who carried the god
was swept away, and though we found the god again (three
lives it cost us, in the finding), the wings, which were not one
with it but fitted into holes in its body, were gone from it, and
so were the shining wreaths that hung from its staff; so that
when we brought it to the Place of Life it was as you saw it
tonight.   Still, we gave it to the Horned One for tribute, and
surely the Horned One was well pleased, for have not our wars
gone well for us ever since, and the deer waxed fat in our
hunting runs?   And I will tell you another thing concerning
the Eagle-god; it is ours now, ours, the Epidaii's; but if ever
the day comes when we host against the Red Crests again,
when the Cran-tara goes out through Albu, calling the tribes
to war, the Eagle-god will be as a spear in the hand of all the
tribes of Albu, and not of the Epidaii alone.'

The bright old eyes turned at last, consideringly, to Marcus's
face.   'He was like you, that Chieftain of the Red Crests; yes.
And yet you say that you are a Greek.   Surely that is strange?'

Marcus said, 'There are many of Greek blood among the
Red Crests.'

'So.   That might be it.'   The old man began to fumble
under the shoulder-folds of the chequered cloak he wore.   'They
were truly warriors, and we left them their weapons, as befits
warriors. . . . But from that chieftain I took this for the virtue

in it, as one takes the tush from a boar who was fierce and valiant above others of his kind; and I have worn it ever since.' He had found what he wanted now, and slipped a leather thong from about his neck. 'It will not go on my hand,' he added, almost fretfully. 'It must be that the Red Crests had narrower hands than we have. Take it and look.'

A ring swung on the end of the thong, sparkling faintly with green fire in the torch-light. Marcus took it from him and bent his head to examine it. It was a heavy signet-ring; and on the flawed emerald which formed the bezel was engraved the dolphin badge of his own family. He held it for a long moment, held it very gently, as if it were a living thing, watching the torch-light play in the green heart of the stone. Then he gave it back into the old man's waiting hand with a casual word of thanks, and turned his attention again to the dancers. But the fierce whirl of the dance was blurred on his sight, for suddenly, across twelve years and more, he was looking up at a dark, laughing man who seemed to tower over him. There were pigeons wheeling behind the man's bent head, and when he put up his hand to rub his forehead, the sunlight that rimmed the pigeons' wings with fire caught the flawed emerald of the signet-ring he wore.

All at once, with over much finding-out for one day, Marcus was tired to the depths of his soul.

Next morning, sitting on an open hill-shoulder where they could not be overheard, Marcus laid his plans very carefully with Esca.

He had already told the Chieftain that he was for starting south again next day, and the Chieftain, and indeed the whole dun, were loath to let him go. Let him stay until spring; maybe there would be more sore eyes for him to salve.

But Marcus had remained firm, saying that he wished to be in the south again before the winter closed in, and now, with the great gathering for the Feast of New Spears breaking up and going its separate ways, was surely the time for him to be going too. The friendliness of the tribesmen gave him no sense of guilt in what he was going to do. They had welcomed and sheltered him and Esca, and in return Esca had hunted and herded with them, and he had doctored their sore eyes with all the skill that he possessed. In all that there was no debt on either side, no room for guilt. In the matter of the Eagle, they were the enemy, an enemy worthy of his steel. He liked and respected them; let them keep the Eagle if they could.

That last day passed very quietly. Having laid their plans and made what few preparations were needful, Marcus and Esca sat in the sun, doing—to all outward seeming—nothing in particular, save watch the delicate flight of the sandpipers above the still waters of the loch. Towards evening they bathed; not their usual plunge and splash about for pleasure, but a ritual cleansing in readiness for whatever the night might bring. Marcus made his sunset prayers to Mithras, Esca made them to Lugh of the Shining Spear; but both these were Sun Gods, Light Gods, and their followers knew the same weapons against the dark. So they cleaned themselves for the fight, and ate as little as might be at the evening meal, lest a full stomach should blunt their spirits within them.

When the time came for sleep, they lay down as usual with Tradui and the dogs and Liathan in the great living-hut; lay down in the places nearest to the door, which also was usual with them, for they had always had it in mind that a time might come when they would wish to leave quietly in the night. Long after the rest were asleep, Marcus lay watching the red embers of the fire, while every nerve in his body twanged taut as an overdrawn bowstring; and beside him he could hear Esca breathing quietly, evenly, as he always breathed in sleep. Yet it was Esca, with a hunter's instinct for the passing of the night, who knew when midnight was gone by—the time at which the priest-kind would be making the nightly offering—and the Place of Life would be deserted again; and told Marcus so with a touch.

They got up silently, and slipped out of the hut. The

hounds raised no outcry, for they were used to night-time comings and goings. Marcus dropped the deerskin apron silently into place behind him, and they made for the nearby gateway. They had no difficulty in getting out, for with the dun full of guests and so many of the tribe encamped outside, the thorn-trees that usually blocked the gate at night had not been set in place. They had counted on that.

Turning away from the camp-fires, the sleeping men, and the familiar things of this world, they struck off uphill, and the night engulfed them. It was a very still night, with a faint thunder haze dimming the stars, and once or twice as they walked a flicker of summer lightning danced along the sky-line. The moon had long since set, and in the darkness and the brooding quiet the mountains seemed to have drawn closer than by day; and as they dropped downward into the valley of the Place of Life, the blackness rose around them like water.

Esca had brought them into the valley from its head, behind the Place of Life, where the sun-dried turf would make no sound at their passing, and carry no track afterwards. But in one place the heather came down almost to the foot of the standing-stones, and he stooped and broke off a long switch of it, and thrust it into the strap about his waist. They reached the lower end of the temple, and stood for what seemed a long time to listen for any sound; but the silence was like wool in their ears; not a bird cried, even the sea was silent tonight. No sound in all the world save the quickened drubbing of their own hearts. They passed between the standing stones and stood in the paved forecourt.

The black mass of the barrow rose above them, its crest of thorn-trees upreared against the veiled stars. The massive granite uprights and lintel were a faint pallor against the surrounding turf; it swelled on their sight as they walked towards it. They were on the threshold.

Marcus said softly but very clearly, ' In the Name of Light,' and feeling for the edge of the sealskin curtain, lifted it back. The bronze discs on it grated and chimed very faintly as he did so. He ducked under the low lintel, Esca beside him, and the curtain swung back into place. The black darkness seemed to press against his eyes, against his whole body, and with the darkness, the atmosphere of the place. The atmosphere: it was not evil, exactly, but it was horribly personal. For thousands of years this place had been the centre of a dark worship, and it was as though they had given to it a living personality of its own. Marcus felt that at any moment he would hear it breathe, slowly and stealthily, like a waiting animal. . . . For an instant sheer panic rose in his throat, and as he fought it down, he was aware of a rustle and a faint glow, as Esca fetched out from under his cloak the fire-pot and glim they had brought with them. Next instant a tiny tongue of flame sprang up, sank to a spark, and rose again, as the wick in its lump of beeswax caught. Esca's bent face grew suddenly out of the dark as he tended the little flame. As it steadied, Marcus saw that they were in a passage, walled, floored, and roofed with great slabs of stone. How long it might be there was no guessing, for the little light could find no end to it. He held out his hand for the glim. Esca gave it to him, and holding it high he walked forward, leading the way. The passage was too narrow for two to walk abreast.

A hundred paces, the darkness giving back unwillingly before them, crowding hungrily in behind, and they stood on the threshold of what must once have been the tomb chamber, and saw, set close before them on the slightly raised flagstone at the entrance, a shallow and most beautifully wrought amber cup filled to the brim with something that gleamed darkly and stickily red in the light of the glim. Deer's blood, maybe, or the blood of a black cock. Beyond, all was shadow, but as Marcus moved forward with the light, past the midnight offering, the shadows drew back, and he saw that they were standing in a vast circular chamber, the stone walls of which ran up out of the candle-light and seemed to bend together high overhead into some kind of dome. Two recesses at either side of the chamber were empty, but there was a third in the far wall, opposite the entrance. In it, too far off for any spark

of light to catch its gilded feathers, something was propped a
little drunkenly, blotted dark against the stones; that must
surely be the Eagle of the Ninth Legion.

Otherwise the place was empty, and its emptiness seemed to
add a hundredfold to its menace. Marcus did not know what
he had expected to find here, but he had not expected to find
nothing—nothing at all, save that in the exact centre of the
floor lay a great ring of what appeared to be white jadite, a foot
or more across, and a superbly shaped axehead of the same
material, arranged so that one corner of the blade very slightly
overlapped the ring.

That was all.

Esca's hand was on his arm, and his voice whispering urgently
in his ear: ' It is strong magic. Do not touch it! '

Marcus shook his head. He was not going to touch it.

They made their way round the thing, and reached the
recess in the far wall. Yes, it was the Eagle all right.

' Take the glim,' Marcus whispered.

He lifted it from its place, realizing as he did so that the last
Roman hand to touch the stained and battered shaft had been
his father's. An odd, potent link across the years, and he held
to it as to a talisman, as he set about freeing the Eagle from its
staff.

' Hold the light this way—a little higher. Yes, keep it
so.'

Esca obeyed, steadying the shaft with his free hand that
Marcus might have both hands free to work with. It would
have been easier to have lain the thing on the ground and knelt
down to it, but both of them had a feeling that they must
remain on their feet, that to kneel down would put them at a
disadvantage with the Unknown. The light fell on the heads
of the four slim bronze pegs that passed through the Eagle's
talons, securing them through the crossed thunderbolts to the
shaft. They should have drawn out easily enough, but they
had become corroded into their holes, and after trying for a few
moments to shift them with his fingers, Marcus drew his dagger,
and began to lever them up with that. They came, but they

came slowly. It was going to take some time—some time here in this horrible place that was like a crouching animal waiting to spring at any moment. The first peg came out, and he slipped it into his belt and began on the second. Panic began to whimper up from his stomach again, and again he thrust it down. No good hurrying; once he started to hurry he would never get these pegs out. For a moment he turned over in his mind the idea of taking the whole standard outside and finding some hide-out among the heather, and doing the job in the clean open air. But the job would have to be done, for the whole standard was too big to hide in the place that they had in mind; time was limited, and he could not work quickly without light, and light, anywhere outside, might betray them, however carefully they shielded it. No, this was the one place where they might be safe from interruption (for unless something went wrong, the priest-kind would not return until the next midnight)—from the interruption of men, that was.

Marcus begun to feel that he could not breathe. ' Quietly,' he told himself. ' Breathe quietly; don't hurry.' The second pin came out, and he thrust it into his belt with the other; and as Esca turned the shaft over, began on the third. It came more easily, and he had just started on the fourth and last, when it seemed to him that he could not see as clearly as he had done a few moments ago. He looked up, and saw Esca's face shining with sweat in the upward light of the glim; but surely the glim was giving less light than it had done? Even as he looked, the tiny flame began to sink, and the dark came crowding on.

It might be only bad air, or a fault in the wick—or it might not. He said urgently, ' Think Light! Esca, *think Light!* " And even as he spoke, the flame sank to a blue spark. Beside him he heard Esca's breath, whistling through flaring nostrils; his own heart had begun to race, and he felt not only the many-fingered dark, but the walls and roof themselves closing in on him, suffocating him as though a soft cold hand was pressed over his nose and mouth. He had a sudden hideous conviction that there was no longer a straight passage and a leather curtain between them and the outer world, only the earth-piled mountain high over them, and no way out. No way out! The darkness reached out to finger him, softly. He braced himself upright against the cold stones, putting out his will to force the walls back, fighting the evil sense of suffocation. He was doing as he had told Esca to do, thinking Light with all the strength that was in him, so that in his inner eye, the place was full of it: strong, clear light flowing into every cranny. Suddenly he remembered the flood of sunset light in his sleeping-cell at Calleva, that evening when Esca and Cub and Cottia had come to him in his desperate need. He called it up now, like golden water, like a trumpet call, the Light of Mithras. He hurled it against the darkness, forcing it back—back—back.

How long he stood like that he never knew, until he saw the blue spark strengthen slowly, sink a little, and then lick up suddenly into a clear, small flame. It might have been only a fault in the wick. . . . He realized that he was breathing in great shuddering gasps, and the sweat was running down his face and breast. He looked at Esca, and Esca returned his look; neither of them spoke. Then he started again on the fourth pin. It was the most stubborn of the lot, but it yielded at last, and Eagle and thunderbolts came loose in his hands. He lifted them off with a long, shaken breath, and sheathed his dagger. Now that it was done, he wanted to fling the staff aside and make a blind dash for the open air, but he schooled himself to take the staff from Esca and return it to its place in the recess, to lay the thunderbolts and the four bronze pegs on the floor beside it, before he turned at last to go, carrying the Eagle in the crook of his arm.

Esca had taken the branch of heather from his belt, and, still carrying the glim, followed him, moving backward to brush out any recognizable tracks they might have left in the dust. His own tracks, Marcus knew, were all to easily recognizable, because, however hard he tried not to, he dragged his right leg a little.

It seemed a long way round to the other side of the tomb chamber, and every few instants Esca glanced hastily aside to the ring and the axehead, as though they were a snake about to strike. But they gained the mouth of the entrance passage at last, and began to make their way down it; Esca still switching out their trail. Marcus moved sideways along the wall, guarding his own back and his friend's. Esca's crouching figure blotted out most of the light from the glim he carried, save where it fell on the dusty flag-stones and the flicking heather-switch, and his shadow swallowed up their way, so that every step Marcus took was into the edge of the darkness. The passage seemed much longer than it had done when they followed it inward; so long that a new nightmare grew on Marcus that either there were two passages and they had chosen the wrong one, or the only one had ceased, since their coming in, to have any end.

But the end was still there. Suddenly Esca's giant shadow ran on to the sealskin curtain, and they had reached it.

'Get ready to douse the light,' Marcus said.

The other glanced round without a word. Marcus's hand was on the curtain when they were plunged in darkness. He drew it back slowly, with infinite care, ears and eyes straining for any hint of danger, and the two of them ducked out under the lintel. He let the curtain ease back into place behind them, and stood with his hand on Esca's shoulder, drawing in great gasps of the clean night air with its scent of bog myrtle and its salt tang of the sea, and gazing up at the veiled stars. It seemed to him that they had been many hours in the dark; but the stars had swung only a little way on their courses since he saw them last. The summer lightning was still flickering along the hills. He realized that Esca was shuddering from head to foot, like a horse that smells fire, and tightened his hand on his friend's shoulder.

'We are out,' he said. 'We are through. It is over. Steady, old wolf.'

Esca answered him with a shaken breath of laughter. 'It is that I want to be sick.'

'So do I,' Marcus said. 'But we have no time, just now. This is no place to wait in until we are discovered by the priest-kind. Come.'

Some while later, having recrossed the hills and fetched a wide half-circle round the dun and encampment, they emerged from the steeply falling woods on to the bleak shores of the loch, just where a spit of rough turf and boulders laced together with alder scrub ran out from the grey shingle beach. Just above the beach they halted, and Esca hurriedly stripped. 'Now give me the Eagle.' He took it, handling it reverently, though it had been no Eagle of his; and a moment later Marcus was alone. He stood with one hand on a low-hanging rowan branch, and watched the pale blur that was Esca's body slip down through the alder scrub, and come out on the spit of land below. There was the tiniest splash as of a fish leaping, then silence; only the water lapping on the lonely shore, and then the faint mutter of thunder a long way off, and a night bird cried eerily in the heavy silence. For what seemed a long time, he waited, eyes straining into the darkness, and then suddenly a pale blur moved again on the spit, and a few moments later Esca was beside him once again, wringing the water out of his hair.

'Well?' Marcus murmured.

'It fits into the place under the bank like a nut into a nutshell,' Esca told him. 'They might search till the loch runs dry, and never find it; but I shall know the place when I come again.'

The next danger was that their absence would have been noticed; but when they came to the dun again, and passed unseen through the gateway, all was quiet. They were none too soon. The sky was still black—blacker than at their setting out, for the cloud had thickened, blotting out the stars. But the smell of the day-spring was in the air, unmistakable as that other smell of thunder. They slipped in through the hut-place doorway. In the darkness only the embers of the fire glowed like red jewels, and nothing moved. Then a dog growled, half sleepily, green-eyed in the gloom, and there was a sudden stirring and an equally sleepy murmur of inquiry from Liathan, who lay nearest to the door.

'It is only I,' Marcus said. 'Vipsania was restless; it's the thunder in the air. Always it makes her restless.'

He lay down. Esca also lay down, curled close to the fire, that he might not have damp hair to explain in the morning. Silence settled again over the sleeping-hut.

XVI

THE RING-BROOCH

A FEW hours later Marcus and Esca took their leave of the Dun, and started out, riding through a world that was clear-washed and as deeply coloured as a purple grape, after the thunderstorm which had finally broken over them at dawn. Southwards they went at first, following the shores of the loch to its foot, then north-east by a herding path through the mountains that brought them down towards evening to the shores of another loch, a long sea-loch this time, loud with the crying of shore-birds. That night they slept in a village that was no more than a cluster of turf bothies clinging to the narrow shore between the mountains and the grey water, and next morning set out again for the head of the loch, where there was a village through which they had passed before.

All that day they rode easily, breathing the horses often. Marcus was eager to be out of this land of sea lochs, through which one had to zigzag like a snipe, in which one could so easily become trapped and entangled, but it was no good getting too far from the Place of Life before the next move in the game could be played. The loss of the Eagle would have been discovered at midnight, when the priest went to renew the offering, and suspicion, though it would be widespread over all outside the tribe who had gathered to the Feast of New Spears, would certainly fall most heavily on himself and Esca. So the tribe would be up and after them long before now. Knowing the way that they had taken, Marcus reckoned that their pursuers could be up with them not long after noon if they crossed the loch by coracle and commandeered ponies on the near shore, as they undoubtedly would do. But he had forgotten to allow for the difficulties of the few mountain passes, and it was much later than he had expected when at last his ear caught the soft drumming of unshod hooves a long way off; and looking back, he saw a ragged skein of six or seven horsemen coming at break-neck speed down a steep side-glen towards them. He drew a quick breath that was almost of relief, for it had been a nerve-racking business waiting for them. 'Here they come at last,' he said to Esca; and then as a distant yell echoed down the mountainside, 'hear how the hounds give tongue.'

Esca laughed quietly, his eyes bright with the excitement of danger. 'Sweff! Sweff!' he encouraged them softly. 'Do we ride on, or rein in and wait for them?'

'Rein in and wait,' Marcus decided. 'They will know that we have seen them.'

They wheeled the mares, and sat waiting while the skein of wild riders swept towards them, the ponies sure-footed as goats among the rocks of the steep glen. 'Mithra! What cavalry they would make!' Marcus said, watching them. Vipsania was uneasy; she fidgeted and side-stepped, blowing down her nose, her ears pricked forward, and he patted her neck reassuringly. The tribesmen had reached the low ground now, and swung into the long curve of the lochside; and a few moments later they were up with the two who waited for them, and reining back their ponies in full gallop, dropped to the ground.

Marcus looked them over as they crowded in on him, seven warriors of the tribe, Dergdian and his brother among them. He took in their ugly looks, and the war-spears they carried, and his face was puzzled and inquiring. 'Dergdian? Liathan? What is it that you want with me, in so much haste?'

'You know well enough what it is that we want with you,' Dergdian said. His face was set like a stone, and his hand tightened on the shaft of his spear.

'But I fear that I do not,' Marcus said in a tone of rising annoyance, pretending not to notice that two of the tribesmen, leaving their own mounts standing, had gone to Vipsania's and Minna's heads. 'You will have to tell me.'

'Yes, we will tell you,' an older hunter cut in. 'We come

to take back the winged god; also for blood to wash out the insult that you have put upon us and upon the gods of our tribe.'

The others broke into a threatening outcry, pressing in on the two, who had by now dismounted also. Marcus faced them with a pucker of bewilderment between his black brows. 'The winged god?' he repeated. 'The Eagle-god that we saw carried at the Feast of New Spears? Why, you——' Light seemed to dawn on him. 'You mean that you have lost it?'

'We mean that it is stolen, and we are come to take it back from those who robbed us,' Dergdian said very softly; and the softness was as though a cold finger gently stroked Marcus's spine.

He looked into the other's face with slowly widening eyes. 'And it must needs be I who stole it?' he said, and then flared out at them. 'Why in the name of the Thunderer should I want a wingless Roman Eagle?'

'You might have had your reasons,' said the Chieftain in the same soft voice.

'I cannot think of any.'

The tribesmen were growing impatient; there were shouts of 'Kill! kill!' And they crowded closer; fierce, rage-darkened faces were thrust into Marcus's and a spear was shaken before his eyes. 'Kill the thieves! There has been enough of talking!'

Startled by the angry turmoil, Vipsania was flinging this way and that, showing the whites of her eyes, and Minna squealed, going up in a rearing turn as she tried to break from the man who held her, and was forced down again by a blow between the ears.

Marcus raised his voice above the tumult. 'Is it the custom of the Seal People to hunt down and slay those who have been their guests? Well do the Romans call the men of the North barbarians.'

The shouting sank to a sullen, menacing mutter, and he went on more quietly.

'If you are so sure that we have stolen the Red Crests' god,
N

you have but to search our gear, and you will surely find it. Search, then.'

The muttering grew fiercer, and Liathan had already turned to Esca's mare, stretching out his hand to the fastening of the pack. Marcus moved distastefully aside, and stood watching. Esca's hand tightened for an instant on the shaft of his spear, as though he longed to use it; then he shrugged, and swung away to join Marcus. Together they watched their few possessions tumbled on the grass; a couple of cloaks, a cooking-pot, some strips of smoked deer-meat flung out with rough haste. The lid of the bronze medicine box was wrenched back, and one of the hunters began to rummage inside like a little dog after a rat. Marcus said quietly to the Chieftain, who stood beside him with folded arms, also looking on, 'Will you bid your hounds be less rough with the tools of my trade. It may be that there are still sore eyes in Albu, though your small son's eyes are well.'

Dergdian flushed at the reminder, and glanced aside at him for an instant, with a kind of sullen half-shame; then he spoke sharply to the man who was delving among the salves. 'Softly, you fool; there is no need that you should break the medicine sticks.'

The man growled, but handled the things more carefully thereafter. Meanwhile the others had unfolded and shaken out the sheepskin saddle-pads, and all but torn the bronze ring-brooch out of a violet-coloured cloak by their rough handling.

'Are you satisfied now?' Marcus asked, when everything had been turned inside out, and the tribesmen stood about, baffled and empty-handed, staring down at the chaos they had made. 'Or is it that you would search us to the skin?' He held out his arms, and their eyes ran over him, over Esca. It was perfectly obvious that they could have nothing a tenth the size and weight of the Eagle hidden on them.

The Chieftain shook his head. 'We must cast our net wider, it seems.'

The tribesmen were all known to Marcus, at least by sight; they looked bewildered, sullen, a little shamed, and they found

it hard to meet his eyes. At a gesture from the Chieftain they
began to gather up the scattered objects and bundle them, with
the torn cloak with its dangling ring-brooch, into the pack-
cloth. Liathan stooped to the disembowelled medicine box,
glancing up at Marcus, and then away again.

They had offended against their own laws of hospitality.
They had hunted down two who had been their guests, and not
found the winged god, after all. ' Come back with us,' said the
Chieftain. ' Come back with us, lest our hearths are shamed.'

Marcus shook his head. ' We are for the South, before the
year closes in. Go and cast your net wider for this wingless
winged god of yours. We shall remember that we have been
your guests, Esca and I.' He smiled. ' The rest we have
already forgotten. Good hunting to you on the game trails
this winter.'

When the tribesmen had whistled up their own ponies, who
had stood quietly by all this while with their reins over their
heads, and, remounting, set off back the way they had come,
Marcus did not move at once. He stood gazing after the
dwindling specks up the glen, with a queer regret, while his
hand mechanically soothed and fondled his upset and angry
mare.

' Do you wish the Eagle yet in the place we took it from? '
Esca asked.

Marcus was still watching those dwindling specks, almost out
of sight now. ' No,' he said. ' If it were yet in the place we
took it from, it would be still a danger to the Frontier—a
danger to other Legions. Also it was my father's Eagle and
none of theirs. Let them keep it if they can. Only it is in my
heart that I wish we need not have made Dergdian and his
sword-brethren ashamed.'

They saw to their gear, tightened the ponies' belly-straps, and
rode on.

Presently the loch began to narrow, and the mountains to
crowd in on it, rising almost sheer from the water's edge; and
at last they caught sight of the village; the distant huddle of
turf bothies at the head of the loch, cattle grazing up the steep

glen behind, and the straight blue smoke of cooking-fires rising pale against the sombre browns and purples of the mountains that towered above them.

'It is time that I sickened of the fever,' said Esca, and without more ado he began to sway from side to side, his eyes half closed. 'My head!' he croaked. 'My head is on fire.'

Marcus reached out and took the reins from him. 'Slump a little more and roll a little less; it is fever, not metheglin, that lit the fire, remember,' he directed, beginning to lead the other horse with his own.

The usual crowd of men and women, children and boys gathered to meet them as they entered the village, and here and there, people called out a greeting to them, glad in their remote way to see them back again. With Esca slumped over Minna's neck beside him, Marcus singled out the ancient headman, greeted him with due courtesy, and explained that his servant was sick and must rest a few days; two days, three at the most. It was an old sickness that returned from time to time, and would last no longer, given proper treatment.

The headman replied that they were welcome to share his fireside, as they had done when they passed that way before. But to that, Marcus shook his head. 'Give us some place to ourselves; it matters not how rough, so long as it will keep out the weather. But let it be as far from your living-huts as may be. This sickness of my servant is caused by devils in his belly, and to drive them out it is needful that I use strong magic.' He paused, and looked round at the questioning faces. 'It will do no harm to this village, but it cannot be looked upon safely by any who have not the signs for protection. That is why we must have lodging apart from the living-huts.'

They looked at each other. 'It is always dangerous to look upon forbidden things,' said a woman, accepting the story without surprise. There could be no question of refusing them shelter; Marcus knew the laws of the tribes. They talked the matter over quickly among themselves, and finally decided that Conn's cow-byre, which was not now in use, would be the best place.

Conn's cow-byre proved to be the usual turf bothy, exactly like the living-huts, save that it was not set so far below ground-level, and there was no hearth in the centre of the trampled earthen floor. It was well away from the main rath, with its doorway at an angle that would make it possible to slip out and in without showing up too clearly to any watchers among the living-huts. So far, so good.

The villagers, feeling perhaps that a man who could conjure out devils was best treated kindly, did their best for the two returned strangers; and by dusk the mares had been taken in charge, fresh fern stacked inside the hut for bedding, an old skin rug skewered up over the doorway; and the women had brought broiled boar's flesh for Marcus, and warm ewe's milk for Esca, who lay on the piled bracken, moaning and babbling most realistically.

Later, with the deerskin rug drawn close across the door, and the villagers crowded about their own hearths with faces and thoughts carefully turned from the outlying bothy and the magic that would be a-making there, Marcus and Esca looked at each other by the faint light of a floating reed-wick in a shell of rancid seal oil. Esca had eaten the lion's share of the meat, for he would need it most; and now, with a few strips of smoked deer meat thrust into the middle of a rolled-up cloak, he stood ready to go.

At the last moment, Marcus said savagely, ' Oh, curse this leg of mine! It should be me going back, not you.'

The other shook his head. ' That leg of yours makes no difference. If it were as sound as mine, still it would be better, quicker, and safer that I should go. You could not leave this place and return to it in the dark, without rousing the dogs; but I can. You could not find your way through the passes that we have traversed only once before. It is work for a hunter—a hunter born and bred, not a soldier who has learned a little forest-craft.' And he reached up to the little stinking lamp hanging from the roof tree, and pinched it out.

Marcus drew back a fold of the rug and peered out into the soft darkness of the mountains. Away to the right, a solitary

glint of gold shone from the chink in a deerskin apron over a
distant doorway. The moon was behind the mountains, and
the waters of the loch were only a lesser darkness, without spark
or lustre.

' All is clear,' he said.   ' You are sure you can find the way? '

' Yes.'

' Good hunting, then, Esca.'

A dark shadow slipped past him, and was gone into the
night.   And he was alone.

He stood for a while in the bothy doorway, ears stretched for
any sound to break the silence of the mountains, but heard only
the wet whisper of falling water where the swift stream
came tumbling into the loch, and a long while later, the belling
of a stag.   When he was sure that Esca had got clear away, he
dropped the rug.   He did not re-light the lamp, but sat for a
long time on the piled bracken in the pitchy darkness, with his
arms across his knees, thinking.   His one comfort was the sure
knowledge that if Esca ran into trouble, he himself would very
soon share it.

For three nights and two days Marcus kept guard over an
empty hut.   Twice a day one of the women, with face averted,
would bring broiled meat and fresh ewe milk, sometimes
herrings, once a golden lump of wild honeycomb, and set them
on a flat stone a little way off, and Marcus would collect them
and later take back the empty bowls.   After the first day there
were only women and children in the village; evidently the
men had gone to answer some call from the dun.   He wondered
whether he ought to provide noises for the benefit of the village,
but decided that silence would probably be more effective; so
save for a little muttering and moaning when he thought someone was near enough to hear, just enough to keep it in their mind
that there were two people in the bothy, he remained silent.
He slept when he could, but he did not dare to sleep much, for
fear that trouble should blow up suddenly when he was not on
the alert for it.   Most of his time, day or night, was spent
sitting just within the doorway watching, through a back-drawn
chink in the rug, the grey waters of the loch and the sheer,

boulder-strewn upward thrust of the mountains towering so high above him that he had to tip his head far back to see their jagged crests where the mist-rags trailed among the peaks and the high corries.

Autumn had come to the mountains almost overnight, he thought. A few days ago, summer had still lingered, though the heather was past its flowering and the flaming rowan berries long since gone. But now it was the Fall of the Leaf; one could smell it in the wind, and the trees of the glen grew bare and the brawling stream ran gold with yellow birch leaves.

Some while after moonset on the third night, without any warning, a hand brushed across the skin rug at the entrance, and as Marcus tensed in the close darkness, he heard the faintest ghost of a whistle: the broken, two-note whistle that he had always used to summon Cub. A sudden wave of relief broke over him, and he echoed the whistle. The rug was drawn aside and a black shape slipped through.

' Is it well? ' Esca whispered.

' It is well,' Marcus returned, striking flint and steel to kindle the lamp. ' And with you? How went the hunting? '

' The hunting was good,' Esca said, as the tiny flame sprang up and steadied, and he stooped and set down something closely bundled in the cloak.

Marcus looked at it. ' Was there any trouble? '

' None, save that I pulled the bank down a little in landing with the Eagle. It must have been rotten, I suppose—but there is nothing in a bank slip to set anyone thinking.' He sat down wearily. ' Is there anything to eat? '

Marcus had made a habit of saving each meal that he was given, and eating it only when the next one came, so that he always had a meal in hand, packed into the old cooking-pot. He produced it now, and sat with his hand resting on the bundle that meant so much to him, while he watched the other eat, and listened to the story of the last three days, told in low snatches between mouthfuls.

Esca had cut back across the mountains without much difficulty, but by the time he reached the Loch of Many Islets

it had been near to dawn, and he had had to lie up in the dense
hazel-woods through the day.   Twice during the day parties
of warriors had passed close to his hiding-place, carrying
coracles, and evidently bound, like himself, for the dun by the
short way across the loch.   Also they had been carrying war-
spears, he said.   As soon as it was dark, he had set out once
again to swim the loch.   It was little more than a mile across
at the place he chose, and that, too, had not been difficult.
He had worked his way down the far shore until he came to the
spit of land that marked the place where they had hidden the
Eagle;   found it, and landed again, pulling down the bank
a little in doing so, and bundled it in the wet cloak that he had
carried bound to his shoulder.   Then he had returned the way
he came as fast as might be, for the dun was thrumming like a
disturbed bees' nest.   Of a certainty the tribe was hosting.   It
had all been very easy—almost too easy.

Esca's voice was growing blurred towards the close of the
story.   He was blind weary, and the instant he had finished
eating, he stretched out on the piled bracken and sleep took him
like a tired hound after a day's hunting.

But before the sun was above the mountains next day they
were on their way once more, for though they were now clear
of suspicion, it was no time for lingering.   The village had
shown no signs of surprise at Esca's sudden recovery;   presumably when the devils were no longer in his belly the man
was whole again.   They had given the travellers more of the
eternal smoked meat, and a boy—a wild, dark-faced lad too
young for the hosting and sulking in consequence—to guide
them on the next stage of their journey, and bidden them good
hunting and let them go.

That day they had gruelling travelling;   no level loch-side
to follow, but a steep thrust northward into the heart of the
mountains, and then east—so far as they could hold to any
course—by narrow passes between sheer heather-washed crags
of black rock, skirting wide mountain shoulders, traversing
bare ridges, across what seemed to be the roof of the world;
until at last the lie of the country turned them south again into

the long downward sweep that ended afar off in the marshes of the Cluta. Here the boy parted from them, refusing to share their camp for the night, and set off back the way he had come, tireless as a mountain buck among his native glens.

They watched him go, easily, not hurrying, at the long, springing mountaineer's stride. He would walk like that through the night and arrive home before dawn, not much tired. Marcus and Esca were both hillmen, but they could never have equalled that, not among these crags and passes. They turned their back on the last glimpse of Cruachan, and set off southward, making for more sheltered country, for once again there was storm in the air, not thunder this time, but wind—wind and rain. Well, that would not matter much; mist was the one thing that would matter, and at least an autumn gale would keep the autumn mists away. Only once before had weather meant as much to Marcus as it did now: on the morning of the attack at Isca Dumnoniorum when mizzle rain had kept the signal smoke from rising.

In the last flush of the evening they came upon the ruins of a broch, one of those strange, chambered towers built by a forgotten people, perched like a falcon's eyrie on the very edge of the world. They made camp there, in company with the skeleton of a wolf picked bare by ravens.

Thinking it best not to light a fire, they simply knee-hobbled the mares, gathered fern for bedding, and after filling the cooking-pot at the mountain stream, which came leaping down through its own narrow gorge nearby, sat down with their backs to the crumbling stones of the entrance, to eat leathery shavings of dried meat.

Marcus stretched out thankfully. It had been a gruelling march; most of the day they had had to trudge and scramble, leading Vipsania and Minna, and his lame leg was aching horribly, despite the ready help that he had had from Esca. It was good to rest.

From their feet the land swept away southward over ridge after ridge into the blue distance, where, a thousand feet below and maybe two days' march away, the old frontier cut Valentia from the wilderness. Far below them, among dark ranks of pine-trees, the northern arm of a great loch reflected back the flame of the sunset; and Marcus greeted it as a familiar friend, for he and Esca had followed its shores on their way north, almost two moons ago. A straight journey now, no more sniping to and fro among sea-lochs and mist-wrapped mountains, he thought; and yet there was a queer superstitious feeling in him that it had all been too easy—a queer foreboding of trouble to come. And the sunset seemed to echo his mood. A most wonderful sunset; the whole western sky on fire, and high overhead, torn off, hurrying wind clouds caught the light and became great wings of gold that changed, even while Marcus watched them, to fiery scarlet. Stronger and stronger grew the light, until the west was a furnace banked with purple cloud, and the whole world seemed to glow, and the upreared shoulder of the mountain far across the loch burned crimson as spilled wine. The whole sunset was one great threat of coming tempest; wind and rain, and maybe something more. Suddenly it seemed to Marcus that the crimson of that distant mountain shoulder was not wine, but blood.

He shook his shoulders impatiently, calling himself a fool. He was tired, so was Esca and the horses for that matter, and there was a storm on the way. That was all. A good thing that they had found shelter for the night; with any luck it would have blown itself out by morning. It struck him that he had not so much as looked at the Eagle. It had seemed better not to, in the village they had left that morning; but now . . . It lay beside him, and on a swift impulse he picked up the bundle and began to unroll it. The dark folds of the cloak as he turned them back caught a more brilliant colour from the sunset, warming from violet to Imperial purple. The last fold fell away, and he was holding the Eagle in his hands; cold, heavy, battered, burning red-gold in the sunset. 'Euge!' he said softly, using the word he would have used to praise a victory in the arena, and looked up at Esca. 'It was a good hunting, brother.'

But Esca's suddenly widened eyes were fixed on one corner of the cloak, outflung towards him, and he did not answer; and Marcus, following the direction of his gaze, saw the cloth at that corner torn and ragged.

'The ring-brooch!' Esca said. 'The ring-brooch!'

Still holding the Eagle in the curve of his arm, Marcus was hastily flinging the folds this way and that, but he knew that it was useless. The brooch had been in that corner. With sudden sharp-edged vividness, now that it was too late, he remembered that scene by the loch-side, the threatening faces of the tribesmen gathered round, the gear tumbled on the coarse grass, the cloak with its dangling brooch all but torn out of the cloth by their furious handling. Fool that he was, it had gone completely out of his mind; out of Esca's, too, it seemed.

'It may have fallen at any time—even while you were in the water,' he said.

'No,' Esca said slowly. 'It rang on the pebbles when I dropped the cloak before I dived for the Eagle.' He rubbed the back of one hand across his forehead, thinking back. 'When I picked up the cloak, it caught for an instant on an alder root; you know how the alders grow right down to the water's edge. I remember now, but at the time I scarcely noticed.'

He dropped his hand and they sat quite still, staring at each other. The ring-brooch was a cheap bronze one, but its design was rather unusual, and the tribesmen must often have seen Demetrius of Alexandria wearing it. Also, to judge by the state of that jagged corner, there was probably a wisp of violet cloth caught in it, to help their memories.

Marcus was first to break the silence. 'If they find it, they will know that one of us has been back since they searched our gear, and there could be but one reason for that.' As he spoke, he began methodically to wrap up the Eagle once more.

'When they speak with the warriors from the village we left this morning, they will know that it was I who went back,' Esca said hurriedly, and checked. 'No, that will not serve, for they will know that I went with your knowledge. . . .

Listen, Marcus. You must push on alone. If you take Vipsania and go now, you may stand a chance. I will put myself in their way. I will tell them that we quarrelled for possession of the Eagle; we fought for it down yonder, and you went into the loch, and the Eagle with you.'

'And Vipsania?' Marcus said, his hands still busy with the folds of the cloak. 'And what will they do to you when you have told them this story?'

Esca said very simply, 'They will kill me.'

'I am sorry, but I do not think much of that plan,' Marcus said.

'There is the Eagle to be taken into account,' Esca urged.

Marcus made a quick, impatient gesture. 'The Eagle will serve no useful purpose when we get it home. I know that well enough. So long as it does not fall again into the tribesmen's hands to be a weapon against Rome, it will lie as worthily in a Caledonian bog as on a Roman scrap-heap. If the worst comes to the worst, we will find means to dispose of the Eagle before they take us.'

'It seems strange that you have not cast a thing of so little worth into the loch before this. Why trouble to carry it south at all?'

Marcus was already drawing his legs under him; but he checked an instant, his gaze holding Esca's. 'For an idea,' he said. He got up stiffly. 'We are in this together, and we will win clear together, or not at all. It may be days before that accursed brooch is found, none the less the sooner we get down to Valentia the better.'

Esca got up also, saying nothing. There was no more to be said, and he knew it.

Marcus glanced up at the wild clouds; hurrying clouds like wind-driven birds. 'How long have we before the storm breaks?'

The other seemed to be smelling the weather. 'Long enough to get down to the loch-side, anyway; there will be some shelter from the wind down there among the pine-woods. We might make a few more miles tonight.'

XVII

THE WILD HUNT

Two mornings later, Marcus lay full length in a hollow of the lowland hills and looked down through the parted bracken fronds. Grey and tawny marshes lay below him, rising to the blue heights of Valentia to the south, and through the flatness of them wound the silver Cluta, spreading westward into its firth: with Are-Cluta, once a frontier town, still a meeting-place and market for all the neighbouring tribes, squatting within turf ramparts on its northern bank. There were coracles on the river, looking, from this distance, like tiny water-beetles; one or two larger vessels with blue sails furled, riding at anchor below the dun, from which the smoke of many cooking-fires rose towards a high grey sky; a sky that was gentle with exhaustion after the autumn gale, Marcus thought while he lay looking back over the past two days as it might be over a wild dream.

The storm had broken over them towards midnight, the wild westerly gale swooping at them down the shoulder of the mountains like a wild thing that wanted to destroy them;

197

whipping the waters of the loch into racing white-caps, bringing with it the bitter, hissing rain to drench them through and through.   They had passed the greater part of the night crouching with the two frightened mares under a steep over-hang of rock, wrapped about with a shrieking turmoil of wind and rain and darkness.   Towards dawn the storm had abated a little, and they had pushed on again until long past noon, when they had found a sheltered hollow under the bole of an uprooted pine, knee-hobbled the mares, and crawled under the upreared mass of torn roots, and slept.   When they awoke it was well into the night, and the rain was falling softly before a dying wind that sobbed and roared through the pines but no longer beat against them like a live thing.   They had eaten what was left of the smoked meat, and pushed on again through the dying storm, until, in the spent calm of the day-spring, with the wet oak-woods waking to the song of chaffinch and robin and wren, they had halted at last, here in the low hills above the Cluta.

As soon as it grew light, Esca had gone on down to Are-Cluta, to sell the mares.   The parting was hard for all of them, for they had grown fond of each other, Marcus and Vipsania, Esca and Minna, in the months that they had been together; and the mares had known perfectly well that it was good-bye. A pity they could not have kept the mares, but with the old cavalry brand on their shoulders they were much too easily recognizable, and there was nothing for it but to trade them for others.   But at least they would be sure of a good master, for the tribesmen loved their horses and hounds, using them hard but only as they used themselves hard, treating them as members of the family.

All would be well with Vipsania and Minna, Marcus told himself firmly.   He stretched.   It was good to lie here on the soft turf of the woodshore, to feel his tunic drying on him, and rest his aching leg, knowing that however fast the hunt came on their trail, they were past the last point where they could be cut off by men pouring down any side glen that linked loch with loch in the misty maze that was behind them.   But how was it going with Esca, down there in the dun? Always it was Esca who had the extra task to do, the extra risk to run. It was bound to be so, for Esca, who was British, could pass unnoticed where Marcus, with his olive skin, his darkness that was of quite a different kind from that of the tribesmen, would be suspect at once. He knew that, but it infuriated him, none the less; all his relief began to ebb away, and as the morning dragged on he grew restless and yet more restless. He began to feel sickeningly anxious. What was happening down there? Why was Esca so long? Had word of the Eagle reached Are-Cluta ahead of them?

It was near to noon when Esca suddenly appeared in the glen below him, riding a shaggy mouse-coloured pony and leading another. Relief flooded over Marcus, and as the other glanced up towards his hiding-place he parted the bracken fronds more widely and flung up a hand. Esca returned the signal, and a few moments later, having joined Marcus in the little hollow, he dropped from the back of the shaggy creature he rode, with an air of duty well and truly done.

' Do you call these mossy-faced objects ponies? ' Marcus inquired with interest, rolling over and sitting up.

Esca was busy with the bundle he had taken from one of them. For an instant his slow, grave smile lifted the corners of his mouth. ' The man who sold them to me swore they were sired out of the stables of the High King of Eriu.'

' Did you by any chance believe him? '

' Oh no,' said Esca. He had looped the reins of both ponies over a low branch and sat down beside Marcus with the bundle. ' I told the man I sold ours to, that they were sired out of the stables of Queen Cartimandua. He did not believe me, either.'

' They were game little brutes, whoever sired them. You found them a good master? '

' Yes, and the same master for both; a little fox of a man, but he had the right hands. I told him my brother and I were taking ship for Eriu. It was a good enough reason for selling the mares, and if anyone should ever ask him, it may serve to start a false trail. We haggled for a long time, because the mares were near foundering. I had to tell him a long story about wolves, to account for that, and so of course he swore their wind was broken, which was obviously a lie. But I sold them to him at last, for a fine sealskin rug and two enamelled war-spears, and a bronze cooking-pot and a sucking pig. Oh, and three fine amber bracelets.'

Marcus flung up his head with a croak of laughter. 'What did you do with the sucking pig?'

'It was a little black pig, very shrill,' said Esca reflectively. 'I sold it to a woman, for this.' He had been busy with the bundle while he spoke, and now shook out a hooded cloak of shaggy cloth that seemed to have once been chequered blue and red, but was now grease-stained and weather-faded to a uni-versal mud-colour. 'Even a small thing will help to change the look of a whole company—at least from a distance. . . . Also for dried meat. Here it is. Then I went back to the horse market and bought these two, with their head-gear on them, for the war-spears and all the other things. The other man had the best of the bargain; ill luck go with him! But there was no help for that.'

'We are in no case to drive a hard bargain,' Marcus agreed with his mouth full. They were both eating by that time. 'I should have liked to have seen you with that piglet,' he added thoughtfully.

Neither of them wasted more time on words. They ate quickly, and not over much, since there was no knowing how long the food would have to last them; and by noon they loaded their few belongings into the yellow pack-cloth, flung the sheepskin saddle-pads across the backs of their shaggy little mounts, tightened the belly-straps, and were on their way once more.

Marcus wore the cloak for which Esca had traded the black piglet, the hood pulled well over his forehead, for he had laid aside the hand-shaped talisman which was too distinctive to serve him any longer; and under the greasy, evil-smelling folds, he carried the lost Eagle. He had contrived a kind of sling for it, with strips torn from the cloak in which it was closely bundled, so as to have both hands free, but as he rode he cradled it in the crook of his bridle arm.

.   .   .   .   .

They fetched a wide half-circle round Are-Cluta, and reached the river again where it swung south-eastward into the heart of Valentia. Their return journey was very different from the outward one. Then, they had wandered openly from village to village, with a meal and a place by somebody's fire at the day's end. Now they were fugitives, lying up in some remote glen through the day, making southward through the night, and somewhere behind them, the hunt was up. For three days they had no sign that it was so, but they knew it in their hearts, and they pushed on grimly, listening always for sounds behind them. They made good speed, for the ponies, though not beautiful, were game little brutes, bred in the mountains, tough as whipcord and sure-footed as goats, and they were able to ride much of the time. Presently, they knew, they might have to let the ponies go, and take to the heather on foot. Meanwhile they pushed on in desperate haste, that they might be as far south as possible before that time came.

The fourth evening found them on their way again, after a day spent lying-up in a thicket of thorn-trees. A murky evening, closing in under a low grey sky. In the low country at their backs it was dusk already, but up here on the high moors the daylight still lingered, reflected back by many little silver tarns among the brown heather.

'Three more days,' Marcus said suddenly. 'Three more days by my reckoning, and we should reach the Wall!'

Esca looked round to answer, and then suddenly his head went up with a jerk, as though he heard something. An instant later, Marcus heard it too, very faint and far behind: a hound giving tongue.

They had reached the crest of a long ridge of moorland, and looking back, they saw a cluster of dark specks cresting a lesser ridge behind them; a long way behind, but not too far to be recognized for what they were: men on horseback and

o

many hounds.   And in that instant another hound took up the cry.

'I spoke too soon,' Marcus said, and his voice jumped oddly in his own ears.

'They have sighted us.'   Esca laughed sharply in his throat. 'The hunt is up with a vengeance.   Ride, brother quarry!' And even as he spoke, his little mount leapt forward, snorting, from the jab of his heel.

Marcus urged his own pony into a tearing gallop at the same instant.   The ponies were fairly fresh, but both fugitives knew that in the open it was only a matter of time before they were ridden down by the better-mounted tribesmen—pulled down by the yelling hounds as by a pack of wolves.   And with one accord they swung a little in their course, heading for the higher ground ahead; broken country by the look of it, in which they might be able to shake off their pursuers.

'If we can keep the lead till dark,' Esca shouted above the drumming hooves and the wind of their going, 'we've a chance among the glens yonder.'

Marcus did not answer, but settled down to ride as he had never ridden before.   The dark heather streaked backward under his pony's thudding hooves, the long harsh hairs of its mane sprayed back over his wrists, and the wind sung past his ears.   For one flashing instant there rose in him the exultancy of speed, the surge and splendour that he had once thought never to know again.   The instant passed, swift as the darting flight of a kingfisher.   He was riding for his life with the dark hunt in full cry behind him, putting out all his skill to keep clear of hidden pitfalls, the hummocks and snags and snarls among the heather that might bring disaster, grimly aware that he could not grip strongly with his right knee, and if the pony stumbled at this flying gallop, he would go clean over its head. On and on they hurtled, now skirting a reed-fringed upland pool, now swerving from a patch of bog luminously green in the fading light; uphill and down, through bronze tides of dying heather, startling here a flock of plover, there a stray curlew from the bents, and always, behind them, the hunt drawing nearer. Marcus could hear the hounds giving tongue above the soft thunder of the ponies' hooves, nearer, steadily nearer; but there was no time for looking back.

On and on. Now the ponies were tiring. Marcus could feel the panting of his little mount's flanks, and foam flew back from its muzzle, spattering against him. He leaned far forward over its neck to ease it; he talked to it, sang and shouted, fondled its sweating neck and dug in his heels, urging it on by every means in his power, though indeed the poor brute was already winged by terror to its utmost speed, knowing as well as its rider the meaning of those sounds behind.

The land was rising under them, and the light fading moment by moment; the little glens and the hazel woods were very near; but so was the hunt. Snatching one glance over his shoulder, Marcus glimpsed a flying blur of horsemen and low-running hounds, smudged out of all clear shape by the twilight, streaking across the open turf, the leading hound scarce a bowshot away.

Near to their last gasp, and with the clamour of the hunt swelling in their ears, they struggled desperately over the crest of another ridge, and saw below them through the dusk the pale streak of running water. Very faintly, an unexpected scent drifted up to them, a sweet, heavy scent like musk, and Esca let out a sound that was half-way between a laugh and a sob. ' Down to the stream before they top the ridge, and we've a chance yet.'

Only half understanding, but content to trust to the other's better knowledge of the wild, Marcus drove his heel again and again into his pony's sobbing flank, urging it to one last effort. Shivering and sweating, the foam that flew from its muzzle blood-flecked now, it plunged forward in one last frantic burst of speed. Neck and neck they hurtled down through the tall bracken, the scent of musk growing every instant stronger; down and down toward the trampled hollow beside the stream, from which two battling, antlered shapes broke at their approach and went crashing away down the glen. Esca was already half off his pony, and in the musk-reeking hollow where only the instant before two great stags had been fighting for lordship of the herd, Marcus half fell, half flung himself from his own mount. His friend's arm was round him almost before he touched the ground. 'Into the water, quick!' Esca gasped, as, snorting with terror, the two ponies plunged on riderless into the dusk.

They dived through the alder scrub and scrambled headlong down the bank, Esca still with his arm round Marcus to help him, and slipped into the ice-cold, swift-running water, just as the first wave of the hunt topped the rise behind them. Crouching under the steep overhang, they heard the ponies crashing away downstream in terrified stampede, heard the hunt sweep down towards them, the check, the baying and the trampling and the sudden splurge of voices; and crouched lower yet, the water flowing almost to their nostrils.

It seemed an eternity that they crouched so, listening to the turmoil just above their heads, and praying that the dusk would hide the traces of their swift descent through the alder scrub, and that the hounds, having been set on to follow horses, would not concern themselves to pick up and follow the scent of men. But in reality it could have been only a few moments before a triumphant yell told them that the movement of the stampeding ponies had been picked up. The hounds were already away yelling on the hot scent of stags or ponies, or both. There was a fresh burst of shouts and trampling, the shrill, angry squeal of a horse, and with the confused speed of a dissolving nightmare, men, hounds, and horses were off in full cry after the flying shadows.

A little farther down, the glen curved, bringing them for an instant into full view of the two who crouched under the bank and stared after them with straining eyes, a shadow chase, sweeping down the dusk-sodden glen, the wild clamour of their passing growing fainter with every beat of flying hooves; swiftly come, and passed, and gone, as though they had been the Wild Hunt, the hunters of souls.

The dusk swallowed them; the last, long-drawn cry of a hound drifted back on the night wind, and that was all. No sound now, but a curlew crying somewhere, and the racing of their own hearts.

Esca rose quickly to his feet. 'They will go like the wind for a while,' he said. 'Lightened of our weight, and terrified as they are; but they will be run down before long, and then the hunt will be back looking for us, so the sooner we are away from here, the better.'

Marcus was making sure he still had the Eagle safe in its sling. 'I feel sick about those ponies,' he said.

'There will be no harm come to them, unless their wind is broken. Those were hunting-dogs, trained to run down and bring to bay, and not to kill until the word is given. With us, I think the word would have been given, but the wanton waste of a horse is not in these hunters unless their tribe be different from all the other tribes of Britain.' Esca had been feeling about under the bank as he spoke, and now brought up his spear with a satisfied grunt. 'Better keep to the stream for a while, and break the trail,' he said, and put out a steadying hand to Marcus.

For what seemed an interminable time they struggled up-stream, now wading knee deep through the shifting shallows, now plunged to the waist in the deep, swift flow where the stream narrowed. It was a fight every yard of the way, against the thrust of the water and the shifting footholds, against time, with every nerve on the stretch for the long-drawn cry of a hound that might rise at any moment above the soft rush of the stream.

It was quite dark now, for the moon was hidden by low cloud; and the hills closed round them, rising blackly on every hand. The stream began to lead them too far eastward, and anyway, they dared not stick to it too long; and at last, where a narrow side glen opened to the south, they scrambled out, chilled to the bone, and thankful to be done with icy water. They shook themselves like dogs, wrung as much water as they could from their clothes, and set off again.

Presently, coming over a steep rise, they dropped down into another glen, wooded with hazel and rowan, through which another burn fell in steep slides and cascades of white water. Indeed, one never seemed out of the sound of running water in these hills.   And stumbling at last on a jagged hollow left by a landslip that the rain had torn away, they more or less fell into it, and sat there, huddled close together for warmth, to get their breath and take stock of the situation.

The little food that they had left had gone with the ponies, and from now on they would have to march empty, since they certainly could not stop to trap for food as they went.   They were still at least two full marches from the nearest station on the Wall, and must cover the distance on foot, through un-familiar country with the wild hunt on their trail.   All in all, their prospects did not look very bright.

Marcus sat rubbing his leg, which was aching intolerably, and staring at the white water through the dark blur of the hazels. The sense of being hunted was heavy on him, and he knew that it was on Esca, too.   The very countryside seemed to have grown hostile and menacing, as though not only men were on their trail, but the whole land up and hunting, the dark hills themselves closing in to the kill.   And yet the Wild had stood their friend once tonight, he told himself, setting a pair of battling stags in their way, just in the moment of their direst need.

They sat silent a short while longer, snatching a breathing space before pushing on again; but they dared not rest long, for they must be much farther from the place where they had taken to the water, and in a much surer hiding, before dawn. Marcus sighed, and was actually drawing his legs under him to rise, when he became aware of Esca grown suddenly tense beside him, and then, above the soft wet rush of the stream, of someone, or something, moving far down the glen.   Marcus crouched where he was, frozen, his head turned to listen, and gradually the sounds drew nearer: a queer confusion of sounds that might be one man or several, a great brushing and rustling through the hazel scrub.   It came slowly up the glen towards them, while they crouched motionless in their hiding-place, nearer and louder until it seemed almost on top of them; and

Marcus, peering up through the overhanging screen of rowan and hazel, made out a pale blur and a dark one. Of all homely and unexpected things, a man leading a cow.

Furthermore, the man was whistling softly between his teeth as he came up the burnside; so softly that it was not until he was within a few feet, that the tune broke through.   A catchy tune.

> 'Oh when I joined the Eagles,
>   (As it might be yesterday)
>   I kissed a girl at Clusium
>   Before I marched away.'

Marcus reached up and parted the drooping rowan branches. 'Well met, Guern the Hunter,' he said in his own tongue.

XVIII

THE WATERS OF LETHE

THERE was a sudden pause; the white cow, startled by the unexpected voice, fidgeting and blowing, with lowered horns; the man, who had checked with a grunt, peering down through the rowan branches. Then the soft growling of the old dog, which Marcus had not at first noticed, rose suddenly to a sing-song snarl, and was checked by a backward thrust of the hunter's heel.

'Well met, Demetrius of Alexandria.'

There was no time to waste in surprise and explanation. Marcus said quickly, 'Guern, we need your help.'

'Aye, I know that well enough. You have brought away the Eagle, and the Epidaii are up after you,' Guern said. 'The word went by at sunset, and the Dumnonii and my own tribe at least will join spears with them.' He came a step nearer. 'What would you have me do?'

'We want food—and a false trail, if you can provide one.'

'Food is easily managed, but it is more than a false trail that you will need to get you in one piece to the Wall. Every pass to the south will be guarded by now, and there is but one way known to me that is likely to be left open.'

'Tell us how to find it.'

'Telling is not enough. It is a way that is death without a guide. That is why the tribesmen will not trouble to guard it.'

'And you know this way?' Esca spoke for the first time.

'Yes, I know the way. I—will take you by it.'

'How if you are caught with us?' Marcus said. 'How if you are missed from your own place, and any think to wonder where you are?'

'I shall not be missed from my own place, for there will be many out hunting these next few days. If any come upon us together I can always knife one of you, and claim the honour of being First Spear among the hunters.'

'It is a pleasant thought,' said Marcus. 'Do we come with you now?'

'Yes. It is best that you come the first part of the way now,' Guern decided. 'We shall have to take the cow; ill luck to her. She is for ever straying.'

Marcus laughed, and got up, catching his breath as his over-taxed leg twinged under him. 'At least her straying has stood us in good stead tonight. Give me your shoulder, Esca, this place is—somewhat—steep.'

Many steep glens and moorland ridges lay between them and the place of the fighting stags, and it was near dawn when Guern at last led them down into an old sandstone quarry that had not been worked since the Eagles flew from Valentia. He thrust them into the crumbling cave or gallery of some sort that seemed to have been the occasional lair of wild pig, and bidding them be quiet until he came again, departed with the cow, who seemed very weary. 'It may be that this will teach you not to wander again, oh daughter of Ahriman!' they heard him say as he hauled her by the horns up the rough slope.

Left to themselves, Marcus and Esca drew the hanging curtain of bramble and dog-rose across the mouth of their hole, and lay down as comfortably as they could. 'If the roof doesn't cave in and the pigs do not come back to challenge our presence, we look like having a quiet day,' Marcus said, pillowing his head on his arms.

Neither of these things happened, and the day dragged slowly by, while Marcus and Esca slept fitfully, trying to forget the emptiness of their stomachs. Beyond the bushes at the entrance the light grew golden and then faded. It was after dusk when Guern the Hunter returned, bringing with him, beside the inevitable strips of leathery smoked meat, a lump of fresh broiled venison. 'Eat the fresh meat now,' he said, 'and quickly.'

They did as he bade them, while he stood leaning on a spear in the cave mouth, with the great dog lying at his feet, and

before it was full dark outside they were on their way again.
They made slow marching at first, for Marcus's leg was stiff
after the day's rest, but the way was easier than it had been last
night, running mostly downhill, and little by little the stiffness
wore off, and he was able to make better going. Silent as
shadows, they followed Guern, by ways that only the hunter
and the deer knew, with never a spoken word between them.
But Marcus was puzzled as the hours went by, for so far there
had been no real difference between this and any other march
that they had made among the hills; no sign of this unguarded
way which it was death to travel without a guide.

And then, as they came down a gentle slope, the air seemed
to change, and with it, the feel of the ground under their feet;
and suddenly he understood. Bog! Bog with presumably
some hidden path across it for those who knew the secret.
They came to the edge of it almost as abruptly as to the edge of
a pool, and the queer rooty smell of it was all around them.
Guern was casting about like a hound cutting across a scent.
Suddenly he halted, and his dog with him.

' Here. It is here,' he said, speaking under his breath for
the first time since their setting out. ' From now on we must
go behind one another. Follow me exactly, and do not halt
for so long as a heart-beat; even on the secret way the ground is
soft. Do as I bid you and you will cross safely; disobey me,
and you will sink.' It was as simple as that.

' Understood,' Marcus murmured back. It was no time or
place for needless talk: Mithra alone knew how near the
scouting tribesmen might be.

With the dog pressed against him, Guern turned outward to
the bog. Marcus moved into place behind him, and Esca
brought up the rear. The ground felt spongy under their feet,
sucking at them gently at every step that seemed taken only
just in time to keep from sinking; and they had gone only a
short way when Marcus noticed that a faint mist had begun
to rise. At first he took it for no more than the breath of the
bog, but soon he realized that it was more than that. Higher
and higher it rose, wreathing upward in faint gauzy swathes

that closed together overhead. Looking up, he could still see the moon shining, but faintly, through mist-wreathes in a glimmering sky. Mist; the weather of all others that they had cause to dread! And that it should come now! There could be no turning back; yet how was it possible for any man to find such a way as they were following, in this murk? And if they lost it? But that was not good to think about.

The mist was thickening steadily. Soon they were walking almost blind, their world made up of a few feet of sodden turf and tufted bog-cotton, and the occasional glint of water, dissolving into a nothingness of glimmering mist; and there was no sign of any path. But Guern seemed never at a loss, walking lightly and steadily forward, changing his course from time to time, and the other two followed. The dank, rooty smell grew always stronger, colder; the moon was sinking low and the mist losing itself in darkness, and still Guern the Hunter walked on. On and on. It was very silent, only a bittern boomed somewhere to their right, and there came small, evil, sucking noises from the bog.

Marcus had long since got over his first unpleasant doubts of Guern's ability to find the secret way in the mist, but now he was beginning to wonder how much longer he could keep on at this light, unvarying stride; and then suddenly it seemed to him that the ground was growing firmer underfoot. A few more steps, and he was sure of it. They were drawing up out of the quag. The mist smelled different, chill as ever, but lighter and sweeter. Soon the secret way was behind them, like an evil dream.

By that time dawn was near, and the mist was growing out of the darkness again, no longer glimmering, but dully grey as the ash of a long-dead fire. In the growing light, clear of the last pocket of bog, they halted thankfully in the lea of a clump of ancient thorn-trees and turned to face each other, while the dog lay down at their feet.

'I have brought you as far as I can,' Guern said. 'Every man to his own hunting grounds, and from now on the land is strange to me.'

'You have brought us clear through the guard of our ene-mies, and we can fend for ourselves now,' Marcus said quickly.

Guern shook his ragged head doubtfully. 'They may be drawing these hills also, for all I know. Therefore travel by night and lie up by day; and if you do not go astray in the mist, nor fall into the hands of the tribesmen, you should reach the wall some time in the second night from now.' He hesitated, tried to speak, and hesitated again. At last he said with a kind of half-angry humility: 'Before our trails divide, it is in my heart that I would see the Eagle once again. It was my Eagle once.'

For answer, Marcus slipped the closely wrapped bundle from its sling, and turning back the folds, laid bare the lost Eagle. It was dark and lustreless in the grey dawn murk; a mere bird-shaped lump of battered metal. 'It has lost its wings,' he said.

Guern reached out eagerly as though to take it, then checked, and dropped his hands back to his sides. The betraying gesture tore harshly at something deep in Marcus's chest, and suddenly he could have howled like a dog. For a long moment he held the Eagle, while the other stood with rigidly bent head, looking down at it, unspeaking. Then as Guern stepped back, he folded the dark cloth once more over it, and returned it to its place under his cloak.

Guern said, 'So. I have seen the Eagle once more. Maybe after today I shall not look on a Roman face nor hear my own tongue spoken again. . . . It is time that you were on your way.'

'Come with us,' Marcus said on a sudden impulse.

Guern's ragged head went up, and he stared at Marcus under his brows. For an instant he actually seemed to be considering the idea. Then he shook his head. 'My welcome might be an over-warm one. I have no yearning after death by stoning.'

'Tonight's work would alter that. We owe our lives to you, and if we get the Eagle back to its own place, that will be your doing.'

Guern shook his head again. 'I am of the Selgovae. I have

a woman of the tribe to wife, and she is a good wife to me. I have sons, born into the tribe, and my life is here. If ever I was—something else, and my life was elsewhere, all that lies in another world and the men I knew in it have forgotten me. There is no way back through the Waters of Lethe.'

' Then—good hunting to you on your own trails,' Marcus said after a silence. ' Wish us well, between here and the Wall.'

' I will wish you well; and it is in my heart that I will wish myself with you. If you win through, I shall hear of it, and be glad.'

' You will have played no small part in it, if we do,' Marcus said, ' and neither of us will forget. The Light of the Sun be with you, Centurion.'

They looked back when they had gone a few paces, and saw him standing as they had left him, already dimmed with mist, and outlined against the drifting mist beyond. A half-naked, wild-haired tribesman, with a savage dog against his knee; but the wide, well-drilled movement of his arm as he raised it in greeting and farewell was all Rome. It was the parade-ground and the clipped voice of trumpets, the iron discipline and the pride. In that instant Marcus seemed to see, not the barbarian hunter, but the young centurion, proud in his first command, before ever the shadow of the doomed legion fell on him. It was to that centurion that he saluted in reply.

Then the drifting mist came between them.

As they turned away, Marcus found himself hoping that Guern would get back safely to the new life that he had made for himself, that he would not have to pay for the faith that he had kept with them. Well, the mist would give him cover on his homeward way.

Almost as though he had heard his friend's unspoken thoughts and was answering them, Esca said: ' He will hear if we come with our lives out of this, but we shall never hear whether he does.'

' I wish that he had chosen to come with us,' Marcus said. But even as he spoke, he knew that Guern the Hunter was right. There was no way back through the Waters of Lethe.

Two dawns later, Marcus and Esca were still a long way from the Wall. The mist that had met them on the secret way had haunted them ever since; a patchy and treacherous mist that was sometimes no more than a faint blurring of the more distant hills, and at others swooped down on them, blotting out all landmarks in a swirling greyness in which the very ground seemed dissolving away. They would have become lost over and over again but for the hunter's sense of direction that made Esca able to smell the south as a townsman might smell garlic. And even with that to help them, they could only struggle on with maddening slowness, covering what distance they could when the mist thinned, and lying up wherever they happened to be when it grew too thick to push on any farther. Once or twice they came very near to disaster; many times they had to cast back for a way round some pitfall that the mist had hidden from them, and Marcus, who was leaving the route to Esca as usual, was having anxieties of his own. His lame leg, which had carried him well enough through the forced marches and weary scrambles of their way south, was beginning to let him down, and let him down badly. He held on doggedly, but he was growing clumsy, and when he stumbled the jar of it made him set his teeth.

That dawn brought them their first warning that the enemy were indeed, as Guern had said, drawing these hills also, when the fitful mist rolled back to show them the figure of a mounted man, evidently on watch, high on a hill-shoulder not more than a bowshot away. Luckily he was not looking their way, and they fell flat among the heather, and spent a bad few moments watching him ride slowly along the ridge, until the mist closed down again.

They spent part of that day lying up in the lee of a great boulder, but started out again while there were still several hours of daylight left. While the mist hung about them, they had had to abandon their plan of travelling only by night, and push on when and how they could.

'How far have we still to go, by your reckoning?' Marcus asked, as he stood trying to rub the stiffness out of his leg.

Esca tightened his rawhide belt, which had become too loose for him, collected his spear and brushed up, as well as he could, the flattened grass where they had been lying.

'It is hard to judge,' he said. 'It has been slow travelling in this murk, but I think that I have not brought us greatly out of our way. By the fall of the land, I should say twelve or fourteen of your Roman miles. There; if any hunter comes close to this place, he will see that we have lain there, but from a few paces distant, it will not show.'

They set out once more on the long march south.

Towards evening a faint wind began to stir; and before it, the mist, which had been thick all day, grew ragged as a beggar's cloak.

'If the wind rises, we may lose this witches' brew at last,' said Marcus, as they halted at the curve of a narrow glen to make sure of their direction.

Esca lifted his head and sniffed, like an animal grown suddenly wary. 'Meanwhile it is in my heart that we should do well to find ourselves a fox-hole until dusk.'

But they had left the finding of their fox-hole too late. The words were scarcely out of his mouth when the mist seemed to curl back on itself. It spread sideways like blown smoke; the brown heather and golden bracken across the burn warmed suddenly through the drifting swathes, and next instant a cry, high and carrying and oddly triumphant, pierced upward from the far side of the glen, and a saffron-kilted figure started from cover and ran, crouching low, for the hill-crest. Esca's spear followed him, but it was too far for a throw. In six racing heart-beats he had reached the sky-line and dropped out of sight, crying his summons as he ran.

'Downhill,' Esca said harshly. 'Into the woods.'

They swung in their tracks, towards the nearest tongue of the birch woods that were spreading like a stain through the ragged mist, but even as they did so, the signal cry rose from among the golden trees in answer. There was no escape that way; and as they turned again, from far up the glen behind them the same cry went up, thin as a bird's call. Only one way lay open for them, and they took it; straight uphill to their right, and what lay over the hill-crest only the Lord of the Legions knew.

They gained the crest somehow, Marcus was never sure how, and as they hesitated an instant on the bare ridge, the cry—it was changing its quality now, becoming a hunting cry—rose again behind them, and was answered and flung up out of the mist below, closing in. They must have blundered into a large band of the hunters. Southward along the ridge, a dark mass of furze seemed to offer a certain amount of cover, and they dived into it like hunted animals going to ground, and began to work their way forward into its heart.

After that all was a blurred confusion of mist and jagged furze branches, and a chaos of dark islands swirled through by tawny tides of bracken and bilberry; of lying rigid among the dagger-sharp furze-roots with a suffocating reek of fox in their throats and the horror of the hunted in their racing hearts, while death with many heron-tufted war-spears stalked them through the dark maze. There were men all round them, on horseback, on foot, thrusting heedless of torn skin through the spiney branches, leaping high on stiff legs like hunting dogs who seek their quarry in long grass, giving tongue like hunting dogs too, now on this side, now on that. Once a probing spear struck like a snake within a span of Marcus's shoulder. And then quite suddenly they realized that against all seeming possibility, the hunt had missed them. It had swept over them and was no longer all around them, but behind!

They began to work forward on their stomachs again, with slow, agonizing caution. They could not tell where they were going, save that it was away from the enemy behind them. A dark and evidently much-used tunnel in the furze opened to them, and they slid into it, Esca leading. The reek of fox grew stronger than ever. The tunnel curved, leading them slightly downhill, and there was nothing to do but follow it, no breaking out through the dense furze that walled and roofed it in. It ended suddenly on the edge of the cover, and before them a spur of rocky, bush-grown turf ran out at an angle from the main ridge. Swathes of mist, drawn up out of the deep glen, were still drifting across it before the rising wind, but at the farthest point, upward of a bowshot away, something that might be a broch loomed through the greyness. It did not look promising, but they could not stay where they were, for it seemed to them that the sounds of the hunt were drawing nearer again, and there could be no turning back.

So they struck out into the open, getting what cover they could from the rocks and scrub, in search of some way down. But it seemed that there was no way down. The north-western slope would have been easy enough, but as they crouched among the bushes at the edge of it, the jink of a pony's bridle-bit came up to them, and the movement of men waiting. That way was securely stopped up. The south-eastern scarp dropped practically sheer into drifting mist-wreaths, out of which rose the indefinable sense and smell of deep water. There might be a way out for the Eagle, there, but there was certainly none for Marcus. Driven on by the sound of the hunt questing through the furze behind them like hounds after a lost scent, they struggled on a few steps, then checked, panting and desperate, looking this way and that, with eyes that strained to find some way of escape. But Marcus was almost done, and Esca had his arm round him. They could go no farther even if the way were clear; they were trapped, and they knew it. The building that they had glimpsed through the mist was quite clear now; not a broch at all, but an old Roman signal-tower. They gathered themselves together and made for it.

It was a very obvious hiding-place, so obvious that it offered a bare chance of safety, or at all events respite, because the hunters might well have searched it already. At the worst it would give them a chance to put up some sort of fight; and there was always the dark coming.

The narrow archway, doorless now, gaped blackly in the wall, and they stumbled through into a small courtyard where grass had long since covered the cobbles. Another empty doorway faced them, and Marcus made for it. They were in

P

the guard-room now. Dead leaves rustled to and fro on the floor, and the milky light filtering from a high window embrasure showed them the foot of a stairway in the wall. 'Up here,' he gasped.

The steps were of stone and still in good condition, though slippery with damp, and they stumbled upward, the sound of their feet seeming very loud in the silence of the stone shell where a little Roman garrison had lived and worked, keeping watch over the border hills, in the short years when the province of Valentia was more than a name.

They ducked out through a low door under the signal platform, on to the flat roof of the tower, into daylight as translucent as a moonstone after the dark below. As they did so, Marcus was almost blinded by a thrashing of great black wings past his face, and a startled raven burst upward uttering its harsh, grating alarm cry, and flew off northward with slow, indignant wing-beats, caaking as it went.

'Curse! That will announce our whereabouts clearly to all who may be interested,' Marcus thought, but was suddenly too tired to care very much. Utterly spent, he lurched across to the far side of the roof, and looked down through a crumbling embrasure. Below him the ground dropped sheer from the tower foot, and through the last filmy rags of the mist he caught the darkness of deep water, far below, a still and sombre tarn brooding on its own secrets, between the spur and the main ridge. Yes, there would be a way out for the Eagle.

On the landward side, Esca was crouching beside a broken place in the parapet, where several large stones had fallen, leaving a gap. 'They are still beating the furze,' he muttered as Marcus joined him. 'It is well for us that there are no dogs with this band. If they do not come before dusk, we may escape them yet.'

'They will come before dusk,' Marcus murmured back. 'The raven has made sure of that. Listen. . . .' A sound came up to them from below the northern side of the spur, a confused, formless splurge of excitement, faint with mist and distance, that told them all too clearly that the waiting man had understood the raven's message. Marcus lowered himself stiffly on to his sound knee beside the other, slipped into an easier position, and stretched out sideways, leaning on one arm, his head hanging low. After a few moments he looked up. 'I suppose I should feel guilty about you, Esca. For me, there has been the Eagle; but what had you to win in all this?'

Esca smiled at him, a slow grave smile. There was a jagged tear in his forehead where a furze root had caught him, Marcus noticed, but under it his eyes looked very quiet. 'I have been once again a free man amongst free men. I have shared the hunting with my brother, and it has been a good hunting.'

Marcus smiled back. 'It has been a good hunting,' he agreed. The soft beat of unshod hooves on turf came drumming up from the mist below; the unseen hunters of the furze cover were casting back towards the open spur, beating as they came, making sure that their quarry did not again slip through them. They would be here soon, but the riders from below would be first. 'A good hunting; and now I think that is ended.' He wondered if any word of that ending would one day drift south across the Wall, would reach the Legate Claudius, and through him, Uncle Aquila; would reach Cottia in the garden under the sheltering ramparts of Calleva. He should like them to know. . . . it had been a good hunting, that he and Esca had had together. Suddenly he knew that, despite all outward seeming, it had been worth while.

There was a great quietness in him. The last of the mist was blowing clear away as the wind freshened; something that was almost sunshine brushed fleetingly across the old signal-tower, and he noticed for the first time that a clump of harebell had taken root in a cranny of the fallen parapet close to him, and, late in flowering because of the place in which it grew, still carried one fragile bell aloft on an arching thread-slender stem. It swayed as the wind blew over, and regained its place with a tiny, defiant toss. It seemed to Marcus that it was the bluest thing he had ever seen.

Up over the edge of the spur, three wild horsemen appeared heading for the gateway.

XIX

TRADUI'S GIFT

As they dropped from their ponies in the courtyard below, Marcus and Esca drew back from the parapet. 'Only three, so far,' Marcus whispered. 'Don't use your knife unless you have to. They may be of more use to us living than dead.'

Esca nodded, and returned his hunting-knife to his belt. Life and the urgency of doing had taken hold of them again. Flattened against the wall on either side of the stairhead they waited, listening to their pursuers questing through storehouse and guard-room. 'Fools!' Marcus breathed, as a shout told them that the stairway had been spotted; and then came a rush of feet that checked at the floor below and then came on, storming upward.

Marcus was a good boxer, and much practice with the cestus last winter had made Esca something of a boxer also; together, weary though they were, they made a dangerous team. The first two tribesmen to come ducking out through the low doorway went down without a sound, like poled oxen: the third, not so completely caught unawares, put up more of a fight. Esca flung himself upon him, and they crashed down several steps together, in a flailing mass of arms and legs. There was a short, desperate struggle before Esca came uppermost, and staggering clear, heaved an unconscious man over the doorsill.

'Young fools,' he said, stooping for a fallen spear. 'A hound puppy would have known better than that.'

Two of the tribesmen—they were all very young—lay completely stunned where they had fallen; but one was already stirring; and Marcus bent over him. 'It is Liathan,' he said. 'I'll see to him. Do you tie up and gag the other two.'

The young warrior groaned, and opened his eyes to find

Marcus kneeling over him with his own dagger to his throat, while close by, Esca was hastily trussing and gagging the two unconscious men with strips torn from the cloak of one of them. 'That was a mistake,' Marcus said. 'You should have kept with the rest of the hunt, not come thrusting in here on your own.'

Liathan lay looking up at him. His black eyes were hard with hate; blood trickled from the corner of his mouth. 'Maybe we saw the raven and we sought to be First Spear, lest a lowland tribe claim the Eagle-god for its own,' he said between shut teeth.

'I see. It was a brave thing to do, but extremely stupid.'

'Maybe; but though we fail, there will be others here soon.' There was a gleam of savage triumph in the black eyes.

'So,' Marcus nodded. 'When they come, these others, you will tell them that we are not here; that we must after all have slipped by in the mist; and you will send them back the way they came, over the main ridge yonder, towards the sunrise.'

Liathan smiled. 'Why will I do these things?' He glanced for a contemptuous instant at the dagger in Marcus's hand. 'Because of that?'

'No,' said Marcus. 'Because when the first of your friends sets foot on the stair, I shall send the Eagle—here it is—into the tarn which lies below this place. We are still a long way from the Wall, and you will have other chances—you or others of the hunt—before we reach it; but if we die here, you will lose whatever chance you have of retaking the Red Crests' god.'

For a long moment Liathan lay staring up into Marcus's face; and in that silent moment there grew a light smother of hoof-beats and a distant burst of shouting. Esca rose quickly and crossed, half crouching, to the broken parapet. 'The hunt is up,' he said softly. 'They have done with the furze cover. Aiee! Like a wolf-pack, they close in.'

Marcus withdrew the dagger, but his eyes never left the young tribesman's face. 'Choose,' he said, very quietly. He got up and moved backward to the far parapet, unwrapping the Eagle as he did so. Liathan had risen also, and stood swaying a little

on his feet, looking from Marcus to Esca and back again.
Marcus saw him swallow, saw him lick the cut on his lip. He
heard the sounds of the in-closing hunt, very near now, the
men giving tongue like excited hounds; and from the emptiness
at his back, only the plaintive cry of a marsh bird in the wind-
haunted silence. He let the last violet fold fall from the Eagle,
and held it up. The evening light, spreading as the mist
thinned, struck on the savage, gilded head.

Liathan made a queer gesture of defeat. He turned and
strode rather shakily to the broken parapet, and leaned over.
The first of the hunt was almost at the gateway, and a shout
from under the walls greeted his appearance. Liathan called
down to them: 'They are not here, after all. They must have
slipped through the other way in this accursed mist.' He
pointed wildly, and his voice broke like the crying of a storm
bird. 'Try the woods yonder; they will likely have bolted
that way.'

A confusion of fierce voices answered him and a pony
whinnied shrilly; he drew back from the parapet as though
coming hot-foot to follow his words, and as the hunt flung back
on itself, turned once more to Marcus.

'It was well done, was it not?'

Marcus nodded without speaking. Through one of the em-
brasures he was watching the hunt streaming back along the spur
and into the furze cover of the main ridge, men on ponies and
men on foot, calling to each other, gathering others as they
went; dissolving into the last shreds of the mist. He brought
his gaze back to the young tribesman. 'Truly it was well
done,' he said, 'but keep your head down, lest any straggler
should look back and think it strange to see you still here.'

Liathan lowered his head obediently—and sprang. Sprang
like a wild cat. But Marcus, warned by some flicker of his eyes
an instant before, flung himself sideways, half falling, with the
Eagle under him, and as he did so, Esca was upon the high-
lander and brought him crashing down.

'You fool,' Marcus said a moment later, staggering to his
feet and looking down at Liathan, who lay squirming under

Esca's knees. 'You young fool; there are two of us and only one of you.'

He crossed to the two bound men, and after satisfying himself that all was well with them, tore off some more strips from the cloak that lay beside one of them, and returned to Esca. Between them they bound the hands and feet of the young warrior, who had ceased to struggle and lay rigid with his face turned from them.

'We can leave the gag for the moment,' Marcus said when it was done. He picked up the Eagle and began to fold it close once more. 'Esca, do you go and make sure the ponies are safe. We shall need them.'

When Esca was gone, he got up stiffly and turned to the southern parapet. The upland tarn lay clear and dark now beneath the steep fall of the spur. The hills were blown almost clear of the mist, though it still scarfed the glen with white; and the evening was coming swiftly, swiftly. And somewhere southward beyond those hills, not far now, surely, was the Wall.

'Why did you come among us, calling yourself a healer of sore eyes, to steal from us the winged god?'

Marcus swung round in answer to the furious voice behind him. 'In the first place, am I so lacking as a healer of sore eyes? At least your brother's son will not be blind.' He leaned one shoulder wearily against the parapet, and stood gazing down reflectively at his captive. 'In the second, I came to take back—not to steal, for it was never yours—*take back* the winged god, because it was the Eagle of my father's Legion.' Instinctively he knew that with Liathan, as with Cottia, that was the part that would make sense; knew also that it was better for the peace of the frontier that the thing be kept a private feud between himself and the tribes.

There was a queer little flicker in Liathan's dark eyes. 'So my grandfather was right,' he said.

'Was he? Tell me about this rightness of his.'

'When the priest-kind found the winged god was gone,' Liathan said, with a kind of defiant willingness to talk, 'my grandfather swore it was you who had taken it. He said you had the face of that Chieftain of the Red Crests he had seen killed under the wings of the god, and that he had been blind and doting not to know you for his son. But when we had followed you and searched your gear and found nothing, we said among ourselves that the grandfather grew old and fanciful. Then Gault the fisherman found your ring-brooch by the shore of the loch, and the bank pulled down and a hollow place under the water-line. And later, we heard a strange tale from the rath where your sword-brother was taken sick; and we knew. And my grandfather said, " I was right, after all, who am never wrong," and he sent for me, for my brother had been savaged by a seal and was too sick of the wound to go to the Hosting. He sent for me, and said: " It may be that it is you who will hunt him down, for there is a link of fate between his line and ours. If it be so, kill him if you can, for he has put shame on the gods of the tribe; but also give him his father's ring, for he is his father's son in more than blood." '

There was an instant's complete silence; and then Marcus said: ' You have it now? '

' On a thong round my neck,' Liathan said sullenly. ' You must take it for yourself, since my hands are bound.'

Marcus lowered himself on to his sound knee, and slipped a hand warily under the shoulder-folds of the other's cloak. But it was no trick; he found the ring, which had worked round to the back, and drawing it out, cut the thong, and slipped it on to his bare signet finger. The light was beginning to fade, and the great stone that had been full of green fire when he saw it last, was coolly dark as ilex leaves, lit only by a faint surface reflection of the sky. ' If the fortunes of war had gone otherwise, and Esca and I had fallen to your spears, you would have had small chance to give me my father's ring. How, then, would you have carried out your grandfather's bidding? ' he asked curiously.

' You should have had the ring to take with you, as a man takes his weapons and his favourite hound.'

' I see,' said Marcus. From the ring he looked back to

Liathan, suddenly half smiling. 'When you go back to your own place, say to Tradui that I thank him for the gift of my father's ring.'

Esca's step sounded on the stairs and a moment later he ducked out into the evening light. 'All is well with the ponies,' he said. 'Also I have looked round a little, and seen that our way lies down the glen westward. That way there is birch cover almost from the first, and moreover the hunt went toward the sunrise.'

Marcus glanced up at the sky. 'The light will be gone in the half of an hour, but much can happen in that time, and it is in my heart that we will go now.'

Esca nodded, reaching him a steadying hand as he rose; and in so doing, saw the flawed emerald, and gave him a quick, questioning glance.

'Yes,' said Marcus. 'Liathan has brought me my father's ring as a gift from his grandfather.' He turned to look down at the tribesman. 'We shall take two of your ponies, Liathan, to carry us to the Wall, but we will turn them loose when we have done with them, and with good fortune you will find them again—later. I hope you do, because you brought me my father's ring . . . See to the gag, Esca.'

Esca saw to it.

Meeting the furious eyes above the gag, Marcus said, 'I am sorry, but we can ill afford to have you shouting the moment we are gone, lest there be someone within hearing. It will assuredly not be long before your sword-brethren return and find you, but to make all safe I will see that word of your whereabouts reaches the tribesmen, when *we* have reached the Wall. That is the best that I can do.'

They crossed to the stairhead. Esca paused to collect the tribesmen's weapons from the place where he had stacked them, and sent them—all save one spear, which he kept to replace his own—over the parapet into the tarn below. Marcus heard them take the water in a stutter of faint splashes, while he bent over the other two captives, both conscious and hating hard by this time, to make sure that they had not yet contrived to slacken their bonds. Then they ducked through the doorway into the descending darkness.

The strain of their escape had taxed Marcus to the uttermost, and the respite in the signal-tower, short as it had been, had been long enough to let the old wound begin to stiffen. He had to nerve himself to every step, and there seemed a great many more steps on the way down than there had been on the way up. But they reached the bottom at last, and came out into the little courtyard, where three ponies stood with their reins over their heads.

They chose the two of them, a black and a dun, who seemed the freshest and, hitching the reins of the third one over a fallen timber to prevent him following, led them out through the narrow gateway. 'The last lap,' Marcus said, drawing a hand caressingly down the neck of the black pony. 'We will break fast in one of the Wall stations tomorrow morning.'

Esca helped him to mount, before he himself swung on to the back of the dun. For a few moments Marcus had all he could do to master his mount, for the fiery little brute objected strongly to an unfamiliar rider, snorting and plunging like an unbroken colt, until, seeming suddenly to tire of the fight, it answered to his hand and set off at a canter, shaking its head and spilling foam over its chest and knees.

Esca ranged alongside on the dun, and they swung over the steep scarp of the spur, and headed downhill for the woods below them. 'Praise be to Lugh, they are yet fairly fresh; for we've a hard ride before us.'

'Yes,' said Marcus, rather grimly; and shut his teeth on the word. That plunging tussle with his mount had taken most of the endurance that was left in him.

The light was going fast, as they swung into the long south-ward curve of the glen. The wind was surging through the birch and hazel of the woods, and overhead the sky between the hurrying clouds was kindling yellow as a lantern.

.   .   .   .   .

A long while later, a sentry on the northern ramparts of Borcovicus thought that in a lull of the tearing wind he heard the beat of horses' hooves somewhere far below him. He checked his pacing to look down, far down where the burn cut through its wild glen a hundred feet below the fortress walls, but a racing, silver-fringed cloud had come across the moon, and the glen was a black nothingness below him, and the wind swooped back, blowing away all sound. Curse the wind! There was always a wind—save where there was mist —up here on the highest lift of the Wall; nothing to hear all day and all night but the wind and the peewits calling. It was enough to make a man hear worse than horses' hooves inside his head. The sentry spat disgustedly down into the dark abyss, and continued his measured pacing.

Some while later still, the guard on duty at the North Gate was surprised by a most imperious beating on the timbers and shout of 'Open in Caesar's name!' So might a bearer of dispatches announce his arrival, if it were at any other gate; but the few who came from the north—horse-dealers, hunters, and the like—did not hammer on the gate as though they were the Legate himself demanding entrance in the name of the Emperor. It might be a trick of some kind. Leaving his gate-guard turned out and standing ready, the Optio clanked up to the look-out above the gateway.

The moon rode clear of the clouds now, and faintly, by its reflected light, the Optio could pick out two figures directly below him in the shadow of the arch. The sheer drop of the hillside was in shadow, but there was enough light to show it empty of men, clear down to the white streak of the burn. Not a trick, then.

'Who demands entrance in Caesar's name?'

One of the figures looked up, his face a pale blur in the darkness. 'Two who have urgent business with the Commander and would fain keep whole skins if possible. Open up, friend.'

The Optio hesitated an instant, then turned and clattered down the few steps. 'Open up,' he ordered.

Men sprang to obey him, the heavy oaken valve swung smoothly outward on its stone socket, and in the opening,

clearly lit now by the yellow light from the guard-room doorway, appeared two wild, bearded figures, who might have been
born of the autumn gale. One of them was leaning heavily
on the shoulder of the other, who seemed to be supporting him
by an arm round his waist; and as they stumbled forward,
the Optio, who had begun curtly, ' Now what——' went kindly
enough to steady him on the other side, saying, ' Run into
trouble, eh? '

But the other laughed suddenly, his teeth showing white in
the dark tangle of his beard; and staggering clear of his
friend's supporting arm, propped himself against the guard-
room wall, and drooped there, breathing hard and fast through
widened nostrils. Clad in filthy rags, gaunt as famine and
well-nigh as dirty, scratched and blood-smeared as though from
contact with many furze bushes, he was as villainous an object
as the Optio had seen for a long time.

As the gate clanged shut behind him, this apparition said in
the cool, clipped accents of a cohort centurion, ' Optio, I wish
to see the Commanding Officer immediately.'

' Ugh? ' said the Optio, and blinked.

Presently, after a queer confusion of changing faces, of
brusque soldiers' voices and clanging footsteps, and long
wavering alleyways between buildings whose corners never
seemed to be quite where he expected them, Marcus found
himself standing on the threshold of a lamp-lit room. It
flowered suddenly golden on his sight, out of the windy dark;
a small room, white-walled, and almost filled by a battered
writing-table and records chest. He blinked at it with a queer,
dreamlike sense of unreality. A square-built man in half uniform rose from the camp-chair, and turned inquiringly to the
door. ' Yes, what——' he began, much as the Optio had done.

As the door closed behind him, Marcus looked at the stocky
familiar figure, the square face with the dark hairs growing
out of the nose, and felt no surprise. He had come back to a
familiar world, and it seemed only natural that he should find
old friends in it. ' Good evening to you, Drusillus,' he said.
' My congratulations on—your promotion.'

The centurion's face was puzzled, and his head went up a little stiffly.

'Do you not know me, Drusillus?' Marcus said almost pleadingly. 'I am——'

But light had already dawned on his old centurion, and the bewilderment in his square brown face became blank astonishment and then lit into incredulous delight. 'Centurion Aquila!' he said. 'Yes, sir, I know you. I would know you in Tartarus itself, now that I come to look at you!' He came tramping round the table. 'But what in the name of Thunder brings you here?'

Marcus set his bundle carefully on the table. 'We have brought back the Hispana's lost Eagle,' he said, rather muzzily, and very quietly crumpled forward on top of it.

XX

VALEDICTORY

TOWARDS evening of a day in late October, Marcus and
Esca came riding up the last lift of the Calleva road.
Having learned at Eburacum that the Legate Claudius
was not yet returned, they had pushed on south, knowing that
they could not miss him by the way, to wait for him at Calleva.

They were rid of their beards and reasonably clean once
more, and Marcus had had his hair clipped short again in the
Roman manner; but still clad in the tatterdemalion clothes
of their adventuring, still gaunt and hollow-eyed and disreputable, they had more than once needed the permit provided by Drusillus to save them from the awkward charge of
having stolen the army post-horses on which they rode.

They were tired, bone tired, and without any glow of triumph
to warm the leaden chill of their tiredness; and they rode with
the reins loose on their horses' necks, in silence save for the
strike of shod hooves on the metalled road and the squeak of
wet leather. But after many months in the wild aloofness of
the north, this gentler and more friendly countryside seemed to
Marcus to hold out its arms to him, and it was with a sense of
homecoming that he lifted his face to the soft grey mizzle, and
saw afar off, beyond the rolling miles of dappled forest, the
familiar and suddenly beloved outline of the South Downs.

They rode into Calleva by the North Gate, left the horses at
the Golden Vine for return to the transit camp next day, and
set out on foot for the house of Aquila. In the narrow street,
when they turned into it, the poplar trees were already bare,
and the way slippery with shrivelled wet leaves. The daylight
was fading fast, and the windows of Uncle Aquila's watch-
tower were full of lemon-pale lamp-light that seemed somehow
like a welcome.

The door was on the latch, and they pushed it open and went in. There was an air of most unwonted bustle in the house, as though someone had lately arrived or was expected to arrive at any moment. As they emerged from the narrow entrance closet, old Stephanos was crossing the atrium towards the dining recess. He cast one glance at them, uttered a startled bleat, and all but dropped the lamp he was carrying.

'It is all right, Stephanos,' Marcus told him, slipping off his wet cloak and tossing it over a convenient bench. 'It is only the Golden Vine that we are sprung from, not the realms of Hades. Is my uncle in his study?'

The old slave's mouth was open to reply, but nobody ever heard what he said, for his voice was drowned by a frenzied baying that rose on the instant. There was a wild scurry of paws along the colonnade, and a great brindled shape sprang over the threshold and came streaking across the floor, skidding on the smooth surface, ears pricked and bush tail flying. Cub, lying dejectedly in the colonnade, had heard Marcus's voice and come to find him.

'Cub!' Marcus called, and sat down hurriedly on top of his cloak, just in time to save himself from being bowled over like a stoned hare as Cub landed with a flying leap on his chest.

They slid together off the bench with a resounding thump. Marcus had his arms round the young wolf's neck, and Cub thrust against him, whining and yelping, licking his face from ear to ear with frantic joy. But by now news of their return had burst through the house, and Marcipor came scuttling with dignified haste to one door while Sassticca ran in through another, still clutching a large iron spoon; and somehow, between Cub's joyful onslaughts, Marcus was turning from one to the other, greeting and being greeted. 'You have not got rid of us, you see, Marcipor! Sassticca, it is like the flowers in spring to see you! The nights that I have dreamed of your honey cakes——'

'Ah, I thought I heard your voice, Marcus—among others.'

There was a sudden hush; and Uncle Aquila was standing

at the foot of the watch-tower stairs, with old grey-muzzled
Procyon at his side, and behind him, the dark, austere figure of
Claudius Hieronimianus.

Marcus got up slowly, one hand still on the great savage head
that was pressed against his thigh. ' It seems that we have
timed our arrival well,' he said. He started forward at the
same instant as his uncle strode to meet him, and next moment
they had come together in the middle of the atrium, and
Marcus was gripping both the older man's hands in his.

' Uncle Aquila! Oh, it's good to see you again. How goes
it with you, sir? '

' Strangely enough, it goes the better for seeing you safely
home once more, even in the guise of a Tiber rat,' said Uncle
Aquila. His glance went to Esca and back again. ' In the
guise of two Tiber rats.' And then after an instant's pause,
very quietly, ' What news? '

' I have brought it back,' Marcus said, equally quietly. And
that was all for the moment on the subject of the lost Eagle.
The four of them were alone in the atrium, the slaves having
slipped out to their own duties when the master of the house
appeared, and Uncle Aquila gathered both young men after
him with an imperious gesture to where the Legate, who had
drawn aside from their meeting, was quietly warming himself
at the brazier. In the general shifting Cub circled for an
instant to thrust his muzzle into Esca's hand in greeting, then
returned to Marcus again. Procyon greeted nobody, he was a
one-man-dog to the point of seldom appearing conscious that
other men existed.

' He has done it! ' Uncle Aquila was announcing in a kind of
triumphant grumble. ' He has done it, by Jupiter! You
never thought he would, did you, my Claudius? '

' I am—not sure,' said the Legate, his strange black eyes
resting on Marcus consideringly. ' No, I am not—at all sure,
my Aquila.'

Marcus saluted him, then drew Esca forward from the
outskirts of the group. ' Sir, may I bring to your remembrance
my friend Esca Mac Cunoval? '

'I already remember him very well,' said Claudius with a quick smile to the Briton.

Esca bent his head to him. 'You witnessed my manu-mission papers, I believe, sir,' he said in a dead-level tone that made Marcus glance at him anxiously, realizing suddenly that there had been no real homecoming for Esca in this return to a house in which he had been a slave.

'I did. But I generally remember men by other things than the papers I may have witnessed for them,' the Legate said gently.

An exclamation from Uncle Aquila cut across the little ex-change, and looking round, Marcus found the other staring at his left hand, which he had unconsciously curved about the precious bundle which he still carried in its sling. 'That ring,' said Uncle Aquila. 'Show it to me.'

Marcus slipped off the heavy signet-ring and passed it to him. 'Of course you recognize it?'

His uncle stood for a few moments examining it, his face unreadable. Then he gave it back. 'Yes,' he said. 'Yes, by Jupiter, I do recognize it. How came you by your father's ring?'

But with Sassticca's voice rising near at hand, and one or other of the slaves likely at any moment to come through the atrium about their preparations for dinner, Marcus could not bring himself to start on that story. Slipping the ring back on to his finger, he said, 'Uncle Aquila, could we leave that—with all the rest, for a fitter place and season? It is a long story, and there are many doors to this room.'

Their eyes met, and after a pause, Uncle Aquila said, 'Aye, well. Both matters have waited long enough for an hour to make little difference. You agree, Claudius?'

The Egyptian nodded. 'Most assuredly I agree. In your watch-tower, after we have eaten, we shall be safe from in-terruption. Then Marcus shall make his full report.' Suddenly his face crinkled into a thousand-creased smile, and with a swift change of manner that seemed to draw a silken curtain over the whole affair of the lost Eagle, shutting it decently from view until the time came to take it out again and deal with it, he turned to Marcus. ' It seems always that I visit this house at a happy hour. The last time, it was Cub who came back, and this time it is you, but the reunion remains the same.'

Marcus looked down at Cub, who was leaning against him, head up and eyes half closed in ecstasy. 'We are glad to be together, Cub and I,' he said.

' So it seems. It is almost past believing that a wolf should be so much a friend. Was he greatly more difficult than a hound, in the making? '

' I think he was more stubborn; certainly fiercer to handle. But it was Esca rather than I who had the making of him. He is the expert.'

' Ah, of course.' The Legate turned to Esca. ' You come of the Brigantes, do you not? More than once I have seen Cub's brethren running among the dog-packs of your tribe, and wondered how——'

But Marcus heard no more. He had stooped quickly, and was running an exploring hand over the young wolf, suddenly aware of something that he had not really taken in, in the first flush of home-coming. ' Uncle Aquila, what have you done to Cub? He is nothing but skin and bone.'

' *We* have done nothing to Cub,' said Uncle Aquila in accents of acute disgust. ' Cub has been breaking his own wilful heart for his own amusement. Since you left, he has refused food from any but that chit Cottia, and since her going, he has pre-ferred to starve. That brute has been deliberately dying in our midst with the entire household buzzing round him like blow-flies round a stranded fish.'

Marcus's caressing hand had checked on Cub's neck, and something seemed to twist and turn cold inside him. ' Cottia,' he said. ' Where has Cottia gone? ' He had scarcely thought of her, save twice, in all the months that he had been away; but it seemed a long, long time before his uncle answered.

' Only to Aquae Sulis for the winter. Her Aunt Valaria discovered a need to take the waters, and shifted the whole household, a few days ago.'

Marcus let go the breath that he had been holding. He began to play with Cub's ears, drawing them again and again through his fingers. ' Did she leave any word for me? '

' She came to me in a fine flaming passion, the day before she was swept away, to bring' back your bracelet.'

' Did you tell her—about keeping it? '

' I did not. Some things are best unsaid until the need comes for saying them. I told her that since you had left it in her charge, it seemed to me best that she keep it until she came back in the spring and could give it into your hands. I also promised to tell you that she would guard it well through the winter.' He held one great blue-veined hand to the warmth of the brazier, and smiled at it. ' She is a vixen, the little one, but a faithful vixen.'

' Yes,' Marcus. ' Yes . . . sir, with your leave I will take the Cub and feed him now.'

Esca, who had been answering the Legate's questions about the taming of wolf-cubs, said quickly. ' I will take him.'

' Maybe if we both take him, we can wash off some of the journey while we are about it. We have time for that, Uncle Aquila?'

' Time and to spare,' said his uncle. ' Dinner will doubtless be put back to Jupiter knows what hour, while Sassticca ransacks her store shelves for your benefit.'

Uncle Aquila was perfectly right. For Marcus's benefit, Sassticca ransacked her store shelves with joyful abandon; and the sad thing was that it was all as good as wasted. To Marcus at all events, that dinner was completely unreal. He was so tired that the soft light of the palm-oil lamps seemed a golden fog, and he tasted nothing of what he ate and scarcely even noticed the handful of rain-wet autumn crocuses which Sassticca, proud of her knowledge of Roman ways, had scattered on the table. It seemed odd, after so many meals eaten in the open or squatting beside peat fires, to eat at a civilized table again, to see the clean-shaven faces of the other men, and the tunics of soft white wool that they wore—Esca's a borrowed one of his own—to hear the quiet, clipped voices of his uncle and the Legate when they spoke to each other. Very odd, like something out of another world; a familiar world, grown suddenly unfamiliar. He had almost forgotten what to do with a napkin. Only Esca, clearly finding it strange and uncomfortable to eat while reclining on his left elbow, seemed real in the queer brittle unreality.

It was an uneasy meal, eaten without lingering and almost in silence, for the minds of all four were on one subject, carefully shut away behind its silken curtain, but making it hopeless to try to talk of something else. A strange home-coming meal, with the shadow of the lost Eagle brooding over it; and Marcus was thankful when at last Uncle Aquila set down the cup after pouring the final oblation, and said, ' Shall we go up to my study now? '

Following the two older men, and once again carrying the Eagle, Marcus had mounted four or five of the watch-tower steps before he realized that Esca was not coming up behind, and looking back, he saw him still standing at the foot of the stairs.

' I think that I will not come,' Esca said.

' Not come? But you must come.'

Esca shook his head. ' It is between you and your uncle and the Legate.'

Followed as ever, by Cub, Marcus came down the few steps again. ' It is between the four of us. What maggot has got into your head, Esca? '

' I think that I should not go to your uncle's private sanctum.' Esca said stubbornly. ' I have been a slave in his house.'

' You are not a slave now.'

' No, I am your freed-man now. It is strange. I never thought of that until this evening.'

Marcus had never thought of it either, but he knew that it was true. You could give a slave his freedom, but nothing could undo the fact that he had been a slave; and between him, a freed-man, and any free man who had never been unfree, there would still be a difference. Wherever the Roman way of life held good, that difference would be there. That was why it had not mattered, all these months that they had been away; that was why it mattered now. Suddenly he felt baffled and helpless. 'You did not feel like this before we went north. How is it altered now?'

'That was at the beginning. I had not had time to—understand. I knew only that I was free—a hound slipped from the leash; and we were going away from it all in the morning. Now we have come back.'

Yes, they had come back, and the thing had got to be faced, and faced at once. On a sudden impulse Marcus reached out his free hand and caught his friend's shoulder, not at all gently. 'Listen to me,' he said. 'Are you going to live all the rest of your life as though you had taken a whipping and could not forget it? Because if you are, I am sorry for you. You don't like being a freed-man, do you? Well, I don't like being lame. That makes two of us, and the only thing we can do about it, you and I, is to learn to carry the scars lightly.' He gave the shoulder a friendly shake, and dropped his hand. 'Come up with me now, Esca.'

Esca did not answer for a moment. And then slowly his head went up, and his eyes wore the dancing look they always wore in action. 'I will come,' he said.

When they emerged into Uncle Aquila's watch-tower, the two older men were standing over the wrought-iron brazier that glowed red in its alcove at the far side of the room. They looked round as Marcus and Esca entered, but nobody spoke; only the rain whispered softly, delicately, against the narrow windows. The small lamplit room seemed very remote from the world, very tall above it. Marcus had a sense of immense depths dropping away beneath him in the darkness, as though, if he went to the window, he might look down and see Orion swimming like a fish below him.

'Well?' said Uncle Aquila at last; and the word fell sharply into the silence, like a pebble dropping into a pool.

Marcus crossed to the writing-table and set his bundle down upon it. How pathetic and shapeless it seemed; a bundle that might contain boots or washing. 'It has lost its wings,' he said. 'That is why it bulks so small.'

The silken curtain had been drawn back now, and with it was gone the brittle surface of ordinariness that they had kept all evening. 'So the rumour was a true one,' the Legate said.

Marcus nodded, and began to undo the shapeless mass. He turned back the last fold, and there, amid the tumble of tattered violet cloth, the lost Eagle stood, squat and undignified, but oddly powerful, on its splayed legs. The empty wing sockets were very black in the lamplight which kindled its gilded feathers to the strong yellow of gorse flowers. There was a furious pride about the upreared head. Wingless it might be, fallen from its old estate, but it was an Eagle still; and out of its twelve-year captivity, it had returned to its own people.

For a long moment nobody spoke, and then Uncle Aquila said, 'Shall we sit down to this?'

Marcus folded up thankfully on one end of the bench which Esca had drawn to the table, for his unsound leg had begun to shake under him. He was warmly aware of Cub's chin settling contentedly on his foot, and Esca sitting beside him, as he began to make his report. He made it clearly and carefully, abating nothing of the stories told him by Guern the Hunter and by old Tradui, though parts of them were hard in the telling. At the appropriate places he handed over to Esca, to speak for himself. And all the time, his eyes never left the Legate's intent face.

The Legate sat leaning forward a little in Uncle Aquila's great chair, his arms crossed on the table before him, his face, with the red weal of his helmet rim still faintly showing on his forehead, like an intent golden mask against the shadows behind.

No one moved or spoke at once when the report was finished. Marcus himself sat very still, searching into the long black eyes for their verdict. The rain sharpened to a little impatient spatter against the window. Then Claudius Hieronimianus shifted, and the spell of stillness was broken. 'You have done well, both of you,' he said; and his gaze moved from Marcus to Esca and back again, drawing them both in. 'Thanks to you, a weapon which might one day have been used against the Empire, will never be so used. I salute two very courageous lunatics.'

'And—the Legion?'

'No,' said the Legate. 'I am sorry.'

So Marcus had his verdict. It was 'thumbs down' for the Ninth Legion. He had thought that he had accepted that from the night when he had heard Guern's story. Now he knew that he had never quite accepted it. In his heart of hearts he had clung, against all reason, to the hope that his own judgement was wrong, after all. He made one desperate appeal for his father's Legion, knowing as he did so, that it was hopeless.

'Sir, there were upward of three cohorts who were not with the Legion when it marched North. Many Legions have been re-formed from fewer survivors than that—if the Eagle was still in Roman hands.'

'Those cohorts were broken up twelve years ago, and distributed among other Legions of the Empire,' the Legate said very kindly. 'By now more than half the men will have finished their military service, and those that have not, will have changed their allegiance to their new Eagles, long ago. On your own showing, the name and number of the Ninth Hispana is no heritage for a new Legion to carry. It is better that it be forgotten.'

'There is no way back through the Waters of Lethe.' Behind the Legate's words, Marcus seemed to hear Guern the Hunter. 'No way back through the Waters of Lethe—no way back——'

Uncle Aquila crashed up from the table. 'And what of their last stand, that Marcus has just told us of? Is not *that* a heritage fit for any Legion?'

The Legate turned a little in his chair, to look up at him. 'The conduct of a few score men cannot counterbalance the conduct of a whole Legion,' he said. 'You must see that, Aquila, even though one of them was your brother.'

Uncle Aquila grunted savagely, and the Legate turned back

to Marcus. 'How many people know that the Eagle has been brought back?'

'South of the Wall, we four, your own Camp Commandant, who I gather knew of the matter from yourself, and the Commander of the garrison at Borcovicus. He was my old Second at Isca Dumnoniorum, and gained his cohort for his defence of the fort after I was wounded. We took pains that no one else in Borcovicus should know what it was all about; and he will say nothing unless I give him leave. Rumour may come down from the North, of course, but if so, I imagine that it will die out as the earlier rumour did.'

'Well enough,' said the Legate. "Naturally I shall lay the whole matter before the Senate. But I have no doubt of their verdict.'

Uncle Aquila made a small, expressive gesture, as though screwing something up and tossing it into the brazier. "What do you suggest becomes of this?' he nodded to the defiant, squatting Eagle.

'Give it honourable burial,' said the Legate.

'Where?' Marcus demanded huskily, after a moment.

'Why not here in Calleva? Five roads meet here, and the Legions are for ever passing by, while the place itself is the territory of no particular Legion.'

He leaned forward to brush the gilded feathers lightly with one finger, his face thoughtful in the lamplight. 'So long as Rome lasts, the Eagles will pass and re-pass under the walls of Calleva. What better place for it to lie?'

Uncle Aquila said, 'When I had this house built, there had lately been a flare-up of unrest hereabout, and I had a small hiding-place made under the floor of the shrine, to take my papers in case of further trouble. Let it lie there and be forgotten.'

.   .   .   .   .

Very much later that night, the four of them stood together in the small alcove shrine at the end of the atrium. The slaves had long since gone to their own quarters, and they had the house and the silence of the house to themselves. A bronze

Q

lamp on the altar sent up a long tongue of flame the shape of a perfect laurel leaf; and by its light the household gods in their niches in the lime-washed walls seemed to look down, as the four men were looking down, into the small square hole in the tesselated floor, just before the altar.

Marcus had brought the Eagle down from the watch-tower, carrying it as he had carried it so many miles and slept with it so many nights, in the crook of his arm. And while the others watched in silence, he had knelt down and laid it in the small square cist that reached down through the hypercaust into the dark earth beneath. He had laid it—no longer bundled in tattered violet cloth—on his old military cloak, and drawn the scarlet folds closely over it with a gentle hand. He had been very proud to wear that cloak; it was fitting that his father's Eagle should have it now.

The four men stood with bent heads; three who had served with the Eagles in their different times, one who had suffered slavery for taking up arms against them; but in that moment there was no gulf between them. The Legate stepped forward to the edge of the square hole, looking down to where the scarlet of Marcus's cloak was all but lost in the depths beyond the reach of the lamplight. He raised one hand, and began, very simply, to speak the Valedictory, the Farewell, as he might have spoken it for a dead comrade.

Suddenly, to Marcus's tired mind, it seemed that there were others beside themselves in the little lamplit shrine; notably two: a slight, dark man, with an eager face beneath the tall crest of a First Cohort Commander; and a shock-headed tribesman in a saffron kilt. Yet when he looked at the tribesman, he was gone, and in his place the young centurion he had once been.

'Here lies the Eagle of the Ninth Legion, the Hispana,' the Legate was saying. 'Many times it found honour in the wars, against foes abroad and rebellion at home. Shame came to it; but at the end it was honourably held until the last of those who held it died beneath its wings. It has led brave men. Let it lie forgotten.'

He stepped back.

Esca looked questioningly to Uncle Aquila, then at a sign from him, stooped to the segment of solid-moulded tessera which stood upreared against the wall, and fitted it carefully back into place over the hole. It had been well contrived, this hiding-place that Uncle Aquila had had made for his papers; with the segment replaced and the pattern completed, no trace of it remained, save for one all but invisible chink just wide enough to take a knife-blade.

' Tomorrow we will seal it up,' said Uncle Aquila, heavily.

Faintly into the silence, down the soft wet wind, stole the long-drawn, haunting notes of the trumpets from the transit camp, sounding for the third watch of the night. To Marcus, still gazing down blindly at the place where the square hole had been, it seemed that they were sounding with unbearable sadness for the lost Eagle, and for the lost Legion that had marched into the mist and never come marching back. Then, as the distant trumpets quickened into the shining spray of notes that ended the call, suddenly his sense of failure dropped from him like a tattered cloak, and he knew again, as he had known in the ruined signal-tower while the hunt closed in below, that it had all been worth while.

He had failed to redeem his father's Legion, since it was past redeeming, but the lost Eagle was home again, and would never now be used as a weapon against its own people.

He raised his head at the same time as Esca, and their eyes met. ' A good hunting? ' Esca seemed to be asking.

' It was a good hunting,' Marcus said.

XXI

THE OLIVE-WOOD BIRD

THAT winter was not an easy one for Marcus. For months he had mercilessly overtaxed his lame leg, and when the strain was over, it quite suddenly took its revenge. He did not much mind the pain it gave him, save when it kept him awake at night, but he did most bitterly mind finding himself shackled by the old wound again, when he had thought that all that was over. He felt ill, and he was wildly impatient; and he missed Cottia through the dark winter days as he had never missed her before.

Also there was the old nagging question of the future still to be settled. For Esca, the future was simpler—simpler as to the outward things at all events. 'I am your armour-bearer, though I am no longer your slave,' he said when they discussed the question. 'I will serve you, and you shall feed me, and between whiles maybe I will turn hunter, and that will bring in a sesterce from time to time.' Even before the year turned Marcus had spoken to his uncle about his old idea of becoming somebody's secretary; but Uncle Aquila had disposed of his capabilities to be anybody's secretary in a few well-chosen and blistering words, and when he proved stubborn in the plan, finished up by making him promise to wait at least until he was strong again.

The year drew on to spring, and slowly Marcus's leg began to strengthen under him once more. March came, and the forest below the ramparts was flushed with rising sap, and the many thorn-trees which gave it its name began to feather the wooded hills with white. And quite suddenly the House of Kaeso woke up. For a few days slaves came and went, scurrying about it; hangings were shaken out of doors, and the fumes of the freshly lit hypercaust fire blew into the slaves'

quarters of Uncle Aquila's house and created unpleasantness
between the two households. Then one evening, returning
from the baths, Marcus and Esca met a hired mule-carriage
being driven away empty from the house of Kaeso, and
glimpsed a mass of luggage being carried indoors. The
family had returned.

Next morning Marcus went down to the foot of the garden,
and whistled for Cottia, as he had been used to do. It was a
wild day of blustering wind and thin, shining rain, and the little
native daffodils in the rampart curve tossed and streamed
before the gusts like points of wind-blown flame, with the shrill
sunshine slanting through their petals. Cottia came with the
wind behind her, up round the end of the swaying hedge, to
join him under the bare fruit-trees.

'I heard you whistle,' she said, 'and so I came. I have
brought your bracelet back to you.'

'Cottia!' Marcus said. 'Why, Cottia!' and stood looking
at her, making no move to take the bracelet that she held out
to him. It was almost a year since their last meeting, but he
had expected her to wait as she had been then. And Cottia
had not waited. She stood before him much taller than she had
been, with her head up, and returned his look, suddenly a little
uncertain. Her soft golden-green mantle was swathed closely
round her over the straight white folds of her tunic; one end
of it, which had been drawn over her head, had fallen back, and
her flaming hair that had been used to blow wild, was braided
into a shining coronal so that she seemed more than ever to
carry her head like a queen. Her lips were touched with red,
and her eyebrows darkened, and there were tiny gold drops in
her ears.

'Why, Cottia,' he said again, 'you have grown up,' and felt
suddenly a little ache of loss.

'Yes,' said Cottia. 'Do you like me grown up?'

'Yes—yes, of course,' Marcus said. 'Thank you for
looking after my bracelet for me. Uncle Aquila told me how
you came to see him about it before you went away.' He took
the heavy gold bracelet from her and sprang it on to his wrist,

still looking at her as he did so.   He found that he did not know how to talk to her, and as the silence lengthened, he asked with desperate politeness, ' Did you like Aquae Sulis? '

' *No*! '   Cottia spat the word between little pointed teeth, and her face was suddenly bright with fury.   ' I hated every moment of Aquae Sulis!   I never wanted to go there;   I wanted to wait for you because you told me you might be home before the winter closed in.   And all winter I have had no word of you save one little—*little* message in some silly letter your uncle sent mine about the new town water supply;   and I have waited, and waited, and now you are not at all glad to see me!   Well, neither am I at all glad to see *you*! '

' You little vixen! '   Marcus caught her wrists as she turned to run, and swung her round to face him.   Suddenly and softly he laughed.   ' But I am glad to see you.   You do not know how glad I am to see you, Cottia.'

She was dragging away from him, wrenching at her wrists to free them, but at his words she checked, looking up into his face. ' Yes, you are now,' she said wonderingly.   ' Why were you not, before?'

' I did not recognize you, just at first.'

' Oh,' said Cottia, a little blankly.   She was silent a moment, and then asked with sudden anxiety: ' Where is Cub? '

' Making love to Sassticca for a bone.   He is growing greedy.'

She drew a deep breath of relief.   ' All was well with him, then, when you came home? '

' He was very thin;   he would not eat after you left.   But all is well with him now.'

' I was afraid of that;   that he would fret, I mean.   It was one of the things that made me not want to go to Aquae Sulis; but I could not take him with me, truly I could not, Marcus. Aunt Valaria would never have allowed it.'

' I am very sure she would not,' Marcus said, his mouth quirking as he thought of the Lady Valaria confronted with the suggestion that she should take a young wolf to a fashionable watering-place.

By this time they were sitting side by side on Marcus's cloak

spread on the damp marble bench, and after a few moments
Cottia asked: 'Did you find the Eagle?'

He looked round at her, his arms resting across his knees.
'Yes,' he said at last.

'Oh, Marcus, I *am* so glad! So very glad! And now?'

'Nothing now.'

'But the Legion?' She searched his face, and the sparkle
died in her own. 'Will there not be a new Ninth Legion,
after all?'

'No, there will never be a Ninth Legion again.'

'But Marcus——' she began, and then checked. 'No, I will
not ask questions.'

He smiled. 'One day, maybe, I will tell you the whole
story.'

'I will wait,' said Cottia.

For a while they sat there, talking by fits and starts, but silent
for the most part, glancing at each other from time to time
with a quick smile, and then away again, for they were unexpectedly shy of each other. Presently Marcus told her about
Esca, that he was no longer a slave. He had expected her to
be surprised, but she only said, 'Yes, Nissa told me, just after
you went away, and I was glad—for you both.' And then they
were silent again.

Behind them, in the bare swaying branches of the wild pear-
tree, a blackbird with a crocus-coloured bill burst into song,
and the wind caught and tossed the shining notes down to
them in a shower. They turned together to look up at the
singer, swaying against the cold blown blue of the sky. Marcus
narrowed his eyes into the thin dazzle of sunlight and whistled
back, and the blackbird, bowing and swaying on the wind-
blown branch, its throat swelling with an ecstasy of song,
seemed to be answering him. Then a cloud came sailing across
the sun, and the bright world was quenched in shadow.

At the same moment they heard a horse coming down the
street, its hoof-beats ringing on the wet roadway. It stopped
before the house, or before the next one; Marcus could not be
sure which.

The blackbird was still singing, but when he turned to look at Cottia, a shadow that was not merely the passing cloud seemed to have touched her. 'Marcus, what is it that you will do now?' she asked suddenly.

'Now?'

'Now that you are strong again. You are strong again, aren't you?' Then swiftly: 'No, I do not believe you are, you were limping more, just now, than you were when I saw you last.'

Marcus laughed. 'I have been lying up like a sick badger all winter, but I am mending fast now.'

'That is the truth?'

'That is the truth.'

'Then—what will you do? Will you go back to the Legions?'

'No. I should do well enough in a skirmish, maybe, but I could not march my cohort down from Portus Itius to Rome at twenty miles a day, and I should certainly be no use on the parade ground.'

'The parade ground!' Cottia said indignantly. 'I have seen them on the parade ground through the gates of the transit camp. They march about in straight lines with all their legs working together, and make silly patterns of themselves while a man with a voice like a bull shouts at them. What has *that* to do with the fighting of wars?'

Marcus hastily gathered his wits together to make Cottia understand what it had to do with the fighting of wars, but he did not have to struggle with the explanations, for she hurried on without waiting for an answer. 'Then if you cannot go back to the Legions, what *will* you do?'

'I am not—quite sure.'

'Perhaps you will go home,' she said; and then seemed suddenly to realize her own words, and her eyes grew frightened. 'You will go back to Rome, and take Cub and Esca with you!'

'I do not know, Cottia, truly I do not know. But I do not suppose for a moment that I shall ever go home.'

But Cottia did not seem to hear him. 'Take me too.'

Suddenly her voice broke almost into a wail. 'They will build the city wall round here soon, and you could not leave me in a cage! You could not! Oh, Marcus, take me too!'

'Even if it were to Rome?' Marcus said, remembering her old wild hatred of all things Roman.

Cottia slipped from the bench, and turned to him as he got up also. 'Yes,' she said. 'Anywhere at all, if only it was with you.'

Two distinct waves of feeling swept over Marcus, so close upon each other that they were almost one. The first was the joyful surprise of finding, and the second the desolation of losing again . . . How was he to explain to Cottia that possessing nothing in the world, without even a trade to his hands, he could not take her with him?

'Cottia,' he began wretchedly. 'Cottia, my heart—it is no use——'

But before he could get any farther, he heard Esca calling, with a note of excitement in his voice. 'Marcus! Where are you, Marcus?'

'Down here. I am coming,' he shouted back, and caught Cottia's hand. 'Come with me now, anyway.'

Rain had begun to spatter round them, but the sun was out again and the rain shone as it fell. Cub met them at the court-yard steps, circling about them and barking joyously, his straight bush of a tail streaming out behind. And hard behind Cub, was Esca. 'This has just come for you,' he said, holding out a slim, sealed papyrus roll.

Marcus took the roll from him, raising his brows at sight of the Sixth Legion's signum on the seal; while Cottia and Esca and Cub all greeted each other after their fashion. In the act of breaking the thread he glanced up to see Uncle Aquila stalking towards them.

'Curiosity is one of the privileges of extreme old age,' said Uncle Aquila, towering over the group in the entrance to the colonnade.

Marcus unrolled the crackling papyrus sheet. He was half blind with the dazzle of the day outside and the written words seemed to float in the midst of red and green clouds. 'To Centurion Marcus Flavius Aquila, from Claudius Hieronimianus, Legate of the Sixth Victrix, Greeting,' the letter began. He skimmed the few close lines to the end, then glanced up and met Cottia's wide golden eyes fixed on him. 'Are you a witch out of Thessaly, to draw down the moon in a net of your hair? Or is it only the Other Sight that you have?' he said; and returned to the letter in his hand.

He began to read it a second time, more carefully, taking it in, as he had scarcely been able to do at first, and giving them the gist of it as he went along. 'The Legate has laid that matter before the Senate, and their ruling is as we knew it must be. But he says that "in just recognition of service to the State, which is none the less real that it must remain unpublished ..."' He looked up quickly. 'Esca, you are a Roman citizen.'

Esca was puzzled, almost a little wary. 'I am not sure that I understand. What does it mean?'

It meant so much; rights, and duties. It could even, in a way, mean the cancelling of a clipped ear, for if a man were a Roman citizen, that fact was stronger than the fact that he had been a slave. Esca would find that out, later. Also, in Esca's case, it was his honourable quittance, the wooden foil of a gladiator who had won freedom with honour in the arena; the settlement of all debts. 'It is as though they gave you your wooden foil,' he said; and saw Esca, who had been a gladiator, begin to understand, before he returned again to his letter.

'The Legate says that for the same service, I am to be awarded the gratuity of a time-expired cohort centurion—paid in the old style, part sesterces, part land.' A long pause, and then he began to read word for word. 'Following the established custom, the land-grant will be made over to you here in Britain, as the province of your last military service; but a good friend of mine on the Senate benches writes me that if you so wish, there should be no difficulty in working an exchange for land in Etruria, which I believe is your own country. The official documents will be reaching both of you in due course, but since the wheels of officialdom are notoriously slow, I hope that I may be the first to give you the news. . . .'

He stopped reading. Slowly the hand which held the Legate's letter dropped to his side. He looked round at the faces that crowded him in: Uncle Aquila's wearing the look of someone watching with detached interest the result of an experiment; Esca's face with an alert and waiting look in it; Cottia's, grown all at once very pointed and white; Cub's great head upraised and watchful. Faces. And suddenly, he wanted to escape from them all; even from Cottia, even from Esca. They were part of all his plans and calculations, they belonged to him and he to them, but for this one moment, he wanted to be alone, to realize what had happened without any-one else entering in to complicate it. He turned away from them and stood leaning against the half wall beside the court-yard steps, staring away down the rain-wet garden where the little native daffodils were a myriad points of dancing flame under the wild fruit-trees.

He could go home.

Standing there with the last cold spattering of the shower blowing in his face, he thought ' I can go home,' and saw be-hind his eyes, the long road leading South, the Legion's road, white in the Etruscan sunlight; the farmsteads among their terraced olive-trees, and the wine-darkness of the Apennines beyond. He seemed to catch the resiny, aromatic smell of the pine forests dropping to the shore, and the warm mingling of thyme and rosemary and wild cyclamen that was the sum-mer scent of his own hills. He could go back to all that now, to the hills and the people among whom he had been bred, and for whom he had been so bitterly home-sick, here in the North. But if he did, would there not be another hunger on him all his life? For other scents and sights and sounds; pale and changeful northern skies and the green plover calling?

Suddenly he knew why Uncle Aquila had come back to this country when his years of service were done. All his life he would remember his own hills, sometimes he would remember them with longing; but Britain was his home. That came to him, not as a new thing, but as something so familiar that he wondered why he had not known it before.

Cub thrust a cold muzzle under his hand, and he drew a long breath and turned once again to the others. Uncle Aquila stood still with arms folded and huge head a little bent, looking on with that air of detached interest.

'My congratulations, Marcus,' he said. 'It is by no means everyone for whom my friend Claudius will sweat as he must have sweated to drag justice out of the Senate.'

'I could lay my head on his feet,' Marcus said softly. 'It is a new beginning—a new beginning, Esca.'

'Of course, it will take a little time to work the exchange,' said Uncle Aquila, thoughtfully. 'But I imagine that you should be back in Etruria by autumn.'

'I shall not be going back to Etruria,' Marcus said. 'I shall take up my land here in Britain.' He looked at Cottia. She was standing just as she had stood ever since he began to read the Legate's letter, still and waiting as a winter-bound withy.

'Not Rome, after all; but you did say, "Anywhere", did you not, Cottia sweet,' he said, holding out a hand to her.

She looked at him for an instant, questioningly. Then she smiled, and making a little gesture to gather her mantle as though she were quite prepared to come now, anywhere, anywhere at all, put her hand into his.

'And now I suppose that I shall have to arrange matters with Kaeso,' said Uncle Aquila. 'Jupiter! Why did I never realize how peaceful life was before you came!'

    .   .   .   .   .

That evening, having written to the Legate for both of them, Marcus had wandered up to join his uncle in the watch-tower, while Esca went to arrange about getting the letter sent. He was leaning at the high window, his elbows propped on the sill, his chin in his hands, while behind him Uncle Aquila sat squarely at the writing-table, surrounded by his History of Siege Warfare. The high room held the fading daylight as in a cup, but below in the courtyard the shadows were gathering, and the rolling miles of forest had the softness of smoke, as Marcus looked out over them to the familiar wave-lift of the Downs.

Down country: yes, that was the country for farming. Thyme for bees, and good grazing; maybe even a southern slope that could be terraced for vines. He and Esca, and what little labour they could afford, little enough that would be at first; but they would manage. Farming with free or freed labour would be an experiment, but it had been done before, though not often. Esca had given him a distaste for owning human beings.

' We have been talking it over, Esca and I; and if I have any choice in the matter, I am going to try for land in the Down Country,' he said suddenly, still with his chin in his hands.

' I imagine that you should not have much difficulty in arranging that with the powers that be,' said Uncle Aquila, searching for a mislaid tablet among the orderly litter on his table.

' Uncle Aquila, did you know about this—beforehand, I mean? '

' I knew that Claudius intended bringing your names before the Senate, but whether any result would come of it was quite another matter." He snorted. " Trust the Senate to pay its debts in the old style! Land and sesterces; as much land and as few sesterces as may be; it comes cheaper that way.'

' Also one Roman citizenship,' said Marcus, quickly.

' Which is a thing apart from price, though not costly in the giving,' agreed Uncle Aquila. ' I think they need not have economized on your gratuity.'

Marcus laughed. ' We shall do well enough, Esca and I.'

' I have no doubt of it—always supposing that you do not first starve. You will have to build and stock, remember.'

' Most of the building we can do ourselves; wattle and daub will serve until we grow rich.'

' And what will Cottia think of that? '

' Cottia will be content,' Marcus said.

' Well, you know where to come when you need help.'

'Yes, I know.' Marcus turned from the window. 'If we should need help—really need it, after three bad harvests—I will come.'

'Not until then?'

'Not until then. No.'

Uncle Aquila glared. 'You are impossible! You grow more and more like your father every day!'

'Do I?' Marcus said, with a glint of laughter and hesitated; there were some things that it was never easy to say to the older man. 'Uncle Aquila, you have done so much for Esca and me already. If I had not had you to turn to——'

'Bah!' said Uncle Aquila, still searching for his missing tablet. 'No one else to turn to me. No son of my own to plague me.' He found the tablet at last, and began with delicate precision to smooth the used wax with his quill pen, evidently under the impression that it was the flat end of his stylus. Suddenly he looked up under his brows. 'If you had applied for that exchange, I believe I should have been rather lonely.'

'Did you think I would be away back to Clusium on the first tide?'

'I did not think so, no,' said Uncle Aquila slowly, looking with surprised disgust at the wreck of his quill, and laying it down. 'You have now made me ruin a perfectly good pen and destroy several extremely important notes. I hope you are satisfied . . . No, I did not think so, but until the time came, and the choice was between your hands, I could not be sure.'

'Nor could I,' Marcus said. 'But I am sure now.'

All at once, and seemingly for no particular reason, he was remembering his olive-wood bird. It had seemed to him as the little flames licked through the pyre of birch-bark and dead heather on which he had laid it, that with the childhood treasure, all his old life was burning away. But a new life, a new beginning, had warmed out of the grey ash, for himself, and Esca, and Cottia; perhaps for other people too; even for an unknown downland valley that would one day be a farm.

Somewhere a door slammed, and Esca's step sounded below in the colonnade, accompanied by a clear and merry whistling.

> 'Oh when I joined the Eagles,
>   (As it might be yesterday)
> I kissed a girl at Clusium
> Before I marched away.'

And it came to Marcus suddenly that slaves very seldom whistled. They might sing, if they felt like it or if the rhythm helped their work, but whistling was in some way different; it took a free man to make the sort of noise Esca was making.

Uncle Aquila looked up again from mending the broken pen. 'Oh, by the way. I have a piece of news that may interest you, if you have not heard it already. They are rebuilding Isca Dumnoniorum.'

List of Place-Names

ROMAN BRITAIN

Aquae Sulis	Bath
Are-Cluta	Dumbarton (Cluta is Celtic for the Clyde)
Anderida	Pevensey
Borcovicus	The next station on the Wall to the modern Housesteads
Calleva Atrebatum	Silchester
Chilurnium	On the Wall just north of Corbridge
Deva	Chester
Dubris	Dover
Durinum	Dorchester
Eburacum	York
Glevum	Gloucester
Isca Dumnoniorum	Exeter
Isca Silurium	Caerleon
Luguvallium	Carlisle
Regnum	Chichester
Segedunum	Wallsend
Spinaii, Forest of	Forest which covered a large part of Southern England, of which all that now remains is the New Forest
Caledonia	Highland Scotland; the Celtic name is Albu
Hibernia	Ireland; the Celtic name is Eriu
Valentia	The Roman province between the Northern and Southern Walls—broadly speaking Lowland Scotland

SCOTTISH TRIBAL TERRITORIES

The Selgovae	Dumfries and Ayrshire
The Novantae	Kirkcudbrightshire and Wigtown
The Dumnonii (the same tribe as in Devon)	Ayr, Lanark, Renfrew, Dumbarton and Stirling
The Epidaii	Kintyre and Lorn, and the country round Loch Awe

12.20.10
$32.99
6L

|||

WORK SONG

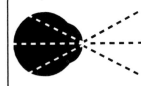

This Large Print Book carries the
Seal of Approval of N.A.V.H.

WORK SONG

IVAN DOIG

THORNDIKE PRESS
A part of Gale, Cengage Learning

GALE
CENGAGE Learning™

Detroit • New York • San Francisco • New Haven, Conn • Waterville, Maine • London

LIBRARY OF CONGRESS CATALOGING-IN-PUBLICATION DATA

Doig, Ivan.
  Work song / by Ivan Doig.
    p. cm. — (Thorndike Press large print basic)
  ISBN-13: 978-1-4104-3252-0
  ISBN-10: 1-4104-3252-1
    1. Single men—Fiction. 2. Miners—Fiction. 3. Butte (Mont.)—Fiction.
  4. Mine rescue work—Fiction. 5. Montana—History—20th
  century—Fiction. 6. Large type books. I. Title.
  PS3604.O415W67 2010b
  813'.6—dc22   2010033731

Published in 2010 by arrangement with Riverhead Books, a member of Penguin Group (USA) Inc.

Printed in the United States of America
1 2 3 4 5 6 7 14 13 12 11 10

*To Carol Doig,
for all the harmony*

1

"Morgan, did you say your name is? Funny things, names." The depot agent, an individual so slow I thought I might have to draw a line on the floor to see him move, was gradually commencing to hunt through the baggage room for my trunk, shipped ahead. "Any relation to old J.P., Mister Moneybags himself?"

I sighed as usual over that. His remark could hardly have been farther from the mark. Nonetheless, I couldn't resist dishing back some of the same.

"Cousins, thrice removed. Can't you tell by looking?"

The railway man laughed more than was necessary. "That's about as removed as it gets, I'd say." Poking into one last cluttered corner, he shook his head. "Well, I'll tell you, Mr. Third Cousin, that trunk of yours took a mind of its own somewhere between there and here. You could put in a claim, if

7

you want."

So much for a storybook *Welcome back!* to the Treasure State, as Montana liked to call itself. While waiting for some sign of life in the agent, I already had been puzzling over the supposed treasure spot in plain view out the depot window — the dominant rise of land, scarred and heaped and gray as grit, which was referred to in everything that I had read as the Richest Hill on Earth, always grandly capitalized. Had I missed something in the printed version? As far as I could see, the fabled mining site appeared rightly christened in only one obvious respect. It was a butte, called Butte.

"You definitely have left me in want." I reacted to the agent's news with honest dismay, equipped with only the battered satchel that accompanied me everywhere. "The bulk of my worldly possessions are in that trunk."

Squinting at me, he tossed aside his agent's cap and donned a businesslike green visor. "Possessions like that do tend to bulk up when the claim form comes out, I'd say." He slipped the pertinent piece of paper onto the counter in front of me, and I filled it out as expected, generous to myself and not the railroad.

The most precipitous chapter of life

always begins before we quite know it is under way. With no belongings to speak of, I gathered what was left of my resolve and stepped outside for my first full look at where I had arrived.

Everything about Butte made a person look twice. My train journey had brought me across the Montana everyone thinks of, mile upon hypnotic mile of rolling prairie with snowcapped peaks in the distance, and here, as sudden and surprising as a lost city of legendary times, was a metropolis of nowhere: nearly a hundred thousand people atop the earth's mineral crown, with nothing else around but the Rocky Mountains and the witnessing sky. The immediate neighborhood on the skirt of land out from the depot, as my gaze sorted it out, seemed to hold every manner of building from shanty to mansion, church to chicken coop, chop suey joint to mattress factory, all mixed together from one topsy-turvy block to the next. Butte stood more erect as the ground rose. In the city center, several blocks on up the slope, lofty buildings hovered here and there waiting for others to catch up, and the streets also took on elevation, climbing the blemished hill until workers' cottages mingled with mines and dump heaps along the top of the namesake butte.

Up there, the long-legged black steel frame-works over the mineshafts populated the skyline like a legion of half-done miniatures of Eiffel's tower.

So, in some ways Butte appeared to me to be the industrial apotheosis of that prover-bial city built upon a hill, and in other aspects the copper mining capital of the world showed no more pattern than a gypsy camp. I have to admit, I felt a catch at the heart at how different the whole thing was from the solitary homesteads and one-room school I had known the last time I tried my luck in this direction. Everything I knew how to part with I'd left behind in a prairie teacherage. But an urge can spin the points of a compass as strongly as the magnetism of ore, and in spite of all that happened back then, here I was once more in that western territory at the very edge of the map of imagination.

While I was busy gazing, a couple of bull-shouldered idlers in the shade of the depot eyed me with too much curiosity; somehow I doubted that they were sizing me up for any family resemblance to J. P. Morgan of Wall Street. With barely a glance their way, I squared my hat and hastened past as though I had an appointment. Which could be construed as the truth of the moment.

The Richest Hill on Earth and I — and, if my hope was right, its riches — were about to become acquainted.

First things first, though. I set out up the tilted city streets in search of lodging. In the business district ahead, proud brick buildings stood several stories above a forest of poles and electrical wires, another novelty I had not encountered in earlier Montana. But the world of 1919 was not that of a decade before in hardly any other way either; the Great War and four years of trenches filled with mud and blood had seen to that.

"Red-hot news, mister? Can't get any newer!" A boy with a newspaper bag as big as he was came darting to my side. I handed him a coin and he scampered off, leaving me with a freshly inked *Butte Daily Post.* The front page could barely hold all the calamitous items there were to post. ATT'Y GENERAL WARNS OF DOMESTIC BOLSHEVIKS . . . BUTTE BREWERY SHUTTERED BY 'DRY' LAW . . . WILSON CAUTIONS AGAINST 'WINNING THE WAR, LOSING THE PEACE' . . . BOSTON POLICE THREATEN TO STRIKE . . . America in that agitated time; not merely a nation, but something like a continental nervous condition.

11

There was little time left in my day for such thoughts: I needed a place for the night. The airy accommodations I could glimpse in the lofty blocks ahead were beyond the reach of my wallet. I dreaded the sort of fleabag hotel that I would have to resort to without my trunk — even the most suspicious hostelry, in my experience, unblinkingly provided a room if the luggage was prosperous enough. While I was studying the lay of the city and trying to divine my best approach, a sign in the bow window of a hillside house with a spacious yard caught my eye.

CUTLETS AND COVERLETS
OR, IF YOU'RE NOT WELSH:
BOARD AND ROOM

Intrigued, I headed directly to the blue-painted front door.

My knock was answered by a woman a good deal younger than I expected a boardinghouse mistress to be. She was compact, in the manner of a dressmaker's form, shapely but with no excess. A substantial braid the color of flax tugged the upper lines of her pleasant face toward quizzical, as though she were being reined by some hand unseen. Whatever proportion of the world

12

had knocked on this door, she seemed freshly inquisitive about a caller such as myself, well-dressed but not well-heeled. Her violet eyes met mine in mutual appraisal. "Madam," I began with a lift of my hat, "I feel the need —"

"I've heard that one before from half the men in Butte. I'm not a madam," she said, cool as custard, "and this is not a house of ill repute. For your information, that's on the next block over." The door began to shut in my face.

"Let me start again," I amended rapidly. "With night overtaking me in a city where I don't know a soul, I feel the need of warm quarters and a solid meal. Your sign appears to offer those."

"Ah, Griff's latest masterpiece. It caught your eye, did it." She peeped around the doorframe to consider the freshly painted words, a lilt coming into her voice. "He'd turn this into Cardiff West if he could. Step on in, please, Mr. — ?"

"Morgan. Morris Morgan."

"Griff will approve, you sound as Welsh as a daffodil." She extended a slender but work-firmed hand, and I noted the less-than-gleaming wedding band on her other one. "Grace Faraday, myself." Appraising the newspaper under my arm and the

13

satchel I was gripping, she paused. "Are those all of your belongings?"

"It's a long story," I said, as if that explained everything.

The upstairs room she showed me was neat and clean, with subdued wallpaper. On the bed was a coverlet of an old style with an embroidered dragon rampant; it would be like sleeping under a flag of Camelot. I can be picky, but I liked everything I had met up with under this roof so far.

As I toggled the switch to make sure the overhead electric bulb worked — another innovation — my landlady-to-be similarly checked me over. "Drummer, are you?"

It took me a moment to recall that the term meant a traveling salesman, one who drums up business. "No, life has given me other rhythms to march to, Mrs. Faraday. My family originally was in the glove trade, until circumstances did that in. I now do books."

"Poetry?" she asked narrowly.

"Ledgers."

"Then you'll appreciate my own bookkeeping, which starts with a week's rent in advance."

"Very wise," I said with composure, although coming up with the sum took nearly every bit I had. Now I really had to hope opportunity of some sort presented itself without delay.

"Welcome to Butte, Mr. Morgan," my new landlady said with a winning smile, complete with dimple, as she pocketed my cash. "Supper's at dark this time of year."

The dining table was laid for four when I came down a few minutes early to scout the premises. There was no wax fruit nor fussy display of doilies on the sideboard, a good sign. Instead, under the blaze of the modest but efficient electrical chandelier, a wedding photograph was propped in the spot of honor. Grace Faraday, even more fresh-faced than now, smiled out as capriciously as if the white of her bridal gown were a field of ermine, while beside her in a suit of approximate fit stood a foursquare fellow I took to be the prominently mentioned Griff. He at least had good taste in women and mustaches, as he wore a full-lipped Rudyard Kipling version not unlike my own.

Just then my hostess popped out of the kitchen with a bowl of boiled potatoes and nodded to where I was to sit, saying, "Make yourself to home, the other pair will be right along. Griff had to stoke the furnace and I told him to go wash up or eat in the street — ah, here's the thundering herd."

15

Through the doorway limped two scrawny half-bald figures that made me think I was seeing double. Both wore work overalls that showed no evidence of work, both held out knobby hands for a shake, and both were grinning at me like leprechauns, or whatever the Welsh equivalent might be.

The nearer one croaked out: "I'm Griff. Welcome to the best diggings in Butte."

"Same here," echoed the other. "I'm Hoop."

Was it humanly possible? I wondered, doing my best not to glance in the direction of the wedding photo during the handshake exchange with the wizened Griff. What manner of marriage could deplete a man from that to this?

With a twinkle, the lady of the house rescued me from my confusion. "These specimens are Wynford Griffith and Maynard Hooper, when no one is looking. They've been part of the furniture here since my husband passed on and I've had to take in boarders." As the duo took their places like old Vikings at a feast, she delivered the sufficient benediction: "We all three could be worse, I suppose."

"I'll try to fit in, Mrs. Faraday."

"Start by saving words and call me Grace, even though this pair of old Galahads

16

refuses to."

"Wouldn't be right, Mrs. Faraday," Griff or Hoop said.

"Manners is manners," said Hoop or Griff.

"I go by Morrie." I dealt myself in, and formalities fell away in favor of knives and forks.

"Didn't I tell you, Hoop?" Griff said as he sawed at his meat. "That new sign works like a charm. What part of Wales do your people hail from, Morrie?"

"Chicago."

"Before they crossed the pond," he persisted.

"Griff, I am sorry to say, the exact family origins are lost in the mists of" — I searched the gazeteer of my mind — "Aberystwyth and Llangollen."

"The grand old names," he proclaimed, adding a spatter of unintelligible syllables that could only have been Welsh. " 'Tis the language of heaven."

"Why nobody talks it on earth," Hoop explained.

By then I was on about my third bite of the meat and ready to ask. "Venison?"

"Close," Grace allowed guardedly. "Antelope."

"Ah." I looked down at the delicate portion. "What a treat to be served cutlets." I emphasized the plural. "Are there seconds?"

She mulled that. "Tonight there are." Off she went to the kitchen stove.

While we awaited replenishment, the history of my tablemates came out. Now retired — "at least the tired part" — the pair had been miners, to hear them tell it, practically since the dawn of Butte. Which was to say, since copper became a gleam in the world's eye. The Hill, as they called it, held the earth's largest known deposit of the ore that wired everything electrical. Much of this I knew, but there was a tang to hearing them recite it with the names of mines such as Orphan Girl and Moonlight and Badger. The crisscross of their conversation about life deep underground was such that I sometimes had to remind myself which was Griffith and which was Hooper. Although they looked enough alike to be brothers, I figured out that they had simply worked together so long in the mineshafts that the stoop of their bodies and other inclinations had made them grow together in resemblance as some old married couples do.

"So, Morrie, you've latched on in life as a bookkeeper, Mrs. Faraday says," Griff was holding forth as Grace appeared with the

18

replenished meat platter, rosettes from the cookstove heat in her attractive cheeks. It was surprising how much more eye-catching she was as the Widow Faraday.

"Except when the books keep me." Both men bobbed quizzically and Grace sent me a glance. Offhand as my comment was, it admitted to more than I probably should have. With rare exceptions, my stints of employment had been eaten away by the acid of boredom, the drip-by-drip sameness of a job causing my mind to yawn and sneak off elsewhere. One boss said I spent more time in the clouds than the Wright brothers ever dreamt of. I had found, though, that I could work with sums while the remainder of my brain went and did what it wanted. "But, yes," I came around to Griff's remark about bookkeeping, "I have a way with numbers, and Butte by all accounts produces plentiful ones. First thing in the morning, I'll offer my services at the office of the mining company, what is its name — Anaconda?"

Forks dropped to plates.

"You're one of those," Grace flamed. Yanking my rent money from her apron pocket, she hurled it to the table, very nearly into the gravy boat. "Leave this house at once, Whoever-You-Are Morgan. I'll not have under my roof a man who wears the copper collar."

"The — ?"

Hooper and Griffith glowered at me. "Anaconda is the right name for company men," Griff growled. "They're snakes."

"But believe me, I —"

"Lowest form of life," Hoop averred.

Enough was enough. Teetering back in my chair as far as I dared, I reached to the switch on the wall and shut off the chandelier, plunging the room into blackness and silence. After a few blank moments, I spoke into the void:

"We are all now in the dark. As I was, about this matter of the Anaconda Company. May we now talk in a manner which will shed some light on the situation?"

I put the chandelier back on, to the other three blinking like wakened owls.

Grace's braid swung as she turned sharply to me. "How on earth, you, can you land into Butte as innocent as a newborn?"

"I have been elsewhere for a number of years," I said patiently. "I knew nothing of this ogre you call Anaconda. To the contrary, I have only seen 'The Richest Hill on Earth' described in the kind of glowing terms the argonauts lavished on the California goldfields in 1849."

Hooper built up a sputter. "That, that's —"

"Hoop, house rules," Grace warned.

"— baloney. The company hogs the whole works. They've turned this town into rich, poor, and poorer."

Griffith furiously took his turn. "Anaconda men sit around up there in the Hennessy Building on their polished —"

"Griff, the rules," came Grace's warning again.

"— rumps, figuring out new ways to rob the workingman. They bust the union, and we build a new one. They bust that, and we try again. Accuse us of being Wobblies, and sic their goons on us."

I looked around the table for the definition. "Wobblies?"

"You really have been off the face of the earth, haven't you," Griff resumed crossly. "The Industrial Workers of the World. They're radical, see, and when they hit town, they tried to edge out our miners' union. The Wobs had their good points, but they riled things up to where the company squashed them and us both."

One chapter spilled over another as Hoop and Grace chorused in on Griff's recital of Butte's story. To hear them tell it, Anaconda was a devilish adversary. The company

21

grudgingly paid good wages when unimaginable millions of dollars flowed in from its near-monopoly on copper, and slashed the miners' pay the instant those profits dipped. Across the past ten years the Hill and the city, I was told, had witnessed a cat's cradle of conflicts among the mineworkers' union, the Wobblies (they were called that, I learned, due to certain members' foreign accents that turned the *double u* sound of "IWW" into *wobble-u*), and the Wall Street–run company. There had been strikes and lockouts. Riots. Dynamitings. The Anaconda Copper Mining Company bringing in goon squads. A lynching, if I understood right, of a suspected IWW labor organizer. And even that was not the worst of the story.

"Then there was the fire." Grace's voice stumbled. "In the Speculator mine two years ago." She drew a breath. "One hundred sixty-four men were killed. My Arthur" — all the eyes in the room, including mine, darted to the wedding picture — "among them."

Griffith and Hooper moved uneasily in their chairs. "We was on the earlier shift," Hoop murmured, "or we'd be pushing up daisies with the rest of them."

In the pause that followed, I sat there before the jury of their faces.

There is something in me that attracts situations, I know there is. Here I was, faced by three people with whom I had spent only forkfuls of time, asked to make one of those choices in life that can dwarf any other. I had to pick a side, right now, or else hit the chandelier switch again and bolt into the night.

I looked around once more at my expectant tablemates. Mentally asking their pardon for what might be called situational loyalty, I made a show of making up my mind.

"The Anaconda Copper Mining Company," I declared, "shall not have my services."

"Now you're talking!" Griff slapped the table resoundingly and Hoop nodded. Grace favored me with a dimple of approval.

"But what am I to do?" I turned out my hands, empty as they were. "I need work with decent pay to it. My funds have been delayed in the course of my journey." If you substituted *trunk* for *funds,* that was perfectly true. Grace's expression changed for the worse at this news.

Griffith looked the length of the table at Hooper.

"Creeping Pete," said Hoop. "Needs a cryer."

"Possible," said Griff. "Too sober?"

"Not for long."

"Righto. Got just the thing for you, Morrie."

2

The C. R. Peterson Modern Mortuary and Funeral Home admitted just enough daylight through leaded windows to let a few sunbeams wander among the casket display as if shopping from heaven. Otherwise, everything in the building was somber as a dead bouquet, and that included Peterson.

"Hmm." His back turned to me, he was leafing through a blackbound ledger that, with professional interest, I tried to peek at. All I could glimpse past his out-thrust elbows were column headings such as *Place of Death, Next of Kin,* and *Payment Due.* "Yes, yes, here they are, Griffith and Hooper, the both of them fully paid up on a 'Miner's Farewell' burial contract, our nicest. Candles and all." He clapped the ledger shut and turned around in creaky fashion. "Sound men, sound judgment. Generally." This last was accompanied by a lidded look that took me in from hat to shoetop.

"I give equal weight to their vouching for you as a possible employer, Mr. Peterson. Your establishment is very, ah, businesslike."

He seemed to brood on that. "Mr. Gorman —"

"Morgan."

"— what would you say recommends you to this line of work?" He swept a hand around the casket display.

You can't just say, *A strong stomach.* I glanced past him to the darkly furnished room that served as the funeral home's chapel, with its waiting bier and an antiquated organ that I could almost tell by looking would wail out notes fit for a Viking pyre. A thought struck me. "My funerary experience is not vast," I admitted, "yet I have been fortunate enough to be an observer at some historically solemn occasions. I happened to witness the funeral procession of Edvard Grieg, to name one."

"In Oslo?" He straightened up like a stork on the alert.

"There under the Scandinavian sky of heroes, with his own music resounding like the heartbeat of the fjords."

"What did they lay him away in?" he whispered.

"Rosewood," came to mind.

"The diamond of woods," Peterson uttered with reverence. "My golly, that casket must have been something pretty to see."

"Unforgettable."

"Hmm." He moved to his desk at such an unctuous pace that I saw where the nickname "Creeping Pete" came from. Picking up a list there, he read off: "*Dempsey, O'Connor, Harrigan* — and that's just this week's deceased. You're hired."

We dickered over the wage and, as we both knew we would, met in the middle. There was a further matter: my attire. Displaying a jacket sleeve nearly worn through at the elbow, I told him my tale of the missing trunk as if it were the loss of a royal wardrobe. "Surely if I am to uphold the name of this establishment, I should be better clothed than circumstances have left me, wouldn't you say?"

Not so much as a *hmm* met that; Peterson apparently took it as a matter of principle that anyone representing the funeral home should be at least as well-dressed as the corpse. He scrawled something on a pad and handed it to me. "Take this over to Gruber the tailor. He'll fix you up."

Tucking the note in my pocket, I turned to go, the vision of a new suit warming me inwardly. "Mr. Morgan," the sepulchral tone

27

stopped me in the doorway. "You have been to Irish wakes before, haven't you?"

I was intimately acquainted with mourning; how many variations could there be? "Uncountable times."

"You start tonight."

"You're gainfully employed? That's not bad for a start." Standing on a chair, Grace took time from feather-dusting the chandelier to nod at me in general approval. "Even if it is when things go 'boo' in the night."

"I am not naturally nocturnal," I admitted, "but that seems to be when wakes take place."

"Just come in quiet, that's the rule of the house." She turned back to brushing at the chandelier with a practiced light touch, its crystals tinkling softly. Turbaned with a towel as she attacked these higher parts of the house, she looked exotic there on her perch, except for the familiarity of the violet gaze whenever she glanced around at me. I watched while she went at the chore, unexpectedly held by her stylish housekeeping. I had intended to go straight to my room and pass the time until lunch relaxing with a book, but the moment would not let loose of me. "You'll get to know the Hill" — Grace's words reached me as if across more distance than was between us — "like it or not."

Rousing myself, I began to say I could blame her prime boarders Hoop and Griff if the job didn't fit, when the floor shook under me, the chandelier crystals rattling as if trying to fly off.

"Jump!" I cried in alarm, my arms out to catch her.

Grace held to where she was, only flashing me a bemused smile. "My, how gallant. It's not an earthquake, if that's what you're thinking. Only dynamite."

Feeling foolish, I toed the floorboards, which seemed to have settled back into place. "What, they're mining here? Right under us?"

"Under every bit of Butte. There are miles and miles of tunnels — Arthur used to say it's like Swiss cheese down there." Her gaze at me had something like a jeweler's appraisal to it now. "Morrie? Do you have a minute?"

"Easily."

She allowed me to help her down from the chair. But as soon as we were settled at the kitchen table, where serious talk is most comfortable, Grace Faraday, landlady, took charge. "There's something you had better know, if you're going to be rooming here

29

for a while." Contemplating me across the oilcloth, she tapped a finger on her cheek as if consulting the dimple. "Besides, you seem the sort who finds out anyway." She inclined her head to indicate the spacious yard that wrapped around the house, then again to include the room we sat in. "The mining company wants to get its hands on this," she confided. "Buy the boardinghouse, that is to say, and tear it down. They send someone around every so often, and I throw hot water at them."

I nearly swooned. "This house is sitting on a copper fortune?"

"Don't we all wish." She clasped her hands in a moment of mock prayer, then crumpled that. "No, it's quite the opposite," she sighed. "Anaconda wants to turn this into a glory hole."

I didn't even have to plead ignorance. Grace took one look at me and laid the matter out:

"A pit, really, but dug from below. If the ore vein they're drilling on happens to head for the surface, they follow it on up. When the ore plays out, it's cheaper for the company to bust through the ground and fence it off than to maintain an empty shaft." She made a wry face. "Glory holes aren't just any old where or we'd fall to

China every time we go across town. The luck of the draw decides when and where Anaconda wants one, the company shysters try to tell me. That's the kind of luck I can do without." She ran her hands up and down her arms, shuddering as she did so. "At first it gave me hives, every time the house shook like that. Right away I'd break out as if I'd been rolling in the nettles." Seeing my reaction, she hurried to say, "Don't be upset, by now it takes more than a little dynamite to make me itch, and this house isn't going away if I can help it. The next time one of those copper collar monkeys comes calling . . ." The towel turban had been slipping toward her worked-up brow throughout this, and now she ripped it off as if it were one more nuisance.

"Grace, let me try to catch up here. Doesn't the mining company offer you a good price? Good heavens, you have what they want, this property. A classic case of supply and demand if I ever heard one, and —"

"That's not Anaconda's way," she set me straight. "They'll only pay the going price for a none-too-new boardinghouse, and that's next to nothing in these times. No, they'd rather set off their blasting every so often to get on my nerves and make me sell.

They don't know my nerves," she said staunchly, hives evidently notwithstanding.

My own nerves still were feeling the quivers of the floor a few minutes before. "I am not an expert on cave-ins, but simply for the sake of speculation: What if they keep dynamiting and digging until a giant hole in the ground becomes a self-fulfilling prophecy, and this house falls in?"

Rather grandly, I thought, Grace shook that off. "The company bigwigs downtown won't let that happen. They don't want a lawsuit even Anaconda could lose."

"Let us hope not. I don't want to sleep in the bottom of a glory hole."

"This place will be as dusty as one if I don't get back to housecleaning." She closed off my concern, only to give me another gauging look before she got up from the table. "I've spilled more to you than I intended to, Morrie. Why do you have that effect? Please, though, don't pass along any of this to Hoop and Griff, promise? I don't want them fretting about whether they're going to have a roof over their old fool heads the rest of their days."

"I shall be a sphinx," I assented.

"I figured you were capable," she said, the dimple adding emphasis.

■ ■ ■ ■

The bantam figures of Hooper and Griffith, each talking into one of my ears, took me around town later that day. Downtown Butte, set into the lower slope of the Hill like the till in a cash register, was as busy as the streets could hold. One moment we had to dodge bowler-hatted Rotarians congregating for luncheon fellowship, and step aside for a covey of nuns the next. The bustling business district was only six or seven blocks long but made up for that size in other ways: amid the shops and stores were saloons (now speakeasies) as big as barns, and every block or so a grandiose hotel or office building stood out, as if bits of Chicago's State Street or New York's Fifth Avenue had been crated up and shipped west. Griff and Hoop took turns pointing out local landmarks: the restaurant where Teddy Roosevelt once ate a steak in plain sight, the theater bar frequented by Charlie Chaplin and other troupers in the prime of vaudeville, and around a corner from other commerce, the red-light district called Venus Alley, said to be the biggest in the West.

What aroused the passion of my tour

guides, however, was the most dominant name in Butte. Passing the *Daily Post* building, where the faint whiff of newspaper ink hung in the air, Hoop spat and said, "Anaconda owns that rag." When I remarked on the architectural preference of brick over stone in so many of the tall office buildings, I was informed the Anaconda Company owned the brickworks. Not to mention — although Hoop and Griff assuredly did — the lumberyard, profiting off the woodframe neighborhoods where the mineworkers lived. Then our stroll brought us to the Hennessy Building, dressier than its neighbors in its terra-cotta trim and window mullions — if buildings could be said to be attired as we are, the Hennessy wore cuff links and a tie pin.

But the pertinent article was escaping my attention, Griff and Hoop had me know, as one or the other profanely attested that this grandest building was where the copper collar was fashioned: the headquarters of the Anaconda Company, up there on the top floor.

My curiosity was tickled. "The copper *collar,* though — why does just that phrase keep coming to your lips and Grace's?"

Hoop looked at Griff. "Might as well let it rip," he said.

"Think so?" said Griff. "Right here?"

"Where better?"

"Righto. Here goes."

There on the sidewalk, Griff squared himself up, took a stance amid the passersby like Caruso among the opera extras, and began to sing in a croaky baritone, to the tune of "The Old Oaken Bucket."

My old copper collar,
It makes my heart so proud.
When I wear the copper collar,
I fit right with the crowd.

No wedding band
Was ever so grand,
So it is always there to see,
The old copper collar,
That Anaconda fastened on me.

Griff finished on a sardonically sweet note that was very nearly a warble. Up in the top floor of the Hennessy Building, someone in a celluloid collar frowned down and the window was shut with a bang.

"The Butte spiritual." Hoop defined Griff's performance for me, and onward we went.

It was when the two of them tramped me

up the streets to the other butte, the rising ground where those long-legged headframes spraddled atop the dozens of mineshafts and piles of tailings spilled down the hillside like gopher diggings, that the two of them truly came into their element. To me, the Hill seemed otherworldly, half mammoth factory, half fathomless wasteland; to my companions, it was home. Their bent backs straightened, and their gait became more spry. The ear-stinging screech of pulleys as ore loads were hoisted from the depths of the earth and elevator cages were let down seemed to reach them as the most melodious of sounds. In accompaniment, Hoop turned suddenly voluble. "We drilled in every corner of this hill, didn't we, Griff. In the Neversweat and the Glengarry and the Parrot and the Nipper and most of these other mines you see. One of us on the steel and the other on the hammer. We was a flash team, if I do say so myself. We'd make the hole in the rock in nothing flat, then set the dynamite, and blooey! Break loose a wall of ore that'd keep a mucking crew busy half a day." In all likelihood it was the effect of Hoop's words, but I thought I felt a tremor in the ground as he spoke. He paused, gazing around at the modern-day mining apparatus. "Now they drill with air."

I took that to mean high-powered compressed-air drills, the throb of giant compressors a steady beat within the industrial medley around the mineshafts.

There is hardly any story more deeply engraved in human experience than a search for the Promised Land, a New Jerusalem where life can flourish and dreams run free. What a saga it was, then, that the barren rise of earth the three of us were standing atop had become such a place, to those unafraid to go into its depths. From what Hoop and Griff had told me the night before, I knew that the Hill's copper diggings, in the course of time and union persistence, had brought forth wages that workingmen anywhere else could only imagine. *Four and a half dollars a day!* my informants chorused with pride, at that time probably equaled only by Henry Ford's assembly line in Detroit. And no man who called himself a miner wanted to bolt fenders onto flivvers for a living. So, dust devils and dump heaps and discolored soil and everything else, the startling land I was gazing at was worshipped by hard-rock miners for its holy wage; in the pits and shafts of the world, the saying was, *"Don't even stop in America, just go to Butte."*

Griff, silent until now, had been watching

the loaded ore cars trundle into view one after another at the Neversweat, a colossus of a mine with seven smokestacks rising from its buildings like a row of stark totems. "Got to hand it to Anaconda," he said grudgingly, "the buggers know how to get the ore out. Looky there, Hoop, they've busted up through the south shaft of the 'Sweat." An obviously fresh fence, its posts unweathered, enclosed a crater so gaping that it looked as if a meteor had struck and blazed on through to the core of the earth. Or at least so deep that anyone who fell in would go to glory, so to speak.

Brows all of a sudden furrowed with thought, my companions exchanged glances. "Morrie," said Hoop, "you maybe ought to know something —"

"— about the boardinghouse," said Griff, and then and there, they chorused the likelihood that in time to come Anaconda would have its greedy eye on Grace's property.

"Don't blab that to Mrs. Faraday," they anxiously cautioned me. "There's no sense worrying her head off beforehand."

"I won't be the bringer of that news," I pledged.

My tour, to hear my guides tell it, now was about to really begin. For there, amid the gray polar wastes of that Richest Hill, were scattered the pockets of populace that I had glimpsed from the train station.

"Here's where the work of the world comes from," Griff pronounced, and Hoop bobbed agreement. Between them, they pointed out each neighborhood. Finntown, straggling below the colossal Neversweat. The Italians, it was stressed to me, occupied Meaderville, not be confused with Centerville, where the Cornish congregated. Griff proudly singled out the smallish Welsh area of St. David's, christened for its church, near our boardinghouse; beyond that, the Serbians had their several blocks, elsewhere the Scandinavians had theirs, and below, at the edge of downtown, lay Chinatown, self-explanatory. My head was beginning to spin, and we had not even come to the sprawl of streets dead ahead, the Irish avalanche of small frame houses and overloaded clotheslines that constituted Dublin Gulch and beyond.

Wisely, Hoop hailed a mailman, and in a brogue that justified his assignment to the route, the postal carrier told me with great elaboration how to find the house of that night's wake.

That job done, Griff proclaimed: "You're all set, Morrie. The only thing to watch out for tonight is —"

Commotion blasted the last of his words away, so sudden and sharp my eardrums winced. The Hill had turned into a calliope, whistles shrieking at every mineshaft. "Change of shifts!" one or the other of my companions yipped as if school had let out.

Those next minutes will never leave me. Down from the mine mouths into the sloping streets cascaded hundreds of workworn men, turning into thousands as we stood watching. The Hill was black with this exodus. Here, on foot, the neighborhoods sluiced together as the miners trudged past, accented English of several kinds mingling with tongues my ear could not readily identify. It was as if Europe had been lifted by, say, the boot heel of Italy and shaken, every toiler from the hard-rock depths tumbling out here. Old habits had followed them across the ocean, husky Finns clustered with other Finns, the Cornishmen not mingling with the Italians, on across the map until each of the nations of Butte came to its own home street.

By now Griff and Hoop were wistfully calling out to fellow Welshmen going by. "Keep fighting for that lost dollar, boys! We're with you all the way, Jared!" This last, I could tell, was addressed to a lean, dark-featured individual at the front of the group, not nearly as far along in years as most of the other miners but plainly a leader. Striding along with a measured tread I identified as military, the younger man grinned through his grime and sent my companions a half wave, half salute.

"What, is there a wage dispute?" I asked in surprise, having heard the hosannas about the riches of the World's Richest Hill.

"There usually is," Griff grumped, Hoop nodding, "but this one's bad. The damn company just told the union it's lopping a whole dollar off the daily wage, can you imagine?" The calculating part of my brain certainly could; a twenty-two percent cut, a severe reversal of the Hill's holy standing. "That's a poke in the eye if there ever was one," Griff was fulminating further. "Jared there and his council are working on how to turn it around, you can bet."

"A strike?" I knew from their earlier recital of labor's struggles that the last time the union leadership called one, the strike had failed when Anaconda's hired thugs broke the spirit of the mineworkers.

"Nobody said that," Griff intoned secretively.

The last of the miners filed past, the next shift went deep underground into the catacombs of copper ore, and we three turned back down the hill toward the brick canyons of streets below. By contrast, the neighborhood I would be coming back to tonight looked made of matchboxes. More than ever I felt like a foreign traveler in the Constantinople of the Rockies. One particular question of the many crowding my mind made its way out first.

"Hoop, Griff, help me to understand something. Why does Peterson, as Scandinavian as they come, pattern his business so strongly here to Dublin Gulch? Hiring me to stand in for him at wakes, for instance."

"Norwegians don't die enough for him to make a living," Hoop imparted. "The Irish, they're another matter."

3

"You're the cryer," simpered the woman, her own eyes red from weeping, who opened the door to me that evening. "I can tell by the cut of your clothes." Truly, I did feel quite distinguished in the olive-brown herringbone worsted suit, vest included, that the tailor had outfitted me with. The boardinghouse trio had assured me I looked freshly spit-shined.

"Ma'am," I began, having learned my lesson in Butte manners of address that first time with Grace, "at this sad time, I wish to convey the deepest sympathy for the loss of your husband, on behalf of the —"

"Ma!" she brayed over her shoulder. "It's the funeral-home fellow, dressed to the gills, come to pay his respects." She all but swept me into the house and steered me toward a tiny elderly woman, attired in the dignity of black and settled in a wicker armchair beside the open casket. "It's my rogue of a father, Lord save his soul, at rest there in the coffin," my escort instructed into my ear as she led me over. "Ma has been expecting you ever so much. Father O'Rourke sent word he can't come tonight, there's a fellow hurt bad at the Neversweat may be needing last rites. So we're awful glad to have a cryer to do the soothing."

This had me blinking. If I was expected to stand in for a priest, I hadn't negotiated wages with Creeping Pete nearly hard enough.

Approaching the shriveled woman perched there on the wicker, I carefully held my hat over the vicinity of my heart and started my recital over. I had made sure with Peterson: I was not expected to actually cry, but a mournful mien, complete with murmurs and respectful remarks toward the deceased, was the order of the night.

"— and you may be assured I speak for Mr. Peterson in offering fullest condolences, Mrs. Dempsey," I concluded the set piece I had memorized.

The widow gazed up at me in her crinkled way, nodded an inch, and broke into a crescendo of sobs.

"There, there, Ma," the daughter consoled but made no other move, "you just cry it out, that's the girl." To me, frozen there as

44

if I had set off a burglar alarm, she hissed: "You'll want to circulate yourself, people will be coming for the next some while."

Shaken by the storm of wailing behind me, I headed for the refuge of the long table where angel food cakes and sliced bread and bologna and a plethora of pickles and preserves and a carnival-glass bowl of tame punch sat. There, I figured, the crowd as it gathered would find its way to me. The thought was the deed. In no time a strapping black-haired man of middle years detached himself from a hushed group that I took to be other Dempsey daughters and their uncomfortable husbands. He came at me like a wind around a corner. "Pat Quinlan," he provided, ready with a handshake. "That's what I like to see, someone with the good sense to wrap himself around the food."

In turn, I told him who I was as he fastened a keen gaze on me. He had the thrust of head I'd noticed in the miners at the change of shift, as if stooping under a mine timber. Facially, he showed the olive skin and conquistador cheekbones that affirmed the tale of Spanish Armada survivors washing up onto the coast of Ireland and contributing to the population.

"Morgan is your handle, is it," he seemed

to taste my name. "Creeping Pete is maybe getting the knack. Last time he sent a scissorbill called George King. How much more English does it get, I ask you?"

"If he had dispatched King George to the occasion, perhaps."

"Sharp as a tack, are we. I like that." With a glint of his own, Quinlan asked, "What brings you to Butte?" His chin came up an inch in the enunciation of that last word, the local habit.

"Reputation." I began to invoke the Richest Hill on Earth, but he cut in with an all-too-knowing grin: "Yours or Butte's? Ah, well, this isn't the time or place to go into that." The widow's wail had settled into a kind of teary drone that still had me flinching, but Quinlan showed no sign it registered on him. Rocking restlessly on his heels, he critically observed the slow traffic of grievers across the room, the men bending a quick knee at the low coffin bench for a muttered Our Father, the women kneeling in earnest to recite Hail Mary. I felt like a heathen, or at least distinctly un-Irish, but my companion at the table clapped me conspiratorially on the shoulder. "Standing around without something that fits the hand, what kind of a wake is this?" Quinlan plucked two glasses from the table. "Here,

46

hold these while I do the needful." Reaching into a pocket of his suitcoat evidently tailored for such an occasion, he brought out a whiskey bottle and began to pour, back and forth, with a heavy hand.

Hastily I asked, "Didn't I read that Montana voted itself dry?"

" 'Dry' doesn't mean 'parched to imbecility.' You could look it up."

"Mr. Quinlan —"

"Quin," he insisted, still pouring.

"Quin, then. I do not normally partake."

"Nobody else does it normal at a wake either."

He corked the bottle and it vanished to its nesting place. "Upsy daisy." Quinlan drank as generously as he poured, while I took a small mouthful that left a sting all the way down. When my eyes cleared, I inquired into the source of the supposedly forbidden liquor. "Bootleg rye." He gestured northerly. "What else is Canada for?"

"You were a close friend of the deceased, Quin?" I asked, to give the whiskey time to settle.

"Scarcely knew him. But a miner stands by another miner, to the last six feet of earth." A moment of brooding came into his dark eyes. Catching me watching this, he resorted to the knowing grin again.

"Drink up, Morgan my man." He set the example. "One swallow is a lonesome bird." As if remembering his manners, he hoisted his glass in salute toward the casket and its occupant. "Tim there knew what thirst is, he was healthy enough in that respect."

"He wore a mighty name," I mentioned, alluding to Jack Dempsey, the heavyweight boxing phenomenon.

"The name was the all. See for yourself — Tim was a shrimp. Add in the bouquets and he's still a lightweight."

"Featherweight, I'd say, the hundred-twenty-pound class." That drew a look from Quinlan. Just then another man with the tilt of a miner came up to us. Like all the others in the room except me, he was in what must have been his church clothes, a tight-fitting suit no doubt worn for both marrying and burying. "Mike McGlashan, meet Morgan, the new cryer," Quinlan did the honors with a flourish of his glass. "Join us in commemorating poor old Tim."

"Never, Quin." McGlashan wagged his head piously. "I'm on the wagon."

Quinlan's expression said he had heard that one before. He produced the bottle again, uncorking it like a magician. "Run that past your smeller and tell me if it's not the scent of heaven."

"Save me from myself, then," McGlashan sighed, covering his eyes and holding out a glass.

During this, the fiery rye splashed into my own glass, and on into me, as Quin and Mc-Glashan gabbed and drank. Inevitably they came around to the lost dollar of wage. With morose acceptance, McGlashan said he and the men on his shift in the Orphan Girl were resigned to waiting it out until the price of copper went back up. That was typical foolishness, Quin said; his shift at the Never-sweat favored a strike if that's what it took. The two argued in the manner of old friends going over customary territory while I took advantage of the food on the table. Conversation and alcohol flowed along in that way until another of those cloudy moments descended on Quin. Gesturing toward the Dublin Gulch neighbors trooping from one black-draped member of the Dempsey female clan to the next with long faces brought out for the occasion, he said in a commanding manner: "This is way too sad, you could cut the air in here like crepe." He reached in another pocket and came out with a small red book. It was about the size of a breviary, but if my eyes and the rye weren't misleading me, musical bars filled its pages. Yet it had none of the binding of a hymnal and I wondered aloud, "What manner of book is that?"

"What's it look like, boyo. It's the Little Red Songbook. Someone slipped it in my lunch bucket the other day, the scoundrels." Quin wetted a thumb and started turning pages. "They know their music, you have to hand them that."

McGlashan snickered. "Evans will think you're a Wob at heart." By then I could glimpse on the crimson cover a drawing of a muscular band of men, sleeves of their work shirts rolled up and arms linked in a chain of solidarity, and the words *Industrial Workers of the World*. The boardinghouse roundelay about Buttes's factions of miners returned to me, and I appraised Quin with fresh interest.

"It wouldn't hurt Jared to look over his shoulder now and then" — he turned aside McGlashan's remark and kept on thumbing through the little book — "but he's stubborn even for a Taffy." I had thought I was the only trace of Welsh amid the wall-to-wall Irish, but now I spotted across the room the soldierly figure whom Hooper and Griffith had called out to on the Hill. "Besides, he's only here with the union tribute." As I watched, the youthful but authoritative miner approached the widow, hat off, and bestowed on her an envelope which from the bulge of it contained a goodly amount of cash. "Are you going to stand there slandering me," Quin was chiding McGlashan now, "or sing? Tim there in the wooden overcoat would appreciate a tune about now, I bet. Ah, here's a nice one," he asserted, crimping open the crimson book to it. "Get Pooch Lampkin over here, he has a voice on him. And Micky O'Fallon, while you're at it."

I ducked away while the musical troops were organizing themselves, not sure my initial night as cryer should be spent in song. Peering over Quinlan's shoulder at the small songbook, the impromptu ensemble squared up and let loose:

Oh Lord of all, of fowl and fish,
Of feast of life, of ev'ry dish;
Observe me on my bended legs,
I'm asking You for ham and eggs.

"They're at it again!" a woman shrieked. "And Father O'Rourke not here to give them what for! Quick, the true music of the faith!" Hastily the opposition vocal force formed up, a number of women in their darkest funereal best and a few older men pinched at the elbow by their wives and conscripted into the choir. Rigid as if they had been called to their feet in church, the bunch of them chorused out:

O'er the sod of God,
O'er the bogs of peat,
Everlasting choirs
Raise a concert sweet!

Undeterred, Quinlan and McGlashan and colleagues soared into their next verse.

And if thou havest custard pies
I'd like, dear Lord, the largest size.

Across the room the choir of the righteous responded in a roar:

Heathendom shall go down,
Though it be everywhere!
God the Father's kingdom
Fills heaven and earth and air!

Sweetly as boys, the Quinlan quartet warbled a last verse:

Oh, hear my cry, almighty Host,
I quite forgot the quail on toast.
Let your kindly heart be stirred
And stuff some oysters in that bird.

"Shame!" cried a particularly broad

woman in black, charging across the room. "My poor uncle, Heaven forgive him, gone on beyond there in the plush box and you singing one of those Red songs. Pat Quinlan, you banshee. May God make your tongue fall out." Over by the door, I saw the young union man cast a rueful look at it all, put his hat on, and slip away from the proceedings.

Quinlan chortled. "Betty, you'd sell tickets to that, wouldn't you. Come have a glass with us, girl."

"I'll girl you, Quin." Nonetheless a glass appeared in her hand. "A taste, if you insist."

"Meet Morgan, the cryer," Quinlan thought to officiate. "He's new to Butte."

"Another pilgrim to the Richest Hill on Earth, have we here?" Betty turned her ample face to me. "Join the long line, Morgan my man." Luckily the bottle made its rounds just then, and while I hid into a gulp from my glass, I noticed that around the room the tone of the wake had lightened into loud conversation and laughter. Centered as I was in the commotion, I apprehensively looked over toward the casket, the item of business I supposedly was here to attend to. The widow seemed to be crying to herself in contentment.

I jumped slightly as Betty fingered the

fabric of my lapel. "My, quite the glad rags Creeping Pete's put you in." With a critical cock of her head, she studied the rest of me. "You look awful learned to be among miners."

"One can never get enough of the school of life," I said with slightly slurred dignity. Tonight was certainly proving that. I had found out that Butte did not sprout shrinking violets.

As if I needed any more proof, Betty batted me on one shoulder and Quinlan on the other. "A man who knows his blarney," Quin commended. "I like that." He aimed his glass at me. "Morgan, a man as cultured as you can't help but have a tune stick to him along the way. Favor us with something, why don't you." The entire crowd around the table loudly seconded that.

"I regret to say, from what I've heard here tonight I'm not equal to the task."

Betty turned indignant. "You don't mean to tell us Creeping Pete's sent a man who can't sing a lick?"

"Really, I —"

"EVERYBODY!" Quinlan let out a shout. "The cryer's going to do us a number! Step on out, Morgan, and show us your tonsils."

I had no choice, and someone gave me a push toward the center of the room besides.

The houseful of people suddenly loomed around me like a crowd at a bullring. Even the widow was wiping her eyes and watching me. My glass half full in one hand, I braced back with the other for some support and found I had put it on the foot of the casket. Inches away, the highly polished toes of the shoes of poor departed Dempsey pointed in the air. Swallowing deeply, I stayed propped there against the coffin wood as if this were the natural spot for the representative of the Peterson Modern Mortuary and Funeral Home, and tried desperately to think of any appropriate snatch of music. What issued forth was as much a surprise to me as to the audience.

I cannot sing the old songs now.
It is not that I deem them low.
'Tis that I can't remember how
They go.

In the silence that met that, I bowed and retreated behind the casket. After long seconds, someone tittered and that loosed a chuckle in someone else, and then the whole crowd gave a collective belly laugh and people pressed in on me, a dozen at once making conversation and clapping me on the back and testifying what an enjoyable wake this was.

It was during this that I realized I was drunk as a gnat in a vat.

The rest of the evening became one long blur of relatives of the man who lay in state beside me and miners telling stories out of an endless supply and black-clad women wanting to know if they couldn't fetch me just a bite more of angel cake, while I concentrated on not tipping over into the casket.

At last everyone wore down, and after a groggy round of farewells and a final whap on the back from Quin, I stepped out into the street and began to make my unsteady way out of Dublin Gulch. The chill air of the Butte night collided with the alcohol in me. The stars were out but, I scolded them, too far to be any help to me. All too soon, I had to skirt the Neversweat glory hole. With the single-mindedness of the inebriated, I crept cautiously past, as if the yawning pit, darker than dark, might empty itself upward over me in an eruption of shadow. Luckily, things were marginally less inky after that. Such splotches of illumination as existed shone from mines that were being worked around the clock, and nearer to downtown I met up with occasional streetlights, so that my route as I wove my way toward the boardinghouse alternated between lit and dim. It fit my condition.

Here is where the mystery begins. I had the eerie sensation that the shadows were following me home from the Hill.

You would think a long walk in shivery weather ought to clear the head of such a phenomenon. The mysterious does not work like that. The more I tottered along, the worse the shivers. Out of the dapple of light and dark behind me, the shadows took shapes as warped as in a bad dream, sometimes huge and foglike, sometimes small and flitting. Like a steady cold breath on the back of the neck, I could feel the darkness changing form. Some small sane part of my mind kept telling me these specters were the distilled and bottled sort, but the corner of my eye was convinced otherwise. A time or two when I suddenly looked back, the shadows nearly became human, then faded into the other patterns of the night. If anyone was there, they were as uncatchable as cats.

Telling myself woozily this was what came of an evening spent in the company of a casket and its contents, I clattered into the boardinghouse and bed.

The morning after, Grace left on the stove

a pot of coffee of a stoutness that would have brought the Light Brigade back to life.

Numb above my shoulders, I sat at the kitchen table and worked cup after cup into myself. I had missed breakfast. The household was well into its day, Hooper in the garden hoeing weeds at a stately pace and Griffith going down the hall with a monkey wrench in hand. Catching sight of me, Griff backtracked and stuck his head in the room.

"How's the crying game going?"

"I can still smell it on my breath."

"Didn't I tell you so?"

"Unfortunately, not quite." How I wished for that moment back, when he was warning me of the one thing to be watched out for at a Dublin Gulch wake and every whistle went off.

Griff waved away silly concern as he limped off. "You'll get used to the elbow-bending. It beats toadying for Anaconda."

I was debating that with myself when Grace bustled in with her shopping basket, fresh from dickering a bargain meat out of the butcher, no doubt.

"Morning, Morrie," she said pleasantly, "what's left of it."

"Short days and long nights are the career of a cryer, I foresee. The coffee was an act of mercy; thank you. Can I help you with those provisions?"

"You had better sit quiet and let your eyeballs heal, I'd say." Putting groceries away, she looked over her shoulder at me curiously. "I've had the good luck never to go to a wake. What was it like?"

I recounted to her what I could remember of the muddled evening. Mostly, the clink of glasses and the clash of singing voices came to mind. At the mention of Quinlan, she bobbed her head. "Quin was a friend of my Arthur, although they didn't see eye to eye on union matters."

"Then there was a Dempsey niece, a rather stout woman named Betty —"

"Betty the bootlegger." Grace had no trouble with the identification. "She knows the right people along the border. Prohibition is the making of her."

I sat wordless, more than ever a novice in the ways of Butte, dumbly considering a mourning occasion fueled with moonlight liquor that redounded to the profit of someone in the family. The C. R. Peterson Modern Mortuary and Funeral Home maybe was in the wrong end of the business.

"Morrie?" Grace closed the cupboard and joined me at the table, settling lightly. Her inquisitive look became pronounced. "I've had a fair number of boarders, besides the palace guard" — Griff could be heard banging in the basement — "but none of them blew in from nowhere quite like you. What was your last place of address, if I may ask?"

"Oh, that. Down Under, as they say."

"Under what?"

"I refer, Grace, to Australia."

"I was teasing. I'm not surprised you have an ocean or so behind you. You have that look."

"It's the mustache."

"My Arthur always said his was the brush hiding the picnic," she reported drily. "Women don't have that disguise."

"Spoken like a high priestess of the plain truth, Rose — I mean Grace."

Before my embarrassment could pool on the table, Grace gave my slip of the tongue the gentlest of treatment. "Whoever she was, was she as pretty as her name?"

"Every bit."

"Maybe it was worth some Down Under, then," she left me with, rising and reaching for her apron. "It's nearly noon, I have a meal to fix or the three of you will have to go in the yard and graze."

Those initial weeks, the job of cryer was an introduction to Butte, definitely, although hardly the one I had sought. Life at the mortuary remained, well, creepy. First of all, there was usually someone dead on the premises, in one room or another. And the wage, while steady enough, was not one of the Hill's swiftest paths to riches; Creeping Pete's ledger was always going to be tipped in his favor, not mine.

What disquieted me more than either of those was that question of shadows. Was it a trick of the darkness and the bootleg rye? The occasional night when I managed to slip away from the conviviality of a Dublin Gulch coffin vigil long enough to dump my drink in the kitchen slop bucket, the shadows on the way home perhaps behaved less like lurking black furies; but they never quite vanished. Something quivers in a person at such times, like a tuning fork set off by phantom touch. You look back along a darkened street that is suddenly limitless and whatever is there keeps eyeing you hungrily. Watching over my shoulder as I zigzagged to the boardinghouse after each wake, I had to wonder whether an old loss was catching up with me. Every footfall, it seemed, brought the thought of my brother and the cold lake waters that took him.

Not all haunting is mere superstition. I'd noticed a certain look in Grace's eyes whenever Griffith and Hooper got going on the evils of Anaconda and the Speculator fire and its perished miners; at such moments Arthur Faraday left his matrimonial picture frame and came to her side, I would have wagered.

One of those suppertimes, as Griff and Hoop hobbled off to their own pursuits, I spoke up as she somberly cleared away the dishes.

"May I be of help?"

She took so long to answer, I wondered if she considered the question hypothetical. But then she looked over with a flicker of interest and said, "You can dry, if you don't have dropsy."

Following her into the kitchen, I took up a dish towel. "As Marco Polo said, I know my way around china. I did dishes at the Palmer House between school terms."

"It seems there is no end to your talents," Grace said with exaggerated wonder, making room for me at the sink. It had been a long while since I settled in side by side with a woman to such a chore. With her braid tucked back and her sleeves rolled up, she was an aproned vision of efficiency at her dishpan task. Still, I could tell something troubled her. I asked, "Have the glory hole grabbers been giving you a bad time again?"

She shook her head. "No, it's not that. It's our anniversary. Arthur's and mine." Slowly washing a plate, she went on: "Seven years ago today we were married. I don't know why this year bothers me so much." She looked cross with herself. "I'm sorry, Morrie, I didn't mean to mope."

"Grief sometimes goes by numbers," I suggested gently. "Seven, that's the copper anniversary."

"I might have known you'd have the answer, you schoolbook." She flicked a few drops of dishwater at me. "I'll simmer down, I promise." By now I was well aware she could also simmer up faster than the law of heat transfer ever predicated, but I was learning to weather that. It seemed worth it for the glimpses of the woman behind the landlady veneer. When something serious was not on her mind, she had the best smile, bright and teasing. That came out again now as she glanced at me and the dimple did sly work. "Let's fish around in you, for a change. Off on a toot again tonight, are you?"

"Grace, it is my job. I seem to recall you being all for it."

"Anyone who runs a boardinghouse needs to be in favor of whatever a lodger does to come up with the rent." That canny glance again. "Within reason."

I smoothed my mustache while I thought that over. I had to admit, presenting myself at a wake most every night made me feel uncomfortably like one of those mechanical statuettes of Death that clank out of a guildhall clock tower at the appointed hour and chase the merrymakers around the cupola. Grace had a point about the reasonableness of that as a lasting occupation. "Life as cryer does have its drawbacks," I conceded to her. "A main one is that I wake up each morning feeling as if my brain were being pickled, gray cell by gray cell."

She prompted: "And while you still have a few to spare?"

"Tomorrow," I said with sudden decision, "I shall find the public library and consult Polk."

Grace paused in her sudsy grapple with the meat platter, puzzled. "Poke who?"

"The Polk city directory." I smiled. "The treasure map to where ledgers are kept."

4

There is an old story that any Londoners with a madman in the family would drop him off at the library of the British Museum for the day. I was given a searching look as if I might be the Butte version when I presented myself at the desk of the public library that next morning and requested both the *R. L. Polk & Co. City Directory* and Julius Caesar's *Gallic Wars* in the original Latin.

The stout woman I took to be the head librarian — she had eyeglasses enchained around her neck commandingly enough for it — scrutinized me some moments more, then marched off into the maze of shelves while I found a seat at a broad oaken table. Everything was substantial, the brass-banistered stairway up to the mezzanine of books in tall rows, the green-shaded electrical lights hanging down from the high ceiling like watch fobs of the gods. I have always

65

felt at home among books, so when the woman from the desk plopped my requested two in front of me, they seemed like old friends dropping by.

Aware that I should get down to business, I nonetheless drew the *Gallic Wars* to me first, unable to resist. I had ordered it up by habit, as a test. To me, a repository of books is not a library without that volume in the mother of languages, but merely a store-house for worn copies of H. Rider Haggard's jungle thrillers and the syrupy novels of Mrs. Mary V. Terhune. No, Caesar's prose that reads like poetry — *Gallia est omnis divisa in partes tres* — is essential in a collection of knowledge, a siren call from Roman words to ours. Handling the book fondly as I was, I became aware of its own touch: tanned leather, not the more common calf-skin cover put on for show. I examined the binding: sewn rather than glued. On the pages, lovely to finger, the sentences practically rose from the paper in a strong clear Caslon typeface. What I was holding was an exceptionally fine copy, so much better than my own that had gone astray with my missing trunk that I momentarily found myself envious of the Butte Public Library.

Just then a drove of schoolchildren came pattering through, herded toward the downstairs by their shushing teacher, evidently to a story hour. Second-graders, I judged, that unhushable age when whispering is as natural as breathing. I felt a pang as the class passed through like a murmur in church. The distance of ten years evaporated, and I swear, for some moments I was back at the Marias Coulee one-room school, my stairstep eight grades there in front of me as intricate and intriguing as a daily circus. And after school, the mental workout of Latin lessons with the keenest pupil a teacher ever had, Paul Milliron. Sitting there, watching this motherly teacher shoo her boys and girls along as they descended the library stairs a whisper at a time, I envied her the job but knew it was too late in the school year for me to even think of such an application. Besides, my credentials were not exactly the standard ones.

Sighing, I patted Caesar and closed him away. Opening the city directory, I began to work my way through the idiom of Polk. There they were as ever, the abbreviated citizens found throughout America, *brklyr, carp, messr, repr,* et cetera. The skills of bricklayers, carpenters, messengers, and repairers were not my own. Nor on subsequent pages could I see myself employed in feather dying, felt mattress manufacture, or fish salting. Dutifully I paged on through, searching for where ledgers that fit my talents might be found. Butte, I discerned, had a modest number of banks for a city of its size; a plenitude of funeral homes; an uninspiring variety of mercantile enterprises; and one Gibraltar of assets, the Anaconda Copper Mining Company. I can't deny, it was tantalizing, that financial colossus which surely needed *bkprs* — bookkeepers — of a certain talent to sluice the riches of the Hill into Anaconda coffers.

Temptation had to vie with distraction, however. Something about the *Gallic Wars* at my elbow kept diverting me. Even when they are closed, some books do not shut up. Why was this beautifully sewn leather edition, a collector's item if I had ever seen one, spending its existence on a public shelf in a none too fastidious mining town? Once more I peered at those tiers on the mezzanine, and if I was not severely mistaken, many other handsome volumes sat there, beckoning, in bindings of royal reds and greens and blues and buffs. Curiosity got the better of me. Up the stairwell I went.

And found myself in a book lover's paradise.

As though some printerly version of Midas had browsed through the shelves, priceless editions of Flaubert and Keats and Tolstoy and Goethe and Melville and Longfellow and countless other luminaries mingled on the shelves with more standard library holdings. I could not resist running my fingers along the handsomely bound spines and tooled letters of the titles. What on earth was the matron at the desk thinking, in scattering these treasures out in the open? Yet the more I looked, the more I met up with the complete works of authors, surely deliberately collected and displayed. Mystified, I was stroking the rare vellum of a Jane Austen title when a loud voice made me jump.

"You look like a bookworm on a spree."

I am of medium height, but when I turned around, I was seeing straight into a white cloud of beard. Considerably above that, a snowy cowlick brushed against furrows of the forehead. In a suit that had gone out of fashion when the last century did, the man frowning down at me had considerable girth at the waist and narrowed at the chest and shoulders; like the terrain around us, he sloped.

Caught by surprise, I had no idea what to make of this apparition confronting me amid the books. The beard was as full as that of Santa Claus, but there was no twinkle of Christmas nor any other spirit of giving in those glacial blue eyes.

Keeping my own voice low, I responded: "Butte is rich in its library holdings, as I assume we both have discovered?"

"Finest collection west of Chicago. Too bad the town doesn't have the brains to match the books," he drawled at full volume. "Quite a reader, are you? Who do you like?"

Appropriately or not, my gaze caught on a lovely marbled copy of *Great Expectations*. "Dickens," I began a whispered confession that could have gone on through legions of names. "There's a person who could think up characters."

"Hah." My partner in conversation reached farther along in the shelves of fiction. "I'll stick with Stevenson, myself." He fondled along the gilt-titled set of volumes from boyish adventure to phantasmagoria of shape-shifting souls. "It takes a Scotchman to know the sides of life." Abruptly he swung around, towering over me again, and demanded loudly: "You like Kipling, or don't you?"

Oh, was I tempted to recite: *'What reader's relief is in store / When the Rudyards cease from kipling / And the Haggards ride no more.'* Instead I put a thumb up and then down, meanwhile murmuring, "His stories are

70

splendid sleight of hand, the poetry is all thumbs."

"Not short of opinion, are you." He fixed a look on me as if he had shrewdly caught me at something. "Saw you down there, pawing at Caesar. English isn't good enough for you?"

"Lux ex libris," I tried to put this absolute stranger in his place, "whatever the language on the page."

"If light comes from books," he drawled back, "how come Woodrow Wilson isn't brighter than he is?"

That stopped me. Was I really expected to debate the intellect of the president of the United States within hearing of everyone in the building?

Just then a couple of elderly ladies entered the Reading Room below, still chattering softly from the street. Frowning so hard the beard seemed to bristle, my companion leaned over the mezzanine railing. "Quiet!" he bellowed.

That legendary pairing, madman and library, seemed to be coming true as I watched. All heads now were turned up toward us, the woman at the desk whipping her eyeglasses on and glowering in our direction. I envisioned arrest for disturbing the literary peace, even if I was barely an accomplice. "Perhaps," I whispered urgently, "we should adjourn to a less public spot, lest the librarian take steps —"

"Ignoramus, I am the librarian." Straightening himself to new white heights of cowlick, he frowned fiercely down at me. "Do you genuinely not know who the hell you're talking to?"

"I remember no introduction," I said coolly.

He waved that off. "Samuel S. Sandison. Come on into my office before you cause any more ruckus, I want to talk to you."

I hesitated before following, but the ravishing books were too much of a lure. Edging through the doorway of his overflowing office at the back of the mezzanine, I made sure that the nameplate on the desk matched what he had told me. Sandison sandwiched himself behind the desk and wordlessly pointed me to a book-stacked chair. I cleared away the pile and gingerly sat. "Mr. Sandison, the books you have here . . ." I hardly had the words. "They're works of art in every way."

"They ought to be." He stroked his beard, as if petting a cat. "A good many of them are mine."

"Yours?"

"Hell yes. From the ranch."

"Ah. The ranch. You were a livestock entrepreneur, I take it? Sheep?"

"Cattle." He delivered me a look that made me want to duck. Well, how was I to know? From the train, Montana expanses appeared to me to be as populous with fleeces as the heavens are with clouds.

Sandison leaned across the mess of his desk as though I might be hard of hearing as well as dim of intellect. "You mean you have never heard of the Triple S ranch?"

"I confess I have not, but I have been in town only a short time."

"It's gone now," he growled. "That's why I'm here. It was the biggest spread in the state; everybody and his brother knew the SSS brand."

"Mmm. By 'brand,' do you mean the practice of searing a mark onto the animal?"

"That's what branding is. It's the Latin and Greek of the prairie."

That startled me. "Intriguing. And so SSS would translate to — ?"

He laughed harshly. "Saddle up, sit tight, and shut up, my riders called it. Most of them stuck with me anyway." An odd glint came to him. "I had an army of them, you know."

"I regret to say, I am not seer enough myself to know the intricacies of reading

73

burnt cowhide." It fell flat with him. "But I am eager to grasp the principle behind alphabetizing one's cows —"

"It's not alphabetical, fool. Brandabetical."

"— excellent word! The brandabetical concept, then. Do you start with the full lingual entity, in this case 'saddle up, sit tight, and shut up,' and condense from there?"

"Hell no," he let out, and immediately after that, "but you're right in a way. SSS stood for Seymour-Stanwood-Sandison. I had to have backers in the ranch operation. Money men." Those last two words he practically spat. Eyeing me as though I were guilty by association, he drawled: "I saw you with your nose stuck in Polk. I suppose you're another refined hobo who heard about the Hill and came here to make a killing."

"A living, I had in mind."

"Hah. You packing around any education worth the description?"

"The Oxford variety."

He looked at me skeptically.

"I bootstrapped my way through."

"Another shoeleather philosopher," he grumbled. "The Wobblies were full of them; they must empty out the bughouse into

Butte every so often."

"I see my little joke did not catch on. Actually, I did work my way through an institution of higher learning — the University of Chicago."

He tugged at his beard. "In other words," he said as if it might be my epitaph, "all you know anything about comes from books."

I bridled. "That is hardly a fair assessment of —"

"Never mind. You're hired."

"You are mistaken, I haven't even made up my mind where to — here?"

"Here is where the books are, ninny."

5

"Sam Sandison? He's meaner than the devil's half brother. If you're gonna be around him, you better watch your sweet —"

"The rules, Griff."

"— step, is all I was gonna say, Mrs. Faraday." Griffith speared a potato and passed the dish onward to me, along with a gimlet gaze. "You must have hit him when he was hard up for help, Morrie. He don't hire just anybody."

"I was as taken by surprise as the rest of you appear to be." Announcement of my sudden employment at the library had set my suppermates back in their chairs, for some reason that I could not decipher. "What can you tell me of my new lord and master? None of you were so bashful about the business practices of the Anaconda Company." The gravy boat came my way, but nothing else of substance from any of the threesome. "For a start, Griff, what exactly is the meaning of 'meaner than the devil's half brother' in regard to Samuel Sandison?"

"He's one of the old bucks of the country, tougher than" — cutting strenuously at the piece of meat on his plate, Griff glanced in Grace's direction and hedged off — "rawhide. Had a ranch they say you couldn't see to the end of. I don't just know where. You, Hoop?"

Hooper gestured vaguely west. "Someplace out there in scatteration."

"Employing, he told me, a veritable army of cowboys — but I would imagine any livestock enterprise of that size needed a rugged crew and a firm hand?"

"You're lucky he's only bossing books around anymore," was the only answer from Griff. Vigorously chewing, he turned toward the head of the table. "Heck of a meal, Mrs. Faraday."

I sampled the stringy meat and sent an inquiring look. "Not chicken."

Grace shook her head.

"Rabbit, then."

"My, you do know your way around food," she remarked, a compliment or not I couldn't tell. It occurred to me how much I was going to miss the tablefuls at wakes.

■ ■ ■ ■

Taking leave of the C. R. Peterson Modern Mortuary and Funeral Home took some doing.

"As I have been trying to say, Mr. Peterson, I am sorry —"

"But you're the most popular cryer I've had in ages." He himself appeared ready to weep.

"— to have to give notice, but another opportunity has presented itself."

He cast a mournful look at the ledger. "One of our busiest times since St. Patrick's Day."

"I am sure an equally qualified cryer will be called forth by the need."

"There'll always be an opening here for you," he said feelingly, the lids of the caskets standing at attention behind him.

That was the end of being chased every night by shadows. Yet something lurked from that experience, the sensation of being trailed through life by things less than visible. I tried telling myself Butte after dark simply was feverishly restless, what with the thirst of thousands of miners built up in the hot underground tunnels being assuaged in speakeasies, and desire of another kind busily paying its dues in Venus Alley — practically nightly, Grace turned away some lit-up Lothario seeking a house of the other sort. In that city of thin air and deep disquiets, wasn't it to be expected that even shadows would have the fidgets? It is surprising how persuasive you can be when talking into your own ear.

So, I set out from the boardinghouse that first morning with a sense of hope singing in me as always at the start of a new venture. Samuel Sandison had instructed me to present myself at the library before it opened at nine, and I knew he did not mean a minute later. When I approached the rather fanciful gray granite Gothic building on the central street called Broadway — modesty seemed to have no place in Butte — I saw a cluster of people outside the front door and was heartened by this sight of an eager citizenry lined up to get at the literary holdings.

In their midst, however, loomed Sandison, and bringing up the rear was unmistakably the Reading Room matron, looking sour. The group proved to be the entire library staff, all the way to janitor. Sandison was counting heads before letting anyone through the arched doorway — the same mode of management, I was to learn, he had used on his cowboys each morning at the horse corral.

He took notice of my presence with a vague gesture. "This is Morgan, everybody. He'll be puttering around the place from now on."

I filed in with the rest of the staff, happily conscious of the palatial grandeur, the Tuscan red wainscoting, the dark oaken beams set against the ceiling panels of white and gold, the all-seeing portrait of Shakespeare above the Reading Room doorway. And beyond, the regal reds and greens and gilts of those books of Sandison's collection, the best of their kind anywhere.

But no sooner were we in the building than he cut me out of the herd, and, just as adroitly, the matron of the Reading Room. "Miss Runyon will show you the ropes," Sandison provided with another of those gestures that might mean anything. "Come on up when she's had her fill of you," he dismissed us and mounted the stairs to his office.

Miss Runyon and I considered each other.

"What foolishness has he put you in charge of?" she demanded, as though she had caught me trespassing.

"That seems yet to be determined."

"That man." Her voice had a startling deep timbre, as if the words resounded in her second chin. "He runs this place to suit himself. The trustees would never have named him librarian but for those precious books of his." Clapping her chained eyeglasses onto her formidable nose, she directed: "Come along, you had better know the catalogue system."

Miss Runyon kept me in tow as we circumnavigated the Reading Room, her realm and her orb, her temple and her fortress, she let me know in every manner possible. I took note of the goodly assortment of dictionaries and cyclopedias, and the respectable selection of magazines and the newspapers racked on spine sticks, all of it recited to me as if I were a blind man in a museum. One oddity, though, she paid no attention to; conspicuously paid it no heed, if I was not mistaken. It was a display case, glassed over, taking up one corner of the room. My mild inquiry about it brought:

"Pfft, that. The boys' dollhouse."

Naturally that increased my curiosity and I went over to it, Miss Runyon clopping after me. Encased there, with plentiful nose smudges and handprints on the glass testifying to the popularity of its viewing, sat an entire miniature mine. It looked so amazingly complete, I half expected it to bring up teaspoonfuls of earth from under the library. Headframe, machine house, elevator shafts, tunnels, tiny tracks and ore cars, the entirety was a Lilliputian working model. With disdain Miss Runyon told me the diorama had been built for a court case over a mining claim and afterward donated to the library. "He" — her eyes swept upward toward Sandison's office — "insists it sit here in the way. It's a nuisance to keep clean."

"Wonders often are," I murmured, still taken with the remarkable model of the workings of the Hill.

"Now, then," Miss Runyon said haughtily, "is that enough of an initiation into librarianship for you?"

"The most thorough, Miss Runyon, since my introduction to the Reading Room of the British Museum."

I seemed to have invoked the Vatican to a Mother Superior. "You, you have actually been — ?"

"Under that great domed ceiling, with its delicate blue and accents of gold, with every word ever written in English at one's beck and call," I dreamily sketched aloud, "yes, I confess I have. And would you believe, Miss Runyon, the very day I walked in, my reader's ticket in my hand, the seat of destiny was vacant."

"The seat of — ?"

"Seat number three, right there in the first great semicircle of desks." I leaned confidingly close to her. "Where Karl Marx sat, those years when he was writing *Das Kapital.* I will tell you, Miss Runyon, sitting in that seat, I could feel the collective knowledge, like music under the skin, of all libraries from Alexandria onward."

With a last blink at me, Miss Runyon retreated to her desk and duty.

When I went up to Sandison's office, I found him standing at its cathedral-like window, trying to peek out at the weather through an eyelet of whorled clear glass. "Damned stained glass," he grumbled. "What do the nitwits think a window is for?" He rotated around to me. His old-fashioned black suit was as mussed as if he had flung it on in the dark, and instead of shoes he wore scuffed cowboy boots that added still more inches to his height. "The downstairs dragon show you every mouse hole, did she?"

"Quite an educational tour. What I am wondering, Mr. Sandison —"

"Hold it right there." He held up a rough

hand as he moved to his oversize desk chair and deposited himself in it heavily. "When somebody calls me that, I feel like I'm around a banker or lawyer or some other pickpocket."

To escape that category, I asked, "Then what form of address am I to use?"

He looked across his desk at me conspiratorially. "I'll tell you what. Call me Sandy. The only other person I let do that is my wife." He chortled like a boy pleased with a new prank. "It'll drive that old bat Runyon loco."

"Sandy, then," I tried it on for size, none too comfortably. "What I need to know is the scope of my job."

"I suppose." Rubbing his beard, he gazed around the cluttered room as if some task for me might be hiding behind one of the piles of books. "Morgan" — there was a dip of doubt in his tone as he spoke it — "how are you at juggling?"

"Three balls in the air at once is a skill that persists from boyhood," I answered cautiously, "but when it comes to ninepins —"

"No, no — the calendar, oaf, the calendar." Irritably he pawed around in the pieces of paper that carpeted his desk and finally came up with that item. "People always want to use this damn place, they need a room to hold this meeting or that, you'd think a library was a big beehive. Myself, I don't see why they can't just check out a couple of books and go home and read. But no, they bunch up and want to cram in here and talk the ears off one another half the night." He squinted as if drawing a bead on the offenders penciled in on various dates. "The Shakespeare Society. The Theosophists. The Ladies' and Gentlemen's Literary and Social Circle. The League of Nations Advocates. The Jabberwockians. The Gilbert and Sullivan Libretto Study Group. And that's hardly the half of them, wanting some damn night of their own to come in here and take up space. They've all got to be juggled."

"I think I can tend to that, Mr. —"

He shot me a warning glance.

"— Sandy."

There may have been a cunning smile within the beard. The librarian of Butte, for everything that entailed, settled more deeply into his chair. "I figured if you're a man who knows his books, you can deal with the literary types who come out when the moon is full." He passed the much-scrawled-upon calendar to me. "They're all yours now, Morgan," said Samuel Sandison with that intonation I came to know so well.

Looking back, that exchange set a telling pattern. You would think, with two persons in one cloistered office, for he had me clear a work space for myself in a corner, that he might sooner or later call me Morrie. Yet that familiar form of address never passed his lips. Each time and every time, he would either preface or conclude what passed for conversation between us with a drawled *Morgan?* even when it wasn't a question. As if it were my first name.

As if he knew.

Morgan Llewellyn. *That* is my rightful name. Yes, *that* famous breed of Llewellyn. I know I carry only a minor share of its renown in the world, but reflected glory is still glory of a sort. It was my brother, Casper, who reigned as lightweight boxing champion of the world, "Capper" Llewellyn in the inch-high headlines every time he won by another knockout. And I was his "genius" of a manager.

Even yet he causes me to lie awake, when the mind tussles with itself before sleep comes, thinking of how life paired us so peculiarly. Casper was magical, if confidence and prowess count as magic. Even as a boy, he had the cocky outlook that nothing was out of the reach of a good left hook, and my role as older brother often amounted to fishing him out of trouble. Which perhaps made it inevitable, when he was matriculating as a boxer in Chicago's West Side fight clubs and I was graduating from the university, that he insisted I become his manager. He did not possess my brains and I did not have his brawn, he pointed out all too accurately, so we had better join onto one another as if we were Siamese, in his words. Casper could be exasperating, but in the ring he was a thing of beauty, a Parthenon statue of a perfect athlete sprung to life, and I have to say, I felt somewhat wizardly in fashioning his boxing career for him. Carefully I chose opponents who would build his record, alternating his bouts between the easy fighters called "cousins" and the tougher ones we stropped Casper's skills on. It became only a matter of time until the name Casper Llewellyn would be on the card of a title fight.

Now the other tussle in the mind's nightly shadows. Rose, delightful maddening Rose.

Along the way, he and she met, a wink served its purpose, and they fell for each other like the proverbial ton of bricks. Brother-in-law was added to my responsibilities. At first I was wary of Rose as an adventuress — why don't I just say it: a gold digger — but soon enough saw that she and my brother were a genuine matching of hearts. Pert and attractive, whimsical and ever whistling, she was a sunny addition to the Llewellyn name. Luck seemed to have found us, as Casper's purses for winning grew and grew, and when he became the lightweight champion, we felt we had truly hit the jackpot. The three of us grew accustomed to high living. Somewhat too high. Rose never saw a satin dress and a saucy hat to go with it that did not appeal to her, while Casper threw money around as if it were going out of style. And I have to admit, money does not stick to me, either. That's why a large supply seemed such a good idea.

It was one of those situations you know you ought not to get into, but do: the pugilistic science, the fight game, the glove trade, boxing in all its guises was uncommonly good to us, yet income did not nearly keep up with outgo. So, it was Casper's brainstorm to throw the fight with the challenger, Ned Wolger. Rose and I might not have listened to him but for the odds on his side — he was a three-to-one favorite to wallop Wolger. That walloping could simply be postponed, as he put it, until the inevitable rematch. In the meantime, all we had to do was put our money on Wolger, spreading those bets around out of town so as not to attract suspicion. Rose and I saw to that, and in the last round of the title match, Casper, shall we say, resigned from the fight. And we collected hand over fist. Too much so. The Chicago gambling mob turned murderous about the amount it had lost on an apparent sure thing.

That part haunts me to this minute: Lake Michigan, blue as sword steel beside the city, and the gamblers seizing Casper and making an example of him, in the infamous fate called "a walk off the dock."

Before they could lay hands on us, Rose and I fled together. Not with the money, alas, which was consigned forever to a biscuit tin wherever Casper had stashed it; he never did trust banks. Left on our own, with the gambling mob ever on our mind if not on our trail, she and I took shelter in Minneapolis, where she had been in household service. Minneapolis was still too close to Chicago for comfort. Then a propitious ad we had placed in Montana newspapers brought Rose a job as housekeeper for a widower and his three sons, and like so many seekers of a new life, we boarded a train for the homestead country of the West.

Events took their own willful course after that. We posed as brother and sister, but in the aloneness of prairie lodgings the two of us became man and woman in the flesh, so to speak.

Only for a season, it turned out. I lost her, fair and square, to the widower, Oliver Milliron, a good man and friend. His eldest son, Paul, was astute in other matters besides Latin, and it was he who drew from me the pledge to mean it when I gave away Rose at the wedding and to never return to Marias Coulee, and the vicinity of temptation. It has not been easily kept. No day since have I not thought of Rose.

"Morrie? Morrie, anyone home between your ears? I asked: How was your day at the library?"

"Sorry, Grace. My thoughts were elsewhere."

"Miles away, I'd say. White meat or dark?" She was majestically carving off slice after slice of turkey, a surprise feast to the other three of us at the supper table. "I hope it's not as hard on the nerves as standing over a corpse every night. Wakes would give me the willies."

"Oddly enough, the library is somewhat more solemn, in a way. May I ask what the occasion is, with this festive bird?"

"The price is down, always to be celebrated." Dishing out judicious servings of turkey, she returned to that other topic: "Just what is it you do all day there in Sandison's stronghold, besides keep the books company?"

An apt question, not easily answered. Day by day, besides my juggling act with the meetings schedule, it had been gruffly suggested to me that I organize the disorganized subscription list of magazines and newspapers, find someone to fix the drinking fountain, deal with Miss Runyon's complaints about squeaky wheels on book carts passing through her sanctum, respond to a stack of letters from people with the kinds of questions only a library can answer — in short, I was tasked with anything Sandison did not want to do, which was very nearly everything.

"This, that, and the other," I replied to Grace honestly enough. "If the library can be thought of as the kitchen of knowledge, I seem to be the short-order cook."

Griff and Hoop were saying nothing. She gave them an exasperated look and sat down at her place. Almost immediately, Griff gasped and straightened up sharply. I had the impression Grace's foot may have given his shin a tap. More than a tap. "I was about to say," he rushed the words, "you getting along hunky-dory with Sandison?"

"We are on" — first-name basis did not quite cover the situation — "what might be called familiar terms. I call him Sandy."

"Heard him called a lot, but never that."

This seemed to bring a sense of relief around the table. Hoop came to life. "Might have plenty of library customers pretty soon, Morrie. Mornings anyway. There's strike talk. We was at the union meeting last night —"

"I could tell," Grace inserted. "I heard you come in." As I unavoidably had, too.

Griff stiffened again, apparently of his own accord this time. "Refreshments are in order after a business session," he maintained, prim as if the pair of them hadn't reeled in around midnight, bumping the furniture and misjudging the stairs.

"Anyhow," Hoop sped past the spree after the meeting, "there's talk that the union might go out if the snakes won't give on the lost dollar." Even I knew that would be something like a declaration of war.

"And bring in more goons and strike-breakers," Grace underscored that, "like the last several times?"

"Those yellow-bellied buggers got on

everybody's nerves a little too much the last time," Griff said, wielding a fork as if fending off such invaders. "The other unions didn't like the way we was treated, they might be next. Evans and his council have made the rounds, they're not as hot in the head as the last fellows were, and they've got most everybody ready to side with us. Even the streetcar drivers. Shut down the whole town this time, we could, if the mine strike gets called." He summed up magisterially, "Things could work out just fine, if them others don't stick their noses in and make trouble."

Grace, I noticed, looked as if strike talk was the kind of thing that gave her hives. Trying to keep up with the nuances of Butte, I asked, "Those others are . . . ?"

"The Wobblies," said Hoop. "Who else?"

"They'd just love to see a strike get out of hand," Griff laid it out for me. "The more blood in the streets, the better they figure it is for them. The Wobs would turn this into Russia if they could." All at once the crimson cover of the jolly Little Red Songbook made more sense to me.

"They aren't the only ones who can play it cute, though." Griff still was wound up, his fork punctuating his words. "Thanks to them, Evans has got Anaconda looking at its hole card in the negotiations about getting the dollar back. It'd rather deal with him than the IWW any day."

"The meek shall inherit, if they are clever enough about it," I mused aloud.

"That sounds like something that shook out of a library book."

"I was merely complimenting the union's strategy at the table, Griff. I am not taking sides on the issue of a strike."

Grace was. She reached to the turkey platter and plucked up the wishbone. "See this, you pair of busybodies?" *Snap,* and she brandished the wish-fulfilling piece of the bone at the supposedly retired miners. "There, now, I've asked that you not get your old fool heads broken on a picket line."

"Aw, Mrs. Faraday, it maybe won't come to that." Griff sounded as if he was trying to convince himself along with her.

Something Hoop had said stuck with me, and I turned to him. "If the men do go on strike, why would any of them frequent the library just mornings?"

"Speakeasies don't open until noon."

In mythology, Atlas alone has the world on his shoulders, but in real life the globe of concerns rests on each of us at any given time. After that suppertime discussion, what weighed on me when I settled into bed as usual with a lovingly done book from the library — *The Education of Henry Adams,* in this instance — was the gravity of the times. The immeasurable shadow of the 1914–1918 war still lay over the affairs of nations; Europe's old jealously held boundaries were being torn up and rewritten, for better or worse, at the Paris peace conference. Russia already had shaken the political firmament by doing away with the Czar and yielding to the new fist of the Bolsheviks. America's habit of throwing a fit to ward off contagion was at high pitch; activists with a leftist tinge were being hounded by government agents, even jailed or deported. Alongside that, the laboring class started at a deep disadvantage whenever it challenged the masters of capital. Strikes were its only effective tool, the way things were, but the powers that be resisted those with force if necessary. It added up to a jittery period of history, did it not? I knew enough of life to understand that every era has a set of afflictions, yet 1919 seemed to be a double dose. The pages in front of me, stylishly written, did little to dispel such heavy thoughts. Henry Adams, descendant of two presidents and with as much blue blood in his veins as there is in America, confessed at length in his autobiographical *Education* to a life contradictorily adrift on oceans of ignorance. Adams had not lived to see the turbulent aftermath of the Great War, but even so he professed little hope of ever finding "a world that sensitive and timid natures could regard without a shudder."

I closed the book on that sentence. There was no point in reading about timid natures in Butte.

The education of Morris Morgan had a new chapter waiting the next day. It began in the Reading Room, where I was poring over the subscription list with Smithers, the young librarian on the periodicals desk, to see how we might squeeze more magazines into the budget we had. I felt a tap on the shoulder and turned around to an angular woman dressed in old-fashioned style, gray and gaunt as a duchess in a Goya etching. "You are the person," she enunciated to me so loudly and clearly that every head in the room snapped up from reading, "in charge of evening groups, I believe? I wish to speak with you."

I looked hopefully toward the mezzanine, but for once, Sandison was not on hand to roar "Quiet!" at the offender. Peculiar characters are drawn to a library like bees to a flower garden, so I turned to this one with the most authoritative air I could, and, indicating I was nearly finished with what I was at, murmured, "If you'll wait in the foyer, ma'am, I'll be with you in just a minute."

"Hsst!" The warning hiss from Smithers came a little late. In an ingratiating tone, he was saying: "How are you today, Mrs. Sandison?"

"Ah. Actually, we can finish this later," I told Smithers, and quickly ushered the visiting personage into the mineralogy section, the nearest room not in use.

Now that we had privacy, Dora Sandison paused to study me, which did not take her long. Even her eyes were gray, and they were the sort that did not miss a trick. She was as tall as her husband, and acted taller. I had heard the library staff refer to the Sandisons as the grandee and the grandora, and could understand why. "I regret taking you away from your other task," she said, her expression indicating nothing of the sort. "However, the evening group of which I am a member has a most pressing need."

"I'm sorry to hear that," I responded warily, trying to imagine which of the clubs that met in the basement auditorium would attract such a personality. The Theosophists, to unravel the mysteries of the Divinity? The League of Nations supporters, to correct the habits of governments?

She surprised me with a conspiratorial smile. "We require music stands."

"Music — ?"

"The Gilbert and Sullivan Libretto Study Group is not provided with music stands, if you can believe that."

"I see." A sense of caution grew in me. "Surely this is the kind of request that your husband has dealt with, up until now?"

"Oh, horsefeathers," she brushed away my concern. "You know how Sandy is about such things."

Now I really did see. I could just about recite what Sandison's response to a request solely on behalf of Gilbert and Sullivan aficionados would have been. *"Don't they have hands? Holding a piece of sheet music in front of their noses shouldn't strain them too much."*

"My husband, bless his soul," she went on in a confiding tone, "sometimes carries matters too far. He takes the ridiculous view that answering the needs of a group I coincidentally am a member of would constitute preferential treatment, can you imagine?"

I chuckled nervously. "There is the point,

Mrs. Sandison, that no other group has seen the need for such, um, equipment."

She snorted, very much like Sandison himself. "That is their failing rather than ours, then," she instructed me with a glint in her eye that wouldn't be argued with. "We sorely lack such equipment, as you call it, to hold our libretto sheets when the member whose turn it is takes our group through the intricacies of the lyrics of the chosen operetta. For example, *'Strike the concertina's melancholy string! Blow the spirit-stirring harp like anything! Let the piano's martial blast rouse the echoes of the past!'* " During this demonstration she waved her arms in my face as vigorously as a semaphore flagger.

She paused and caught her breath. "You can surely understand," she said as if I'd better, "the presenter needs to be free to gesture, or the spirit of Gilbert and Sullivan is lost."

Sometimes it is wise to bend before the gale. "I'll see what can be done about music stands."

She smiled slyly again. "I'm so glad Sandy put a reasonable person in charge of such matters."

With that, Dora Sandison departed in as grand a fashion as she had arrived, and I was left with the equipment problem. I searched the building high and low, but the marvelous holdings of the Butte Public Library did not include music stands. Somehow a purchase would have to be made, and I groaned at what was ahead of me, knowing how tight Sandison was with a dollar when the purchase of anything other than a book was involved.

"Sandy? If I could have a minute of your time?" Grumpily he left off reading a rare books catalogue and creaked around in his desk chair to face me. "Spit it out, Morgan."

"We have a request from an evening group for some freestanding smallish reading racks to hold the sheets of paper they work from, and —"

"Hah. You've been hearing from the Giblet and Mulligan Society about those damn music stands. My wife is in that group, and I've told her the same thing I'll tell you: the library can't show favoritism to any one bunch."

"Naturally not. But those rather modest implements would be of use to other groups as well."

"What for? Don't they have —"

"— they do have hands, but there are occasions when they would welcome some

100

kind of device to hold certain items." I groped for some sort of example. "The Ladies' and Gentlemen's Literary and Social Circle, for instance, when they wish to have photo displays to go with their discussion of the works of Robert Louis Stevenson. The mystical castle in Edinburgh." My fingers conjured that citadel in the air. "The sinister backstreets of London where Jekyll transmogrifies into Hyde." I turned my hands into claws and made a grotesque face.

Sandison watched my little performance incredulously. "That's what goes on with that la-de-da bunch? Dry-goods clerks and young women afraid they'll be old maids sit there and actually follow Stevenson's stories from scene to scene?"

"Stranger things have happened," I said, true as far as it went.

He smacked a hand to his desktop, a sound like a shot. "That's genius for you. What a writer." I was given the kind of look a cowboy probably received for coming late to the corral. "Why didn't you tell me this before, Morgan? Go on over to Simonetti's music store and buy the things." He jerked open his bottom drawer, dug into the small strongbox that held petty cash, and handed me some money. I waited for him to jot down the sum or have me sign for it or however he handled a disbursement, but he simply waved me out of his sight and went back to pawing through the list of books he craved.

Out on the street in the freshness of the day, and having survived both Sandisons, I sauntered along with snatches of song in me; Gilbert and Sullivan can do that to you. The Montana weather for once was as perfect as could be, sunshine slanting between the tall buildings, checkerboarding the busy street, passersby in their downtown clothes brightening or dimming according to warmth or shade. The street tableau of shoppers and strollers seemed removed from talk of a strike, even though the Hill and its clashes were never far off. The day was so fine I tried to put such thoughts away and simply enjoy being out on my errand.

Emerging from the music store with my arms full of music stands I felt like an itinerant choirmaster, but Butte apparently saw stranger sights every day and no one paid me much attention. I was passing a haberdashery when my own eye was caught by the window display. An Arrow collar mannequin was admiring itself in a mirror; I could do without the collar, but draped on the mannequin torso was an exemplary suit

— blue serge, librarianly. I stopped to admire the cut and material, smiling to myself as I thought of something Casper would say when about to commit an extravagance: *"How's a guy ever going to be rich if he doesn't practice at it?"* Riches were still eluding me — I needed to do something about that at some point — but my library wages were adding up a trifle, and that suit beckoned, come payday.

Turning to go, I glimpsed past the mannequin into the mirror and froze in my tracks. In the reflection, I could see across the street, half a block down, to where two bulky figures were assiduously studying the plate-glass display of a pet store. They were not the type to be in the market for parakeets.

Window men.

I would know the species anywhere, but in Chicago they had been rife enough to be a civic nuisance. Private detectives spying on lovers who happened to be married to other people. Pinkerton operatives lurking on some mission. Plainclothes policemen trying to keep an eye on the mob, or mobsters trying to get something on the police. Sometimes it seemed every Chicagoan was trailed by another, half a block behind. And whenever the one in front paused to tie a shoelace or buy a newspaper, the one trailing had to evince sudden interest in the nearest store window. The duo in the mirror — why should I rate two? — still were rapt over pets.

As I committed their sizable outlines to memory, another mental image was jostled: these two together were a near fit to the worst of those shadows that had followed me from wakes. But that was too much imagination. Wasn't it?

Casually as I could manage, I walked back to the library, the music stands feeling like an armful of lightning rods with a storm on the horizon. When I reached the big front door, I opened it slowly so that I could see behind me in the glass. The window men were gone, naturally.

That evening after supper, I knocked on Griffith's door.

The shuffle of carpet slippers, then the door flung open and Griff stood there in his long underwear and workpants, like a watchman roused by an out-of-place noise in the night. "What's up, Morrie?" Down at his side, in his right hand, something sharp glinted. "Need a new notch in your belt?"

For the second time that day, my feet felt planted in quicksand. "I didn't mean to intrude, I'll come back another —"

"Naw, step on in." The pointed instrument cut a circle in the air as he indicated a table and chair crammed into the far corner of the room. "Fixing Grace's purse strap for her." Ushering me in, he went on over and put down the awl he was holding, atop the leatherwork. "Guest gets the chair." He perched on the edge of his bed, toes of his slippers barely reaching the floor. "What's on your mind? You look spooked."

"This will sound silly, but I think I'm being followed around town."

Griff perused me, his wrinkles wrinkling even more. "Let's get Hoop in on this." He banged the heel of his fist on the wall, and shortly Hooper came in, bringing his own chair.

I described to them that morning's experience, and the unlikelihood that the two idlers were pet fanciers. "Keep this to yourselves, please. I don't wish to worry Grace about this."

"Or have her kick you out of here on your can," Hoop said.

"Well put."

Griff hopped off the bed, went to the window, and pulled down the blind. "Tell me this," he intoned, turning to me. "When you lit down from the train, was there a

105

couple of bruisers hanging around?"

"Big and bigger," Hoop specified.

"Beefier than ordinary, yes, now that you say so, there was such a pair at the depot."

"That's them," Griff said. "Anaconda's goons. The one big enough to eat soup off the top of your head is Typhoon Tolliver."

I felt as if the seat of my chair had just pinched me.

Hoop was saying, "Jim Jeffries flattened him —"

"— in the second round of the title bout, right hook to the jaw," I finished for him. "What on earth is he doing in Butte?"

"Beating people up," Griff had no trouble answering that. "The Anaconda Company don't play pattycake."

"But —" Some questions scare off words. Why was I a candidate for a beating from an ex-heavyweight pug?

Hooper answered that without it being asked. "That bunch in the Hennessy Building sics the goons on any union organizers who come in from the outside." He and Griff looked at me critically.

I shook my head.

"Especially anybody working for the Wobblies," Griff prompted.

I shook my head harder.

"Somebody who'd lay low until the right

time," said Hoop.

"Then stir things up like poking a hornets' nest," said Griff.

"Anaconda don't like that kind of thing," Hoop added.

Another shake of my head, as much to clear it as anything else. "I am not any kind of an organizer, believe me. I simply came here to get ri— to find decent work." Both old men watched me mutely. "The goons, as you call them, are wasting their time on me."

One or the other of my listeners, like ancients who had heard it all before, spoke up. "You better hope they get tired of it."

The next day was Sunday, day of rest for the library, but not for the boardinghouse. Scarcely was I seated for breakfast, wondering where the others were, when Grace forged out of the kitchen all but wrapped in a tie-around apron over a nice dark dress. Along with my plate of sidepork and eggs, she delivered with a flourish:

"I wondered if you might like to go to church."

"Church." I hadn't meant for it to come out quite like that, but it sounded as though I was trying to identify the concept.

Hooper came through the doorway, also

dressed in surprising Sunday best and smelling of musky cologne. "What this is, Griff's filling in with the choir. They're hard up."

"Ah. And bringing his own audience, insofar as it can be conscripted?"

"He'll be in much better voice if he sees us there, he happened to mention," Grace coaxed with a nice example of a Sunday smile.

"He can stand all that kind of help he can get," Hoop chipped in.

I put up my hands. "I know when I'm outnumbered." Obligation takes strange shapes. Back in Casper's earliest bouts, I had mastered the tactic myself of "papering the house," as it was called, by giving away tickets by the handful if necessary to fill the seats of the arena. If Griffith dreamed of a sellout crowd for his star turn with the choir, I understood intrinsically.

The snug redbrick church with its peaked hat of cupola looked as if it had been smuggled in from a vale in Wales, and no sooner had Grace and I and Hooper slid into seats at the back of the congregation than the creased little minister, peering over half-moon eyeglasses like a veteran counter of crowds, nodded to himself and launched into prayer. In Welsh. Evidently Grace had not anticipated this any more than I had, both of us trying to keep a straight face at not understanding a word of what plainly was going to be an hour of many hundreds of words. Actually, some time into the minister's spate my ear figured out the repeated invoking of "Iesu Grist," and I sat there caught up in the wayward notion of Christ as grist, the mills of faith grinding fine the belief in a clear-eyed savior at that moment across half the world. Sunday certainties, which left only the rest of the week.

The praying rolled on like thunder until the minister reached a final crescendo of syllables that sounded like *tragwyddoldeb!*

"Eternity!" Hoop translated to the other two of us in a hoarse whisper, and that was definitively that.

"Welcome, all ye, the accustomed and the new faces." The surprise lilt of English from the minister sent Grace and me melting toward each other in relief. Not much taller than his pulpit, the elderly man of faith again peered around the church as if counting the house, this time shook his head instead of nodding, and declared: "A sufficiency will be heard from me soon enough. Let us get on with the singing." With that, the male choir filed up, all in severe black suits and blinding starched white shirts, two dozen strong, Griff at one end, proud as a parrot. Church or not, he sought out the three of us with a broad wink, welcoming us to the occasion he plainly saw as the Welsh Miners' Choir of Butte, starring Wynford Griffith.

The choir director, burliest of the bunch, stepped from the ranks, gave a steady bass hum, which was picked up by the others in a communal drone that seemed to vibrate the building. Then, as if in one glorious voice the size of an ocean's surf, they swept into hymn after hymn. I sat there enchanted, Grace swaying gently next to me. Music makes me almost willing to believe in heaven.

Then, though, came a chorus I could have done without.

> Were I to cherish earthly riches,
> They are swift and fleet of wing;
> A heart pure and virtuous,
> Riches and eternal gain will bring.

There is that about the Welsh: they can sing their way under your skin, to the bones of your being. I needed no reminding that riches, in what pursuit I had given them, had proved to be elusively swift and winged. Yet why did a Richest Hill on Earth and its supposed opportunities exist, if not to be tapped? Was I really supposed to count my gains in life only afterward, in the time of *tragwyddoldeb?* Eternity did not seem much of a payoff if you had to scrimp to get there.

My spell of brooding broke off when the old minister, frail as a leaf after the gusts of the choir, ascended to the pulpit once more.

" 'Tis no sense to maunder about, when but one thing is on every mind." He gazed severely over the settled moons of his glasses. "There is talk of a strike in the mines, is there not?" The rustle of the congregation answered that.

"I have had my say any number of times before," the ministerial voice sounded weary, "on the stopping of work and the negotiating of wages. The two seem as bound together in this town as the two sides of a coin." Aha! Not even the man of the cloth could set aside the propensity for earthly gain. Perhaps I was imagining, but his own choir seemed to be looking at him as though he had just caught up with a main fact of life. "The shepherd does not leave his flock, even when it may have wool over its eyes," he went on drily. "If the mines do shut down, the church shall again have a strike committee. We'll again gather food and clothing for the families left bereft. Depend on that." He paused, drawing on the silence. "A word of caution, however. If you men do go out" — he looked out over the stooped miners' shoulders that filled half the church — "or you women march in their support" — a similar gaze to the upturned faces of the wives — "as you have been known to do, walk the line of the law very carefully. The times are not good. The sedition laws that came with the war are not fine-grained as to whether a person is the Kaiser in disguise or a Bolshevik with a bomb under his coattails or an honest miner seeking honest pay. Some of you had a taste of that last time, when I had to go down to the jail and bail you out for the hitherto unknown crime of 'unlawful assembly.' " Reaching in over his glasses, he pinched the bridge of his nose as if to shut off that memory. "The church coffer is no longer sufficient for bail," the words came slowly now, "nor can we keep contributing to legal defense funds. This time around, it will all be up to your union. You can help its cause and your own by being mindful of that pernicious statute until wiser heads can change it. Otherwise, Butte's finest, to call them that" — it was well known that Butte policemen were Irish, and not the Dublin Gulch ore-shoveling type — "will pick you off like ripe apples. For now," his voice rose, "render therefore unto Caesar the things which are Caesar's."

I squirmed at that. I perfectly well knew it to be a biblical parable, but it was not Caesar up there in the Hennessy Building, pulling strings attached to the police department.

The minister took off his spectacles, folded them, and seemed to shake his head at himself. "Let us return to the singing."

As we walked out after the service, Grace pursed a look at me as if to see what I thought. "My Arthur used to say there are those who make a scarecrow of the law." I thought it best not to say Arthur had read some Shakespeare along the way. Directly ahead of us, Hoop and Griff were stumping along, sleeve cuffs flying as they dissected the sermon. Watching them, Grace said soberly: "The union is going to have its hands full, isn't it."

There was no knowing how these things come about, but somehow that Sunday spate of Welsh sermonizing and song rinsed away the window men. The way was clear, to and from the library, the next day and the next and those after that, and while I habitually peeked over my shoulder for figures lurking half a block behind, they were notable only for their absence. It was as I indeed hoped, I could tell myself: the goons or their bosses saw me for what I was, a glorified library clerk sauntering meek and mild to church, and were wasting no further time on me.

Which was a lucky thing, because I was falling in love with the Butte Public Library. Walking up to it each fresh morning, its Gothic turret like the drawbridge tower into the castle, I warmed to the treasures within those softly gray granite walls. Sandison standing there at the top of the steps counting us off as if checking his herd came to seem patriarchal rather than high-handed. The staff softened toward me — with the exception of Miss Runyon — as I picked up stray tasks that they wanted to dodge. The nooks and crannies and grandiosities of the old building intrigued me, like an ancient mansion labyrinth leading back to Gutenberg's printing press and the start of everything, and always, always, there were the lovely classic books tucked away here and there for stolen snatches of reading. Down any aisle, Stendhal or Blake or Wharton or Cather or Shakespeare or Homer or any of

114

the Russians waited to share words with me, their classic sentences in richly inked typefaces as if rising from the paper. I suppose the best way to say it is that the library's book collection, courtesy of that snow-topped figure with the Triple S initials, was the kind I would have had myself if I were rich.

In short, work of this sort fit me from head to toe. I could even put up with sharing office space with Sandison, as his chain-lightning moods kept a person alert. The old saying had his name on it: he may have been hard to get along with, but harder to get along without.

The library ran on one principle: Samuel S. Sandison was next to God. Whether above or below, opinions varied. His style of administration was as effective as it was unpredictable. For hours on end he would stay holed up in the office, apparently oblivious to anything happening elsewhere in the building. Then without warning he would barge out of his lair and prowl from floor to floor, wearing the expression of a man who took pleasure in kicking puppies. The result was an amazing library: the staff was on its toes every second, and its offerings were, of course, first-rate. I have to say, the man responsible for all this was not exactly an officemate easy on the nerves. The only mirth Sandison showed was when he spotted a bargain book in some catalogue of rarities and he would let out a *"Heh!"* and smile beneath his wreath of beard. Mostly, being around him was like having the Grand Inquisitor grading one's homework.

"Goldsmith," he characteristically would snap over his shoulder from where he was enthroned in his desk chair, and I had mere seconds to figure out whether he meant for me to trot across town to the dealer in fine metals or commence a conversation about the poet of England's peasantry.

Guessing, I recited: " *'Ill fares the land, to hastening ills a prey / Where wealth accumulates, and men decay.'* Rather daring for his day, wouldn't you say, Sandy?"

"Romantic twaddle about how nice it was to live in huts, I'd call those elegies of his."

"That's too dry a reading of him," I protested. "He had a wicked wit. Who else would have said of Garrick that onstage he was wonderfully simple and natural, it was only when he was off that he was acting?"

That brought a snort. "Doesn't mean old Goldilocks could tell a hoe from a hole in the ground. Robert Louis Stevenson, now, he knew his stuff about how life really is." And with that, Oliver Goldsmith, or whom-

116

ever, would be consigned to the vast second rank and remain unbought.

"Morgan?" The dubious drawl that met me this particular day told me I was in for another assignment of the Sandison sort. "You started something with those music stands. Now Miss Runyon claims she can't function unless she has a corkboard on a tripod to pin pictures on for the kids' story hour. Go down there and see what you can rig up."

As I was passing his desk, he looked askance at me over one of the catalogues of rare books that were perpetually open in front of him. "Oxford flannel?"

"Serge." I brushed a bit of lint off the new blue suit. "Like it?"

"You look like an undertaker."

Down the stairs I went, past Miss Runyon's cold eye, to the spacious meeting room all the way in the basement. The basement had originally been intended as an armory, and its thick walls made it a fine auditorium, no sounds escaping to the outside. You could about hear the spirited echoes of the Shakespeareans and the philosophical ones of the Theosophists lingering amid the pale plaster foliage of the scrollwork around the top of the walls. A curtained stage presided across one end of the room, and at the other stood a spacious supply cabinet. I was rooting around in the cabinet for anything resembling corkboard and a tripod when I heard the entry door swish closed in back of me.

I glanced over my shoulder and there the two of them were, big and bigger.

"Look at him, Ty." The one who was merely big had a pointed face with eyes that bulged like those of an eel, probably from so much time spent planted in front of store windows peering sideways. "In that prissy suit, you'd almost think he's the real item, wouldn't you."

The response from the figure half a head taller than him clip-clopped in at a heavy pace: "If we wasn't smart enough to know he's up to something, yeah."

The lesser goon was alarming enough, but Typhoon Tolliver I knew to be made of muscle, gristle, and menace. In the boxing ring his roundhouse blows stirred a breeze in the first rows of seats — hence his nickname — and had he been quicker in either the feet or the head, he might have become an earlier Jack Dempsey. As it was, his career of pounding and being pounded made him no more than a punching bag that other heavyweights needed to get past on the way to a championship bout. His flattened features and oxlike blink were the kind of thing I had been afraid would happen to Casper, another reason behind cashing in on our fixed fight and the intention to steer the ring career of Capper Llewellyn into early retirement after he regained the title. Trying not to stare at Tolliver and his ponderous bulk, I brushed my hands of my cabinet task and managed to utter:

"The business of the library is conducted upstairs, gentlemen. If you would follow me —"

My break for the door was cut off by Eel Eyes, barring my way with a coarse left hand that justified the Latin *sinister*. "We like it down here," he said lazily. "Nice and private, we can have a talk." He sized me up with a tilt of his head. "Let's start with what brings a fancy number like you to Butte. You slipped into town real easy, didn't you, no baggage or nothing."

That threw me. "Just because the railroad lost my —"

"You're pretty slick," Eel Eyes gave me credit I did not want. "But you can't pull the wool over Ty and me. We get paid good dough to be on the lookout for wise guys like you. Some gold-plated talker who just shows up out of nowhere," his tone was mocking, "if you know the sort. And sure enough, you no sooner hit town and that Red songbook starts doing its stuff at those burying parties. Then you latch on at this joint, where all kinds of crackpots come out at night. It all adds up to one thing, don't you think, chum?"

This was a nightmare. "I can explain every one of those —"

"I bet you can, fancy-pants." He leered at me. "After what happened to the last organizer for that Red pack of Wobblies, you have to come sneaking into town all innocent-like, don't you. You can maybe fool those stupid miners up on the Hill, but Ty and me got you pegged."

"One of them outside infiltrators, yeah." Tolliver's belated utterance unnerved me a great deal more than anything from the other goon. His conversation came off the top of his head and out his mouth seemingly without passing through his brain. It was as if he had speaking apparatus on the outside of his head, like English plumbing.

"I am a denomination of one," I protested hotly, "employed by no one but this library, whose gainful work you are keeping me from. Now if you will accompany me upstairs, I can lead you to someone who will set you straight about —"

Typhoon Tolliver took a flatfooted step

and planted himself in front of me. "You look like somebody, under that face spinach. Ain't we met somewhere?"

"Surely I would recall such a mishap."

"Don't get smart on us." He loomed in on me. "You been somewhere I been, I just know it. Chicago, how about?"

Here was where family resemblance was a danger. I looked like my brother, whose face had appeared on boxing posters on every brick wall in that city. Maximum as my mustache was, it amounted to thin disguise if someone concentrated hard enough on the countenance underneath to come up with the name Llewellyn. Goons do business with other goons, and this pair would not waste a minute in transacting me to the Chicago gambling mob. Which meant I was a goner, if Tolliver's slow mental gears managed to produce the recognition he was working at.

I snapped my fingers. "Aha! The World's Fair, of course! The African native village and the big-eyed boys that we were." Wiggling my eyebrows suggestively, I took a chance and leaned right into the meaty face. "The bare-breasted women of the tribe, remember?"

Tolliver blushed furiously. "Every kid in Chi was there looking."

"We know of two, don't we, although the passage of the years has dimmed my recollection of you more than yours of me."

"Yeah, well, sure, what do you expect, a mug like yours —"

"Knock it off, both of you." The one with those aquarium eyes moved in on me. "Let's try another angle on what kind of four-flusher you really are. What did you do in the war?"

"I was elsewhere."

"Like where?"

"Tasmania."

"Say it in English when you're talking to us," Tolliver warned.

"It's in Australia, stupe," the other one rasped. "And you weren't in any rush to come back and enlist, is that it? You look like a quitter if I ever saw one. No wonder this country is full up with pinkoes and —"

"Infiltrators," Tolliver recited mechanically.

"— and stray cats from half the world and —" The lesser thug's yammering broke off and he eyed me suspiciously. "What're you cocking your head like that for?"

"Just listening for the clink of your own medals."

You find concern for reputation in strange places. The pointy face reddened to the same tint Tolliver's had. "I kept the peace here at home."

"I can imagine."

"Hey, punk, a smart aleck like you can end up in a glory hole if you don't watch your —"

Swish, and then *bang!* All three of us jumped.

Samuel Sandison towered in the doorway, the flung-open door still quivering on its hinges behind him. "What's this? The idlers' club in session?"

All at once there was more breathing room around me, both goons stepping back from the perimeter of authority Sandison seemed to bring with him. What was I seeing? He was twice their age, and though of a size with Tolliver, no physical match. Yet the two burly interlopers now looked very much like spooked schoolboys. Why the white-faced wariness all of a sudden?

Sandison's ice-blue gaze swept over them and onto me, and I blinked innocently back. "We're only here because this helper of yours is up to something," the pointy-faced one was saying, not quite stammering, "and the people we work for need to know what he's —"

"Quiet!" Sandison boomed, the word resounding in the enclosed room. "You tell them on the top floor of the Hennessy Building that they maybe run everything else in town, but not this library. Clear out of here, and I mean now."

The pair cleared out, but not without glares over their beefy shoulders at me.

Now all I faced was the stormcloud of beard. Sandison inspected me as if having missed some major feature until then. "Miss Runyon told me you were taking an unconscionably long time down here. Morgan? Are you up to something?"

"Sandy, I swear to you, I am an utter stranger to the battles of Butte." That left Chicago out of it.

He shook his head. "If you weren't such a bookman, I wouldn't have you on the payroll for more than a minute." Turning to go, he said, as if he was ordering me to head off a stampede: "Get the damn corkboard rigged up so we don't have to hear any more from that old heifer Runyon about it."

I picked at my food that suppertime, drawing a look of concern from Grace. "More turkey, Morrie? It's not like you to be off your feed."

Down the table, two sets of bushy gray eyebrows squinched in similar regard of me. Neither Hoop nor Griff asked anything about my disturbing day, however, in respect of our pact not to bother Grace's head about the goons' interest in me. Pushing away my plate, I alibied: "A touch of stomach disorder, is all. Nothing a restful evening in my room can't fix, I'm sure."

Upstairs, flat on my back atop the dragon coverlet while I stared at the ceiling and waited for inspiration of some sort to show up, I never felt less sure of fixing anything. The zigzags of life were more puzzling than ever. There I lay, in the most comfortable circumstances I had known for a long while, with work that nicely employed my mind, and the goons of the world were sure I was a secret operative for the most radical wing of the laboring class. It was dizzying. If America was a melting pot, Butte seemed to be its boiling point. The Richest Hill was turning out to be also a Cemetery Ridge of copper to be fought over, and some trick of fate had dumped Morris Morgan — all right, Morgan Llewellyn — right in the middle of it. Not the spot I thought I was choosing when I stepped down from that train.

A train runs in both directions, the ceiling reminded me, as boardinghouse ceilings tend to do. Lying there looking up at the map of plaster imaginings, I felt an old restlessness. It was a lamplit evening in the Marias Coulee teacherage, when I knew I was losing Rose, that a faint stain in the beaverboard ceiling seemed to suggest the outline of Australia. Even here in Grace Faraday's well-maintained accommodations, did that swirl in the plasterer's finish-work over by the window resemble South America?

Fate comes looking for us, often when we are most alone. Stealthily the conclusion I was waiting for crept down from the ceiling and took shape in the corner of the room. My gaze followed it to my satchel, shabby reliable companion in a portable life.

I swore softly to myself. Ordinarily I do not use profanity, but that was the least of what had been fanned up in me by the bluster from Eel Eyes and Typhoon Tolliver. Bouncing off the bed, in a hurry of resolve now, I crossed to where the satchel waited. Grappled it open wide. Dug to the bottom of it, past spare socks and the poetry of Matthew Arnold, to where they lay.

Brass knuckles. The "Chicago pinky ring," weapon of choice for the streetwise combatant facing an unfair fight.

It had been years since I needed to resort to these, but they never aged. As I tried them on now, they fit across the backs of my hands cold and secure. Even the most vicious street fighter had to hesitate at the dark sheen of armor on a fist, the set of nubs that could gouge into skin like a can opener. Of course, knuckles of metal did you any good only within striking range of an opponent. But I had sparred enough as a warm-up partner for Casper in training camp; I knew at least as much footwork as that lummox Tolliver. And unless I had lost the knack of sizing up an adversary, the more mouthy goon was the type who would blink hard at the sight of brass knuckles. He would not rush to have that well-shaven pointy face marred to the bone.

Quitter, he'd called me. We'd see.

Wouldn't you know, no sooner was I prepared to put my fortified knuckles on the line against Anaconda's lurkers than they ceased lurking. Even when I deliberately dawdled on downtown streets, passing the time of day with the blind newspaper seller or picking up the latest gossip from the hack driver at the nearby hotel, I could not draw the goons out. As the days lengthened, their cloak of shadow shrank, further discouraging any encounters. Fondling the brass knuckles in my suitcoat pocket as I went to and from the library, it was as if I were rubbing amulets that kept away evil spirits. Although I knew the real force that had stopped the goons cold in their tracks was Samuel Sandison, whatever that was about.

As for me, the lord and master of the books kept me hopping. It was a mystery how the Butte Public Library had managed to operate before I was there to catch all the tasks delegated from that kingly desk of his to mine.

This particular Friday had started as usual, with Sandison drawling, "You know what needs doing, or at least should," and disappearing off to somewhere undisclosed, while I faced tabulating the week's checkout slips sent up from the issue desk. He was a demon promoter of the library and wanted the list of current favorite books unfailingly in the newspaper at the end of each week. It was not an inspiring task, as the most popular book of the past seven days invariably turned out to be Mrs. Mary V. Terhune's *My Little Love,* and I sometimes had to adjust the arithmetic to get Thomas Hardy and Edith Wharton onto the list at all; Proust of course was hopeless. So, by the time I fiddled with the citizenry's literary taste to more or less satisfaction, the messenger would be there waiting to rush my compilation to the *Daily Post.* Messengers raced across Butte, jumping on and off the trolleys and trotting the edge of the sidewalks as they carried typed instructions back and forth between the downtown headquarters and the mine offices, workers' cashed paychecks from stores to banks, small goods from the department store to the wealthier homes, and so on. Our stretch of street was served by a gnomelike courier named Skinner. Old enough to be thoroughly bald, Skinner nonetheless had the pared build of a jockey and was never motionless, on one foot and then the other as he waited to be handed whatever was to be delivered. I had learned to let him jitter there in the doorway; the man apparently was not constructed to sit in a chair.

I was nearly done typing up that week's list from Miss Runyon's checkout slips when Skinner, waiting restlessly as usual, blurted:

"Where you from, pal?"

"Mmm? Chicago."

"Small world. Me, too." I stiffened. "Maxwell Street and Halsted, know it?" he said from the side of his mouth, sending a deeper chill through me. The toughest neighborhood of the toughest section of that hardknuckled city. Was this going to be a repeat of Tolliver and Eel Eyes? Another message of the threatening sort from the Anaconda Company? Panic began to set in as I realized I was in my shirtsleeves, with my suitcoat — and its protective cargo of brass knuckles — on a hanger across the room. A disturbing look on him, the wiry man now bounced toward me on fleet feet as I grabbed for an inkwell, anything, in self-defense. Practically atop my desk as he leaned in face-to-face with me, Skinner demanded:

"Cubs or White Sox?"

I relaxed somewhat; baseball rivalry was not necessarily lethal. But it is surprising how an old grudge can hold up. In a ring constructed over the infield of the White Sox stadium, Comiskey Park, Casper on a cool clear Columbus Day had defeated Kid Agnelli — knockout, third round — before twenty-five thousand paying customers, and the owner of the White Sox and the ballpark, Charles Comiskey, had shorted us on the purse. Not for nothing was he known in Chicago sporting circles as Cheap Charlie. I would root against him and his team if they were the last baseball nine on earth. "My allegiance is to the Cubs," I put it more temperately to Skinner. "I once saw Tinker to Evers to Chance produce four double plays in one game. Masterful."

Skinner hooted. "The Cubs ain't what they used to be. The Sox got the real players these days, they're going to the Series, you watch."

"I shall." Sealing the book list in a gummed envelope, I handed it to him indicatively. "Now, do you suppose this missive could possibly find its way to the *Daily Post*?"

No sooner had the messenger scampered off than Sandison filled the doorway. Bypassing his desk, he lumbered over to the stained-glass window and peered out through one of the whorls like a boy at a knothole, a sign that something was on his mind. Something on his desk that he did not want to face.

"Sandy, you seem perturbed," I said diplomatically.

"I've just been with the trustees. They raked me over the coals about the library budget. Wanted to know where every damn penny goes." Turning from the window, he shook his head, the wool of his beard quivering. "They have a reason, I suppose. Few months ago, the city treasurer took off with everything he could lay his hands on."

"Bad?"

"Enough that the elected fools downtown see an embezzler under every bed now.

131

Damn it, I thought it was hard to keep track of a few thousand cows — that was nothing compared to running this outfit." He passed a hefty hand over his cowlick as if trying to clear his head from there on in. "Spending that much time on numbers drives me up the wall. I don't see why the idiot trustees can't just trust a man."

I remember it exactly. Opportunity was in the air of that office, distinct as ozone. Idly piling paperwork from here to there, I said as though his bookkeeping burden were merely something I could add to the other stacks on my desk: "Thank heaven you have an arithmetical person on hand."

"Who?" Sandison eyed me. "You? You mean you can handle books that don't have mile-long words in them?"

"Assuredly."

"Are you telling me you're a certified accountant?"

"Mmm, *certified* perhaps is too confining a term. As you might imagine, standards are different from here to there. But along the way in life, I've had considerable experience with ledgers."

Sandison dropped into his desk chair, his weight sending it wheeling toward me. "Morgan? You just said you're not an accountant. What the hell then do you do with these ledgers you're talking about?"

"Oh, mend them. From the inside out." From his furrowed look, I could tell Sandison was not satisfied with that reply. "Let me put it this way, Sandy. Numbers are simply a language I happen to understand — Latin, numeracy, both have certain principles, fundamental in themselves. Surely you know the story of the bookkeeper and the desk drawer? No? Allow me. Every morning, a certain bookkeeper would come into the office of the firm, hang up his hat and coat, seat himself at his desk, pull out a drawer and look in it for a few seconds, shut it, and only then turn to his work. For forty years this went on — the same drawer, opened and shut, every morning. Finally came the day he retired, and the minute he left the office for the last time, the rest of the office staff crowded around his desk and one of them slowly opened that drawer. In it was a single sheet of paper. On it was written: 'Debits go on the left, credits on the right.' "

Sandison did not find my little tale as entertaining as I had hoped. "The long and short of it is," came his rumble, "you claim you know how to balance the books."

I nodded. "To the last penny, if it comes to that."

He sat there and frowned for some time. He could be intent as a fiend when he was mulling a matter. "All right," he grudgingly granted at last, "you probably can't make any more mess of the arithmetic than I have. You're in charge of the damn bookkeeping. Come over here and start getting acquainted with the ledgers."

I walked on air back to the boardinghouse at the end of that day. The one fundamental principle of bookkeeping that had always stood out to me was that if you know how and where the money flows, you are hard to get rid of.

6

Live it up while you can, Mister Man
    About Town,
Because what you gonna do when the
    rent comes roun'?

Whistling it softly to myself, I contradicted the catchy popular tune by counting out my rent money as usual, that subsequent week, as I came down a few minutes early for supper. Grace was not there to take it. The table was not yet set. This was a new experience; generally the Faraday Boarding House ran like a seven-day clock.

I peeked in the kitchen, to find supper uncooked but Grace steaming.

"Make yourself useful, please," she said testily, bent low to the opened oven. "Yell up to the others that supper will be a while yet. This bird refuses to get done."

In double defiance — pale and dry — the latest turkey lay there in the roaster, and

135

after calling upstairs to Hoop and Griff to hold on to their appetites, I returned to the kitchen, rolling up my sleeves. "If I might suggest, it is time to baste the beast."

"Baste," Grace said, with a fry cook's doubtfulness.

"Allow me." Crouching where she had been, I spooned the turkey's drippings over the breast and drumsticks, then stoked up the kitchen stove with a couple of pitchy sticks of wood. "There, now, the meal has no choice but to cook."

No sooner had I said so than the floor did a little dance. Silverware jingled, and Grace steadied a cream pitcher. After a moment, she dismissed the latest shake of everything. "That could have been worse."

"Grace," I let out along with my breath, "I will gladly take your word for that." I doubted I could ever get used to dynamite going off beneath the house.

Pushing a rather fetching flaxen wisp of hair off her forehead, she studied me as if I was the newest distraction. "Sit down for a minute, star boarder. There's something we need to talk about."

I went still. Was I in for another grilling about whether I was an IWW secret operative? What was I supposed to do, march around Butte wearing a sandwich board that read I AM NOT A WOBBLY?

"If it's about an unfortunate event in the library a while back," I fended as I settled across the kitchen table from her, "that was sheerly a case of mistaken —"

"It's church," she announced, rolling her eyes. "There's talk. About us. 'Ye and me,' " and she did not a bad imitation of the wee Welsh preacher. Griff had been asked to fill in with the choir a few more times, and the two of us and Hoop duly had made command performances as audience. What was wrong with that? Answering my inquiring look, Grace fanned with a hand as if brushing away pests. "What some of the nosy ones around the neighborhood are saying is" — she reddened at the exact words — "I'm taking up with a boarder. The old biddies."

Gossip, forever the whisper in the wind. "Mmm," I met Grace's report with uncertainty.

"Morrie?" Her violet eyes took in mine, a test that wouldn't go away. "Do you feel, um, taken up with?"

"I am about to fork over my week's rent," I said, unsure of how much honesty beyond that was a good idea just then. "That tends to put matters in a certain perspective."

Carefully folding my money away into her

apron pocket, she allowed: "It does, doesn't it." Still hesitant, she went on: "There's the matter of appearances, though. A boardinghouse has to be extra careful not to be lumped in with —" She gestured off toward the fleshly neighborhood of Venus Alley.

Now Grace looked at me, but not quite straight at me. "So you know what this means. I'm sorry, but —"

I waited, dreading the prospect of trying to find any other lodging in Butte as cozy as this.

"— you'll have to go to church just with Hoop," she finished off her decree. Then bounced up to take out the perfectly roasted turkey.

Reprieved at the boardinghouse, I could now busy myself learning the ins and outs of the library's finances. Sandison's style of bookkeeping had been what might be called extemporaneous, with occasional casual entries of *Miscellaneous book purchases* followed by sums that might well make a library trustee gulp. Trying to untangle his method, if that's what it was, I finally spotted in the ledger pages of staff wages and hours his hole card, so to speak. Me. Counting up, I could see there was not quite as much staff as was budgeted for — always a position or two short — and he covered those gaps in service, and doubtless put what would have been the wages into that bland expenditure on books, by shuttling employees from job to job during the course of a day. That works until, say, the board of trustees' president's wife is kept waiting at the temporarily vacant genealogy desk. My arrival plugged a lot of slots. Shunting me from task to task as Sandison did took those burdens off the other staffers; on a ranch I believe I would have been called the chore-boy. I didn't mind; variety has always been more to my taste than its opposite. I even was growing fond of the diverse evening groups, catching the end of the discussion those nights when it fell to me to go back to the library and close up, enjoying the verbal volleying about Hamlet's nervous condition or Wilson's strategy at the Paris peace conference. (However, I prudently waited for the Gilbert and Sullivan clan to vacate entirely before I tended to the music stands, lest Dora Sandison pounce on me with some other demand.) And on a more daily basis, when needed at a desk, I happily stepped into that role of librarian as bar-tender of information. Presiding over shelves of intoxicating items, dispensing whatever brand of knowledge was ordered up, I am sure I poured generously. At least Sandison must have thought so, the morning he told me to get downstairs and fill in for Miss Runyon at the Reading Room main desk as she made her grand descent to prepare for story hour.

Elevated there at the high desk, I was coping with patrons' questions when commotion broke out in the foyer.

"*Don't,* pigface."

"Can't take it, huh, bag ears?"

"Jack and Molly, quit that or I'll have your hides."

The purr of threat in the teacherly voice settled things down, at least momentarily, and in trooped as rough and tough a crowd, male and female, as I had seen yet in Butte. On the other hand, they were twelve-year-olds and a freckle epidemic was loose among them. In flat caps and pigtails, hand-me-down britches and mended pinafores, plainly these were children from one of the neighborhoods on the Hill, spruced up for the library visit, but the sprucing could go only so far. Watching casually as edgy girls and pushing boys milled down the stairwell to the auditorium, I took a bit of guilty pleasure in the thought that Miss Runyon would have her hands full with this mob.

"Mr. Morgan." The purr was close at my

side. "Your mustache is back."

I turned and was nearly startled off my sitting place.

"Rabrab!" I blurted, drawing nasty looks and one severe *shhh* from the Reading Room patrons.

A knowing laugh arrived with the same throatiness as the purr. "You remember. But you would, wouldn't you. Did you know the whole school used to call you the Walking Encyclopedia?"

I had last seen Barbara Rellis as a sixth-grader, a dark-eyed willow of a girl on the lookout for intrigue. Foremost in my memory was my first day of teaching at the Marias Coulee one-room school, when she ever so innocently raised her hand during roll call and asked if for the sake of keeping up with certain contrary stunts of the boys she couldn't turn her name around, most of it at least, just on the schoolground where name-calling ran every direction anyway? I found an appealing flavor of logic in that and let her. The Rabrab of then had filled out into a fashionably bobbed young woman, still slender but with a substantial bodice, and those eyes that so often held mischief like a flash of struck flint now had authority to them as well. She called over to the tail of the brigade dragging its feet in

141

the stairwell. "Margie, mind them, please, give them a swat if you have to. Tell the story lady they're all hers, she can start. I'll be there in a minute." An older schoolgirl, obviously conscripted for the outing, took charge and the last of the children were hustled down the stairs.

Rabrab's — Barbara's — attention swung back to me. "I see that little smile," she said with one of her own, "don't try to hide it. You caused this, you know, my ending up a teacher. A number of us have. Paul Milliron is already a county superintendent, had you heard?" She was studying me, from my mustache on in, a faint wrinkle of puzzlement at the side of her eyes. "At first I didn't think it could be you, perched here like the head canary. In Butte, of all places. We were told you'd gone to — where was it? Transylvania?"

"Never mind. In the here and now, I —"

"Have you been back to Marias Coulee, since?"

"Not in person. I mean, no. Rab — Barbara, that is —"

This time her smile was the sly schoolgirlish one I remembered so well, as though she had something sweet tucked in her cheek. "You can call me that. It would make two of you who do. That's rather nice."

We were conversing in spirited whispers, not the best etiquette for the Reading Room, and I summoned Smithers from periodicals to sit in for me. Hurriedly escorting Rab out into the foyer, where there was only Shakespeare to overhear us, I began trying to contain the situation.

"About Marias Coulee. I must take you into my confidence, Rab." It worked. The racehorse keenness she had always shown at any prospect of conspiracy was immediately there to see. "It is best if no one in our old neighborhood knows I am back in Montana," I went on, "because of — well, possible hard feelings, you'll understand." I paused for what I hoped was drama's sake. "Rose and I had a falling out. A family matter."

She swooped on that. "It happens over and over, doesn't it. A brother and a sister, you'd think they were built to get along, but no, they find every way there is to get crosswise with each other. I see it all the time in my pupils. So I'm not surprised — those of us at school thought you and Rose were born in different phases of the moon, as the saying goes. And you won't go back now because you don't want to stir up old trouble — that is so like you, Mr. Morgan."

"I could not have put it better myself."

143

Rab leaned closer, back to whispering. "Now I'll let you in on a secret. It just happened, the other night. I'm betrothed. E-n-g-a-g-e-d," she rattled off as if in one of Marias Coulee's spelling bees. She wrinkled her nose, turning in an instant into the perfect facsimile of a pretty and mischievous bride.

There was no hiding my smile this time. "The lucky man is getting more than he bargained for."

"But keep the news to yourself for now," she added anxiously. "My pupils can be such awful teases, and I want to wait until the school year is over to —"

As if the word *pupil* had triggered open a gate at the head of the hall, here toward us came one of the schoolgirls, mostly knees and pigtails. Undoubtedly she had put up her hand in that urgent way that allowed her to go to the lavatory, but she marched right past it until she was practically at the hem of Rab's smock.

"Just so you know, Miss Rellis, Russian Famine snuck off."

"Not with you around, Peggy, I'm sure. Now do your business and scoot back downstairs." The class tattler flounced happily into the lavatory, and Rab spun to me. "Is there another staircase?"

144

I took her down the hallway toward the set of stairs at the back of the stacks. "Rab," I questioned as we quickstepped along, "isn't your class somewhat advanced for story hour? They look very much like —"

"Sixth-graders," she sighed. "Don't you dare laugh, Mr. Morgan." She herself had been a ringleader — it was the kind of class that had many — in the populous sixth grade that had been my biggest handful in the Marias Coulee schoolroom.

"I won't bother to say justice is served," I told her archly. "But story hour at that level — what sort of story?"

"First aid."

It was always hard to tell with Rabrab whether she was pulling your leg. She shook her head as I scrutinized her. "It's the school board's big idea." Her expression sharpened. "Most of the boys will be in the mines in just a few years, and most of the girls will be hatching other children, up on the Hill. The thinking is, it might spare the public treasury in the future if they learn some first aid before what is going to happen to some of them happens. In theory, I suppose I can't argue with that." Another sigh. "In any case, your Miss Runyon here is looked upon as the apostle of first aid. I'm told she was greatly disappointed that she was too far up in years to boss the nurses in France during the war."

"I can imagine. Here we are." I unlocked the delivery door to the stacks, and we stepped in.

To be met with sounds such as I had never heard put together before: a shoeleather *chuff-chuff-chuff* spaced what seemed a dance step apart, followed by a drawn-out soft whizzing like a very long zipper being drawn down.

"That'll be him," Rab said under her breath. "See?"

Beyond the bookshelves sheltering us, a boy as spindly as any I had ever seen was racing up the long staircase to the floors above. As if built on springs he bounded up the stairsteps three at a time, on the brink of trying for four, and when his leaps carried him to the top, the race against gravity, against himself, momentarily over, he in one swift mounting move jockeyed his legs over the banister and slid back down. There was a heart-stopping pneumatic grace, a fireman's fearless ride down a twisting pole, in the way he shot to the bottom. The instant he touched the floor again, he was back into motion, *chuff-chuff-chuff,* trio after trio of stairs flown over by the broomstick legs.

"He does it at school whenever he can,"

Rab's murmur was close to my ear. "You should see him on the fire escape." Just watching him here was mesmerizing enough; I felt as the audience must have when Nijinsky first flew out of the wings onto a ballet stage, and human ability would never be seen the same again. This pint-size dervish seemed determined to spring at the steep staircase until he could sail up it in one weightless jump.

"Wladislaw, that's enough," Rab called to him. I could have told her a teacherly tone was not effective in cases of extremity; it took something more.

Oblivious, the boy launched off on another waterbug skim up the cascade of stairsteps. Rab cupped her hands to her mouth and let out a shout that would have cut fog: "Russian Famine, do you hear me?"

"Yes'm. Can't not."

Strawy hair flopping, he slowly glided off the banister and dropped on the balls of his feet in front of us. He did not appear guilty, simply caught. I could see how his classmates came up with the nickname, brutal as it was. Gaunt as an unfed greyhound, the hollow-cheeked boy did resemble a living ghost from starvation times on some distant steppe. He met our gaze with a bleak one. "I was just fooling around a little."

147

"While you are supposed to be in class learning about first aid," Rab chided, combing his hair out of his eyes with her fingers. "Come, say hello to Mr. Morgan — the library couldn't run without him."

The boy's reluctant handshake was like squeezing a puppy's paw. As quick as seemed decent, he rubbed his hand on a hip pocket and cast an appeal to his teacher. "Can't I skip that aid junk, Miss Rellis? Pretty please? All it's gonna be is rags and sticks," he maintained, with a certain degree of clairvoyance. "I seen them bring that Bohunk mucker up the other day at the Neversweat, wrapped up like a mummy and just as dead anyhow. The roof comes down on them in the mine and they're goners. How's rags and sticks gonna help that?"

Wisely not debating the point, Rab instructed with firmness: "You're going to be a goner of another kind — after school until the seat of your pants wears out — if you don't get down there in that room with the rest of them, right now."

"Yes'm. Pretty please don't do no good with you." The spring was gone from him as he hunched off to class.

We watched him trail away, Rab making sure he went down to the auditorium rather than out the front door. "He's an acrobatic marvel," I remarked, "especially since he's so thin you can see through him."

"Wladislaw has been given the thin edge of life in every way," she filled in the story for me. "His parents and a baby sister died in the flu last year. He's being brought up, if you can call it that, by an old uncle. The man has a peddler cart, he sharpens knives around town." She shook her head somberly. "What they live on is anybody's guess." As if having taken a cue from her rubber-legged pupil, she pirouetted to leave. "I'd better go or your Miss Runyon will be sending out a search party. We still have catching up to do, though." She peered at me quizzically, schoolteacher and schoolgirl merged into a single soul of curiosity. "Such as, why *does* that mustache come and go?"

I had my answer ready, along with a slight smile. "We all have our disguises in the masquerade party of life, don't we, Rabrab?"

She took that with a laugh and another crinkle of her nose. "That sounds just like you. But I'm not letting you get away that easily. You have to meet my Jared. Tomorrow night? Join us for supper at the Purity."

The Purity Cafeteria, I found, prided itself on its snowy tablecloths, the forest of tables and chairs that could hold a couple of hundred customers at a time, and, the dubious piece of progress that demarcated it from a café, a total absence of waiters. NO WAITING! YOUR FOOD AWAITS YOU! proclaimed a large sign in red, and across the rear of the ballroom-size dining area stood a line of counters with the menu's offerings, condiments, cutlery, glassware, and so forth. "A new customer! They must be cleaning out heaven!" I was greeted by a plump bow-tied individual, evidently the owner, presiding over the cash register. "Sir, I can tell from here, your belt buckle is hitting your backbone. Skip right in and fill on up."

Smiling thinly at that gust of Butte bonhomie, I cast around for Rab and her fiancé amid the eating crowd. I spied him first, with a prickle of inevitability up my backbone.

Rabrab had been leaning in, tasting something off his plate, as lovers will, and as her bobbed head came up into view, she spotted me and waved.

Mindful of his manners, the young man stood and turned to me with a soldierly correctness that I could have predicted. He'd had that same deportment while tendering the union's envelope of benefit to the widow Dempsey, and in marching like a Roman at the head of the miners in shift change on the Hill. Rabrab gazed up at him as if she'd had him made to order.

"The men in my life," she announced fondly. "Jared Evans, this is Morris Morgan."

"Morrie," I amended over the handshake, to put us on familiar terms.

"Jared," he said, perhaps humorously, perhaps not.

As soon as chairs were under us, he sat back and regarded me through dark deep Welsh eyes that reminded me of Casper's, only more reflective. Beyond that, he and Rab together were like matched cutouts in charcoal paper by a scissor portraitist, his slicked-back hair black as hers. Any children of these two would be ravens. Yet there was something even more striking about this lean chiseled man, and it took me a second to single it out. His ears were different sizes; the left one was missing its earlobe, clean as a surgery. Together with the fathoms in that gaze, it gave him the look of a reformed pirate. I tried not to stare at the foreshortened ear, which of course only creates another level of attention.

Still examining me with those grave eyes, Jared spoke as if I were a question brought before the podium. "You're the cryer. You get around."

"A temporary appointment," I brushed away my career of wakes. "The best kind to have where a coffin is involved."

Rab rippled a laugh. "Now he's the resident genius of the library, aren't you, Mr. Morgan? Have you read every book in it by now? I remember when you knew everything there was to know about comets, and that was just the start of —"

"Flattery does not have to be laid on more than an inch thick, Rab," I waved that to a halt. Basking in her words more than I should have, I shared to Jared: "You must know how she is by now — when her enthusiasm gets going, she'll talk your ear off."

Immediately I wanted to crawl under the table. Jared's dark brows drew down as he leaned in and pointed a cocked thumb and finger at me like a pistol, and I wildly wondered what I was in for. Then, of all things, he winked.

"A German bullet took care of that for me. I got off lucky — they didn't call that sector Dead Man's Hill for nothing. A medical corpsman slapped a patch on me and I went right back into the thick of it." Fingering what was left of the ear, he dispatched a droll half of a smile to the rapt Rab and around to me. "I have to watch out not to be too proud of it — the earmark none of the rest of the herd has."

As when Sandison plunged off into live-stock terminology, I chuckled uselessly.

Rab came to my rescue. "Mr. Morgan, you need to hunt up some food. We had to start, Jared has a meeting. He usually does."

"To dicker the lost dollar out of the Anaconda lords and masters?" my natural interest in wages prompted me to ask.

The question was flicked right back to me. "How is it that you know we're in there dickering?" Over a deliberative sip of his coffee, the union leader held me in that compelling gaze again. What was it about the Richest Hill on Earth, that I seemed to be a suspect of some kind no matter which way I turned?

"My usual dining partners," I alibied hast-ily, "are Griffith and Hooper at the board-inghouse. They discuss matters."

Jared's look softened somewhat. "If that's who you're hanging around with, you prob-ably know more about anything and every-thing in town than I do."

In the time soon to come, I would learn that Jared Evans had been thrust from the thick of one war into that of another. The combat between the hierarchies of Europe had at last reached a mortal end, while the struggle he came home to on the Hill showed no sign of abating as long as there was corporate capital and there was unionized labor. Flint and gunpowder had the same relationship. Put simply, although Hoop and Griff in their telling of it to me seldom did, the Great War had crippled the once-mighty Butte miners' union; its bargaining power had been hampered by government decrees, rivalry from the IWW, and Anaconda's imperious determination to fatten profits at the expense of wages and workers' lives. Jared alit back into the middle of all this, chosen for that sense of capability he carried as naturally as the set of his shoulders. The better I came to know and observe him, I could not help thinking of Rab's beau as a paradoxical version of Lucius Quinctius Cincinnatus, the Roman soldier who fought his battle and returned to his plow; Jared had been summoned from the battlefield to plow the ungiving ground of Butte's conflicts.

"You two," Rab broke in now, her napkin a flick of white flag between us, "would rather talk than eat, I know, but that's not me." She was onto her feet, poised in the direction of the dessert counter. "Rhubarb pie. I can't resist. Jared, sweet, can I bring you some?"

He leaned back in his chair and stretched

mightily, a man with much on his mind and a long night of negotiating ahead of him. "Just some more java, thanks, if you have enough hands."

"Back in a jiffy," she promised. She sailed off, spiffy as a Riviera princess in the shorter style of dress that was coming into fashion; you could actually see she had legs.

"I had better follow Rab's example," I said, starting to get up to find a meal for myself. Only to be stopped in mid-rise by Jared's thumb pinning the sleeve of my suit-coat to the table. It was a very substantial thumb.

"How does it come to be" — unmistakably the words were those of a stern young fiancé — "that you call her 'Rab'?"

"I, ah, officiated on that name."

That didn't seem to help. "Officiated how?"

Rapidly I told the story of Barbara's verbal somersault into Rabrab in my classroom. The thumb grudgingly lifted from the fabric of my sleeve. "All right," he granted, "it makes two of us who call her that. That's a great plenty."

With a measure of relief I moved off toward wherever the food waited. "You're lagging," Rab scolded as she passed me, bearing a tray with her slice of pie and

Jared's cup of coffee. "Only until I can track down the breaded veal," I assured her. Grace had many virtues as a landlady, but it had been a considerable time since I had seen a cutlet.

Cafeteria dining, Butte style, evidently meant that half the clientele was fetching mounds of food for itself at any given moment, and so I had to work my way through the crowd to the counter where the meat dishes were listed, past a huge mahogany breakfront stacked with glassware and coffee cups and saucers. Squeezing around that furniture, I popped into an opening in the meal line, nearly bumping into the larger-than-life figure piling a plate with liver and onions.

Typhoon Tolliver and I stared at each other.

"The rumor is wrong, then, Typhoon. You don't eat hay."

"You," he said thickly. Beside his tray, I saw his fists ball up.

Something about the way I thrust my hands into the side pockets of my coat halted any further movement from him. I had decided that if it came to blows, I would try to hit him on the left fist with my brass knuckles, in the hope of putting his best punch out of action. But I did not particularly want to test that tactic, and from his slow, perplexed blinks, Typhoon seemed not sure he wanted to initiate anything either. Before he could think it over too much, I rushed to say: "The crowd in here is not going to be entertained by you beating me up in public — this isn't the boxing ring."

"No, it ain't," he agreed with that.

"Where's" — I cast a hasty glance around for the telltale set of sideways eyes — "your partner in crime?"

"Who, Roland? He goes for that Chinee stuff." Typhoon swiped a dismissive paw in the direction of Chinatown and its bill of fare. "Noodles and chicken feet or something. I can't stomach it myself." Independence seemed to be linked to appetite somewhere in that big thick head. "He and me ain't joined at the rib cage."

"Then he doesn't need to know we're showing the good sense not to whale into each other in front of two hundred witnesses and get ourselves arrested, does he."

"I guess maybe not." The mention of witnesses caused the flat-faced pug to look around nervously, peeking over the top of the breakfront for anyone watching our impromptu meeting. I did the same, around a corner of it. We both had more than enough reason to be jittery. It was perilous for me to be seen talking to a prime Anaconda goon, and just as detrimental on his side of things to be caught conversing with me, possible Wobbly that I might be. Luckily, back at the table, Jared's attention centered on Rabrab, and Typhoon's jerky scan around the room evidently did not pick up any watchers either. Rolling his big shoulders, he huffed to me:

"There'll be another time, punk."

"Until then, I'd be careful if I were you," I responded in a concerned tone. "You see the union bug there?" I inclined my head toward the small but significant Federation of Labor emblem in the bottom corner of the wall-hung certificate attesting that the establishment proudly employed members of the Cooks and Dishwashers Brotherhood. "I hear that if the crew in the kitchen knows you wear the copper collar, they slip ground glass in the onions."

I left him staring down at his plate.

"What, did the calf have to be butchered first?" Rab bantered when I returned to the table with my cutlet.

"Something like that." No sooner had I sat down than Jared leaned my way and spoke in a low tone. "Morrie," he tried the name out, "I maybe jumped on you a little too hard there at first, about union matters.

Rab worked me over and says you can be trusted." His face said, *We'll see.* "Keep this under your hat, but there might be a work action, sometime soon. I'll make sure Hoop and Griff stay out of it. I'm telling you now so you don't have to worry about the old devils, all right?"

"I'll try not to. From what they've told me, though, doesn't Butte turn into a hornets' nest during a strike?"

"I didn't say 'strike,' did I?"

"We went through enough of that, last time," Rab said as if instructing both of us. "Anaconda's squads of bullies in our streets. You'd think we weren't Americans."

"That smarted," Jared admitted, his brow creased. He looked over at me. "A year ago I was getting shot at in a trench in France, and I come home to the mines, and next thing I know, a bunch of muscleheads who never even got overseas are ambushing me on the picket line. We're going to try to get around that this time."

Rab traced a chevron on his shoulder. "My sergeant."

Covering Rab's hand with his own, he made a wry face, again in my direction. "You tell me, is it a promotion or a demotion to head up the union council when Anaconda is trying to make us eat dirt?"

The question lingered in those agate-dark eyes. "When the company goons broke the strike last time, the men kicked out the council leaders." He spoke the next very levelly, as if sharing it between Rab and me. "The same way they'll kick me out if I don't deliver the lost dollar."

"Can't not, as Russian Famine would say," Rab said confidently. "You have to budge Anaconda somehow, so you will. I'll bet on it."

For their sake and Butte's, I hoped she was right. Jared got up, saying he had to get to his meeting, and Rab moaned that there was a school board session she had to attend, while I had to make sure there were enough chairs for the Shakespeare Society's Merry Wives' Night back at the library; and I imagined Typhoon and Eel Eyes would be flexing their shoeleather and muscles somewhere in the night, too.

7

Sometime soon, in the vocabulary of Jared Evans, turned out to mean the very next morning. As I rounded the corner to the library, I saw that the usual line of staff and a few patrons at the door had grown mightily and fanned out like a peacock's tail, the entire street filled with new faces. For a moment my soul lifted at this surge of literary interest from the citizenry of Butte. Then it dawned on me that the atmosphere of the city had changed overnight. The Hill's normal throb of labor was not to be heard: no ore trains were running, the seven smokestacks of the Neversweat were empty pipes in the air, the headframes stood as stark and still as gallows. And the mass of fidgeting men here in the light of day ordinarily would have been at work in the everlasting night of the mines. Whatever Jared's definition of a "work action" was, it closely resembled a wildcat strike.

A crowd is a temperamental thing. I could tell at once that as watchfully quiet as this one was, it would not take much to make it growl.

The minute I arrived, Sandison — grim as thunder — beckoned me up. The library staff nervously held its place at the closed door as he and I stepped to one side and conferred.

"What are these lunkheads doing here, Morgan, instead of out on a picket line somewhere?"

"Sandy, I know no more about this gathering than you do."

"Some help you are. What are we supposed to do about all this mob?"

"Put out more chairs? There are stacks downstairs from when the Shakespeareans —"

He cut me off with a look. "Let them in and make them at home, are you telling me? Hell, man, the Butte Public Library isn't supposed to take sides in some damn dogfight of this kind." Then the oddest thing. There on the topmost step, Sandison turned and gazed out at that sea of workingmen's faces, much the way a pharaoh might have looked down from a pyramid. In that suspended moment, he seemed to draw something known only to himself from those so

162

many eyes. Then he gave a laugh that made his belly heave.

Shaking his head, he climbed onto the base of one of the doorway pillars. I feared he might fall, but he clambered up as if he did this all the time. The sight of him perched there, with the white aureole of his beard and cowlick against the grave Gothic stone of the building, made the crowd fall silent; once more, I could feel that strange mixed mood of apprehension and fascination that followed Samuel Sandison like the shadow at his heels.

"It looks as if the library has some new visitors today," his voice rang off the building across the street, "and I have one thing to say to all of you. It pertains to behavior that will not be tolerated in this public institution." Throughout the crowd I saw faces darken, the phalanx of idled miners readying for yet another warning against "unlawful assembly" even here. "You maybe do it out of habit up there on the Hill or down in the shafts," Sandison blazed, hands on his hips, "but this is not the place for that kind of thing, understand? I am only telling you once." He glowered down at some of the hardest men in Butte as if they were schoolboys playing hooky. "No spitting."

With that, although I would not have thought it possible, his voice rose to another level. "Let us in, Morgan."

Once inside, I made straight for the cash-box Sandison kept in his desk, grabbed a fistful of money, and sent someone scurrying to the newsstand down the street to buy all available reading material. I would worry later about a ledger entry for *Miscellaneous diversionary matter*. Next, several of us lugged chairs from the auditorium to the Reading Room, the mezzanine, even the foyer. Meanwhile the miners circulated, speaking in hushed tones if at all, as they got the feel of the grand paneled rooms and the tiers of the world's writings. With the arrival of the newsstand supplement of newspapers and such, so many men settled at tables and in corners with newsprint spread wide that the Reading Room took on the look of a schooner under sail. The library staff, originally taken aback as I had been, caught a fever of enthusiasm at having constant customers, cap in hand, requesting guidance; librarians do not ordinarily receive such worship. I detected a warm gleam of triumph even from Miss Runyon when a stooped miner asked in a thick Italian accent for *L'avventura di Cristo-*

foro Colombo and she was able to produce a pristine Florentine edition from the mezzanine treasure house.

One thing I particularly noticed: the display case in the far corner drew onlookers as though it were magnetized. Man after man crouched to contemplate the mine model, so complete from tip of headframe to deepest dungeon of tunnel, the compressed vision of the mines standing empty on the Hill this day. It was as if the glass of the case was a smudged crystal ball, with hints of what lay ahead if one could only make them out.

Busy with everything, I was hastening down the hallway and past the drinking fountain when a familiar voice caught up with me. "Just a suggestion, but the flavor of the water in this place would be improved by piping in some rye."

"Quin!" The Irish conquistador face looked more solemn in this circumstance than it had at wakes. "I had no idea you were the library-going type."

"Funny, boyo." Quinlan winked and indicated toward the horde in the Reading Room. "A lot of us feel the call of culture today. In about a hundred percent of those cases, the wife told us to get out of the house."

"Why not on a picket line, showing solidarity?"

He arched an eyebrow, amused or the opposite. "Tsk, Morgan, for a sighted man you're deep in the dark, aren't you. There's no picket line. No negotiating session. No anything whatsoever. Jared Evans just made some kind of safety excuse and pulled us out at the start of morning shift like that" — he snapped his fingers — "and is letting Anaconda stew about it." He hardened as I watched. "Whether it gets us our fair wage or we need to try stronger persuasion —" The shoulders of his coat lifted, and I was aware that the Little Red Songbook, in some pocket or other, could find an adherent in more than musical ways. "We'll see if the lop-eared Taffy knows what he's doing." Quinlan's expression suggested it would not be easy to prove to Dublin Gulch.

At the end of the day, I had to resort again to the higher powers to uncloud the bafflements of Butte for me.

Hooper was several rungs up, against the weather side of the house, industriously slapping on paint while Griffith held the ladder. "Everything still standing, downtown?" Griff called out upon sight of me.

"Every brick in place, when I left. Why weren't the pair of you in the middle of things today?"

Hoop dipped his brush and stroked a comet of paint onto the siding. "Told not to."

"Saving us for when we're really needed, Jared says," Griff reported. He wagged his head in general acknowledgment. "Caught Anaconda with its pants down today, he sure did. Put a Welshman in charge and you start to get somewhere. Look at Lloyd George." He gestured as if the prime minister of Great Britain might materialize to set things straight in Butte.

"Yes, but —"

"Your turn," Hoop called down.

I waited while the two of them traded places, like two aged sailors scrambling in the rigging. "But why this so-called *work action* instead of a genuine strike?"

"No strike, no strikebreakers." Holding the ladder with both gnarled hands, Hoop looked around at me as if deciding how much more tutoring I was worth. "Besides catching that other gang —"

"— with its pants down," Griff contributed, along with an emphatic swipe of his paintbrush.

I must have looked blank. Top and bottom of the ladder, both of them eyed me. The silence grew until at last Hoop spelled out:

"The Wobblies. They'd cut in on a strike, try to take it over if they knew it was coming."

"Send in infiltrators." To hear Griff echo Typhoon Tolliver was an unnerving experience. I drew myself up.

"As a mere bystander" — it was hard to tell if that registered on those walnut faces — "it appears to me the union council won the day, as you say. But what happens tomorrow?"

The last word was Hoop's. "Things go back to their normal confusion."

Trudging upstairs to my room to wash up before supper, I reflected again on that zigzag pattern of life. There I was, simply a hopeful empty-pocketed climber of the Richest Hill on the planet, and suspected of something more by nearly everyone except Rabrab, who usually saw connivance behind every mustache. At least, I told myself with a grim smile, tonight I could look forward to a meal not garnished with a goon.

But when I opened the door, my room looked as if it had been visited by a typhoon.

The bedding lay in a heap on the floor, the pillows flung onto the dresser top. The truly alarming thing, though, was the mattress, standing on its side and teetering toward me like a falling wall, while someone grunted in exertion behind it.

"You thugs!" I cried, wildly fishing in my pockets for the brass knuckles, expecting the pointy-faced Anaconda man to burst from the closet while the bigger one mashed me with the mattress. "Get out of here or I'll —"

The mattress stopped its waggle. Around an edge, Grace's face came into view. "Morrie!" She appeared as startled as I was. "Is it that time of day already?"

"Room devastation time, you mean?" The brass knuckles swiftly pocketed out of her sight, I stepped toward the disarranged bed.

"I'm glad you're here, you can help me turn this mattress," she said reasonably. "I do this every so often, so you don't have to sleep on lumps." I took an end and we flopped the mattress into place. As she unfolded fresh sheets she looked across at me curiously. "You came in sounding like you were declaring war. What were you so worked up about?"

"Oh, that. Everything upset as it was, I thought I'd caught Hoop and Griff playing a prank on me," I alibied. "Tossing the room — all boys do it, and aren't they that at heart?"

"They're supposed to be painting the bad side of the house."

"I must have come around the other way."

Grace cocked an eyebrow. " 'Thugs'?"

"The word comes from *thuggee,* Hindu for someone who sneaks around and, ah, does mischief to you."

She shook her head, making her braid dance. "I always learn something around you."

I made no answer. A fresh apprehension was coursing through me. Over in the corner of the disheveled room, my satchel was missing.

Busily fluffing a pillow, Grace took a few moments to catch up to my alarmed gaze. "Oh. I had to move your bag out of the way. It's in the closet."

Undisturbed or gone through? I nearly asked. Suspicion was the contagion of Butte; now I was the one catching it. For once I was glad my trunk was not there, to disclose any of its secrets.

My landlady, dimpled with either innocence or guile, by now was done with the freshened bedding, the room miraculously back in order, and she announced she had

170

better see to supper. "Grace?" I halted her before she could swish out the door. "You've been through the war of nerves between the men and the mining company before. What's your sense of this one?"

She bundled her hands in her apron as she considered my question. "My Arthur," she invoked somberly, "used to say taking on Anaconda is like wrestling a carnival bear. You have to hope its muzzle doesn't come off."

The speed of sound is slightly less than that of a shock wave, and so the tremor in the dark of that night shook my bed, and every other in the city, a few instants before the noise of the blast arrived.

Even foggy with sleep, I knew this was no usual detonation, no dynamiting at the depth of a glory hole. I stumbled to the hallway. Half-dressed, Hooper struggled from his room, yanking into the remainder of his clothes, while Griffith already was putting on coat and hat. At the head of the hall, Grace clutched her bedgown around her throat as she witnessed the exodus, then sent me an agonized look.

She did not even have to deliver my marching orders aloud. I dressed hastily and set off with the limping pair of old boarders to the Hill.

Up there, in the ghostly light of the head-frames, a murmuring crowd was clustered around a mineshaft called the Flying Dutchman. When people gather from the nooks of a mining town to the surface of a disaster, they bring every degree of dread, and as the three of us edged through the throng I could feel the mood of apprehension, the air was sticky with it. Each arriving set of eyes, mine included, expected the sight of bodies laid out on the hard ground. But Griff and Hoop, pointing and muttering, saw at once this was no mineshaft accident, no explosion and flash of deadly flame deep in a tunnel. Instead, over near the machine house, beneath a now askew sign reading PROPERTY OF THE ANACONDA COPPER MINING COMPANY, the mine's pay office stood open to the night, its front wall blown out.

Blue-uniformed policemen were chiding the crowd to stay back, while burly civilian types who could only have been plainclothesmen prowled the blast site. Reporters were clamoring out questions and receiving no answers. Flash powder kept going off, the hollowed-out pay office in rinses of light that would put it on front pages all across the state.

My companions were not impressed. "Mighty poor job of setting the dynamite," either Hooper or Griffith appraised there in the deep shadows of the Hill.

"Could've done that much with firecrackers, couldn't we?" said the other.

To me, the building looked devastated enough, the huge ragged hole in its front displaying broken bricks like snaggled teeth. I moved closer to the skeptical experts. "Do I hear that this blast wasn't up to your standards?"

"The stupid pay office is still standing, isn't it?"

"Well, yes."

"That's no kind of a result, if you're gonna blow something up."

"Waste of a good fuse and a match."

"But," I wasn't able to budge from the evidence of my eyes, "the front of the building is by and large gone."

"So what? They'll get bricklayers in here in the morning and have it fixed back up before you can say boo."

"Spell this out for me, then," I gave in. "How would someone who was an old hand at blowing things up have done it?"

"All it would have taken," Hoop explained patiently, "was to set the dynamite at the corner of the building."

"It'd slump over like a dropped cake," Griff mused, practically smacking his lips as he envisioned it.

By now the cloud of reporters and chain lightning of photography flashes were concentrated around one small circle of men next to the Flying Dutchman's headframe. Even though I had expected something of the sort, my heart sank. As flash powder flared again, I saw in the glare the strong but strained features of Jared Evans in the midst of his beleaguered union officials. Although I had nothing to lend but moral support, I headed over.

An arm slipped authoritatively through mine, nearly scaring the life out of me. "I just knew you'd show up, Mr. Morgan," Rab's warm voice was next to my ear. In stylish scarf and jumper, she cut an unlikely figure there in the industrial spoils of the Hill. With perfect prepossession, she assessed the cordon of newspapermen surrounding Jared and the other union men. "Look at the mob of them. They're like pecking birds."

As the two of us sorted our way there in the semidark, we could hear the volley of questioning. Peppered from all sides as he was, Jared raised a hand for quiet.

"We're told no one was hurt," he chose

what to deal with and what not to. "Given that someone is killed in the working conditions in these mines every week of the year, in this nasty incident only bricks suffered any harm, for a change."

"Anaconda says provocation like this will make it take 'all necessary measures' to deal with a strike," called out a newspaperman in a better topcoat than the others, which marked him as working for the *Daily Post,* the mining company's mouthpiece. "What's the union think of that?"

"There is no strike," Jared deliberately raised his voice above the clanks and clatters of the night shift in the other mines around. "When the miners of this hill go out, there's never any mistaking it — you can hear the grass grow, up here. That's it, gentlemen, no more chitchat, thanks." To his council members: "I'll catch up with you at the union hall. We're in for a late night." Jared's expression had lifted measurably when he spotted Rabrab, and she and I skirted the pack of reporters to join him. As we did so, Rab "accidentally" tripped the *Post* man, sending him stumbling into an oily puddle and cursing at the splatter on that spiffy coat.

Smiling tiredly, Jared chucked his feisty fiancée under the chin. "You'll get us a big headline."

"They'll smear you no matter what," Rab predicted, "in that waste of ink they call a newspaper." Making a face at the mangled pay office, she went on: "So the sneaks resorted to this. I suppose they think they're clever."

"They're not far from it," Jared let out a slow breath of judgment. "They've put us in a hole about the size of that, for now."

By then I felt reasonably sure that in the company of Jared and his union followers, I was not in with dynamiters — even inept dynamiters. To catch up with the conversation, I contributed in a confidential tone: "The Wobblies, you mean. It's in their interest to stir up all the trouble they can, so they did it with a bang, hmm?"

Jared and Rab looked at me as though I were speaking in tongues. He shook his head. "If the Wobs wanted into this, they'd more likely blow up a machine house. Something that would really cripple this mine."

I was back to bafflement. "Then who?"

"Mr. Morgan, put your thinking cap on," said Rab. "It's so obvious."

Weary as he was, Jared took pity on me. "Anaconda. Their goons. To blame it on the union."

■ ■ ■ ■

There are moments in a lifetime when you can taste history as it is happening. When the flavor of time, from one hour to the next, somehow is not quite the same as any day before. So it was, at the start of the intense summer of 1919, as the miners of Butte and the mining corporation cooked up strategies against each other. Dickens should have been living in this hour to tell the tale of the two cities, the one of the neighborhoods of the Hill, and the other of the tall offices downtown, in the double-numbered year.

The morning after the bombing of the pay office, along with breakfast Grace delivered a firm suggestion. "This might be a good day for everybody to stay in."

"How come, Mrs. Faraday?" Griff could have taught innocence to a cherub. "Nice weather, it'd be a shame not to take a little walk downtown."

Hoop went to the point: "We wouldn't want to miss anything."

"And I suppose you," Grace turned to me in exasperation, "are going to say the library will curl up and wither away if you're not there."

"Not at all," I said from behind my coffee cup. "But my job might, if I don't show up as usual."

Off the three of us went, into the tense center of things. There is an atmospheric condition known as earthquake weather, a blanket stillness that forecasts a shaking-up; this day was like that. Hoop and Griff and I hiked up the Hill to that vantage spot of my first day in town and waited. With the city braced, with squads of policemen at the ready, we held our breath as it came time for the morning shift of miners to appear. They did so in eerie silence, the long files of men spilling into the streets of Meaderville and Centerville and Finntown and Dublin Gulch as if forming a somber parade. They marched toward the police lines with barely a murmur. And then turned in at the gates of the mines and went to work as if all was normal.

At supper, Griff and Hoop were downcast and Grace was not serving up sympathy. "No blood in the streets, how disappointing. Jared Evans must be more sane than some I could mention."

"He'd better have something up his sleeve," Griff said.

Three mornings later, I rounded the corner of the library into a teeming streetful of miners and Sandison frowning down at them.

I worked my way through the crowd, dropping questions as I went. Sandison met me at the top of the steps, looking even more disgruntled than usual. He drew me aside behind a pillar, while the library staff and the miners gawked back and forth. "What do the knotheads say?" he pumped me without preliminary. "Have they quit fooling around and actually gone on strike this time?"

"Not as such," I reported. "It's another work action — just the morning shift, they told me."

"How many more times is this going to happen?" he demanded, as if I were in charge of that.

Knowing Jared Evans, I put up my hands helplessly. "Doubtless as many as it takes. Wouldn't you say it's a tactic that goes back to Roman history, Sandy? You will recall the great delayer, Fabius Cunctator, who out-generaled his foes with skirmishes that put off the climactic battle time after time. It appears to me that the union similarly is using these stoppages to wear on Anaconda's nerves and —"

"They're practicing on mine, I can tell you that much," he disposed of my discourse. "Are we running a library or a union hall?" Scowling at his own question, he heaved himself around for another look at the packed street. I barely caught the words in his gust of exhalation: "Oh, hell, let them in, Morgan."

Full as a church on Christmas, the library brimmed with activity, much of it mine as I sped from task to task. Sandison commanded from the mezzanine, on the lookout for anyone forgetful enough to spit on the sacred floor, and things seemed to be going well until midway through the morning, when he flagged me down with the news:

"Miss Runyon has gone home in a nervous fit, the excitement has been too much for her. You'll have to take over the story hour."

"Now? How? Whatever short notice is, this is less."

"The tykes are on their way," he overrode my protest. "You wouldn't want to break their young hearts, would you?" Did the man actually have a sense of humor? I would have had to part that beard of his like a curtain to be sure. "Get yourself down there," he ordered.

I raced to the basement, hoping against hope that the auditorium's supply cabinet held some storybook that Miss Runyon had in reserve for emergencies such as this. Rummaging frantically, I came up with a dog-eared *Mother Goose Tales.* Well, it wasn't Aesop, but it would have to do. I breathed easier; from my experience in the one-room school, even jaded fifth-graders eavesdropped keenly enough when those old nursery tales were read to the younger children.

Then I heard the thumps and scuffles on the stairs.

By the time the freckled heathens of the sixth grade spilled into the room, with Rab riding herd behind them in a harried way, I had given up on Mother Goose. More like a rough-dressed horde than a class, boys and girls alike threw themselves into chairs and looked me over. *Who's this gink?* I heard the loud whispers. *How come so much of him is mustache? Where's Old Lady Bunion?*

"Everyone, shush, or else," Rab recited as if by rote, meanwhile shooing the final straggler in from the hallway. Pale as a chalk figure, Russian Famine slouched past her, sending me a prisoner's gaze as he took the farthest seat of the last row.

His classmates ignored him but not one another, pinching, poking, prodding, and generally provoking disorder. How well I remembered it all. Grade six somehow transforms obedient schoolchildren into creatures with the bravado of bandits and the restlessness of overage Sunday schoolers. Rabrab herself had turned into a schoolyard Cleopatra at that time of life; the Marias Coulee sixth-grade boys went dizzy in her presence. Now I watched her brightly approaching me, while behind her a pugnosed boy and a redheaded girl swatted each other over the issue of elbow room. If Rab, with her battlefield experience, couldn't command best behavior from this bunch, what chance did I have? The dismaying thought occurred to me that, in Butte, perhaps this *was* best behavior.

"Mr. Morgan, what a treat," her velvet murmur greeted me as we stepped aside to confer. "My pupils don't know how lucky they are."

"I can see that. I was hoping for a second-grade choir of angels."

Rab wrinkled her nose at her squirming tribe. "They're somewhat worked up today."

"I wonder why."

"The Hill is a little excitable this morning," she hedged, "but Jared is only doing what he thinks is necessary."

"Maybe so. The question is, what am I to do with this mob of yours, Rab?"

"Anything you like, as long as it teaches first aid," she said contradictorily. "That's a must — we don't want the school board on our necks." She thought to add: "Nor, I imagine, Sam Sandison."

I had forgotten the medical aspect. Seeing my blank look, Rab prompted: "Your Miss Runyon starts off with Florence Nightingale as a nurse in, oh, say the Crimean War, with shot and and shell whizzing everywhere, and somehow jumps from there to strapping one of the pupils up in bandages. Then, next story hour it is Florence Nightingale happening upon some awful accident in London, and —"

"I get the picture."

There was nothing to be done but square myself up and advance to the stage of the auditorium. Restive in the seats below, the class eyed me like cub lions in the arena waiting for a Christian meal. So be it; I took off my suitcoat and tossed it to a surprised Rab, then rolled up my sleeves as if for a fight.

"Blood," I said in a tone practically dripping with it.

The word did its work, for the moment at least. Two dozen sulky faces showed flickers of interest.

"Blood is red as fire, and thicker than rain," I did not let up. "Blood percolates secretly all through us, from finger to toe. It outlines our family, whom we speak of as our own flesh and blood. When we are afraid, we feel our blood run cold, and when we are angry, we are hot-blooded. No other substance carries the magic of life so tirelessly." As I talked on, I pressed a set of fingers to my wrist. "The heart beats in its mysterious way, day and night, so blood never sleeps." I finished taking my pulse. "While I have been speaking, my heart has pumped blood sixty times. If it had stopped doing so, back there when I rolled up my sleeves to test it, by now I would stand before you dead."

Several more heartbeats went by as my audience caught up with that. A litany of gasps, a lesser peal of nervous laughs. One girl crossed herself.

Before such attention wore off, I swept my listeners through the Greek suppositions of Hippocrates and Galen — that blood simply sloshed in us like water in a jug — to William Harvey's discovery that the substance in fact goes around and around.

184

"The circulatory system, as it is called, sends this miraculous fluid circling through us." There is a glaze that comes over a class if too much of a topic is pressed on them at one time, and I could tell from a first few restless feet and territorial elbows that I was reaching that limit.

Folding my arms on my chest in thinking mode, I paced the stage. "Roll up your sleeves, everyone." This was a gamble. Hardboiled boys and pouty girls among the group showed no inclination to do so. But Rab got on the job, patroling mercilessly, and soon enough I had a forest of naked arms in front of me.

"There is a superstition that your life can be read in the palm of your hand," I began, "but really, it is written there on the underside of your wrist." I bustled them through taking their own pulse, emphasizing that the underskin rhythm was actually the contractions of arteries as blood was pushed through by the pumping of the heart. As intended, even the most heedless twelve-year-old could not ignore the message of existence there just beneath a surface barely thicker than paper. "And," I rounded off the arm lesson, "the blood that keeps us going has to find its way back to the heart to be pumped again. See the blue tracings between your wrist and elbow? Each of those is a vein. A word you have heard at home, am I right? Your fathers and perhaps your brothers descend into the body of the earth to find those streaks of ore. If you think about it, copper is the blood of Butte."

As I said so, a part of my mind filled with visions of what lay ahead of these youngsters in this veined city. By all odds, at least one among the fresh-faced boys who would follow the family path into the mines would die underground in that relentless toll of a death a week. A greater number of their classmates in pigtails and curls, women-to-be, would experience perilous childbirth and the innumerable ills of the Hill. Yet others sitting here today would go on uneventfully to what passed for average life in Butte. Those flashes of precognition were hypnotic; I could see as if it were written in me the circlings of fate which would single these young lives out, as always happens in the human story, within the rushing bloodstream of time.

"Mr. Morgan?" Rab prompted me out of my trance. "You were saying . . . ?"

"Ah." I scrambled for new ground. "Blood provides life to our language, too, doesn't it. Shakespeare could scarcely write a page without bloodshed ahead or behind. Poets would have nothing to rhyme perfectly with *flood.* Who can tell me some everyday ways we use this essential word?"

"Bloody murder!" blurted a freckled scamp who seemed to relish the thought.

"Red-blooded," a bossy girl overrode that, impatient at not having been first.

"The blood of our Lord," said a cauliflower-ear tough who nonetheless must have been an altar boy.

"Bloodshot eyes!" rang out from one end of the increasingly enthusiastic audience, and from the other, "Blood poisoning!"

Amid the hubbub came a muted utterance from the back row. Everyone looked around. I encouraged: "A little louder, please?"

Russian Famine wriggled in his seat, scratched behind his ear, gazed over our heads as though that would make us go away, and finally muttered:

"No getting blood out of a turnip."

"A well-known saying, thank you very much," I honored that. Before I could get another word out, a hand was up and waving strenuously. Its owner was the impish enthusiast for bloody murder. "I perceive you have a question."

"Sure do. Back there a ways when you had us taking our pulse, how come we couldn't do it on our veins just as good as on those archeries?"

"Clean out your ears, dummy," the girl next to him jumped on that. "It's not *arch*eries. That's bows and arrows. It's *arth*ries, like *arthritis*. Isn't that right, Mr. Teacher?"

"You are both nearly correct." But not near enough. While explaining that the returning blood in veins was too dispersed to register a pulse, I despaired of ever making my words stick in minds as flighty as these. Then an idea hatched.

"Miss Rellis?" Rabrab was startled to hear me call her that for the first time since she was the age of these students. "Do your young scholars ever sing?"

"They most certainly do. Why?"

"Can they sing this one?" I whistled a snatch of it.

Confidently, Rab swept to the front to lead the command performance. "Class, serenade Mr. Morgan such as he has never heard."

Whether it was the song's mischievous endorsement of betting on bobtail nags or the familiar sassy tune or simply the chance to bawl at the top of their adolescent voices, the sixth-graders attacked the old favorite with gusto, making the auditorium ring with the final galloping chorus:

Camptown ladies sing this song, doo dah,
    doo dah!
Camptown racetrack's five miles long, oh
    the doo dah day!

"Unforgettable," I said with a congratula-
tory bow to the class when the last high-
pitched note had pierced the rafters. "And
would you believe, the exact things we have
been talking about go nicely with that same
tune. Hum it for me and I'll show you."
With the room practically vibrating to Ste-
phen Foster's jingle-jangle rhythm that
practically anything can be fitted to, I improvised:

Arteries and veins and pulse, heartbeat,
    heartbeat!
They all deliver life to us, that's the job of
    blood!

"Ready to try it?" I challenged. They
couldn't be held back. Rab looked radiant
as the young voices romped through my version a number of times.

"One last thing." I rolled my sleeves down
at the conclusion of the songfest. "At next
week's story hour, I am sure Miss Runyon
will be happy to show you the knack of

the tourniquet."

"I hope you didn't do too much damage to the minds of the youngsters."

Sandison was back to prowling the mezzanine when I came upstairs. "Just imagine" — he swept a hand over the scene of the miners tucked in every conceivable sitting place in the Reading Room below — "if we had this kind of patronage on a usual day. The trustees would think we're geniuses." He looked resentfully at the Roman-numeraled clock high on the wall. "And at one minute past noon, ninety out of a hundred of our involuntary scholars will hightail it out of here to the nearest speakeasy. The poor fools."

"That's an altogether gloomy view of humanity, isn't it, Sandy?" I protested. "Surely a good many of the men apply their minds while they're in here like this."

"Hah." He rested his bulk against one of the grand bookcases, the gilt-edged works of George Eliot over one shoulder and Ralph Waldo Emerson over the other. "Let me tell you a story, Morgan." A distant look came into those iceberg-blue eyes. "It was back when I was just starting out in the cattle business, before I could get things built up into the Triple S. I was wintering in

190

by myself — Dora and I hadn't been to a preacher yet. It was a bad winter, down around zero a lot of mornings when I'd have to pitch hay to the cows. Other than the feeding, I had all the time in the world on my hands, and the winter wasn't half over before I'd memorized every damn word of all the reading material in the house." He turned his hands up empty, still in the distance of remembering. "There wasn't a library or bookstore in fifty miles in those days. The only neighbor was an old prospector, up a gulch a couple of miles away. I'd seen a beat-up copy of *Robinson Crusoe* in his cabin." Sandison fixed his disturbing gaze on me. "You're a bookworm, maybe you savvy: I had to have that book or go crazy. I saddled up to go get it. Snow was starting to come down heavy, but I didn't give a damn, I wanted something to read. When I got there the old coot drove a hard bargain — I had to promise him a veal calf in the spring. Anyhow, he finally handed over the book and I wrapped it good in a piece of oilcloth and stuck it under my coat. Rode all the way home in a blizzard, and both ears were frostbitten, but I still thought it was worth it." One more time he scowled down at the mineworkers, some of whom were starting to watch the clock. "See there?

Do you think any of these would have gone through that for the sake of a book? Look at them, they'd rather educate their tonsils than their brains."

Maybe I thought he was scanting the capacities of the Quins and the Jareds and others from the Hill whose minds were as lively as could be asked for. Maybe I was still sailing on air after my session with Rab's young minds. In any case, I indignantly invoked the bard of us all, presiding open-eyed as an owl above the entrance to the jam-packed Reading Room. "You leave me no choice but to bring down Shakespeare on you, Sandy. 'The music of men's lives' is not so easy to call the tune of, we must remember."

At that, the expression under Sandison's beard was unreadable, but the rest was plain enough. Shaking his head conclusively, he moved off toward his office, leaving these words over his shoulder: "You're an optimist, Morgan. That's always dangerous."

"You have a caller."

Along with Grace's knock on my door came the distinct note of curiosity in her tone. I was as inquisitive as she was. With my head still full from that day in the library, I could think of hardly anyone in the entire city who would be paying me a call here, with two shadowy exceptions. But Grace, of all people, would know an Anaconda goon when she saw one. Wouldn't she? To be on the safe side, I made sure the brass knuckles were in my pockets before I went downstairs.

The parlor was empty, as was the dining room; no caller, no Grace, anywhere.

Just as panic was setting in on me, she called from the kitchen: "In here, Morrie. Your visitor is making me tired just looking at him."

At the first glimpse of my guest, I relaxed the grip on my weaponry. Dealing with a twelve-year-old may take a lot of one's resources, but usually not brass knuckles.

Skinny as the sticks of kindling in the woodbox behind him, in dusty patched pants and a hand-me-down shirt, Russian Famine was only barely occupying a chair, one leg jittering and then the other, ready to bolt. Grace, as usual in crisp apron and a dress so clean it practically squeaked, was looking at him as if one or the other of them was at the wrong costume party. So as not to confound her even further, I retrieved the boy's given name with a smile: "Wladislaw, we meet again. What brings you?"

Even his words were thin and fidgety.

"Miss Rellis needs to see you. At that Poor-ity place."

"It's another long story," I fended off Grace's quizzical look. Gesturing toward our surprise caller, I made a supping motion. "Perhaps . . . ?"

"Good heavens, yes." She cut a thick slice of bread, put it on a plate, and set it in front of the famished-looking youngster. Pouring from the syrup can, she said, "Say when."

"I like it sogged."

The syrup pooled on the plate before the boy nodded. As he tucked in to the food, Grace wordlessly cut another slab of bread for him. I excused myself to fetch my hat from upstairs. When I came back down, Grace's guest reluctantly licked his fork and edged out of the chair to go with me. "I may be a while," I told her. "Skip me at supper."

"The larder can stand a chance to recover," she bade us off, still looking mystified.

Another side of Butte showed itself in the route I was now led on. With a nonchalance you might not expect in a sixth-grader, my guide took an immediate shortcut through Venus Alley. Overhead in one of the red-curtained windows, the sash was flung up and a woman in a kimono leaned out. "Hey, kid! How about running over to Betty the bootlegger's and getting us a bottle of her best?"

"I'm busy, can't you see?" the boy called back importantly.

"Then how about you, Mustachio? Come on up and we'll cure what ails you."

"I'm busy keeping up with him," I tipped my hat, "thank you very much anyway."

Block after block, we wound our way past buildings that put all their respectability out front, their back ends grimy with the detritus of coal chutes and the leavings of garbage. Around every other corner a view of the Hill was framed between brick walls, the tower over a mineshaft like a spiked ornament on the roof of the city. I could hear the throb of ore lifts and other machinery, so pronounced after the silence left behind when the morning shift walked off; Jared and his tactic of work actions was turning the Hill off and on like a master switch. If, that is, the Anaconda Company didn't find a way to break his hold on the matter. Or already had. I wondered again why Rab was summoning me.

Suddenly my hotfooted escort was talkative. "How come you work at the library 'stead of the schoolhouse? I was just telling Miss Rellis she's the best teacher in the whole world and she said not as long as you're on two legs."

That touched me deeply. Yet it also mandated an answer. "Life likes to surprise us, Wladislaw, and so —"

"I hate getting called that," he muttered, squirming as if to dodge the name. "It sounds too much like *coleslaw*."

"Russian Famine, then —"

"Don't like that no better. I ain't any kind of a Russian. My unk says if we're anything, it's Glishians." I tried to remember if Galicia was central to what the Europeans from time immemorial called the Polish Problem, and whether that part of Poland was another jigsaw piece on the table in front of Wilson and Clemenceau and Lloyd George as they sought to remake the world with the peace treaty. In any case, the Old Country was forever off the map of a peddler whose only ware was the sharpening of knives, and a skin-and-bones street tough nephew, wasn't it. The thought clutched at me: the fostering places that we are exiled from, in the irreversible twists of life.

Back to the question at hand, though. "Young citizen of the world, we are running out of possibilities — what would you like to be called?"

He thought for the next some steps, slow-ing his pace to mine. "Famine ain't too bad. It'd be one of those nicked names, huh?"

Gravely I took off my hat and in due ceremony tapped him on a narrow shoulder with it. "By whatever authority is vested in me, I dub thee Famine." He bounced a little higher his next couple of steps. "Now, then, Famine, as I was saying. Sometimes a person finds himself doing the unexpected. And so you give each job everything you have, but stay on your toes for what comes next. Isn't it that way with you at school?"

A shrug. "I guess. Miss Rellis's flame says it's the same in the army — now you're peeling spuds and next thing you're shooting back at somebody."

"Jared is at the Purity with her?"

"Uh-huh." The boy flopped his hair out of his eyes and looked around at me hopefully. "That sure was good about blood. Are you gonna do story hour some more?"

"We'll see," I said, smiling. "That's up to the man who runs the library."

"With all the whiskers? The one they call the Earl of Hell?"

That stopped me in my tracks.

"Where did you hear that?"

Famine slowed himself to wait for me by walking backwards. "Down around the stockyards. Those cowboys riding the fence are always yakking about something."

I felt relieved. I could easily believe Samuel Sandison had been high-handed in his ranch days and gained that name in the Triple S bunkhouse. That had me thinking about the doggedness of reputation, fair or not, when Famine, curiosity on as much of his face as there was, wanted to know:

"What's a earl?"

"Someone who owns everything but a good name, usually. That other word, I'd advise you not to use around Miss Rellis."

"Uh-huh, she's death on cussing." Restless as a hummingbird, Famine now was talking to the top of my head. I had frowned him off clambering on fire escapes along our backstreet route, but he couldn't resist hopping up onto the loading docks at rear entries to stores. He teetered along the planked edge of this latest one, his sense of balance making a mockery of gravity. I watched with the envy of those of us who have outgrown the blind bravery of a twelve-year-old. Perhaps it was the pale sharp cheeks or the flatly factual eyes beneath the toss of uncombed yellow hair, but he looked oddly pristine up there, more like a trainee in an acrobats' academy than a schoolboy. I thought back to the blood enthusiasts among his classmates, and to the black eyes, bent noses, scabs, and bruises that my Marias Coulee pupils accumulated in the average mayhem of the schoolyard. Skinny and milk-skinned as he was, my young friend seemingly would be a bullies' delight, yet there was not a mark on him. "Famine, I'm not trying to be nosy, but the bigger boys don't give you trouble?"

"Would if they could catch me."

"You're quite the runner, then. Don't they ever catch you?"

"Huh-uh." He continued along the outmost inch of the loading platform with the aplomb of a tightrope walker. "I run until they drop."

After depositing me at the entrance to the Purity Cafeteria, Famine vanished at a high lope. The owner, a scarlet bow tie blazing under his set of chins, met me with a glad cry. "I knew you'd be back," the gust of welcome nearly parted my hair. "Your appetite wouldn't let you stay away! Help yourself, this is the spot to fill that hollow leg!" I slipped in line behind a broad-beamed couple who obviously had partaken of the menu many times before. First things first, as ever; I peeked from behind the glassware breakfront to make sure the Typhoon goon was not on the premises, then gathered a meal for myself and joined Rab and Jared at their corner table.

Fatigue showed on Jared, but so did something like the sheen of a winning streak; Rab's pride in him stuck out all over her. He had not backed down after the dynamiting of the Flying Dutchman pay office, simply skipped aside from any blame with the kind of remark Butte loved — even the *Daily Post* could not resist quoting him — to the effect that anybody who worked for Anaconda maybe should have his head examined, but no miner was dumb enough to blow up the place his wages came from. In boxing parlance, I knew, he and the union were winning the early rounds on points, with the shift stoppages he was invoking about some faulty working condition or another in the mineshafts; the danger was whether the company would be provoked into unloading a haymaker, such as a lockout or a show of force, brutal and bloody, by its goons. Well, he was the tactician and I wasn't. I simply remarked, "On behalf of the library, I should thank you for our unprecedented number of users, lately."

"Always glad to encourage the cause of learning," Jared responded, wearing that droll expression somewhere between pious and piratical. "I hear you're quite the expert on blood." He eyed me as if curious to find any evidence to back that up.

"In a pedagogical sense," I said, between bites of my food. "All in all, though, that is likely the wisest approach to the substance. For instance, Shakespeare invoked the word some seven hundred times in his works, but there is no evidence he ever actually experienced the shedding of blood. Christopher Marlowe, now, sadly did undergo —"

"My pupils want you back next week to talk about skulls and skeletons," Rab sought to pin me down.

"While you're handing out favors," Jared was quick on the heels of that, "I could use one, too. Rab tells me you're a whiz with figures."

With a modest gesture I admitted to something of the sort.

"Good. Anaconda has us bamboozled on the production figures." As if scouting a battlefield, he scanned the entirety of the restaurant to make sure we were not being observed. "Show him, Rab."

Covertly she cracked open her sizable purse to give me a peek at a vivid sheaf of papers. "Those are the pink sheets the mine managers hand in at the end of each week," Jared went on in a low voice. "The janitor at the Hennessy Building is supposed to burn them, but he has a nephew working in the Neversweat shafts, so he slips the batch to us." Rapidly he explained that the famously fought-over wage was tied to the Hill's production total and subsequent price of copper, but the union was suspicious of the company's numbers in the negotiations. "They're playing it cute on us, we're pretty sure. It seems like the bulk tons that come out of the mine" — he indicated Rab's trove of pink sheets — "ought to add up to more processed tons at the smelter than the company tells us. But the differential is the problem. No two mines assay out at the same percent of copper in the ore, and there are three dozen Anaconda mines on the Hill." Jared tugged ruefully at his lopped ear. "It's driving us batty trying to come up with a complete figure to argue against theirs."

"I told you Mr. Morgan would have a solution," Rab snuggled nearer him with the scheming expression I remembered so well, "just wait and see."

With the situation delineated to their satisfaction, the two of them, ravens of collusion, waited me out.

This, I realized with a churning in my stomach that caused me to lose interest in my meal, was another of those moments when choice was forced upon me. What was being asked of me was exactly what Sandison inveighed against, taking sides in the dogfight, as he not inaccurately characterized the Butte feud of labor and capital. Here was where a headful of learning was a burden. Intuition, instinct, some mental gremlin, whispered to me that the library's extensive mineralogy section, complete with the annual mining reports of the state industrial board, with a bit of calculation might yield the set of ore differentials the union needed. But why should it be up to me to coax out that magic arithmetic? Unfortunately the answer kept coming back: *Who else?* Resist it as I tried, a certain line of reasoning insisted that the Anaconda Company had an army of bookkeepers on its side and the union deserved at least one.

Besides, around Jared Evans you felt you were made of stronger stuff than you previously imagined, and Rab's guile was as infectious as ever.

"All right," I sighed as she glowed in triumph, "let me see what I can do." Jared watched keenly as she slipped me the pink sheets and I tucked them well out of sight inside my vest. "I may live to regret this, but I'll help out in the name of the holy cause of the lost dollar."

"Oh, we have the wage back up to where it was," he answered matter-of-factly. "Now we need to fight to hang on to it."

"You have the — Since when?"

"Since some Anaconda bigwig with a lick of sense looked at a calendar and realized Miners Day is almost here." He grinned fully for the first time. "Just after the next payday."

"It's Butte's biggest doings of the year," Rab leapt in on that. "The whole town turns out for Miners Day. You'll have to, too, Mr. Morgan."

My brain felt weak. "Are you telling me the Anaconda Company gave in about the dollar because a holiday is coming?"

"Look at it from their side," Jared instructed. "Every miner in Butte will be perfectly legally parading through town that day. If you were up there on the top floor of the Hennessy Building, would you rather have them happy or ready to tear things up?"

"Then this is a kind of truce," I wanted to make sure of what I was hearing, "of the moment?"

"That's not a bad way of putting it," he commended in his best sergeant manner. "The one thing sure about dealing with Anaconda is that the war is never over."

■ ■ ■ ■

Whatever lunar power Miners Day possessed that the year's other three hundred and sixty-four did not, things settled down ahead of it. Work actions ceased and the Hill pulsed day and night with the excavation of rich copper ore. The coveted dollar a day, as Jared had said, was added back in to the wages of ten thousand temporarily soothed union men. Without the morning tide of miners, library life quieted to its usual seashell tone of whispers. Miraculously, I nearly caught up with the chores Sandison pushed my way. He himself, of course, constituted a sizable task as often as not.

This day I came back into the office after some errand to find him pacing from his desk to the window and back, his bootsteps sharp as a march beat. Barely acknowledging me with a glance, he delivered: "That robber Gardiner in New York I deal with has a fine copy of *The Bride of Lammermoor.* What do you think?"

Quick as a fingersnap, I calculated what a transaction of that sort would do to the delicate balance I had achieved in the library's ledger. "Sir Walter Scott himself regarded that as one of his lesser works," I responded breezily. "Rather like *Ivanhoe*, but done with a trowel."

He grunted. "All right, I'll think it over." The boots retraced their route as if following dance steps imprinted on the floor. I grew uneasy as he prowled the room, more often than not a signal that something was on his mind. I could only hope no one had blabbed to him that I was staying late after the Jabberwockians and other evening groups packed up and went home, and immersing myself suspiciously deep in the mineralogy section.

Just then Miss Mitchell from the cataloguing section, young and rather pretty and somewhat of a flirt, came in with a question. I dealt with it in no time and she pranced out.

Sandison watched the back of her until she shimmied out of sight, then turned to me with a frown. "Morgan, I don't see you making eyes at young things like that even when they're asking for it. What are you, some kind of buck nun?"

This turn of topic took me off guard. Good grief, did my social situation look that dusty to someone whose own idea of mating in life was the grandee and grandora sort? Trying not to show how much that smarted, I stiffly assured my white-bearded interrogator: "I enjoy female companionship when it presents itself, never fear."

"This day got away from me." Grace guiltily bustled past me, trying to tie her apron and control her braid at the same time, when I came in at the end of my own hectic day. "How do you feel about cold turkey for supper?"

"Rather tepid. Let me see what can be done." Following her to the kitchen, I scrounged the cupboard, coming up with cheese that was mostly rind, some shelled walnuts, and macaroni. Yielding the culinary arena gracefully, so to speak, Grace stood aside while I whacked chunks of the turkey into smaller pieces and set those to simmering in cream and flour in a baking pan.

"Such talent." She watched with folded arms as I did my imitation of Escoffier. "If all else fails, you can get on as a cook at the Purity," she ventured.

Up until then, I had not offered any explanation of Rab mysteriously summoning me to the cafeteria, nor, for that matter, of Rab herself. "Yes, well, Miss Rellis you heard mentioned by our fleet young friend the other day," I fussed with the meal makings some more while coming up with a judicious version of the past, "and to make a long story short," by which time a pot of water was boiling merrily and I dumped in the macaroni for what was going to approximate turkey tetrazzini, "someone I knew when she was just a girl ends up as the fiancée of none other than Jared Evans. Isn't it surprising how things turn out?"

Grace's expression had gradually changed from puzzlement to a ghost of a smile. "You lead an interesting life, Morrie."

As I combined the macaroni and turkey and added the walnuts, I took the opportunity to bring up the question that was in my mind and doubtless Hoop's and Griff's these past many suppers. "Now you tell me something — why is a holiday bird like this such a perpetual bargain at this time of year?"

Razor-sharp shopper that she was, Grace looked at me as if I did not understand basic commerce. "Don't you know? The homesteaders' crops dried up, so they tried raising turkeys. The whole dryland country is gobblers these days, and what that does to the price, you see, is —"

"I can guess, thank you." I tried not to show it, but the news of hard times in the other Montana, the prairie part of the state where agriculture drank dust if rain did not come, hit into me all the way to the hilt. My hands took over to grate the cheese atop the other ingredients while the remembering part of myself was transported to Marias Coulee and the parting of the ways there, Rose's and mine. So deep in thought was I that I barely heard Grace's expression of relief as the turkey dish went into the oven looking fit for a feast. "You've turned the trick again, how do you do it?" She patted my shoulder as she passed. "I'll call you and the Gold Dust Twins to the table when it's done."

My mood refused to lift during supper; the boardinghouse blues are not easily shaken once they get hold of you. The same exact faces that had seemed so companionable three times a day now surrounded me like random passengers in a dining car, right, left, and center. The four of us were at that table because nowhere in our solitary lives was there a setting for just two. I knew Hooper was a widower, and no one had ever been willing to put up with Griffith as a matrimonial mate. Grace still was beholden to her knightly Arthur, touchy as she was about any appearance of being "taken up with" by an unworthy successor. And I, I had to be classified as something like an obligatory bachelor, always mindful that for a woman to be married to me would be like strapping her to a lightning rod. A quartet of solitudes, sharing only a tasty meal.

Tired from brooding — tired *of* brooding — I excused myself from small talk after eating and went up to my room to lose myself in a book. The one I had brought home was a lovely blue-and-gold volume of letters titled *Let Me Count the Ways.* The illustrious surname incised twice on the cover caused me a rueful moment; Casper used to tease me whenever he caught sight of my Browning collection, asking if I was reading up on how to get a suntan.

I tucked into a pillow and the coverlet, hoping to be transported, and was. In the marriage of poets, I found from the very first page, each wrote with the point of a diamond. Dazzled and dazzling, Robert Browning was a suitor beyond any that Elizabeth of Wimpole Street could have dreamt of:

I love your verses with all my heart, dear Miss Barrett . . . the fresh strange music, the affluent language, the exquisite pathos and true new brave thought; but in this addressing myself to you — your own self, and for the first time, my feeling rises altogether.

I do, as I say, love these books with all my heart — and I love you too.

The quality in that. The pages fell still in my hands as I thought of such a matching of souls. The ceiling became a fresco of Marias Coulee as I sank back on the pillow and imagined my version.

"Morrie! You're back! Even though you promised not to be."

"Rose, run away with me."

"Oh, I can't."

"You did before."

"I did, didn't I. But that was to save our skins, remember?"

"You might be surprised how little the situation has changed."

"Tsk, don't spoof like that. I know you. That tongue of yours calls whatever tune it wants to."

"If you won't listen to reason, my dear, let me try passion. We have ten lost years to make up."

"Where's the clock that can do that?"

Rose always did know how to stump a good argument.

Wincing, I put away reverie and sat up. My mind took a resolute new posture as well. You don't need to be an Ecclesiastes devotee to realize there is a time to equivocate and a time to do something.

Still in my slippers, I trotted down the stairs. In the living room, Grace whirled from the sideboard where she was putting away her mending, looking flustered at my hurried arrival. I halted at the foot of the stairs, she braced at her end of the room. Practically in chorus, we blurted:

"I was wondering if you might want to —"

"If you don't have anything better to do —"

Both of us stumbled to a pause. She caught her breath and expelled it in saying, "You first."

"I'd be impolite."

"Morrie, out with it, whatever it is — we can't beat around the bush all night."

"I suppose not. I, ah, I wondered if you might like to go to Miners Day. With me, that is."

Grace covered her mouth against a wild laugh. I felt ridiculous and, calling myself every kind of a fool, was ready to slink back upstairs when she put out a hand to stop me. "Great minds run in similar tracks. I was about to knock on your door and ask you."

8

"Never seen you quite so dolled up, Morrie. Mrs. Faraday will have to go some to keep up with you."

I smoothed the fabric of my new checked vest and adjusted the silk necktie bought to match it. "Everyone tells me Miners Day is a holiday like no other. You are quite the fashion plate yourself, Griff."

"Better be, on account of the parade. We've marched in every one of them, haven't we, Hoop."

"Since parades was invented."

The brand-new work overalls on both of them looked stiff enough to creak, and underneath were the churchgoing white shirts and ties. Their headgear, though, was the distinctive part. Each wore a dingy dented helmet that must have seen hard duty in the mineshafts.

"Are you expecting a hailstorm?" I asked with a straight face.

Hoop proudly tapped his headpiece. "The Hill tried to knock my brains out any number of times, but nothing ever got past this lid. Anymore we only wear it the one day a year, don't we, Griff."

Telling me they had to form up early with the other marchers or spend the entire parade looking at hundreds of behinds, the pair hustled out while I waited for Grace to come down from her room. With the Hill not operating due to the holiday, a stillness had settled over the city, and the boarding-house was in rare quiet. A silent room that is not your own tends to breed long thoughts. Around me now, the boarding-house's furnishings seemed to sit in arrested attitude, as if arranged in a villa in Pompeii. The mood of timeless deliberation drew me in and I became more aware than ever of the wedding photograph on the sideboard, where Arthur Faraday stared levelly at me. Something in that everlasting straight gaze reminded me of Casper, likewise gone too early from life and a bride who idolized him. Introspection is a rude visitor. An unsparing look into myself went to the heart, in more ways than one. I know myself fairly well: I am solo by nature. Incurably so, on the evidence thus far. But what a hard-eyed trick of fate — perhaps reflected in Arthur's stare? — if I was destined, around women, always to be a stand-in for better men.

"Sorry to keep you waiting," I heard Grace behind me, her footsteps quick on the stairs. "I had about forgotten how to dress up."

I turned to look at her, and looked again. She had gone some, in Griff's phrase for it. Her hair was done up in a crown braid, and atop that sat a broad-brimmed summer hat with a nice little swoop to it and a sprig of red ribbon. Her dress, attractively tailored to her compact form, was of a sea green with a shimmer to it. Even her complexion had a new glow, assisted by just enough rouge to give her cheeks a hint of blush.

"Very nice," I fumbled out.

"You, too," she managed.

With Arthur in the room, we stood there, shying away from further compliments, until she remembered to check the clock. "We should get a move on," landlady back in her voice, "everyone turns out for the parade. I hope we can still find a place to see."

"Spare yourself that worry," I rallied. "I know just the spot."

Man, woman, and child, the populace of Butte lined the downtown streets a dozen thick. I shouldered a way for us, Grace with a grip on the tail of my coat, to the block by the library. She looked dubious as I led her past people picnicking on the steps to the big arched doorway. "Isn't the library closed for today?"

"Except to the privileged." I displayed the key.

We slipped in, the ornate front door sweeping closed behind us. Inside the thick walls, the din of the outside world was shut out. The foyer, its Tuscan paneling and dark timbered beams as royal as ever, stood staidly empty. I glanced up to see whether Shakespeare winked at us as we passed through the Reading Room doorway, and he may have. Grace gazed around the elegant quiescent chamber with a trace of awe, and then at me. "Sam Sandison must trust you."

"Mmm, I suspect he simply doesn't want me to have any excuse day or night for not being in here doing all the things he piles on me to do."

As we passed through the Reading Room, I could not help but stop for a minute and run my eyes over the mezzanine's ranks of books, silent but eloquent. I was smitten every time by the finest collection west of Chicago, and to have its literary riches almost to myself this way seemed like a scene in a dream. Housed in their volumes, the souls of writers waited in this great room to come out into the light of day. I would not have been surprised right then if Joseph Conrad materialized at the railing like a stalwart first mate on the deck watch, or Emily Dickinson came tiptoeing out of the shelves to peer down to the unattainable life below.

"My. It's so different in here without anyone around, isn't it."

"Grace, you needn't whisper."

"Oh, right." She trilled a laugh in relief. "If you promise not to shush me."

A last lingering moment, I gazed at the varicolored bindings as a person would cast a final glance at the jeweled colors of a cathedral window. Then I motioned Grace to the stairway, but she stayed as she was, studying me. "This is the love of your life, isn't it. What's in these books."

"I suppose it is," I conceded. "As the phrase goes, for better and for worse."

Off the corridor to Sandison's office was a small balcony, like a flex in the stonework over the main entrance's keystone arch, and the parade coming down Broadway would pass practically beneath us. Grace went straight to the balustrade and took a full look around, adjusting the swoop of her hat to keep the sun out of her eyes. Smiling her best, she plucked at the cuff of my suitcoat. "This is such a treat, you devil."

The rising roar from the street announced that things were under way. The copper capital of the known world knew how to stage a spectacle. Everything in shoes walked in the parade. The lodges — Masons, Elks, Templars, Odd Fellows, you name it — all of them sashed, some plumed. The firemen, prideful of their new hook-and-ladder Ford. The suffragists, resolute with their signs championing the correction to the Constitution that would give women the vote. The trade unions, and in Butte that was every trade; bakers, tailors, cooks, carpenters, even blacksmiths went by with their banners in the breeze. Most groups were led by a drum, the boom of march step resounding off the buildings. Then behind those marchers came the big horses, the brass of their harnesses gleaming, pulling delivery vans of every sort, and other horse-drawn conveyances polished up for the occasion. A traveling carnival, calliope and all, rolled past in gold-spoked wagons; a stilt-walker ambulated by nearly at eye level with us. The next group on wheels were putt-putting automobiles with dignitaries trying to maintain dignity in the herky-jerky progress.

Eventually, more pedestrianly, came contingents of schoolchildren. Rab, gaily dressed, went by in charge of a flock of beribboned girls representing her school. She spotted me, waved, and blew me a kiss. Grace looked at me with a slightly raised eyebrow. "She must have been quite something as a girl."

By now the Miners Day processional had gone on for a considerable time, and I leaned out to see how much more there could possibly be. "Good heavens!" was all I could say.

Bearing down on us was what looked like an army of toy soldiers magnified to heroic size. Each marching man wore a uniform of emerald green with gold-thread embossing across the chest and down the sleeves, and their cap visors were set identically low to their brows. The mix of gaudy uniforms and shiny musical instruments suggested an orchestra conscripted onto the stage of an operetta. As the marching mass neared the library, its leader spun in his tracks and, walking backward, lifted his arms. Instantly instruments sprang to lips, and at his signal, a Sousa march roared to life. Sun glinted off a tuba, the extensions of trombones, the squadron of cornets. The bass drums produced a beat that could be felt on the body.

"The Miners' Band," Grace managed to make herself heard into my ear. "They're nationally known. Not for lullabies, as you might guess."

And in the wake of the powerful music, here came the miners in their hundreds and hundreds, beneath a forest of banners with the union council proudly at the front. Leading them with his level stride was Jared Evans, in suit and tie and a snappy hat that might as well have been a crown. With his triumph in the wage battle, he was the hero of the day; Caesar coming home to Rome after victory could have received no greater tribute from the crowd. Grace and I added our cheers. The banners dipped and rose and swirled in back of Jared and the other council members, where the ranks of men who worked in the mineshafts stretched for blocks, each national group distinct to itself as I had seen them that first day on the Hill, but now scrubbed and tidied and in their best clothing. We strained to see, and tucked in between the Finns and the Serbs were the retired miners, with Griffith and Hooper and dozens of stooped replicas all in their vintage helmets.

By now the band had wheeled about and

strutted back, facing the mineworkers. The resplendent bandleader lifted his arms and everything halted. He bowed from the waist toward the council, and a great cheer went up for the union and the restored wage. The other council members pushed Jared, grinning and not objecting too much, out for recognition by himself. The bandleader spun, up went the arms, and in tribute the band thundered into the mighty Welsh anthem "Men of Harlech."

Men of Harlech, march to glory!
Victory is hov'ring o'er ye!
Bright-eyed freedom stands before ye —
Hear ye not her call?

"I've never been within five thousand miles of Wales," Grace was sniffling when it was over, "and that old thing always makes me want to bawl."

I was somewhat misty myself. "A very wise man once said mankind's two great magics are words and music."

Meanwhile Jared had doffed his hat to the band and the crowd, and the marchers were starting to shuffle into motion again.

Then it happened.

From somewhere, perhaps an alley or a rooftop, came a lone singing voice, just short of a yodel but with a devilish lilt to it. The refrain sliced through the parade mood:

Wear the copper collar,
Swallow dirt for your dollar.
You'll get pie in the sky
When you die.

Jared looked up as if the mocking ditty had hit him like an arrow. A squad of policemen at the intersection, whom I had assumed were on hand to hold back the crowd, jumped into action toward where the derisive singing seemed to come from. Before they made much headway, the invisible songster was at it again.

Work and pray,
Live on hay.
You'll get pie in the sky
When you die.

Now a couple of the council members shouted to the bandleader, a march tune was struck up, and the parade slowly snaked into motion once again. Looking back from now, what strikes me in the whole episode was that although I had never heard the pie-in-the-sky stanza before, I knew its origin almost from the first few insidiously catchy notes. So did Jared, according to his reaction. That kind of serenade rose straight from the Little Red Songbook.

"That's Butte for you." Grace had been waiting as patiently as she could for me to return to myself. "The top of the world one minute, the glory hole the next."

Now it was her turn to surprise. With the parade over, I assumed we would follow the crowd to the next attraction, down at the depot. Butte was a regular stop for political speakers traveling through, in that ritual of a suspender-bursting oration from the rear platform of a train. Today's portable statesman was the imported variety, Eamon de Valera, a leader in Ireland's struggle against British rule, and judging by the sprigs of green in lapels and bonnets of everyone rushing by us, Dublin Gulch was avalanching off the Hill to hear him. Grace, though, firmly headed us the other direction. She would not tell me our destination — "You know what curiosity did to the cat, don't you?" — as we bundled onto a trolley. All I saw ahead as the trolley tracks continued past the outskirts of the city were mine dumps and the wall of mountains that topped out at the Continental Divide. Yet Grace and the other holiday-goers packed in with us were as merry as if we were bound for paradise.

The last stop on the line, in the tuck of a valley at the foot of the mountains, may not have been my notion of paradise, but it was somebody's idea of a fantasy land. We stepped off into an enormous amusement park, with COLUMBIA GARDENS spelled out in floral design against an entire hillside. Everything but the flowers seemed to be in excited motion. As I tried to take it all in, a roller coaster galloped through the treetops, and beyond, a Ferris wheel spun against the sky. Across acres and acres of the only green grass I had seen since coming to Butte, there were picnic groves; a playground featuring a brilliantly striped maypole and high-flying swings and a labyrinth of monkey bars; a merry-go-round; a zoo; a baseball diamond; a boxing ring; a trout pond; flower gardens; on and on. And the populace of the city had arrived in force to absorb the pleasures, it looked like. There is an unforgettable painting by Bruegel of swarms of children, serious about their fun, each bunch engaged in a different game and oblivious to the larger world. This panorama was like that.

Directly ahead from where Grace and I stood was a huge central pavilion, vaguely Italianate, surrounded by a soda parlor and other refreshment stands. "Pinch me," I told her, "I seem to have been whisked off to Coney Island. Who runs this?" She only gave me a certain kind of look.

"Don't tell me," I groaned. "The Anaconda Company."

"You're getting better at the facts of life," she awarded me.

The extravaganza surrounding us, then, was the other side of the copper coin, at least for this one day. Shaking my head at the turnabout of Anaconda's conduct, I asked Grace what she would like to do first. "Stroll the gardens," she chose without hesitation. "I haven't had an outing like this since — it's been a few years."

For as long as there are men and women, some things in life will best be done arm in arm, and strolling a flower garden is one. We exclaimed together at a hillside burst of blooms planted in the design of a giant lyre, as if a Gulliver had temporarily laid aside his music-making. Grace's grip on my arm was an exclamation in itself as we happily competed in naming off blossoms while we walked. Under the spell of the aromatic surroundings, we soon were sharing more than just the pleasure of the day. Grace's story was entirely rooted in Butte, I learned. "The mapmakers don't get rich on some of us,

Morrie." To help support the family she had been a bucket girl, selling sandwich lunches from a pail as the men trooped to the mines on the Hill. There she caught the eye of a young miner on the same shift with her father; Arthur Faraday, as patient as he was gallant, had his reward when she reached marriageable age. The toils of Butte took her parents before their time — heart and lungs worked to death — leaving the young couple the gift of property. I listened raptly, the makings of a life always casting a spell on me. "We thought we had it made, Arthur and I, with the house in our name and his job in the Speculator." Instead, the fire, the worst in American mining history, widowed her overnight. There had been no children. "Nature did not provide." Left on her own, Grace used what resource she had — the house — and boarders such as present company were the result. "You and the matched pair are good about the rent," she patted my arm, "but it's still a hard go. The taxes and the upkeep and all. I get by, though. No sense in waiting for my ship to come in when there's none in sight, I've decided." She tilted her head in my direction, putting the question lightly enough. "What about yours, is the library it? You seem at home there." I cocked the same kind of look to her. "Do I? I don't always have the Butte Public Library all to myself, understand."

We laughed, duly self-conscious about the day's unexpected glimpses into each other. So much private time on the most public day of the year surely was too good to last. "Aren't Hoop and Griff joining us?" I checked. "It's not like them to miss this kind of spree."

"They're off to their own pursuits, they told me," Grace reported in that tone of fond exasperation the pair customarily produced in her. All at once she clutched my arm hard enough to leave a mark. "Look, dear!"

Companionable as our promenade was, I was surprised silly by the sudden endearment. I had to wonder if I was keeping up with developments. Was this a forward side of Grace Faraday, hitherto hidden in the house rules of landlady and boarder? Then, thoroughly abashed, I saw the deer she meant, several does and fawns flitting through a stand of blue spruce in the near distance.

"Cutlets on the hoof," I jested feebly and drew a swat on the arm, but also Grace's teasing smile.

Something surprising seemed to be the

constant at Columbia Gardens. Fresh riots of flora in exuberant designs kept showing up as we strolled. Around any curve of the path, we were apt to be met with flower-holding ceramic gnomes of the European sort. And down at a pond off to our side, evincing great interest in the ducks, was Typhoon Tolliver.

There in broad daylight, the awful sensation of being stalked by shadows came over me. Luckily, Grace was distracted by the next riot of flowers. Taking a neck-stretching look around as if I could not get enough of admiring the grounds, I caught sight of Eel Eyes behind us, lurking around a corner of the soda fountain.

Apprehension rose in me like the mercury in a thermometer with a match under it. There is no law that goons have to take holidays like the rest of us, but why was this pair of dunces on my tail at all? The miners and the Anaconda Company were at peace, at least temporarily. Were Typhoon and his sidekick simply in the habit of following my every move? Whatever the notion in their thick heads, I didn't like it.

I scanned around some more. Back toward the pavilion and its huddle of refreshment stands, a photographer with his hood and flash powder was busily taking pictures of posing couples. "Let's," I said, pointing. "What's a day like this without a keepsake? My treat."

Grace hesitated, no doubt hearing from the spirit of Arthur. Verve won out. She primped her extensive hat and provided me a practice smile. "I suppose we shouldn't let all this gussying up go to waste."

The waiting line to be photographed was considerable, as I was counting on. "You hold our place," was my next proposal. "How about a root beer fizz?"

"Morrie, are you made of money all of a sudden?"

"I hope you're not turning down a root beer fizz."

"Of course not."

Off I strode, nonchalantly enough, to the soda parlor and its line of customers. The instant the angle of the building concealed me from Eel Eyes, I darted around to the back.

I crept along until I could sneak a look around the far corner. Eel Eyes, his back to me, was slouched against the building, dully watching for me to return to the photography line. I was scared to do what I was about to do, but more scared not to. The one advantage I had was musical; the Miners' Band had arrived somewhere on the park premises, and the triumphal march from *Aïda* was blaring loudly enough to drown any sound I could possibly make. Whatever Nile god is in charge of brass knuckles I said a quick prayer to, and fitted the metal onto my fists. Coming up unheard behind the bored goon, I clipped him hard on the crazy bone of his left elbow.

He yelped like a coyote and flopped around clutching the elbow, his business hand unable to reach for the blackjack or gun or whatever he carried in his coat. Grabbing hold of his shirtfront, I backed him against the rear of the soda parlor. While he was still squirming in pain, I rested a fist on the point of his chin, where at any sharp move the brass knuckles could knock out his front teeth.

"Typhoon isn't close enough to be any help to you," I uttered with so much bravado I hardly recognized my voice, "so you're going to have to tell me a thing or two. Why do the pair of you keep following me around like collie dogs?"

"Coincidence," he said sullenly, looking down his nose at the brass knobs threatening his teeth.

"Come now, Roland. Before one of us gets hurt" — I tapped his chin hard enough to make him wince — "you need to rid yourself of this ridiculous notion that I'm worth tagging after. Where does it come from, anyway?"

"How am I supposed to talk with those things half in my mouth?"

"Try."

He drew his lips over his teeth and munched out the words. "Let's square with each other, Morgan, or whoever you are. You're up to something, but Ty and me are on to you — so what do you say we cut a deal?"

"I am not 'up' to anything, you idiot, and whatever the pair of you think you're 'on to' is a figment of your overcooked imaginations."

"Oh yeah? Try this for size," he mustered hardily for a person in his situation. "Butte ain't been quite the same since you showed up. You got off that train and funny stuff started happening. Wildcat strikes. That old mug who runs the library wakes up and throws his weight around. And today you're up there on that balcony like a royal highness and at just the right time some Wobbly belts out a song and throws the whole parade bunch into a fit. Don't that add up to something in anybody's book?"

"That is all coinci—" I caught myself from using his exculpatory word. "I swear to you, man to man, I did not come to Butte to stir up trouble. What more can I do to convince you?"

"Leave town. Vamoose."

I hated to admit it, considering the source, but there was a lot of sense in that. Something else outweighed it, though. Maybe this was a wrong reading of the human condition, but it seemed to me there ought to be a limit to the number of times in life a person was obligated to vamoose.

Eel Eyes took my brief silence to mean I was thinking it over. "Ty and me will put you on a train tomorrow, how about?" he blurted. "We won't lift a hand to you except to wave good riddance, I promise. Him and me can find better things to do with ourselves than trailing you around."

"Then go find those, starting about now. But I'm not leaving. Butte is too interesting at the moment." His left hand was creeping toward the inside of his coat, so I rapped his knuckles with my brass ones. "Ow!" He sucked his lips over his teeth again. "And one more thing while we're at this," I leaned in on him instructively. "In case you're told to deliver any messages about a glory hole to a certain boardinghouse, save yourself the trouble on that, too. Now go collect your fellow idiot and" — I have to admit, I took nasty pleasure in the word — "vamoose."

I gave him room, and he backed around away from me. At a safe distance, he spat out: "Okay, we're done following you since you're on to it, but that ain't the only way to nail you. We'll get the goods on you yet."

"Tsk, Roland. You really ought to take up some other line of work."

He looked at me with sneering pity. "There's goods to be got on anybody, sucker."

"Did you have to brew the root beer for those?" Grace inquired when I came back. We sipped our fizzes while the last few couples ahead of us in line were posed to wait for the click of the shutter, then it was our turn.

If memory serves me right, it was Balzac who believed that the human body has layers of self, and each time we are photographed one of those ghostly images is peeled off us irreparably onto the photographic print. In our case, Grace posed cautiously beneath the shelter of her hat, and I'm sure I looked as though I had too many things on my mind, which I did.

"Perfect!" cried the photographer as the flash powder went off with a *poof*.

He emerged from under his black cloth to

hand me a numbered receipt. "Here you go, you can pick up your picture at the gate when you leave."

Grace startled me by taking my arm again. "Now I have a surprise for you."

Surprises come in two sizes, good and bad. Hers remained indeterminate while she steered me through the holiday throng toward the grandstand by the playing fields. The area was buzzing with activity as sporting events took shape; I could not help but notice two boxers going at it in the ring at a corner of the grassy expanse. After Eel Eyes, a boxing match appealed to me as restful. But Grace did not guide me up into the stands to spectate the various contests as I expected. With a flourish, she led me to the lip of the grass where the surprise came into sight.

I laughed helplessly. "Why didn't I think of this?"

"You must be slipping," she teased.

"I'll try to make up for it. Wait here, I'll be right back."

She frowned. "Has anyone ever told you, Morrie, you are restless company?"

Off I went in search of a gnome that moved, and found him circulating in the vicinity of the men's lavatory, as expected.

"What's up, buddy?" the halfpint messenger, in Sunday suit and bow tie for the day, called out when he spotted me. "Hey, how about those White Sox? They're burning up the league."

I sighed. Chicago follows a person like a botanical name. "The Comiskey Cheap Sox," I scoffed as I came up to him. "They'll unravel."

"You Cubs guys don't know real baseball when you see it."

"I shall keep looking." I left it at that and got down to business. "Skinner, I believe you might know how a man could place a bet."

"Think so?" He scanned the grounds. Satisfied that no strolling policeman was going to intrude on his working territory, he whipped out a much-used notebook. "What's your pleasure? The boxing matches? The mucking contest?"

"The boys' hundred-yard dash."

Indignantly Skinner pushed away the money I held out to him. "You kidding me? Use your noggin, buddy. Not till I look this over. How do I know you're not running some junior-size Jim Thorpe in on me."

Russian Famine was shambling back and forth at the edge of the field of contestants like a stray keeping his distance from the herd. All the boys in the race wore jerseys cut down; the stenciled FARADAY BOARD-ING HOUSE practically wrapped around him.

I went over to lend encouragement. I needed some myself after a closer look at our entrant. His gangly arms and legs were as pale as if the bones beneath were reflecting through, the strawy hair had not been combed in days, and for lack of a handkerchief in his racing outfit he was busily wiping his nose with the tail of the jersey. I had to hope the rest of him was as runny as his nose. Bending down to him, I urged in a low voice: "When you're in the race, Famine, just imagine the other boys are trying to catch you and beat you up."

"Doesn't take much imagination," he said stoically.

"To the victor belongs the spoils, remember."

"Huh?"

"Just run like the wind." I patted him on a barely existent shoulder, then joined Grace on the sidelines. She looked worriedly at the bigger boys in the race. "You're the one who told me he's lightning on two legs. He'll need to be." She inclined her head indicatively at a lanky redheaded lad, Irish as Saint Paddy, wearing a jersey with

PETERSON'S MODERN MORTUARY across his chest, and on the back: AND FUNERAL HOME. "Look at that one, he makes two of poor Famine. This had better be worth the five dollars," she muttered, meaning the sponsoring fee.

"At the very least, it will distinguish the boardinghouse." I did not need to say with precision that it would distinguish it from the different sort of houses a block or so away in Venus Alley.

Catching Skinner's eye, I stepped over to place my bet. Observing this wagering side of me, Grace bit her lip but said nothing. Skinner wasn't happy to see me either. He shook his head, squinting skeptically at the assortment of boys, and Famine in particular. "Huh-uh, I don't bet blind. How do I know this kid of yours isn't some kind of freak of nature?"

The gambling spirit took another leap in me. "Then let's try this. I'll bet he wins by at least ten yards."

"Ten out of a hundred?" Skinner exclaimed. "A racehorse couldn't do that. You're on, let's see the color of your money."

He bolted for the far end of the track to gauge the finish, and I swept Grace along, despite a little protesting squeal. Meanwhile at the starting line, eleven of the dozen boys took determined stances while the Faraday Boarding House entrant stood there, fidgeting from one scuffed foot to the other. Somewhere the band played "When You and I Were Young." The starter's pistol fired. And Russian Famine was in full flight while the others were getting their speed up. He ran as if the devils of the steppes were pursuing him with red-hot pitchforks. He ran however fast it is a boy can run. Down the track he came, flying toward us, leaving the puffing pack of other runners in his dust, if there had been any. He crossed the finish line so far ahead of the others that Skinner simply turned away.

While Grace hurried over to congratulate her winner, I stepped aside to settle up with Skinner. Disgusted, he ponied up my bet. "Hardly fair. That skin-and-bones kid is like a streak."

"Exactly." I made a show of taking out my wallet and plucking the money from his bookmaker hands. "Don't you think he would make a messenger, if the right someone were to put in a word for him?" Skinner was giving the money hovering over my wallet a sad farewell gaze. "Who knows, I might forgive the bet if that were to happen."

Skinner perked up. "I guess I could see

about it."

"At," I emphasized with a riffle of the money, "the Hennessy Building."

"At the Hen? Whoo, that's tough." He scratched his head as if digging out a thought. "They do hire an office kid for the summer. Usually it's some bigwig's fat nephew."

"Put it to them that in the relay of their messages, they have a choice between a flatfooted chair-warmer and winged Mercury."

"I'll skip that lingo, but those top-floor guys are always on fire to get their messages delivered fast." He watched in dismay as I tucked the wagered sum into my wallet. "Hey, when do I get my bet back?"

"At the time my friend Wladislaw becomes a messenger you-know-where."

While I was at that, Grace had flagged down a vendor and provided our victor with a feast of salami and cheese. Famine was devouring the victuals as if living up to his name when I joined them. I ruffled his hair, telling him that's where the laurel wreath should reside for a race so splendidly run and won, and in professional interest asked what he was going to do with his winnings.

He burped. "Eat some ice cream. Then go

on the rolly coaster."

Grace and I watched him bound away. By then our own next diversion was hammering at us, literally. At the end of the field was what seemed to be a carnival of clang and clamor — even in its entertainment, Butte flexed its muscles — where contests of mining skills were being held. Arm in arm without thinking about it, we strolled over to spectate as the Miners' Band set the mood with "The Anvil Chorus." I saw Grace turn somber amid the displays of strenuous skills that had been her husband's working life. The mucking contest was almost too fatiguing to watch, as men competed to see who could shovel a ton of ore into an ore car the fastest. Moving on, we came to a series of drilling contests, divided, I was interested to note, into weight classes like those of prizefighting — lightweight, middleweight, heavyweight — and competitors stripped to the waist readying for the match. Fit, muscular, confident of their skill, plainly these were the pick of the Hill, which meant of all the copper miners on earth.

Which is why I thought I was seeing wrong — Grace's reaction was even more pronounced than mine — when just ahead of us, swinging a sledgehammer and hoisting a drilling bar to loosen up, were Griffith and Hooper, shirts off, in their overalls and long underwear.

The weight of years defined this competition, as the placard bluntly announced: OLDTIMERS DRILLING CONTEST.

"No wonder they were so full of themselves this morning," Grace burst out. "I hope they don't fall over dead, the old fools."

Across on the other side, there seemed to be no similar trepidation around their competitors, a pair of Finns who had lost no huskiness to age. Their supporters were whooping and clapping and singing in Finnish as if the contest already was won.

Wordlessly I assessed the matchup, although it didn't take much study. I reminded myself that the gambling spirit should be harkened to only when the gamble carries a discernible chance of reward. I protectively patted the winnings Russian Famine had supplied to my wallet. In short, I took myself through the whole breviary of common sense, then told Grace I would be right back and went in search of Skinner again. She bit her lip even harder this time.

The rival teams were poised to start by the

time I rejoined Grace, each pair of men at a block of bluish granite the size of a packing crate. These drilling matches were of the old classic type, before compressors and air hoses replaced muscle and diligence at the rockface; in other words, by hand. Two sets of hands, and two steel tools. The holder knelt with a five-foot drill of tempered metal, like a slim crowbar, gingerly in his grasp. The hammerman, swinging a sledge, would strike the end of it, and as he drew back for the next stroke, the holder twirled the steel a quarter-turn for the drill head to make another flaking cut. In the early rise of Butte to mining eminence, I gathered, this blow-by-blow assault on rock — off-handedly called "breaking ground" — was an essential skill; the hole drilled in this laborious but effective way would be tamped with dynamite and the resulting blast would bring down the wall of rock for the ore to be separated out. Life tells tales as strange as those we can make up: the copper that wired the world for electricity was set loose, like fresh water from a struck stone in a fable, by those pairs of hands and driven steel in the chinks of the Hill.

Fortunately, dynamite was not involved in this match, which was to be a race to see which team could drive the deeper hole in a given time. Grace and I, already tense, watched intently as the judge fondled his stopwatch and instructed the two teams to get ready. Hoop, the hammerman, spat in his hands; Griff, the drill holder, flexed his fingers. The hardy Finns at the other block of rock did the same.

"Ready," the judge chanted, "set . . . DRILL!"

The ear-ringing sound of steel hitting steel echoed off the hill where flowers spelled out COLUMBIA GARDENS, on up into the mountains beyond, and in not many seconds resounded again. The strokes of the sledge-hammers set up a clanging rhythm best described as Hell's bells. Yet the process was strangely hypnotic and suspenseful to watch; the hammerman had to hit, each and every time, a target no bigger than a nickel, while the holder had to absorb the sting of the blow and make his fingers turn the drill the correct fraction. It was inherently danger-ous, the eight-pound head of the sledgeham-mer arcing at the holder if the hammerman missed, the shaft of steel thrusting spearlike toward the man with the hammer if the holder mishandled it. I watched in fascina-tion as Hoop, scrawny as he was, swung his sledge in a pace steady as a pendulum, and Griff, equally meager, knelt fearlessly over the drill as if his life depended on its next turn. Their opponents meanwhile seemed built for the job. One of them gravely white-haired, the other with a mustache that would have been white except for tobacco stains, both Finnlanders looked as sturdy as the granite.

As the clamor of the hammers went on and the drills chewed into the rock particle by particle, Grace nudged me hard enough to make me grunt. "Tell me, you," she fanned herself with her hat as though the exertion of the competitors was getting to her, "which team did you bet on?"

"I'm surprised at you, Grace. How could I not be loyal to the boardinghouse?" She was not the only skeptic. Skinner had chortled as he took the money I put on Hooper and Griffith. "Don't know how to quit while you're ahead, huh? Those old gimps have seen their day. You better stick to footraces and baseball, pal."

"Loyalty is one thing, using your head is another," Grace now added to that, fretfully watching the spectacle of old men attacking hard rock.

"Never fear, I still have enough to pay my rent."

"I wasn't worried about that." She fanned herself more rapidly, giving me a sidelong look. "Well, maybe a little."

It was no doubt true that in a world where chance operated as surely as gravity, I would have bet on the Finns. And perhaps regretted it, for Hoop was matching the mustached Finn blow for blow, their sledgehammers chorusing together. I was no stranger to contests, and this one could not have been closer, one team ahead by a fraction of an inch, then the other.

"Switch!" cried the judge at the five-minute mark, and, fantastically, the men of both teams changed jobs without missing a stroke. That fast, Hoop was on his knees minding the drill, Griff was banging away with the sledgehammer, and the race into the rock thundered on.

Grace sat on the edge of her seat, urging Griff on and muttering aside to me about the bawling-out he and Hoop were going to get from her at home. Griff's long underwear darkened with sweat across the shoulders as his turn at hammering went on. It was incredible to think of, the human muscle that had gone into the extraction of ore before machinery came to the mines, and Griff and Hoop and their opponents were part of it then as they were now.

"Switch!" cried the judge again, and like the flash team Hoop had told me they were, he and Griff switched jobs for the last stint of the quarter-hour contest.

"If only they don't kill themselves," Grace breathed. My concern, too, with money thrown in. As the contest drew down, Hoop was red with effort. I ached in some of my parts just from watching his exertion. Yet the beat of his hammer stayed steady. By the time the judge shouted that they were coming to the final minute, I could see no measurable difference in the extent of the drills into the blocks of stone.

Then, like a broken note between the rhythm of the hammers, came an anguished cry from Griff. His hand had cramped, freezing onto the drill and pulling him, bent by the pain, toward the path of the sledge-hammer. Grace gasped and started to her feet and I vaulted toward the scene along with several other men. Hoop with miraculous presence of mind buckled his back leg at the last second, driving the hammer head into the dirt instead of Griff. The two of them stayed hunched that way, gulping for air, to the sounds of the Finnish team driving its drill the last inch to victory.

In the aftermath, Grace and I consoled Hoop. Griff was avoiding everyone, staring at the hand that had betrayed him. I saw him wipe his eyes with his shirttail. "We'll see you at breakfast," Hoop told us wearily as we watched Griff disappear, shoulders bowed, into the holidaying crowd. "He's gonna need some liquid refreshment to get over this. Me, too."

"I'm spent," Grace sighed, sounding already wistful when we ended our stay after a silent last tour of the gardens.

"Wait, we have to see how we're immortalized." I plucked the photographer's result out of the envelope I'd picked up at the amusement park exit and she pressed close to me. At the sight, we both burst out laughing and teasing. She claimed I looked like a scared preacher, and I expressed amazement that Queen Marie of Romania had got into the picture with me.

"Such a day, Morrie," Grace wound down as the trolley back to town toddled along the tracks to us. Her violet eyes sought mine. "I feel as if I've been on that roller coaster with our star runner."

With a pensive smile to match hers, I provided my arm to help her up the step as the trolley rattled to a halt. "I know the feeling."

9

"Now we can get back to business," Sandison met me with as the staff reluctantly queued up on the library steps to be let in, the morning after. "I never have understood the meaning of holiday. Didn't have time for loafing of that sort on the ranch. Cows never took time off from eating."

"The nomenclature, Sandy, I think you'll find goes back to Middle English — the term recognizably became 'holy day,' and subsequent centuries of quickening pronunciation have given us —"

"Damn it, Morgan, did I ask for the history of the universe? Didn't think so." His shaggy gray eyebrows knitted, he contemplated me in either amazement or extreme irritation, it was always hard to tell which. "You have the damnedest brainbox ever created, I swear. Anyhow, get yourself caught up on the usual chores" — a near impossibility the way he kept adding to them —

"the next couple of days. I have something I want you to do. Tell you when the time comes."

Grace had been quiet as a mouse at breakfast, as had I, out of respect for the kingsize hangovers Hoop and Griff brought to the table. I was unprepared, then, when I came home from the library and heard the urgent stage-whisper from the kitchen: "*Hsst.* In here, Morrie."

Expecting to perform an act of rescue on whatever was cooking for supper, I stepped in and found Grace miserably seated at the kitchen table, her face a smeared mask of white. A bottle of calamine lotion was standing ready for more application. Wrapped around her forehead was a rag soaked, according to its eye-stinging odor, in vinegar. Not that I needed any further evidence, but the red welts on any inch of her skin not yet daubed with calamine told me I was seeing a prime case of hives.

"What on earth — ?" I sat down quickly and reached over to hold her hand, trying madly to think what to do beyond that. If the goons had shown up here on a glory hole mission despite my warning, I was going to have to find some way to make them regret it; I did not look forward to that. She continued to gaze at me with a forlorn expression, her eyes smarting from the acrid vinegar cloth, which, truth to tell, did not seem to be cooling her troubled brow appreciably. "Grace, you have to put it into words. What's the matter?"

"You are."

This was worse than if she had said, "The goons were here, breathing fire." My hand withdrew. Apprehensively, I asked, "How so?"

"By being you, whoever, whatever —" She started to scratch her arms, thought better of it, and instead dug her elbows into the table and leaned practically flat across to confront me. "I tossed and turned all night trying to figure out who am I with when I'm with you. Take yesterday. One minute I'm on the arm of someone I enjoy thoroughly" — her reddened eyes blinked more rapidly at that emotion — "and the next, you're gambling away money like you're feeding the chickens."

"Russian Famine won by at least eleven yards," I pointed out.

"All right, then," she said, no less miserable, "half the time when you're busy getting rid of any wrinkled money, the wind blows a little back."

Still trying to catch up, I asked hoarsely:

"What brought this on? Just a few bets I happened to place when the opportunity seemed ripe?"

Wordlessly she gazed past me, through the kitchen doorway, to the wedding portrait on the sideboard, and my heart sank. The ghost of Arthur hovered in from the next room, and how could I ever compete with such a paragon of domestic virtue? Her whitened, rag-wrapped countenance as tragic as a mummy's, Grace leaned farther toward me as if to deliver that verdict more fiercely. But what came out was practically a whisper.

"Arthur was a betting man."

Silence followed this shocking news. Grace sat back as if exhausted, scratched under an arm, and with an angry swipe slathered on more calamine. I still was trying to imagine which competitions of skill so manly a miner would be enticed to wager on. "Boxing matches? Drilling contests?"

"Dogs."

My jaw dropped. "Believe me, I never have and never shall put money on the velocity of a canine."

"Arthur was hopeless about it," she half-whispered again, her voice carrying the strain of the memory. "He would be perfectly fine for a while, bringing his wages

251

home, sweet as anything. Then would come a payday when he didn't show up for supper and I knew he'd gone to the dogs again. The races, that is." She folded her arms, wincing as she did so. "And there you were yesterday, one minute as perfect a companion as a woman could ask for, and the next, behaving as if you were trying to break the bank at Monte Carlo. Which one is the real you? I can't tell from one moment to the next whether you're the best creature that ever wore pants, or, or — I don't know what." Her tirade ran down. "How can a person ever hope to get a straight line on you, Morrie?"

I nervously smoothed my mustache, dreading where this was leading. It had to be faced, it always does.

"Grace" — I used her name as if patting it before putting it away for good — "I don't know any cure for being myself. The lotion for that hasn't been concocted yet." The next had to be said past the lump in my throat. "Do you want me to pack my satchel and go?"

No man is a hero to his butler, it is said; nor is any boarder a model of perfection to his landlady. Grace Faraday straightened up and scrutinized me, blinking harder. "If I had a lick of sense, I should push you out

252

the door right now, shouldn't I." As I watched, her dubious self struggled with the proprietorial side of her. "But when you're not a pile of trouble, you're no trouble. You're on time with the rent every week, although heaven knows how. You aren't a steaming drunk, at least since you gave up wakes. You don't throw a fit when dynamite goes off under the place. And Griff and Hoop don't seem to drive you crazy. That counts."

Had she been ticking these off on her fingers, she now was out of fingers. Looking as doubtful as she sounded, she concluded:

"For now, you may as well stay. One more thing, though. We need to be as clear as we can about each other. Yesterday was too, um, too forward of me, Morrie, and it wasn't really fair to you." Something more than an itch was making her chalky face twitch. "You shouldn't get the wrong idea and feel . . ." There she faltered.

"Taken up with," I finished for her, and I was surprised at how sad it sounded.

This was one of the nights of the week when I had to go back to the library and lock up after the evening groups, and I trudged off to do it with the old weight of disappointment on me.

First Rose, now Grace. Rejection as soon as someone personable and pretty took a good look into me, whatever it was they thought they saw.

Women were the fairer sex? What was fair about their fingersnap judgments of me? Even Sandison, grumpy and flatfooted around women, had found someone to put up with him, the redoubtable Dora. While my best efforts caused them to dust their hands of me or break out in hives.

I felt lonely as a castaway, and, what was worse, from present indications I had better get used to it.

My acidic mood was at odds with the gentle summer dusk, spreading down from the Hill over the brick canyons of the city, casting the streets into picturesque shadow. That sank through to me, and a couple of times I whipped into a doorway and looked back. There was no sign of goons, at least. Brass knuckles seemed to get the job done, although I couldn't see how to apply that to courtship.

In the library basement when I arrived, the Ladies' and Gentlemen's Literary and Social Circle was still going strong. A balding young man with the look of a bank clerk was onstage, reciting in round tones: *". . . now when heaven holds starry night in its* keep / and on moonlit Olympus, the Muses gently sleep." Ordinarily I am all in favor of the Muses, but tonight I shooed the literature lovers mercilessly, and they filed out of the auditorium in shy pairings. The big room echoing with emptiness now, I was stacking away the chairs when I heard a single set of footsteps rapid on the stairs. The goons always traveled as a pair. Or did they? Just in case, I hefted a chair, ready to hurl.

"What the devil," Jared stopped short as he came through the doorway and saw me with the chair in my hands, "are you cutting the janitor out of his job?"

"It's his lodge night, so he's excused early," I said crossly. "My employer has a habit of bending the rules for this, that, and the other, except where I'm concerned."

"You need a union," he joked, or not, lending a hand with the stray chairs. He looked at me curiously. "That poor thing who's your landlady told me you've about taken up residence in the library."

"It's a long story."

"I imagine. Anyway, I'm glad I could track you down." He glanced around to every corner of the auditorium even though we were alone. "Any luck with you know what?"

"Luck is the residue of endeavor, in some

situations," I responded, still not in my best mood. "Come on up to the office."

Our footsteps were magnified in the empty darkened building as we went upstairs, and I sensed Jared was jumpy in the unfamiliar surroundings. But if situations were reversed, I would not be particularly at ease in a mineshaft, would I. When I switched on a light in the office, he stayed by the door and took everything in. "So this is the lion's den." His gaze came to rest on me, with that flavoring of curiosity again. "I have to hand it to you, you've got guts, holed up in here with him all day long. I've heard about old Triple S since I was a kid."

"He hasn't taken my head off my shoulders, so far," I muttered, my attention on the contents of the hiding spot in the cabinet where the ledgers were kept, the one place I was sure Sandison would not go near now that he had shed the bookkeeping to me. I brought out the pink sheets and my pages of calculations of each mine's differential between raw tons of ore and tally of processed copper. "Is this what you had in mind?"

Not wasting a moment, Jared laid out my pages on the nearest desk — Sandison's — and ran his finger down the figures. When he reached my totals, he pulled a slip of paper from his shirt pocket and compared. His whoop startled me, and probably the pigeons on the library roof. "You've nailed it! Anaconda's been feeding us low numbers on the finished copper. We'll give them holy hell in the negotiations now and they won't even know how we figured it out." Exuberantly he batted my shoulder. "Rab thinks you're the greatest thing going. I'm starting to see why, Professor, if I can call you that."

"I'm flattered, I suppose."

As the two of us headed downstairs, I could make out just enough of Jared in the library's moonlit atmosphere to know he could hardly wait to turn the tables on Anaconda. Now I was curious. "You have the lost dollar back. What are you still negotiating about so urgently?"

"You name it. Working conditions. Hiring and firing. Safety." His voice turned hollow. "On first shift, just this morning, one of our men in the Muckaroo was killed when a tunnel roof fell in on him. Left a wife and six kids." I recalled his delivering the union tribute — cash and consolation — to the widow at my first wake as a cryer; again and again, from the sound of it, he faced that duty.

Mustering himself now, Jared went on with what he had been saying. "All of it causes bad feelings in the union. There are those who say getting the wage back is what counted, let's don't beat our heads against the shed on these other matters until we get some paydays behind us. And then there's plenty who are ready to shut down the Hill again like that" — he snapped his fingers — "if the company doesn't give us every last thing we want."

He glanced sideways at me. "Professor?" In the splendid acoustics — we were in the foyer by now — he sounded like a messenger of fate in a Greek drama as he laid matters out. "I wouldn't guess you're a military man at heart, but you maybe know what an accelerated march is. It covers ground a lot faster than parade cadence, but it's not a run that makes your tongue hang out. That's about what I'm trying for. We can't let up much on Anaconda or things slip back. But we're never going to turn copper mining into a picnic, no matter what we try. Either way, as I see it, those of us on the council have to keep things moving, just fast enough." The next came out as if he were thinking to himself. "Particularly now."

When I halted short of the front door and gave him a questioning look, Jared hesitated. "All right," he granted, "Rab will probably blab this to you if I don't. Anaconda isn't our only problem — we're scrambling to stay ahead of the Wobblies. The word is, they're going to make a big push to take away our members." He tilted his head to one side as if trying to see the situation from a fresh angle. "Who knows, if things had been different, maybe I'd be on their side. But I was born a union man. The union stuck up for the workingman on the Butte Hill all those years, every day of my father's life when he went down into the mine. The Wobs always say they would, too, and take over the mines and everything else besides." He shook his head. "I don't trust that, Professor. It would go to hell in no time, I think. Look at Russia. The Bolshies did away with the Czar, and now they're knocking off anybody they don't like the looks of."

I just listened, Jared needing to get the weight of fate off his chest; he had earned the right in the trenches that were the maw of the Great War.

"I have to hand it to the IWW," he was saying ruefully, "they're a persistent damn bunch. The last time they sent a bigtime organizer in here, the goons hung him from the railroad trestle. Lynched him. The old remedy, the Montana necktie." With a laugh that had no humor in it, he gazed around at the grandeur of the library as though wondering how it and a lynching site a dozen blocks away could exist in the same realm of time. "Maybe I have Wobs on the brain," he mused. "That one at the parade yesterday, singing that damn thing?" Jared Evans startled me again by mimicking, quite presentably, the phantom voice that had mocked the parading miners' union with *pie in the sky, when you die.* He banged his head with the heel of his hand. "It gets in there and I can't get it out."

"It's called a mnemonic effect," I informed him. "Something that prompts remembering, usually voluntary but not necessarily. A musical phrase is particularly suited. For instance, 'Camptown —' "

At the library door now, Jared put up his hands to hold off my discourse.

"I appreciate the definition. But I'll just call it trouble. Good night, Professor."

I was wary in every direction I could think of, those next few days. But there was no sign of lurking goons, and on the home front, Grace — still a picture of misery, under the ghostly layer of lotion — did not come up with any further charges against my personality. She and I were painfully polite with one another, to the point where Hoop and Griff grew nervous around us. They talked a blue streak at mealtimes to cover our silences, and while I learned a lot about assorted topics of interest to retired Welsh miners, it was a relief each morning to go off to work at the library.

Until, that is, the pertinent day when Sandison spun around in his chair as soon as I stepped into the office and announced, "Morgan, it's time we get some ammunition to use on the trustees."

I knew "we" meant me, so I simply cocked my head to listen.

"You've done a good enough job of balancing the ledger, the board can't find anything to kick about in there," he went on. "Now they're fretting about where the money is going to come from for new carpets, all the wear and tear we've had in here lately. I keep telling them any board of trustees worth its name would just pony it up, but they want to steal it out of the book budget, the damn thieves."

He hunched forward as if about to rake in a poker pot. "That's where you come in. I want to remind that pack of meddling fools which side their bread is buttered on." He looked at me craftily. "I've never signed my book collection over to the library," there

261

was a sly note in his voice I had not detected before, "it's here on loan, like museums have with paintings of people with their clothes off." That explained much: for Butte to house the finest collection west of Chicago, the obsessive keeper of the books came along with it.

"Told you there's something I have for you to do," he was saying, as though I were looking for a way to fill my time. "Draw up an inventory of what's mine out there on the shelves," he waved in the direction of the prized books on the mezzanine. "That'll bring the trustees to their senses," the grandee of the library finished, sitting back and cracking his knuckles in satisfaction.

"I shall need a helper."

That caught him by surprise, and before he could cloud up enough to tell me I was out of my mind, I said, "Fortunately, Sandy, the staffing has been a little light for some time, hasn't it." I flipped to the ledger page that listed library positions and wages, his piggybank for those *Miscellaneous* expenditures when irresistible books showed up in dealers' catalogues. He eyed me as my finger singled out positions budgeted for but chronically unfilled. "Very wise of you," I drove the point home with a final finger tap, "to leave leeway for an occasion just

262

such as this."

Sandison coughed. "Let's be reasonable about this. We can't be cluttering up the place with some moron we don't absolutely need, just because —"

"No, no," I headed off that objection, "summer help will do. A teacher, perhaps, with free time now that school is out. In fact, I think I know of one."

"Don't waste time talking about it, then." He heaved himself around in his seat as if compelling business awaited on his desk. "Hire this summer wonder you have your eye on, and get going on the inventory. You have to make decisions in this life, Morgan."

"This is exciting, working for Sam Sandison. It's like being on a pirate ship."

"Rab, contain your imagination. This is a library."

"You know what I mean," she whispered back secretively, there on the mezzanine. "Everyone in Butte has an opinion about him. What's yours, Mr. Morgan?"

"It's too deep to go into. Pull down *Pride and Prejudice* and see if it has the book-plate."

She took a peek inside the tanned leather cover and giggled. "It does. Just like on a heifer." Volume by volume, our library lord's collection bore the bookplate lettered in bold SSS, with the smaller, uncompromising line below, *Property of Samuel S. Sandison*. I hadn't put this together until Rab's remark, but now my first conversation with the man came back to mind, when he berated me for not knowing that the most famous cattle herd in Montana history had borne the Triple S brand. Leave it to him to put a brandabetical stamp on the world's literature.

Rabrab — or Miss Rellis, as I had to make myself call her in front of other staff members — was a diligent worker, as we were both going to need to be. Already we each had a heaping armful of exquisite books, and this was only Adams, Arnold, and Austen. As we tottered off to the sorting room, where Sandison had let us set up shop for the inventorying, she marveled: "Say what they will about him, he really does have a soft spot for books, doesn't he."

And Ivan the Terrible perhaps loved his staghounds. My private opinion of Sandison, inconstant in the best of times, varied almost hourly during those first busy weeks of summer. He was as demanding as ever in the office chores he foisted onto me, the Earl of Hell with a list in his head, and between those I would dash back to the sorting room to work with Rab on the inventory. Sometimes we would look up and see the snowy beard and cowlick pass by as he came stalking out of his office to stand there on the mezzanine and contemplate the ranks of books on the shelves. When he loomed there in one of these trances, white as a sacred elephant, Rab and I simply detoured around him in our task. I was certain as anything that *bibliomania* did not mean a maniac loose in a library, but there were times Sandison made me wonder whether the definition needed adjusting. Yet, fume at him and his high-handed ways as I so often did, there were the immortal books, which would not have graced the Constantinople of the Rockies but for him. In life's list of complications, this one seemed to carry an acceptable price.

Volume by plated volume, Rab and I kept compiling and adding up the Sandison library-within-the-library. If the edition in hand matched a listing in a rare books catalogue, it was no problem to assign a value. Any we could find no listing for, one or the other of us would take, several at a time, for appraisal by old Adamson, the coldblooded antiquarian book dealer across town. As you might guess, there is a secret satisfaction in going through the streets with your arms around the Artful Dodger and Natty Bumppo and Emma Bovary, no one knowing you are hugging a monetary fortune as well as a literary one.

So, its hectic moments aside, the inventorying was the most pleasant kind of work, engaging the mind, and no unduly heavy lifting involved. Rab was sparkling company, as I had counted on. She showed up each morning bright-eyed for whatever the day might bring, and in plucking the SSS books from the shelves, she whisked in and out of the mezzanine stacks as if on jeweled skates. From the number of upturned male heads among the Reading Room patrons as she winged past overhead, I was not the only one appreciative of her presence.

I suppose I should not have been surprised when Sandison called me in to his office, and there, like one of the frowning Easter Island stone heads, was Miss Runyon.

"It seems there is a distraction in our otherwise flawless service to the reading public," Sandison addressed me pontifically from behind his desk. "State your case, Miss Runyon."

She drew herself up as if to huff and puff and blow me away. "It's that helper of yours. She wears those little dresses, you can see everything she has."

"You can? I mean, I had not noticed."

"Then you are the only man breathing who hasn't," she declared.

I looked from her to Sandison and back again, both of them dressed twenty years behind the times. "Perhaps it is natural that the younger people take a different view of wardrobe than, ah, we do."

Rousing himself, Sandison abandoned his chair and clomped out from behind the desk. "Your concern for propriety is notable, Miss Runyon," he said soothingly as he escorted her to the door, "and I'm sure Morgan can deal with the issue."

When she was gone, he rounded on me. "The next couple of days, you be the one to prance out there on the mezzanine and fetch the books," he directed, "just on the chance that people may not be quite as interested in seeing everything you have." His frosty eyebrows were hoisted high as he studied me. "You're a sharper operator than I thought, Morgan." He laughed bawdily. "Make the most of your time with Miss Rellis."

I look back on that midsummer stretch of weeks as a season of life that went up and down with the regularity of a carousel. Each day divided itself according to the female company of the time. At the boardinghouse, Grace and I stayed as self-consciously civil as schoolchildren who had been told to mind their manners or else; her hives had gone away, but her allergy to being taken up with me had not. Then I would go off to the library and the short-hemmed zephyr that was Rabrab Rellis.

With her keenness for being in on things, Rab was as intrigued with the inventory books as I was, both of us beaming like babies at the chance to handle lovely volumes that even the most omnivorous reader would miss out on in a lifetime. On nice days we carried the mood outside, joking to one another, and ate lunch on the library steps. Butte sunned itself those noon hours, as if storing up for rougher weather ahead. Gangs of boys swarmed down from the Hill neighborhoods, heading for the swampy attractions along Silver Bow Creek. On the next street, the *Post* building had put up a baseball scoreboard on its front, and the amplified voice of the sports telegraphist relaying diamond drama as it took place in Cincinnati and Washington and other major-league outposts carried to us like opera arias: *"Flash! It's a home run! The Redlegs lead one to nothing!"* Sometimes Russian Famine, scrubbed and neatened, would stop by on his errands as a Hennessy Building runner, and one of us would share a sandwich with him before he sprang to his duty again.

"Mr. Morgan, there's something I've been puzzling about," Rab broached during one of those pleasant noontimes when we were alone. "I noticed it all the way back at Henry Adams and his *Education.* That was published only last year." She had her old look of a schoolgirl circling what might be a trick question. "Aren't the Sandison books supposed to be what he collected when he was on the ranch, ages ago?"

That had tickled my interest, too. By now we were at Kafka, Keats, and Kipling. The romantic poet was sadly gone, but the other two were up and writing and I had just catalogued recent contributions to literature by both that also carried the SSS bookplate.

So as not to heat up Rab's instinct for intrigue, which never needed encouragement, I shrugged past the matter of newly minted books among the old: "An occasional stray may have wandered into his literary herd, large as it is. Isn't there a ranching word for that?"

"Maverick, you mean? An unbranded cow that someone slaps their own brand on?" Rab wrinkled her nose as if sniffing some-

269

thing spicy. "Oh, that's so funny."

It was more so than she knew. Possibly Sandison, from long habit, was simply buying valuable books out of his own pocket and folding them into his collection, as he had every right to do. But the more tantalizing possibility, I sensed, was that those *Miscellaneous* purchases drawn from the library's payroll budget were being cunningly mingled into his earlier holdings. If I knew anything about Samuel S. Sandison by now, it was that he never saw a thing of worth that didn't look better to him with SSS on it.

Brushing away lunch crumbs as though that took care of the topic, I told Rab, "We had better get back at it, there's a shelf of Longfellow ahead."

"How's that inventory coming?" Sandison rumbled when I passed by the office that afternoon.

"Sandy, you are to be commended for your buying eye," I stuck to what I could honestly say. "The books you have gathered amount to a financial fortune as well as a literary one."

"They damn well ought to," he said as he hunched over an antiquarian catalogue and some notations to himself which, I was quite sure, added up to more books for the Sandison collection.

"Oh, by the way," the issue of expenditure reminded me, "a cyclopedia salesman this morning left us a sample of his newest." I stepped to my desk for the brochure as Sandison groaned at the distraction. "Here you go, the sales pitch for *Prominent Figures of Montana, Past and Present.* He assured me no self-respecting library should be without such a volume. As an added inducement, he told me you will find yourself prominently in it, Sandy." I passed the brochure to him for inspection.

He took one look, informed me it was nothing more than the usual attempt by some robber to steal names and sell them back to flattered fools, and tossed it aside. "Bury it in Section 37," I thought I heard him mutter as he turned back to what he had been doing.

"Excuse me, please" — by then I thought I knew every corner of the library — "but you'll have to tell me where that section is."

"Eh?" His head jerked up and around as if I had been eavesdropping. Catching up with himself, he waved me off the subject. "Never mind. Get back to the inventory and making eyes at Miss Rellis, why don't you."

■ ■ ■ ■

Not long after, I was met at the breakfast table by two long faces. Griff asked mournfully, "You heard what they're doing to us now?"

"I am barely out of bed, Griff, how could I?"

"They're cracking down," said Hoop, equally doleful.

I waited, but both informants were too overcome to provide anything more. Mystified, I had to look to Grace for an explanation.

"The police have heard from a higher power," she said with a frown. From the look on her, I translated that to mean the top floor of the Hennessy Building, home of the copper collar. "They're arresting characters who hang out downtown without any business for being there." For a change, she spoke to me in the old dulcet way, I supposed to make two sets of deaf ears perk up and listen in. "A couple of those come to mind at this table, don't they."

"Spitting on the sidewalk, the cops call it," Hoop said with disgust.

"Vagrancy is another way of putting it," Grace provided for my benefit.

Griff burst out, "It's that 'unlawful assembly' crap" — Grace did not rebuke him — "whatever name the buzzards put on it."

Still behind, I asked around the table: "What put the authorities on this rampage?"

"The Wobblies," Hoop and Griff answered together, while Grace's expression said she had heard all this too many times, and she went off to the kitchen. The IWW wanted to cut in and take the lead in the miners' struggle with Anaconda — it just wasn't right, my tablemates stated. From what they heard, the specter of operatives filtering into town to mold discontented workers of the Hill into a radical legion had thrown Butte's powers that be into a tizzy. Hence, jail awaited anyone deemed a "vagrant."

When the law is bent that way, a detour around it is sometimes needed. That morning I went to the library by the back-alley route shown me by Russian Famine, just to be on the safe side.

To my surprise, that lunchtime, Rab was mum about this newest tussle over who would control the Hill. I don't know what I expected to be in sight when we settled at the top of the library steps as usual — the Hennessy Building being stormed like the

Bastille by maddened Wobblies, perhaps — but the streets were placid, only punctuated here and there by strolling policemen who looked vaguely embarrassed. Rab was chattering on about Melville and whether anyone who wasn't vitally interested in blubber actually ever read every page of *Moby-Dick*, but there was something bubbling under that which should have alerted me. Nonetheless, I was caught by surprise when a lean figure, brisk and businesslike in a somber suit but with his hat pulled low, peeled away from the concourse of patrons in and out of the library and dropped onto the steps beside us. "See what I mean about the Wobs spelling trouble, Professor?"

"I suppose I do, Jared," I answered him as equably as I could. "There seem to be a lot of ways to spell that in Butte." I watched with envy as he nestled in next to Rab and was rewarded with a kiss and a sandwich. Curious as to why he was dressed up, I asked: "What's the occasion?"

"None in particular," Jared provided between bites. "I just don't want to look like somebody who might spit on the sidewalk." A policeman went by on leadfooted patrol, giving us hardly a glance. "You can almost feel sorry for the dumb cops," he mused. "Almost."

The police on puppet strings were not the only ones entitled to sympathy in the situation, I could tell; the crackdown plainly hindered the activities of the miners' union, and I charitably said something of the sort to Jared.

"An opportunity for a strategic withdrawal, we called it in the army," came the dry response.

"Extra syllables aside, I believe that means 'retreat'?" I made sure.

"You might say that," he granted. "But going a different direction, even backwards," he munched on the matter along with his sandwich, "gives a chance to gain some ground somewhere else, doesn't it?"

Rab, eyes alight, had been flicking glances back and forth between us. "You'd better ask him, love," she prompted. "Mr. Morgan and I have to get back to whaling all too soon."

The ancients who invented storytelling knew to the instant when drama must put on a human mask. The soaring ambition of Icarus to consort with the sun, before the first feather melted from his wings and wafted down and down to the waiting Aegean Sea. The echo of the knight's heartbeat within his armor before he slays the dragon. Some such flutter in the curtain of fate, now that I look back on everything that was about to happen, came with Jared Evans that noontime.

"You brought this on yourself, Professor," he said as though I didn't know any better. His dark eyes held a glimmer as he went on: "Remember when you were telling me why 'pie in the sky' gets in a person's head and won't leave? The 'nimo gizmo' side of things, you called it?"

"The mnemonic aspect," I was glad to clarify. "It derives from Mnemosyne, the Greek goddess of memory, and —"

"That's what I'm saying, the union needs that kind of brain food." Past the brim of his hat I could see Rab glistening with interest. Jared scanned around as if scouting enemy terrain and lowered his voice. "I got to thinking about what you'd said and it hit me — why shouldn't the union have a song like that?" He made a fist. "Something that shows our spirit. There on Miners Day, when the band played 'Men of Harlech,' I damn near bawled and I wasn't the only one. That kind of thing. I mean, hell, up against Anaconda, we're in a fight just as much as any army." I practically had to shield my eyes in the face of his fiery determination. It took only one look at Jared to know he was purposeful as a harpoon, and another at Rab to remind me that the whiff of anything venturesome was catnip to her. I had to admit, the two of them were made for Butte.

"Professor?" He spoke now as if taking me deep into his confidence. "You see where I'm going with this?"

"Vaguely. You have in mind musical phraseology that will rally —"

He didn't wait for me to finish. "A song of our own that will make the Wobblies sound like sick cats. And that's where you come in."

Well, who would not want to be the author of "La Marseillaise" or "Marching Through Georgia" or even "Yankee Doodle"? However, sometimes I know my limits. "Jared, that's generous of you, but songwriting is actually not among my talents."

"Doesn't matter," he sped right over that. "All I want you to do is to make the case to a few people for a hell of a good song for the Hill. Miners can be contrary. We have more factions than a henhouse." He gazed up at the dark strutworks over the mine-shafts and the spill of neighborhoods between. "The Finns would join up with the Wobblies lickety-split if the union gives them any least excuse. The Italians think the union is getting too radical. The Irish are itching to run things themselves, and the Cornish think they could do a better job than the Irish or any of the rest of us. So on down the line." Abruptly he batted my shoulder, which was going to develop a callus if this kept on. "You're just the right one to set the bunch of them thinking about a song that will pull everybody together instead of their own grumbles. Rab swears you're a wonder when you get going." Her smile ratified that.

"Ah." Flattery is a quick worker. "I suppose I could lend whatever modicum of musical knowledge I have. If you'd like, the next time you hold a meeting, I could come by the union hall and —"

"That's the rub," Jared said quickly. "The bunch we want won't come near the union hall, the way everyone is being watched like sin these days."

The rogue had already calculated the next, I later realized, but he offered it as if the notion just then strolled up to him.

"Come to think of it, though, there's one place in all of Butte where the cops and goons know better than to go. Down the shaft."

No three words in the language could have been more unwelcome to me. I am not subterranean by nature. Quite the opposite;

I tend to look up, not down, in life. The sky has held fascination for me since I was a boy sneaking out to the Lake Michigan shore on clearest nights, tracing out the constellations shimmering over the water. Above me in the hypnotic dark, Sagittarius the archer bent his everlasting bow while Pegasus flew on wings of light; those and all the other patterns etched in star-silver define heaven to me. I know of no mine pit in the sky. Now I was being asked to reverse my basic inclination and point myself into the blind paths under the ground. Down where a glory hole led to.

"Must we?"

Jared brushed aside my quavery question. "It's our only shot at getting the right people in one place at the same time." Rabrab watched him with adoration as he tackled tactics. "How are you at being somebody else?" he asked me and didn't wait for an answer. "Your pals Griff and Hoop never took themselves off the extra gang list, it makes them feel like they're still miners. We can sneak you onto the night shift on one of their work tickets." He wrinkled his brow. "First we have to get you past that pair of apes at the gate."

I groaned. "Big and bigger? One of them with eyes that belong on a sea creature?"

Jared showed surprise. "How'd you know? The company stuck them there to watch for Wobs."

"It's too long a story to go into." I felt a guilty kind of relief as I explained that Eel Eyes and Typhoon Tolliver would know me on sight; with them on lookout at the gate, it was impossible for me to enter the mine.

During this, Rabrab had been studying me.

"Your mustache, Mr. Morgan. If that were to come off, you'd look like a different you."

My upper lip smarting, I trudged up the Hill in the company of Griff the next night. I felt undressed without the mustache, although I was in the same regalia as the hundreds of other miners around us: substantial trousers, a workman's jumper, and an old hat.

Griff was practically hopping with anticipation. "You're in luck," he had me know as we trooped along. "The Muckaroo is as nice a digging as there is on the Hill."

"Is it," I responded without enthusiasm; doubtless there was a similarly prime spot in the salt mines of Siberia, too. To try to bolster myself for this, after the library closed I had gone down on my knees and examined the mine model in the glass case long and hard, but right now that seemed like no preparation whatsoever for the real thing. The screeching of pulleys and the throb of machinery sounded louder than in the daytime. Ahead of us, lit harshly, the headframe of the Muckaroo mineshaft towered into the darkness. The graveyard shift — how I wished it wasn't called that — converged at the pinch of the mine gate and then spread out as men filed off to their eight hours of labor beneath the surface of the earth. Jared was a steady but discreet number of strides behind us, which was somewhat reassuring, but Griff hustling along next to me, madly eager to redeem himself after the Miners Day drilling contest, was not. I kept hearing Grace's strained words when my conscience made me draw her aside after supper and confess what we were up to: "Think twice about this, Morrie, please? The Hill is the most dangerous place on earth, even for those who know what they're doing."

By now I'd had those second thoughts and many more, with no result but Griff to show for it. Allegiance to a cause is a prickly thing. Put your hand to it just right, and there is the matchless feeling of being part of something greater than yourself. Grab on to it the wrong way, though, and it draws blood. Back and forth this scheme of Jared's wavered in me as our rough-dressed procession tromped out of the dark to the mine entrance.

The enemy was at the gate, the oversize pair of them scrutinizing every passing face, Eel Eyes with that sideways stare, Typhoon with doggish concentration. Griff braced up beside me as we neared that inspection. "Here we go, Mor— Hoop, that is." He sneaked a look toward the weedy shadows along the high fence, muttering: "If that kid's gonna do it, he better be doing it."

"He will," I said with more confidence than I felt.

Just then a rock clanged off the tin siding of the gatehouse behind the goons. "Scabs!" came the taunt. "Anaconda stinks and so do you!"

As hoped, Tolliver reflexively bolted off after the stone thrower, although he had no chance in the world of catching up with Russian Famine. Eel Eyes angrily stayed sentry, but his gaze kept dodging toward the darkness or in search of the jeering laughs from the rank of passing miners, while Griff and I, prim as monks, flashed our work tickets and slouched past him.

Jared caught up to us in the mine yard.

"Nice work. When we get in the lamp

room, stay at the back" — he was addressing me — "and keep your head down. Griff, you know what to do."

The lamp room, jam-packed with men and equipment, was where we were to outfit ourselves with helmets with a small head-lamp atop like a bright Cyclops eye. Finding one that more or less fit, I plopped it on, hoping it would help to hide me. No sooner was it down around my brow than the night supervisor stepped into the room, a list of names in his hand.

"Hooper and Griffith on the extra gang," he sang out. "Oldtimers' night, is this?"

"Don't fret yourself, Delaney," Griff bridled. "We can still turn out the work."

"We'll see about that." The mine overseer peered to the right and left of Griffith. "Where's Hoop?"

"Taking a leak against the office."

"He would be." Comparing the rest of the names on his list to the crowded roomful of faces, now the supervisor craned to see to the back, where I was keeping my head down. "Who else we got here, anybody I don't know?"

Jared broke in on that. "Just so you have it in mind, Delaney — we voted not to go on the twenty-hundred level until more shor-ing gets put in."

"Nobody's asked you to yet," the mine boss said sourly. "Don't push it, Evans."

"You call that pushing, when it's our necks at risk?" Jared harped on the matter to create a distraction. "I'm just saying, that shoring better go in before any of us set foot onto that level or —" During this, Griff and I slipped out.

The open air of the mine yard chilled me. With the helmet weighing on me, I felt even more like a blockhead for agreeing to this scheme. Happy as if he had good sense, Griff gimped along ahead of me, carrying on about the old days on the Hill and this rare chance to have a look at the workings of the Muckaroo. "So, all we need to do," he chatted over his shoulder as if we were out for a stroll, "is get ourselves down to the thirty-hundred level."

That snatch of enthusiasm sounded reassuring. Wait, though; multiply those offhand numbers and the result is —

"Three thousand feet?" I jammed to a halt as if an abyss of that depth had cracked open beneath the toes of my shoes. "I just can't. You'll have to tell Jared."

Without saying a word, Griff circled back and clamped a sinewy old hand on my shoulder, steering me toward the mineshaft.

The Muckaroo's headframe stood over us,

black metal casting blacker shadows in the glare of the night lights, as we approached. Griff headed us straight in under the girders toward a narrow plate-metal box hung from a steel cable. "Here we go, Morrie, I mean Hoop. Hop in the cage."

Rust-spotted and dented, the thing looked like some torture chamber left over from the Spanish Inquisition. Rationally I knew it was simply an elevator, a way to travel to work the same way an accountant in a celluloid collar would step into wood-paneled circumstances downtown and pleasantly tell the operator, "Fourth floor, please." Except that this express traveled more than half a mile between stops, straight down. With Griff's firm aid I edged in and stood rigid against the back plating, as far away from the flimsy accordion gate across the doorway as possible. He shouldered in next to me as other miners packed in with us.

The hoistman peeked in, counting heads, then snicked the gate closed. He called out, "Everybody ready for China?"

"Let 'er drop," the miner nearest the front called back.

No sooner were the words out than the cage plunged like a shot, for about a dozen feet. Then stopped with the kind of yank that comes at the end of a scaffold rope.

Everything dangled there, shuddering wildly; I include myself in that. The walls of the mineshaft had closed in around us and overhead there was a terrific clatter and continuing commotion. I believe I would have whimpered if the power of voice hadn't been scared out of me.

"It's okey-doke," Griff tried to soothe me with a whisper. "They're loading a couple more cages over us, is all."

Oh, was that all. Merely piling people on top of our heads, to make sure of calamity if anything went wrong in the descent. Hearing Griff's rushed words or perhaps my breathing, the other passengers glanced over their shoulders curiously at us.

"My partner here is a greenhorn, I'm breaking him in," Griff confided to them. "He's got a little case of heebie-jeebies." That brought knowing laughs and a round of wisecracks about how lucky I'd be if I didn't get anything worse than that from digging copper.

In a minute came another sickening jolt downward and one more shuddering wait. Then *swish!* The next thing I knew, the cage was dropping at top speed, so fast that I feared we had been cut loose and were free-falling to our doom. I shut my eyes, not wanting to see death coming. Then, though,

I heard the steady whine of the cable, and I cautiously peeped past the darkened outline of Griff and the others. Down and down and down, the shaft walls flew past in a terrifying black blur. My ears popped. I was trying to work my jaw when everything stopped with a hard bounce. The cage yo-yoed for long seconds as the springiness of three thousand feet of cable settled down.

Someone outside flung open the cage gate and I was blinking into a harshly lighted concrete chamber. Hot air rushed into the elevator shaft as the other men clambered out ahead of Griff and myself. A staccato chorus, like invisible riveters, emanated from various tunnels where compressed-air drills were noisily cutting into walls of ore. "Here we are," Griff announced as if it were a tourist destination, "as deep as it goes in the Muckaroo."

As I gawked around, the next cage settled to a stop and Jared climbed out. Giving us a thumbs-up, he disappeared off into a timbered tunnel across the way. By now the underground traffic was thick, files of miners passing us by, their talk trailing away as they vanished into various tunnel portals. Griff had been orienting himself. "C'mon, we want to scoot off over here."

He had picked out what looked to me like

an abandoned tunnel, except that steel rails were aligned in the center of it. Our head-lamps cast bobbing beams as we hiked deeper into the darkness. Every so often, the light caught a gleam where water dripped down a rock wall. The stammer of drilling followed us at first, gradually drop-ping to a distant murmur that was simply in the air, like the metallic smell that smarted in my nose. I kept waiting for where this burrow led to, some larger cavern, timbered and more secure, where actual mining was done. Then something occurred to me, from my session of studying the mine model in the library.

"Griff?" I sounded like I was in the bot-tom of a well. "I believe this is what is called a drift tunnel —"

"Righto. You know more about this than a person might think."

"— and if I am not mistaken, the only purpose of a drift tunnel is the excavation of ore. It isn't a passageway to any of the rest of the mine."

"Right again. You are a whiz."

"Then where's the crew that's supposed to be in here doing that digging? I don't see or hear anyone."

"That's because we're it."

I stopped almost in mid-step.

Griff plowed along for a few more paces before noticing I was missing. Turning around, he examined me critically. "I don't want to worry you, Morrie, but you look kind of milky."

"Where did this notion come from that you and I are going to dig copper in this crypt?" I burst out. "My understanding was, I came down here to meet with the men from the other mines."

"Well, yeah, sure," Griff said, patience and reason combined. "When meal break rolls around, Jared is gonna see to that. I bet he's got it worked out slick, don't worry. But we need to make some kind of showing until then. We get caught loafing around" — the beam of his helmet lamp shined past me as if in search of assailants following us through the tunnel — "and Anaconda will make it rough for us. I don't know how you feel about it, but getting turned over to their goons doesn't appeal to me."

"Lead on," I said with resignation.

Like tramps on a railroad track, we trudged along the narrow set of rails deeper and deeper into the reaches of the mine. It was hellishly hot; I would not have been surprised to see lava oozing out at us. Every so often, small rocks dribbled down disconcertingly beside us. At last a covey of ore cars, squarish troughs on wheels, showed up in our lamp beams. Here we were, Griff declared with a flourish, at the ledge of ore. Above us the tunnel wall opened into an arched excavation, and he skimmed up the ladder to it, with me gulping and following.

What awaited at the top was a large cave; blasting had hollowed out the far wall of the ledge and left a litter of ore. I clambered in behind Griff, barking my shin in the dark as I did so. "Whoopsie-daisy," he advised absently, "watch your footing." As I stepped over to a rock where I could sit and rub the sore spot, he cautioned: "Let's just sort of hang back and look things over before —"

At that instant I felt a familiar tremble. Not my own, but the kind of glory-hole tremor that shook the boardinghouse every so often; somewhere in the catacombs of copper, dynamite had been routinely set off. I had just started to say to Griff, more than a little nervously, that I supposed I'd better get used to that down here, when half the cavern ceiling caved in, with an avalanche roar and a blinding boil of dust.

Choking on dust and my ears ringing, I staggered a few steps this way and that in the murky cavern. My headlamp barely penetrated the filth, thick as smoke. Desperately I tried to fan away the cloud and find

290

Griff, or what was left of him.

In the gloom, something darker yet appeared, also disturbing the dust. It stopped and I stopped. Through a swirl of murk, Griff and I became visible to each other by the whites of our eyes.

Wiping off a mask of dirt, he said, "That's why it's not a good idea to rush into this kind of place." He squinted around as the dust settled. "Lucky thing is, it was the ceiling toward the back that came down." Turning to say something more to me, he stopped, and very slowly raised a pointing finger. "Morrie," he said quietly, "don't be passing the time of day under a Creeping Pete like that." I looked up, to where he was indicating. Overhanging me was a wicked-looking slab of rock, which, if it dropped on a person, definitely would necessitate the services of the undertaker.

Hurriedly I backed away from beneath it as Griff explained that blasting throughout the mine loosened overhead rock in unpredictable places. Studying this cracked mass, he concluded: "Nasty. We're gonna have to bar it down."

He went over to the tool stash in the corner and fished out what looked like a very long, skinny crowbar. Armed with that, he began to pry at the slab. After many thrusts and grunts, he succeeded in breaking it loose. When it hit the floor of the mine with a deafening crash, he grinned at me. "There's one that won't come down on our heads."

Griff moved on to the next overhang, eyes peeled to find the right crack to insert his bar. I stood back as far as I could, spitting out dust, and watched him jab away at the rock until I noticed he was favoring a hand. Remembering the cramp that had done him in during the drilling contest, I took a deep breath and shuffled over to relieve him of the rod. "Here, let me give it a try."

Poking and prodding as if I were using a lance to find chinks in a dragon's hide, eventually I was rewarded with the fall of a chunk about the size of a gravestone. "See there, we'll make a miner out of you yet," Griff commended from the far corner where he was sitting in apparent contentment.

"Not if I can help it." I fanned away more dust and scanned the ominously uneven surface overhead. Trading back and forth, we pried more chunks down until Griff at last called a halt. "Let's have a listen." He took the bar from me and struck the rock ceiling with it. The timbre was surprisingly musical, a high lingering note that resounded rather sweetly. "There, hear that

nice clean sound? It ought to be safe now."
He tossed the bar aside with satisfaction.
"Now we better get to work."

"Digging, you mean?"

"Nope. Mucking."

I waited, but that seemed to be the entire explanation.

"Griff, really, not only aren't we anywhere in the same pew on any of this, we're not even in the same church. The best thing I can see for us to do is to go back and get on that elevator and —"

"Don't worry none, you'll get the hang of mucking in no time."

That turned out to be true if a person had brains enough to operate a shovel. The loose ore strewn on the floor of the ledge had to be scooped — "mucked out," in Griff's terminology — into those ore cars waiting in the tunnel.

"We might as well get at it. The sooner done, the sooner finished," he philosophized unarguably.

We commenced shoveling. Copper ore proved to be the peacock of rocks, mottled blue and green showing off the mineral wealth within. I was up to my shoetops in the wealth of the Richest Hill on the planet, but in raw lump form. As the task heated up, with Griff tossing two shovelfuls to my every one, he remarked sympathetically:

"It's kind of tough on the muscles at first. Some people can't stay with it."

"I can sweat with the best of them."

"Sweating isn't necessarily the same as hard work, in my experience."

That pricked my pride. "I'll have you know, I am not a total stranger to manual labor."

He eyed me. "Lately?"

There he had a point. As time wore on, I wore down. I thought our amount of copper-bearing rock flung into the ore cars was heroic, but Griff was not inspired by it. He shook his head reminiscently. "Hoop and me could fill an ore car while other guys was standing there thinking about it."

"I'm not the second coming of Hoop," I panted.

Just then a baby-faced flunky stuck his head above the edge of the ledge. "Jared says to tell you," he piped in a high voice, "the shifter is coming through."

The youngster vanished while that was still sinking in on me. "Quick!" Griff rubbed dust on my face, even though I already felt grimy as a coal stoker. "Keep those lily hands of yours out of sight."

We heard the crunch of heavy footsteps, and then the shift foreman came climbing the ladder to us. Our helmet lights dimly lit the chamber as he stepped in. Long-faced and gray-mustached, he had the same miner's stoop as Griffith; they leaned toward each other like apostrophes. "Griff, you old poot. I heard you were on the extra gang — can't stay away, eh?"

"You know how it is, Smitty. It gets in your blood."

I was standing back as far as I could in the shadows. It didn't help. The shift boss cocked an unblinking look in my direction. "Who's this?"

"Hoop's kid," Griff said blandly. "He's trying his hand as a fill-in. Been down on his luck, haven't you, Junior." He confided as if I weren't there: "A little too much of the booze."

The shift boss shook his head. "The company let us know it doesn't want stew bums down here anymore. These aren't the old days, Griff."

Trying to backtrack from his mistake, Griff scuffed at the mine floor. "Aw, Smitty. What am I gonna tell Hoop, that our old buddy from when we was all working in the Neversweat tied a can to his kid? Hardly seems fair, after Hoop told me: 'Make sure to get Junior in at the thirty-hundred level, I don't want him on anybody's shift but

Smitty's. Smitty'll understand, he's had a few under his belt himself, like the time you and me and him were celebrating payday in the Bucket of Blood and —' "

"Don't pour it on," the shift boss managed to stem the tide. He sucked at his mustache as if straining the dubious impression of me through it. "So, Junior, how do you like mining so far?"

"It's a sobering experience."

He grunted, still studying me skeptically. Walking over to the brink of the ledge, he peered down at our loaded ore cars. I held my breath and could see Griff doing the same. With a last doubtful look at us, the shift chief backed around and started descending the ladder. "Keep the rock flying, you two."

We more or less did, although even Griff eased off somewhat now that we had survived inspection. Still, I was sweating so much I felt like a sponge, and every muscle on me was protesting. I was nearly done in by the time a bell signaled somewhere in the distant tunnels.

"Chow time! Here we go." Griff bounded down the ladder and scuttled off, and I followed as best I could.

The route he led me on was as twisty and unpredictable as the wildest of the streets of

Butte somewhere over us. Here, however, the thoroughfares were a mere few yards wide, and all the way there was the encroaching roof of solid rock or splintery timbering barely overhead. People speak of the ends of the earth, places beyond all normal geography: the South Pole, the Amazon, the Sahara. The deep mine was that extreme to me; even though I knew the Hill was as pierced as the catacombs of Rome, the unending tunnels we were trekking through made me feel trapped in a maze. That feeling redoubled when we came to a place where borehole pathways diverged left and right and Griff abruptly halted. "Let me just kind of sort this out a little."

I waited, twitching, while he studied the two choices, fidgeting considerably himself. At last he swayed into motion in one direction, declaring, "The left one's the right one." Was I imagining, or did I hear him mutter to himself, "I think"?

This passage showed no signs of recent mining; the dead air of abandonment was unpleasant to breathe. Except when our boots met rocks on the uneven footing, the silence was absolute. And the going became increasingly narrow; I did not have to put out either arm very far to touch a side of the tunnel. This was what the circle of Hell for claustrophobics must be like. Long minutes passed, and as far as I could tell, we were not getting anywhere except deeper into a labyrinth.

"Griff, are you sure this is the way?"

"Pretty sure. Watch your head on that overhang."

You wonder sometimes where your common sense disappeared to, just when you most needed it. Over and over I asked myself that as I followed Griff toward nowhere. I could not stop remembering the Miners Day drilling contest when his hand had so miserably failed him. My only hope was that the part of his brain which held the instinct of a badger wasn't similarly cramping up.

The tunnel, though, seemed to have no end, and I was frantically wondering whether we had left the Hill behind and were doomed to roam some crevice of the earth where no other human existed. Finally I could contain my doubts no longer.

"I really and truly think we ought to turn back and —"

"Shh. Don't talk so much, Morrie. Let's just have a listen."

We did. Water dripped somewhere. Our own breathing was loud. But faintly, some immeasurable distance ahead, there were voices.

In the beam of my helmet lamp, my guide gave me a silent frogmouth grin. For the life of me, I couldn't tell whether he was as relieved as I was or just being the essential Griff.

We emerged into a musty chamber which had been mucked out and abandoned. A few glowing helmet lamps hanging from spikes driven into the rock walls illuminated this cavern, showing a scene of open lunch buckets and grimy faces as darkened as my own, as though the bunch of us were in vaudeville. Naturally Griff seemed acquainted with everyone in sight. There were a dozen or so of these miners of various persuasions and nationalities, Jared in their middle. The only other one I recognized was Quinlan, who grinned a wolfish welcome. I couldn't care about manners, I was famished. Collapsing onto a convenient rock, I grappled open my lunch bucket and tore into a turkey sandwich Grace had fixed. Jared cleared his throat and announced: "Here's the gent I was telling you about."

After a silence broken only by my munching, someone in the jury-like assembly posed the question prevailing in them all:

"He's the brains?"

Quinlan chortled. "They're running out his ears. He has to stick corks in at bedtime, don't you, Morgan."

Swallowing a major bite of sandwich, I managed to respond: "Mental miracles are in short supply with me at the moment. Music lore, I perhaps can provide as Jared has requested."

A man built like a small haystack stirred from where he was squatting against the inmost side of the cavern. "Why should we fiddle around with music," he demanded of Jared in the declarative accent of Cornwall, "when there's every kind of thing to fight Anaconda about?"

"Tell it to the Wobblies, Jack. I can't get to sleep at night without hearing about pie in the sky. Can you?"

"Thee be right, it's somewhat like a bug in the ear," the Cornishman acknowledged, "but a ditty is just a ditty."

"Ah, but it is much more than that," I was roused in defense of melody and lyric. "A song says something to us that we can't hear in any other way. There is a kind of magic to it. Music does not simply soothe the savage breast, it reaches to our better nature, wouldn't we all agree?"

Not a word nor nod from this uncooperative audience.

"A tune keeps us company," I refined that, "when we need a bit of cheer. We don't whistle just to let air out of ourselves, do we?"

Whistlers in their spare time or not, the entire bunch sat there with lips firmly clamped.

"Or," I tried a different tack, "sing in the church choir merely to show off the starch in our shirts?"

Even Griff was looking stony now, in the frieze of unmoved faces.

Frustration giving way to desperation, I burst out: "How else was the Erie Canal dug but to the chant of workmen who had come from the world over *'to see what they could see / on the Ee-rye-ee'?* Nor would railroads such as the Union Pacific have conquered the continent without the chorus of Irish tracklayers" — a hopeful glance toward Quinlan here — "swinging their sledgehammers to the rhythm of *'No leshure in your day, / no sugar in your tay, / working for the U Pay Railway.'* " By then I was onto my feet. "And I would bet any amount some of you lately marched in the service of your country to the memorable strains of *'You might forget the gas and shell, parlee voo! / You might forget the gas and shell, / but you'll never forget the Mademoiselle, / hinky dinky parlee voo!'* " Head up, chest out, I tramped in place to make the point. Jared's expression said he remembered that anthem of soldiery all too well.

In the dim and shadowed light, expression among my other listeners was mostly limited to brows and eyeballs, and I could see some widened gazes by the time I registered a final ringing *parlee voo!*

After that died away, one of the most grizzled miners spoke up. "All them songs you been reaming our ears out with are for bunchwork, while we're scattered just a few at a time in every mine on the Hill. So what kind of thing are you talking about that would ever fit us?"

"Mmm." Inspiration is hard to produce on demand. "A work song does have to fit the job and its circumstances, you could not be more right," I stalled. "In our instance here, now don't hold me to this as a finished product, but perhaps something along the lines of —" Insidious as ever, the catchy rhythm of "Camptown Races" crept to mind, and in what I like to think of as a passable tenor voice, I improvised:

I'm a miner through and through; you too, you too!

We dig all day and nighttime too, in the
    Muckaroo!

Utter stillness met the finish of my performance. Eyebrows came down like dropping
curtains, and I saw a wince on Griff. "That
was merely one of many possible examples,"
I offered up feebly. Shaking their heads, the
miners began gathering themselves, lunch-
boxes were snapping shut — Jared looked
as defeated as I felt. Any hope for a song for
the union cause was walking out with these
men.

"Wait!" The requisite bar for breaking
treacherous slabs loose lay in a corner.
Grabbing it up, I stepped front and center
in the cavern and struck the ceiling as hard
as I could.

The same high sweet tone that Griff had
produced in our workspot filled the cavern.
Its clarion call halted everyone in mid-
motion.

"There, hear that?" I hurried to capitalize
on the frozen moment: "That sound — let
us call it a musical note, because it has such
a ring — is one you would know anywhere,
any time of day or night, am I correct?" I
noticed both Quinlan and the Cornishman
now looking sharply interested, and other
faces attentive as well. "The point is, the

right kind of song stays in the mind that same way. It's a melodic message that never wears out, in there. And that's what I was endeavoring to tell you about the magic of a work song."

"A work song for us against Anaconda," Quinlan said slowly, the rest of the miners letting him speak for them. "I like that." Off to one side, Griff rocked on his heels as if he knew all along it would come out this way.

Jared jumped in. "We've got Morgan here for brains, we've got over ten thousand voices on this Hill if we just had the right song for them. It's worth a shot, everybody agree?" One by one around the disparate circle of men, heads nodded and *yes, yup,* and *aye* were heard.

"With one understanding," I made sure to have this generally known. "Your response to my first little ditty was indicative. The work song will have to come from you and the men themselves."

"How's that supposed to happen?" a bearded miner demanded. "If any big bunch of us try to get together for it, the cops will be right on us for unlawful assembly."

Jared's gaze of appeal was more than I could turn down. I said:

"Leave that to me."

10

You meet yourself in the mirror one morning and wonder if you know the revealed face in the glass. My reflection, after the night spent three thousand feet beneath the surface of the earth, seemed to mockingly remind me that the head on my shoulders is mostly bone, not brain. What had dropped away from me, due to Jared's tricky scheme hatched down there in the Muckaroo, was the visage of self-confidence, the appearance of a sure-thinking person that had carried me largely unscathed through the world. Now as I blinked dumbly at myself in the light of day, I seemed to be missing the countenance I had always counted on. Although perhaps it was only the absence of my mustache.

By the time I pulled myself together sufficiently, I was late to breakfast. Griffith and Hooper were done with theirs, but lingered at the table to greet me. Hoop hopped up from his chair and shook my hand as if operating a pump handle. "So you're pitching in with the union, Griff says. We knew you came to Butte for some good reason."

"That remains to be seen," I said woodenly.

"Don't worry," said Griff, he and Hoop grinning their ears off. "We'll help out on the work song business. You just tell us when and where."

Off they went to their day's puttering, and Grace emerged from the kitchen with my warmed-over breakfast. Her arched eyebrows expressed all that was needed.

"I know, I know," I responded to what had not been said. "You told me the Hill is a dangerous place."

Shaking her head, she slipped into a chair and passed me the jam for my cold toast. "What an honor for the Faraday Boarding House to have the singing master for the union on the premises," she said apprehensively.

"I am not the —" I gave up and poked at my plate. "Butte has a way of making a person line up on one side or the other, you may have noticed."

"You like to place a bet now and then," she observed, as though I might not have noticed this about myself. "You've just placed a big one."

"It is only a bit of music," I tried to convince us both. "Who is going to be overly bothered by that?"

"Other than the police, the Anaconda goons, and the Wobblies, do you mean?" She crimped a worried frown at me, scratching under an arm. I hoped she was not going to have to reach for the calamine. No, the affliction of the moment was entirely mine, her attitude made clear. "You really have taken on trouble, Morrie, with this. Just where do you think you're going to hold these sing-alongs and no one will notice?"

"Somewhere near the surface of the earth, definitely." I stroked my upper lip nervously. My eyes met hers. That violet gaze cast its spell on me even when she was being severe. "Your honest opinion, please. Should I grow the mustache back or not?"

Grace being Grace, she provided a deeper reckoning than I had asked for. She smiled the old bright way, or at least close to it. "Try life without it, why don't you. Men are lucky, you can change your face overnight. That's not bad for a start."

Hers was a more lenient view of me than Sandison's opinion, which was that I looked like a skinned rabbit.

With that, he dismissed my presence in the office and went back to opening the small bundle on his desk that had come in the day's mail. With practiced flicks of his jackknife, probably learned from skinning cows, he slit open the brown paper. There the treasure lay, the latest from a rare book dealer, swaddled in cotton wrap. Sandison lifted it out tenderly. I could see it was an exquisitely tanned edition of *David Copperfield.* "This does it!" Sandison congratulated himself. "The complete Dickens in leather and gold." Deftly he opened the novel to the sumptuous first page. " *'Whether I shall turn out to be the hero of my own life, or whether that station will be held by anybody else, these pages must show.'* Heh heh. The old scribbler knew his business, wouldn't you say, Morgan?"

He always was in his best mood at such moments, so this was my chance. Hovering at the bulwark of his back, I spoke with forced casualness. "Just so you are apprised, Sandy, there's a new group that will be meeting in the basement."

"What is it now," he drawled without turning around, "some weak-kneed bunch that wants to hold seances?"

"These are not spiritualists, although now

that you mention it, spirit is of interest to them."

"Don't let me die of suspense — what's the name of this pack?"

"I believe it is the, um, Lyre Club."

"Liars?" His shoulders shook as he laughed long and loud. "You slay me, Morgan. The majority of Butte is already a liars' club."

"No, no, you misconstrue. The meaning in this instance is the stringed instrument that accompanied the words of bards. When Homer smote his lyre, he heard men sing by land and sea, remember?" I drew a breath. "To launch this group, I have been asked to be the guest speaker for a series of sessions."

"You're the main attraction? They must be hard up. What are you going to yatter to them about?"

"Versification," I said, honest enough as far as it went.

"Aren't there enough bad poets in the world already?"

"You never know where the next bard will derive from, Sandy."

"If you want to spend your nights making up nursery rhymes, I guess I can't bring you to your senses." He looked around at me as though I had lately lost more than my mustache. "If you ask me, you're going about things all wrong. Why don't you spend your nights sparking Miss Rellis like a red-blooded human being, instead of preaching verse to some bunch of sissies?"

"Actually, she will be on hand at these meetings."

"Oho. Maybe there's hope for you yet, Morgan. Make the most of your Homeric opportunity." Chortling into his beard, he turned back to fondling his latest bound-and-engraved prize.

Rab was lingering near the office doorway when I came out. "Is he going to let you?"

"We have his blessing," I said moodily.

"I knew you'd make things click. Jared will get word to the others and we're in business, presto!"

"I can hardly wait," I said, my mood not at all improved.

"Aha! There you are."

Dora Sandison made it sound as if I had been hiding from her, when in point of fact she was the one lurking like a lioness at a watering hole as I emerged from the lavatory later that morning.

"Everyone is somewhere, nature's way of housekeeping," I responded, skipping back a bit from her overpowering height. "I

310

expect you're in search of your husband, and I believe I just saw him disappear into the mezzanine stacks. May I escort you to —"

"Not at all," she crushed that with a smile. "My evening group has a wee problem that is beneath Sandy's notice."

"I see. How wee would that be, Mrs. Sandison?"

"Simply a book we are in desperate need of," she said airily. Her enunciation of the title lacked only a drum roll: *The Gilbert and Sullivan Musical Treasury, Complete and Illustrated.*

"You're in luck!" I exulted, really meaning that I was. "If I am not mistaken, such a volume already exists at the reference desk."

"That is precisely the point," she said, that sly note coming into her voice. "The book can't leave the Reading Room. But our meetings are held not there but in the auditorium." She fixed me with the look I had come to dread. "A downstairs copy of our own is absolutely essential when major questions arise, such as what costumes the three little girls from school wore in the original Shaftesbury production of *The Mikado.*" Confident that even I could see the justice of that argument, she added, generously: "Storing it would be no problem

311

whatsoever for you. It could fit with the music stands, could it not?"

My mind was whirring with the cost of a fat reference book of that sort, the kind of duplicate expenditure that would send Sandison through the roof. Fortunately, though, there were a lot of Gilberts in the world, and if I slipped merely the author's last name and a reference like *costumery in foreign lands* into the general book budget, chances were our mutual bugaboo wouldn't pay any attention to it.

"Mrs. Sandison, I think I can accommodate you."

"Good. You haven't disappointed me yet." She pursed the smile of one weaned on a pickle, and turned to go.

"Now I have a favor to ask of you," I halted her.

A pause. "And what would that be?"

"A dual favor, actually. I need to squeeze a new group into the meetings calendar. So, I would like your group to change its meeting night for the next several weeks, and to amalgamate with another group during that period."

Dora Sandison looked at me as if I had lost my mind.

"Preposterous," she snorted when she had regained enough breath for it. "We could

312

not possibly —"

"The other group," I sped on, "is the Ladies' and Gentlemen's Literary and Social Circle. Your husband rather scoffs at them as junior aesthetes, but just between us, Mrs. Sandison, they would make ideal new adherents to Gilbert and Sullivan. Think of it: maidens and swains, already listening hard for the music that makes a heart go pit-a-pat. You'd be doing them a favor, really."

The sniff of conspiracy had its effect on her. I swear, her nostrils widened a tiny bit with anticipation as she eyed me. "This might work to everyone's benefit, am I to understand? Yours included?"

"Your understanding is pitch-perfect."

She gave me the queen of smiles, as lofty as it was crafty. "You still have not disappointed me." With that, she swept out of the library.

When I got back to the inventorying, Rabrab looked at me curiously and asked where I had been.

"Reinventing the calendar," I said, mopping my brow.

"Good evening, fellow lyrists."

Among the upturned faces as I took center stage in the auditorium only a faithful few showed any appreciation of my greeting. Rab sent back a warm conniving smile, and Jared grinned gamely. In the front row Hoop and Griff looked eager for whatever mischief the night might bring; Quinlan's expression was similarly keen, but with a sardonic edge. Most of the others, union stalwarts coaxed by Jared and his council to represent their neighborhoods, showed curiosity at best, and at worst a variety of misgivings. These hardened miners had sifted into the library basement one by one or in pairs; several had brought their wives, weathered women in dark-dyed dresses usually worn to weddings, wakes, and funerals. Life on the Hill was written in the creased faces staring up at me in my blue serge, and I needed to tap into whatever inspiration I could find, without delay.

"Why the lyre, you may be wondering, as a fitting symbol for our musical quest?" I whirled to the blackboard I had rigged up on Miss Runyon's story-hour tripod and sketched the flowing curves of the instrument, then chalked in the strings. "Poets and singers of ancient Greece took up the lyre to accompany their recitations, wisely enough. It is a civilized instrument that honors a song's words without drowning the intonations out."

"You draw a pretty picture," Quinlan called out, "but come right down to it, Morgan my man, the thing is only a midget harp. How's that going to compete with anything in the Little Red Songbook" — in back of him Jared pained up at those words — "where all you have to do is oil your tonsils a little and bawl out the verse?"

"Just the question I was hoping for, Quin. What the lyre gives us is the word we must strive toward."

There was a waiting silence, which I could tell would not last beyond one more fidget from the audience.

"Lyrical," I pronounced, and drove the matter home. "The lyrics of the work song for the union cause must sing to the heart as well as the mind."

A miner with a bristling mustache objected. "What'd be wrong with a song that just out and out gives Anaconda hell?"

"I believe that already exists." I warbled the first few lines of "The Old Copper Collar" in illustration. "As apt as that may be, it seems to have had no measurable effect on the top floor of the Hennessy Building, do we agree?" Griff looked hurt.

The audience absorbed my performance uncertainly until the Cornish miner from the Muckaroo called out. "Thee speak a

315

good spoke. But what's the first bite of the bun to get this done?"

"Aha! You have just put your tongue to it." I spun to the blackboard and wrote *bun* and *done.* "Rhyme is the mother of song."

That was the overture, musically speaking, in the quest for a battle hymn for the miners of the Hill.

With the union contingent now regularly showing up, a martial set to their jaws and unpredictable stirrings in their throats, I had to enlist Hoop and Griff to direct traffic in and out of the library; it would not do for top-hatted downtowners to come face-to-face with restive Dublin Gulch and Finntown, for example. (I could just imagine Quinlan at close quarters with a library trustee.) No, at all costs I needed to keep the so-called Lyre Club from being brought to Sandison's attention by any complainers. Only too well I remembered how he fumed against "taking sides" when the idled miners sought shelter in the library during the work actions. If he ever divined that the crowd of us in the basement were, shall we say, less than legally assembled to generate a rallying song for the union, all he had to do to be rid of us was to summon the authorities. What other choice would he have?

Jail was only one worry. Authoritative in their own way and answering to their own shadowy purposes, there were always the goons.

But where were they?

Jared reported that the pair of them had vanished from the mine gate, replaced by uniformed guards not so apt to be taunted as scabs and bombarded with rocks in the night. Accordingly, I watched the shadows more sharply on my way home from the library in the dark, but the inky shapes at alley mouths and lightless doorways never once materialized into Eel Eyes and Typhoon Tolliver. Which did not put to rest my sense of apprehension. In broad daylight, I was carrying a beautiful matched set of Shakespeare plays to the antiquarian shop for appraisal when I rounded a corner and nearly bumped into a hulking figure with an upraised club. I jumped back, shielding myself and the works of the Bard against a blow from Typhoon, but it was merely a hod carrier transporting bricks into the building. So, maybe the goons were nowhere to be seen, but to my mind that didn't mean they were not, as the one called Roland had said of me, up to something.

My imagination kept asking: Up to what?

"Do me a favor, please, Rab," I felt compelled to ask, when I was sure we would not be overheard in the book stacks as we tackled Tennyson, Thoreau, and Tolstoy. "Just as a hypothetical exercise, mind you, find out from Jared how much granite it takes to withstand dynamite."

"Mr. Morgan, since when are you such a scaredy-cat?" she scolded. She clucked as if I were one of her more dismaying schoolboys. "Besides, I already checked. The walls of the basement auditorium are three feet thick."

"Rhythm." I turned to the next session of miners and wives sitting immobile as birds on a wire while I paced the stage. "The ebb and rise of sounds, the heartbeat that gives life to the alphabet."

I paused, which never hurts in building up drama.

"In other words, the vital pattern within each line of a verse. Art imitates nature in this, for we live amid natural rhythms, don't we? For instance, the *pit-pat, pit-pat* of rain," I clapped gently in time with that.

Climatology evidently did not stir this audience. Not even Hoop and Griff in the front row responded with more than stifled yawns.

"Or," I resorted to, "let us take the example of oceanic sound, the anticipatory *swish* of the tide coming in" — I illustrated with my elbows out and my hands sweeping grandly to my chest — "and the conclusive *hiss* of it going out," my arms spreading wide to imaginary watery horizons.

High tide did not seem to register in Butte. Clearing my throat as though the problem of communication might be there in the windpipe, I tried once more:

"In strictly musical terms, a song can attain a distinctive rhythm with repetition of certain syllables or sets of sounds. An example, please, anyone?"

I had not encountered that many mute faces since trying to explain the Pythagorean theorem in the Marias Coulee schoolroom.

Walking a circle on the stage as if surrounding the problem, I thought out loud for the benefit of the passive gathering:

"I assume many of you have children at home? A show of hands, please."

A good proportion of the audience admitted to parenthood.

"And all of us here are former children, am I correct?"

An unsettled chuckle went around the room.

"Therefore, let us approach this matter from that younger time. We are fortunate to have with us someone who, I happen to know, excelled in schoolyard serenade. Miss Rellis? Would you come up, please, and demonstrate?"

Rab colored prettily. Beside her, Jared tried to look as though he was not present during this. "You're too kind, Mr. Morgan," she made a show of demurring, "I'm badly out of practice."

"One never forgets one's specialty. Recess was never complete without it, I have reason to believe."

"Ooh, that. Do you really want me to?"

"Desperately."

"You asked for it, then."

Rab sprang from her seat and paraded up onto the stage. As I had counted on, she showed the admirable zeal of a schoolgirl, but of more interest to this mostly male audience, also the chest and legs of a Ziegfeld chorine. She proceeded to deliver the playground song in a voice as pretty as she was, her hands instinctively hoisting the hem of her dress a trifle at just the right words:

Two little lovebirds sitting in a tree,
K-I-S-S-I-N-G!
First comes love!
Then comes marriage!
Then comes a baby in a baby carriage!
That's not all! That's not it!
Now there's another before they quit!
That's not it! That's not all!
Now comes twins, Peter and Paul!

I had no more trouble explaining the vital nature of rhythm.

Hectic nights or not, the library went about its daytime business at its own whirligig pace. Rab and I were kept hopping to finish the inventory before she went back to teaching in a few weeks, and on top of that was my never-ending round of chores devised by Sandison. Reaching the end of a typically crammed week, I was somewhat behind in tabulating the most popular books of the past seven days and typing up the list for the *Daily Post,* and still was slaving away at the checkout slips when I heard footsteps approaching the office at a near trot. Why, just once in his life, couldn't the courier be less than prompt? Glancing up to say something of the sort, I discovered the speed demon coming in the door was not Skinner, but an even skinnier messenger.

"He's busy running bets on some fight," Russian Famine explained nonchalantly. "Said it don't take any brains to do this kind of thing."

"Nice to see you, Famine. Make yourself comfortable," I pointed him to a chair, "I'll be a little while yet at this."

Making himself comfortable was the opposite of sitting still, as I should have known. After a bit of trying to put up with his fidgets, I suggested he work off that energy on the back staircase and I'd meet him there. Bouncing up to go, he spun into the doorway and collided with Sandison's belly. The boy gawked up the slope of body, gasped out a strangled " 'Scuse me," and darted into the hallway.

Sandison stared after him. "What the hell now, do you have us taking in orphans?"

"You have just met our current messenger to the *Daily Post,* Sandy. Butte's version of winged Mercury."

"If he was any scrawnier, he'd be transparent. Where's he off to?"

"Oh, just out among the books. Fam— Wladislaw is interested in higher learning."

Only barely assuaged, Sandison steamed on into the room, took charge of his chair, and wheeled it around to face me. Lately he seemed even more testy than usual. "Something's not quite right around here, and for once I don't just mean the library. You've got ears like a donkey when it comes to what's going on in this town. Catch me up."

I hesitated. Saying anything about the rising resolve of the miners' union might brush too close to the fact of the sessions in the basement. I chose to concentrate on the Wobblies and recited the gossip about the arrival of phantom operatives to poach membership from the miners' union.

"Outsiders," Sandison pronounced flatly. "They're always trouble." With that, he heaved himself out of the chair and marched over to the stained-glass window to broodily peer out as if watching for trouble to come.

Russian Famine was flying up the top steps when I went to the back staircase with the book list for him to deliver to the newspaper office. For a minute I stood watching, not daring to interrupt the dizzying ballet on the stairs. As before, the scissor-thin legs flashed up the steps three and almost four at a time, then straddled the banister and rode gravity *zip-zip-zip* to the bottom. Reluctantly I called to him after one of these precipitous rides, and, shaking his thatch of hair as if coming awake, he trotted over to me.

"Has anyone ever told you, my young friend, you give new meaning to the word *restless?*"

"Huh-uh. You're the only one who talks that way."

I thought it best to walk him out of the building, lest he run into Sandison again. While we made our way through the standing ranks of books Rab and I had tallied, the turn of season was on my mind, with her impending departure back to the classroom, and, as adults always foolishly do, I asked Famine if he was ready for school to start.

The boy put on a long face. "Flunked is what I shoulda done. Hung on in Miss Rellis's class. Now I'll get some old biddy for a teacher." He sent me a sideward look, his eyes as quick as the rest of him. "I maybe won't be going to school too much longer anyway. Skinner says I'm in luck, the Hennessy bunch has its eye on me when they do any more hiring."

That knifed through me. So much for my bright idea of having posted him to the almighty top floor, just for the summer, to watch for any message of a certain sort dispatched by the goons; true to its nature,

Anaconda was ready to swallow him up.

"What does your uncle think?" I asked, afraid I knew the answer.

"He says it's up to me." Famine scuffed along, head down. "I don't much want to, but a kid has got to eat."

So, things flew at me like that during those days; and the hours after work the fledgling lyricists of the Lyre Club were steadily ready to consume. "You're quite a night owl again," Grace waylaid me as I was about to hustle back to the library one of these times.

My spirits instantly shot upward. How good to have her popping out of the kitchen to trade small talk as she used to. "These evenings, though," I responded in relief, "everyone involved is healthy enough not to require a casket."

"That's not bad —"

"— for a start, yes, yes, you needn't remind me." That drew nothing more from Grace; she just hovered in the hallway. The recent distance between us had shrunk to within reach. I chanced hopefully: "If you're feeling daring, would you like to come with me tonight?"

She shook her head, but still made no move to let me by.

"Hoop and Griff, bless their incurably

Welsh souls, have taken practically a proprietary interest in the song sessions," I gabbed to break the silence.

Grace pinched her lip, restricting her response to a careful "Mm-hmm." I waited, willing her to find whatever words she needed to put us back on the good terms of Miners Day.

Finally she wound her hands in her apron and said:

"Rent day was three days ago, Morrie."

Deflated, I paid up and exited into the night.

At my second home, the library, once more the miners and wives and Rab and Jared and Hoop and Griff and I filed into the basement without the whole passel of us being hauled off for unlawful assembly. It was a critical night: by dint of my tugging and hauling, we had reached melody, in the steps of song construction. However, I was making scant progress by standing on the stage and humming famous melodies as illustration, and in frustration I bemoaned the auditorium's lack of any means of musical accompaniment.

To my surprise, that put life in my audience. For once, there was unanimity in the knowing grins of everyone but me, even

Jared and Rab.

It was left to the Cornishman to ask:

"Has thee not heard of the Butte Stradivarius?"

"I confess I have not."

"Thee shall have that remedied."

The concertina, rapidly fetched and in Cornish hands, could produce any melody I could think of, and plenty more. The wheezebox, as I came to think of it, my point that a good tune was essential to a good song.

"That completes the three parts of musical invention," I announced exultantly as the last wheezy strains of "Camptown Races" wafted away into the plaster foliage atop the auditorium walls.

"Rhyme, rhythm," I smacked my fist into my hand with each word, "and melody. Keep those in mind and the Hill and its union shall sing a work song to rival that of the angels in their airy labors." (Or, in my mind and Jared's, to challenge that infernally mocking ballad of pie in the sky.)

This was a proud moment, and the craggy miners who had manfully sat through nights of musical instruction now slapped their knees and batted their neighbors on the shoulders and shouted out, "Good job, Professor!"

I took a modest bow. "I have done my utmost, and now it is up to you. Appropriately enough, creating the right song will take work, don't think it won't," I exhorted further. "Inspiration most often follows perspiration. Now, then," I advanced to the lip of the stage and made a beckoning gesture to the group, "what ideas do I hear for that song?"

Discord ensued.

The Finns wanted something grand and sonorous, in the manner of a saga.

The Cornish wanted something brisk.

The Irish wanted something rollicking that would tear the hide off Anaconda.

The Welsh, who legitimately had music in their blood, were outnumbered and outshouted by the others, as usual in history.

The Serbs wanted something that dripped blood.

What the Italians wanted was not clear, but it was nowhere close to what the other nationalities had in mind.

Standing up there trying to referee the musical wrangle, I wondered what it took to get committed to a mental institution in Montana.

At last Jared dutifully climbed onto the

stage beside me and in his best top-sergeant manner managed to institute some order.

"This is a start," he took command of the chaos in an unarguable style Napoleon might have admired. "There are a few differences of opinion, but talk those over with each other, with your shift partners and anybody who can carry a tune, all right? We'll sort out what's promising and what isn't, next time. After that, we'll get the union delegates from each shift at every mine together, and settle on the best song." Without breaking his cadence of being in charge he asked over his shoulder: "How many people does this place hold, Professor?"

"Hmm? Perhaps two hundred. But you can't —"

"It'll be the damnedest thing they ever heard on the top floor of the Hennessy Building," Jared vowed with a fist, "our song when we get it. Folks will sing it in this town as long as there's a chunk of copper left in the Hill." He clapped his hands, once, sharply. "Now let's go home and get to working on the work song, everybody."

As the group dispersed, I stood by numbly, still jolted by Jared's fervent promise to assemble two hundred miners here in a library space where they were not supposed to assemble at all. Knowing perfectly well that if I asked him, "How?" the reply was going to be, "Professor, I leave that to you."

Quinlan passed by me with a troublesome grin, humming to himself. That tune at least was unmistakable. *"Same song, second verse. / Could get better, but it's gonna get worse."*

When I closed up the library, Rab and Jared were waiting for me down on the steps. "Come with us to the Purity for pie," he invited, direct even when he was being pleasant. "I'll even buy."

I joined them, and the sound of our footsteps was our only company on the lamplit streets. Of course Rab had a dozen enthusiasms about what the sought-after song should be like, and Jared winnowed those in his wry fashion. I contributed what I could, although my head was a swirl. A crowd of a couple hundred, to get past the police, the goons, and, perhaps most consequential, Samuel Sandison, without attracting attention? My mind went back and forth over this, which simply dug the problem in deeper. My mood was not helped when we passed the *Daily Post* building and I saw that even the so-called autumn classic, the World

Series, was jinxed this wayward year; the scoreboard being set up for the forthcoming games announced the Chicago White Sox — Skinner would crow to me unmercifully — versus the Cincinnati Red Stockings, as purists knew the team that sports pages habitually shrunk to the Redlegs or Reds. The Anklet Series, I thought of it with disgust. Where were the teams with good sound contentious names, Cubs, Tigers, Pirates? When even baseball starts to go downhill, I grieved, there's no telling what will follow.

My brooding spell was broken by Jared as we neared the cafeteria. He tugged at his short ear as he did when thinking hard, and Rab attentively shut up. Looking around to make sure we couldn't be overheard, he said in a voice low but firm:

"Just so you know, Professor. The Hill might have to go on strike, maybe pretty damn quick."

I hoped his wording was a slip of the tongue. "Another work action, you mean."

"That's the farthest thing from what he means, Mr. Morgan," said Rab.

"She's right as usual," Jared acknowledged, giving her a wink. He was all seriousness as he turned to me again. "We've negotiated until we're blue in the face, and

331

Anaconda still won't meet us halfway on anything that counts. Worse than that, those of us on the council have a hunch the company is getting ready to cut the dollar off the wage again. If that happens," his tone became even more resolved, "we won't have any choice. The union will either have to curl up and die or call a strike." In the streetlight there outside the cafeteria, I saw Jared square his shoulders as he looked up at the lights of the Hill and listened for a moment to the drivewheel sound of the mines at work. In another battle, of another sort, he must have sized up Dead Man's Hill similarly before the attack up the slope. Now he shifted his gaze to the slumbering city around us. "It's always tough on the town, to shut everything down," he said solemnly. "But Butte has been through strikes before. They're part of life here. Everybody understands it's our only way to fight back against Anaconda."

"Jared, I must know," another apprehension creeping up on me, "how quick is pretty damn quick?"

"After the next payday, more than likely. Doesn't leave you any too much time, does it."

I blanched. That soon? To come up with the union song necessary to rally his forces?

From an aggregate of miners who didn't agree on anything musically except the sublime charm of the concertina?

Jared nodded as if reading my mind. "I know it'll take some doing. But we'll need all the ammunition we can get when the strike comes." He touched my shoulder. "The song counts for a lot, Professor. I want it in the head of every miner on the Hill, to hold us together."

"Inspiration follows perspiration, you did say, Mr. Morgan," Rab contributed all too helpfully.

At least one thing stayed the same in the Butte night: the owner of the Purity with a glad cry ushered us in to serve ourselves.

Thus, there was everything but library business on my mind during business hours at the library the following day. Which may explain the next thing to happen. My thoughts elsewhere, I was on my way between one chore and another in a rear hallway when a shadow not my own loomed on the wall beside me. In a fit of panic, I whirled and put my back against the wall, digging with both hands for my brass defenders.

"Famine!" I exhaled with relief. "You surprised me a little."

333

"Didn't mean to spook you." He handed me an envelope. "Told me you wanted to see anything with Shycago on it."

I glanced at the Chicago postmark and the kind of chill that supposedly occurs when some creature of the night treads across one's gravesite came over me.

"Have yourself some ice cream," I rewarded my trustworthy messenger with enough money for a vat of it, "and then come back." He vanished in leaps and bounds, and I trotted downstairs to the auditorium. The Theosophists' electric tea kettle steamed the envelope open quite nicely.

Two pieces of paper shook out, dire as loaded dice.

"There's goods to be got on anybody, sucker." Eel Eyes' parting shot resounded in me like a cannonade as I examined the sheets one by one. You should never underestimate even the most thickheaded adversary. The goons had been a lot more determined to get something on me than I imagined. Who knew how many underworlds they'd had to try, but they hit pay dirt in a certain den of high rollers beside Lake Michigan. What I was holding was a print of the photograph from Miners Day, Grace and myself frozen-faced as missionaries with the splendor of Columbia Gardens around us. My head was circled in red crayon like a target.

The letter that came with was even worse.

"Photo you sent is positive identification: real name Morgan Llewellyn. Capture him and deliver him to us. We have an old score to settle."

There was more, but that told the story. The Chicago gambling mob did not forgive; it never even forgot. Like hounds stirred from sleep by an old hunting scent, the betting sharpies were roused all over again about Casper's last fight and our winnings, and I had to act fast.

Reflex and logic agreed on the same piece of advice: take the next train out of town. Put all possible distance between the contents of the envelope and myself. But that left Grace, literally in the picture next to me, and in for nasty interrogation by Eel Eyes and Typhoon if I wasn't available. Besides, if I fled now I would be leaving other loose ends flapping in this Butte chapter of life, and that would bother me for the rest of my days.

With the troublesome pieces of paper tucked inside my suitcoat, I made my way upstairs to the mezzanine, thinking as hard as it is possible to think. Rab had gone out with an armload of books for appraisal by the antiquarian dealer; that helped. And further luck: Sandison was down there in the Reading Room, trying to deal with Miss Runyon, highly indignant over something, and would have his hands full for a while. My path was clear, and indicatively it led through an aisle of fiction. Passing through the ranks of Twain and Defoe and the others as I slipped into the office, I was in the company of those who best knew that a greater truth can sometimes be told by making things up. And those wise old heads did not even have my magic kit to work with, the typewriter and fountain pen.

I had two envelopes waiting for Famine to deliver when he scampered back. In the one from Chicago, the goons now were informed in nice fresh typing with a copied signature that, alas, this was a case of mistaken identity, no one back there had ever laid eyes on the nobodies in the photo. In the one to go into the mail to Chicago, the gambling mob was notified that, regrettably, its message had arrived too late, the miscreant Morgan Llewellyn had vanished from Butte.

"You look sunny this morning," Grace observed.

As I sat down to breakfast that next day, it was all I could do not to reach over and pat her on the dimpled cheek in celebration of our mutual survival. "A sound night's sleep does wonders," I restricted myself to. She herself looked refreshed by something, taking time off from the kitchen to sit and sip coffee until Hoop and Griff appeared. I still was only a boarder and she still was the landlady, but when Grace wasn't having to doctor herself against her own nerves, she also was a very attractive companion at the table. Right now, with her freshly braided hair a coil of gold, she resembled the sunshiny maiden on the lid of tinned shortbread. The sovereign maiden in charge of all such tinned goods, that is. While I was in the midst of such thoughts, she gave me, in the words of the poet, a brightening glance, and I smiled gamely back. Maybe this was only a mild degree of thaw between us, but it improved the climate. She watched me expectantly as I settled into eating. "Well, have you noticed?"

Whatever it was, it hadn't caught my attention yet; certainly the cold toast was the same as ever.

"The house, Morrie," she prompted, "the house!"

"Ah." I scanned around. "New curtains?"

"All right, you," she said in mock exasperation — at least I hoped it was mock. "There hasn't been any dynamiting for days and days, has there?" She knocked on wood, but her smile was triumphant. "I was curious," she continued in a confiding tone, "so I had Arthur's old partner in the mines look into it for me. And guess what? The shaft under here is played out and Anaconda has had to seal it off. You can quit worrying about sleeping in a glory hole," she teased.

Little did she know that the Chicago watery version had just passed me by. "Grace, that's nice news," I could say unreservedly. "Butte would not be the same without the Faraday Boarding House."

Bouncing up when she heard Hoop and Griff on the stairs, she went off to fry their breakfast.

The two of them came in grinning, grinned at each other, then grinned at me some more as they sat at the table.

"We been thinking," said Hoop as if it was something new.

"You've got yourself a lulu of a problem, slipping a couple hundred people into the library the night the song gets voted on," Griff said as if that fact might have escaped me.

"Wouldn't be the first time the cops broke

up a meeting and arrested everybody in sight," Hoop went on, tucking in his napkin.

"Righto," Griff confirmed, spooning sugar into his coffee. "So we figure what you need, Morrie, is an *eisteddfod.*"

I did not want to say that something pronounced *eye-steth-vod* stumped me as much as if he had been speaking mumbojumbo. But it did.

"Perhaps you could elaborate on that just a bit, Griff."

"Glad to. Like everybody knows, an *eisteddfod* is when the finest singers and the greatest bards in Wales gather from the hills and the valleys and every mine pit from Caernarvon to Caerphilly" — he swept a knobby hand around like an impresario — "and try to outdo one another."

"Kind of a jollification," Hoop put in. "Like Miners Day that just don't stop."

With that, my tablemates sat back and slurped coffee, magnanimously ready for all due praise.

"I see," I coughed out. "Actually, I don't. The Welsh miners are the only ones who would have any idea what an *eye — eisteddfod* is, and they're just a handful among the song bunch. Everyone else — ?" I spread my hands.

Griff squinted at me. "You're a little slow

on the uptake today, Morrie. Everyone else *outside* of the song bunch, after we clue those in."

"Nobody is gonna go near the thing," Hoop expanded on that, "who don't know the lingo."

Thinking back to the Welsh minister and the tongue-tying eternity of *tragwyddoldeb,* I couldn't argue with that.

Somewhat against my better judgment, I tested the matter out loud.

"Such as the public at large and the police, you mean." Both wrinkled heads bobbed at my response, gratified that I was catching up. My tablemates now took turns expanding on why an indecipherable event that would unobtrusively slip a couple of hundred people into the basement of the Butte Public Library was such a surefire idea.

Grace came from the kitchen with a plate in each hand, stopping short at Griff's grand culmination:

"Hoop and me can handle the whole proceedings for you, don't worry none."

I had not really started to, until he said that.

It was like trying to rein in runaway horses, but I managed to make the pair promise to contain their eisteddfod enthusiasm until I could test the notion on Jared. Meanwhile, I was late and had to bolt for the library. People were out and about in unusual numbers, I couldn't help but notice, all heading down toward the railroad tracks where a sizable crowd had already gathered. I presumed another political figure was arriving to make a speech off the back of a train; but President Wilson himself would not be a shield against Sandison's displeasure if I weren't in the head count of staff before he opened the library.

Too late. When I got there, everyone had gone in but Rab, who was practically dancing with impatience as I hastened up the steps.

"Mr. Morgan, you came from that direction," she spoke so fast it was nearly all one word, "did you see it?"

This was not my day, linguistically. "Do you suppose, Rab, you could take a deep breath and define *it* for me?"

She was as disappointed in me as Hooper and Griffith had been. "Oh, here." Whisking over to a stack of newly delivered *Daily Post*s beside the doorway, she handed me one with fresh ink practically oozing from the EXTRA! atop the front page.

Beneath that, the even larger headline:

And below that, a jolting photograph of the railroad overpass where the IWW organizer had been lynched a few years before. From the middle of the trestle girders dangled a hangman's noose. Attached to the rope was a sign readable even in the grainy newsprint reproduction:

THE MONTANA NECKTIE
YOU ONLY WEAR IT ONCE
WOBS AND OTHER
TROUBLEMAKERS —
LEAVE TOWN BEFORE THIS FITS YOU

Digesting this, I had mixed reactions. Plainly the goons, stymied about me after Chicago was no help, had broadened their approach to include any other strangers in the vicinity of the Hill; when you are a target, I have to say, you do appreciate having that kind of attention shared around. On the other hand, a noose just down the street from where you lay your head at night is still too close for comfort.

"Jared says the police are taking their sweet time about removing it," Rab confided over my shoulder, again as fast as words could follow one another, "so Anaconda gets to scare everybody."

"We have to let Jared handle that," I stated, "while we have to get inside and handle books or face the wrath of our employer."

Her mischievous laugh surprised me. "We wouldn't want that, heaven knows."

Dispatching Rab to take out her ardor on the book collection, I had to tend to a few office matters before joining her. If I was in luck, Sandison would be out on one of his prowls of the building. But, no. There he sat, stormy as thunder. Before I could utter any excuse for being late, he flapped the *Post*'s front page at me. "Did you see this damn thing?"

"By this hour of the day, I believe everyone in the city has seen either the newspaper or the actual piece of rope, Sandy."

"This town," he said in a tone that it hurt to hear. "It just can't resist having dirty laundry out in the open. Hell, anyone knows outsiders are asking for it, that's where rope law comes from." Saying that, he took another furious look at the front page photograph, his gaze so hot I thought the paper might singe.

"The 'Montana necktie,' " he ground out the words, "what's the sense of dragging that up?" He started to say something more, but instead crushed the newspaper in the vise of his hands and thrust it into the wastebasket.

I stood there, gaping at the outburst, until his glare shifted to me. "Don't you have anything to do but stand there with your face hanging out?"

I left in a hurry. The calm ranks of the books on the mezzanine were particularly welcome after that. Was there any way in this world to predict the actions of their combustible collector?

Hearing me come, Rab spun from the shelf where she had been flicking open covers to look for the SSS bookplates. "This is the day, you know."

From my experience, that could be said about every twenty-four hours in Butte. But I did know what she meant.

"The sixth grade is about to meet its match," I said with a smile. Tomorrow was the start of school and the teaching year of Miss Rellis, as she had to turn into. I was going to miss Rab's company and the noble ranks of the inventory. Reaching to the shelf nearest her, I asked: "Ready?" She nodded. Into her waiting arms I stacked the plump volumes of *Thérèse Raquin, Nana, Germinal,* and on top the slim, elegant masterpiece *J'accuse;* Zola, the end of the inventory alphabet.

"The ones we've been looking for," she joked a little sadly as we went to the sorting room to tally these treasures in with the rest.

"Maybe the full inventory will improve Sandison's disposition," I thought out loud. "The commotion about the noose seems to offend his civic sensibilities."

The mischievous laugh again. "Quit being funny, Mr. Morgan."

"Rab, really, you are not being fair to our employer." For whatever reason, I felt tender toward Sandison in his upset mood. "I grant you he has a bit of a temper, but we shouldn't judge him entirely on that. It is a truth as old as humankind that the presence of a shortcoming in a person does not preclude the existence of other worthier attributes in that same — Why are you looking at me like that?"

Rab had the magpie gleam of possessing the hidden morsel. "Don't you know who Sam Sandison is? He's the Strangler."

11

Rabrab's words went directly to my windpipe.

When I recovered enough air to speak, it was little more than a squeak. "Rab, you might have said so before now. Are you telling me the man I share an office with goes around throttling people?"

"Not that he was ever caught at it himself," she said, as if explaining etiquette to a child. "He had mugs who worked for him do the dirty work. 'Necktie makers,' they were called. Vigilantes." She looked at me closely. "You know: types who hang first and ask questions later."

"I grasp the terminology," I fumbled out. "What I am uninformed about is who my employer has had strangled, and why?"

"Cattle rustlers," she answered both of those. "Or anybody who looked like one, to those cowboys of his." Rabrab calculated with the aplomb of a hanging judge herself.

"Plenty of them had it coming, probably. But some might have been small operators whose herds some Triple S cows and calves just got mixed in with. You know the saying about a rope" — she looked at me as if I likely did not — "one size fits all."

"But —" Still stunned, I tried to reconcile the two Samuel Sandisons, the one who petted rare books as if they were living things and the other who used lethal means without thinking twice. "How can a, a vigilante be permitted to run a public institution such as this?"

"Oh, I suppose people think those old hangings were a long time ago," Rab reasoned. "After all, Butte is where a lot of people get over their past. Mr. Morgan, are you feeling all right?"

"The start of a headache," I replied, truthfully enough. It was scarcely twenty-four hours since I had wriggled free from the grasp of the goons and the Chicago betting mob, and now I found out my library refuge was in the grip of a hangman. Whose method of tapping the library payroll budget to accumulate literary treasures in his own name was known only to me. This was an unhealthy turn of events, to say the least.

"MORGAN!"

I nearly jumped out of my hide, but managed to face around to the white-maned figure looming at the end of the aisle of bookshelves. Sandison looked as if he had grown even more enormous since I saw him minutes before.

"Drag your carcass to the office," he bawled out, turning away, "I want to talk to you."

Rab bade me off by wrinkling her nose prettily. "He really is something, isn't he."

I went in, determined not to tremble. I suppose the blindfolded man facing a firing squad tries that, too. At the other end of the office, Sandison's black suit was the darkest kind of outline against the stained-glass window jeweled with colors. He swung around to face me, saying nothing, sizing me up. Between us, on his desk, lay the smoothed-out newspaper with the emphatic photograph of the noose.

"Sandy?" I gambled, not for the first time, by taking the initiative. "I believe you wanted to see me about some minor matter?"

He grunted and advanced toward me as if he needed a closer look. The gleam in his eye seemed diamond-sharp. "You're an odd duck, Morgan," he declared, halting an uncomfortably short distance from me, "but you're cultured, I have to hand you that. You damn well mean it when you jabber about the music of men's lives, don't you."

A weird hope sprang up in me. Maybe he had discovered I was flouting his orders against "taking sides" by letting the miners congregate in the basement in search of a song and was merely going to fire me. I would take that instead of a death sentence any day.

"Anyhow," he immediately brushed aside that hope, "we can talk about that tomorrow. You're coming with me in the morning."

"Where to?" I asked over the thump of my heart.

The white whiskers aimed at me. "A place you ought to see. Section 37."

Was that a joke from Samuel Sandison? If so, it was his first. I cleared my throat, to try to speak without a quaver.

"Perhaps, Sandy, you could elaborate a bit on that destina—"

Somewhere within the whisker cloud he snorted. "What's the matter, sissy, coming down with a case of *Hic sunt dracones?*"

I had to bridle at that. A measure of caution about traveling in the company of someone nicknamed the Strangler did not equate me with skittish mariners of old who feared sailing off the edge of the map into the abyss that carried the warning *Here be dragons.*

"That's hardly fair, I am only naturally curious as to —"

Sandison didn't pause over my hurt feelings. "Never mind." He briefly stared at me again with that strange gleam. "Don't tell anyone we're going, eh? Tongues are already too busy in this town." Turning back impatiently to the newspaper spread on his desk, he told me to meet him at the depot, good and sharp, for the six a.m. westbound train.

There was a midnight train. Eastbound.

Why not be on it? the ceiling posed the question, a certain seam in the plaster straight as a railtrack as I lay fully clothed on my bed. I was as alone as ever in this latest dilemma. At supper, Hoop and Griff had been as animated as carnival pitchmen, while Grace put actual cutlets on the table in evident celebration of the boarding-house's new lease on life. No one seemed to pay particular attention to my unmoored state of mind; when that happens, it makes you wonder about your normal mien.

The bed was crowded with debate. Sandison was a latent noose-wielding unpredictable madman. Or not. He'd had the perfectly sound sense to hire me, I tried telling myself. Just to be on the safe side, though, pack the satchel for the train; saying a permanent goodbye to Butte would be only a strategic withdrawal, after all. But so was Napoleon's retreat from Moscow.

My head now really did ache from going back and forth. I checked my pocket watch again. Midnight was not far off. Abruptly my mind made itself up, almost as if I had not participated. I scrambled off the bed.

Quietly as I could, I opened the door of my room and tiptoed into the hall. Snores emanated from Griff's room, and Hoop's next to his; at the end of the hall, Grace's bedroom kept a silence. Feeling like a burglar in the darkened house, I slipped past one door. Then another. And stealthily turned the doorknob of the end one.

I crept to the sleeping form and, hesitating just a bit, shook the bare shoulder where the nightdress had slipped down.

"Grace, I hate to interrupt your slumber. But I must talk to you."

My whisper penetrated as if I had jabbed her. Bolting upright in the bed, she clutched the coverlet around her, huskily reciting: "In the name of decency, Morrie, we really ought not —"

"This is imperative or" — I looked at the ivory slope of shoulder still showing — "I would not come uninvited. Please just listen, Grace."

Vigilantly, she did so while I told her she had to be my witness, to attest that I was alive and in one piece before boarding the train early in the morning with Samuel Sandison. "Just in case worse should come to worst."

"Worse coming to worst, is it." There was just enough light in the room that I could see she had let down her flaxen hair when she went to bed, and now she ran a hand through the long tresses. "Morrie, you are the most complicated boarder there ever was."

"I wish I could dispute that."

"Why do I have the honor of this, why not Griff and Hoop?"

"They've been at a union meeting, and you know the condition they come home in after that."

Grace gave an extended sigh. "All right, you want a sober witness. But why go with Sandison at all?"

"He's the kind who will not let loose of an idea — the man is a bulldog. If I don't humor him on this, he'll do away with my job at the library. Then I won't have charge of the auditorium. Then the eisteddfod can't be held in the — It's, well, complicated."

All that was wordlessly weighed on the landlady scale of things. Then she reached to the bedside table, opened the drawer, and took something out. "Here."

In the dimness of the bedroom, I peered down stupidly at the cold metallic item, with some dull opalescence to it, that she put in the palm of my hand. If I was not mistaken, it was the type of small pearl-handled pistol called a Lady's Special.

"You're — you're armed," I stammered.

"I'm a widow, sleeping alone," she said quietly. "And Butte is a rough and tough place, as you may have noticed." Again she passed a hand through her hair, looking at me as if memorizing me. "That little thing is called an equalizer for a reason, don't forget, Morrie."

I hesitated, then pocketed the gun. "I'm sure I am in better health than when I came in here, thanks to you."

An expectant silence. She patted my hand there in the dark, in a feathery way that was either shy or sly. "I would only be telling the truth if I said you had life in you the last I saw of you, wouldn't I."

An honest enough affidavit, under the circumstances. I returned her caress pat for pat. If I could trust anyone in Butte, it was Grace.

If I could trust anyone in Butte.

"Sandy, how are we to do this?" Stumbling along before dawn in Sandison's wake, I dubiously approached the depot platform. "If I am not mistaken, those are ore cars." The line of heaped railcars stretched off as far as I could see in the dim light.

"Keep walking, don't be a nervous Nellie." Sandison strode along recklessly enough himself that I wished the pair of depot goons would pop around a corner and be steamrollered by him. No such justice, however, at that early hour. Only a yawning conductor, beside what I perceived to be one lone Pullman car behind the train engine, stood in our line of march.

I followed Sandison aboard, feeling tipped to one side by the unaccustomed gun in my coat pocket, even if it was the most decorous of firearms. He and I were the only passengers at that hour. As the train lurched into motion, I could contain the question no longer. "West is a long direction — where exactly do we get off?"

My traveling companion grumpily pawed at his whiskers as if herding the word out.

"Anaconda."

"The company?"

"The town."

It turned out to be both. A company town, Anaconda was as orderly and contained as Butte was sprawling and unruly. The train pulled in past boxy workers' houses lined up in neat rows, along streets laid as straight as shelves. Sandison appeared to pay no heed to the town itself, gazing away into the valley beyond. At least, I thought as I looked out the window on that side of the train, it was a bright clear day for this. I happened to look out the other side, and the sky was clothed in heavy gray.

When the two of us climbed off at the trim crenellated depot, another chess piece of municipal order, the division in the sky over Anaconda was made plain. On a slope above the murky side of town could be seen the immense smelter for copper ore such as had accompanied us from Butte, and dominant over the smelting works stood a sky-scraping smokestack, thickly built and hundreds of feet tall. The scene leapt from every accusatory line ever written about dark satanic mills — the smokestack like the devil's forefinger, black fume trailing evilly as it pointed its challenge to heaven.

Dumbstruck as I was by this sight, only

slowly did I register the other product of the smelter besides copper and smoke, a series of slag heaps surrounding the town like barren hills.

"That's Anaconda for you," Sandison growled. "Let's get a move on." So saying, he stalked off toward a livery stable across the tracks.

Now I was alarmed. A saddle horse is not my preferred mode of transportation. Of necessity, I had spent some time on horseback during my prairie teaching career, but no more than I had to. Sandison brayed to the stableman that we wanted genuine riding stock, not nags, and shortly I found myself holding the reins of a restless black horse with a bald face, named Midnight. When a rangy steel-gray steed was brought out for Sandison, he looked in disgust at the stirrups on the rented saddle and lengthened them six inches to account for his height. That done, despite his bulk he swung up onto the horse as easily as a boy and waited impatiently for me to hoist onto mine.

"Going to be a blisterer out in the valley. Here." He tossed me a canvas water bag to tie to my saddle and spurred his horse into motion, leaving Midnight and me to catch up.

We managed to do so at the edge of town, past one last ugly dark slag heap where children ran up and down. With the cries of their playing fading behind us, the horse-back pair of us cantered into another existence entirely, a sudden savannah-like landscape that seemed to exhale in relief at leaving the pall of Anaconda behind.

The valley extending before us was a classic oval of geography, broad and perfect as a French painting. Rimmed by mountains substantial enough to shoulder snow year-round, the valley floor was uninterrupted except for a few distant settlements strung out near a willowed river like memory beads on a thong. Gazing wide-eyed at the breadth of landscape — truly, here a person was a fleck on the sea of ground — I said something about this startling amount of open country so near the industrial confines of Butte and Anaconda.

Unexpectedly Sandison reined to a halt, and I pulled up beside him. He massively shifted in his saddle to turn in my direction. "Take a good look, Morgan. I owned it all."

At first I thought he meant the plot of land we were riding across. Then I realized he meant the entire valley.

I cannot forget that moment. Picture it if you will. A woolsack of a man, surely two hundred and fifty pounds, nearly twice of me, sitting on his horse, looking down on me like a wild-bearded mad king.

Suddenly he raised a meaty hand and swiped it toward me, his action so swift I had no time to grab for the pistol.

Paralyzed, I felt the swish of air as the thick palm passed my face and descended to mash a horsefly on the neck of my mount.

Flicking away the fly carcass, he rumbled, "Don't just sit there with your face hanging out, we've got a ways to go."

He put his horse into a trot, and mine followed suit. I rode holding tightly to the reins and my Stetson. In Montana, it is a good idea to keep your hat on your head so the wind doesn't blow your hair off. Besides, it gave me something to concentrate on, other than the thought that I might have shot a man for swatting a fly. But Sandison's behavior still unnerved me. Keen as a tracker, he stood in his stirrups every so often to peer ahead at the print of ruts we were following; it might once have been a road but looked long unused.

Leading to where? There were wide open spaces around us to all the horizons, but no arithmetic of logic that I could find in the destination Sandison had set for us. I knew from my time among the homesteads of

Marias Coulee that land is surveyed into townships of thirty-six sections, each section a square mile. The numbering starts over at each township. Where, then — and for that matter, *what* — was Section 37? Was I going to survive to find out?

After an eternity of joggling along, we came to a plot of land boxed by a barbwire fence. We — rather, I — opened the treacherously barbed gate, and the horses stepped through, skittish enough about it that they had to be reined hard.

It could be said they were showing horse sense. The ground changed here. The soil, to call it that, had an unhealthy grayish hue, like the pallor of a very sick person. The sudden change was puzzling to me. I did not know thing one about the raising of cattle, but what was beneath our horses' hooves would not pasture any creature, I was quite sure.

My riding companion now simply sat in his saddle, lost in contemplation of the expanse of valley. I resorted to my water bag. The day was warming to an extreme, and I could see sweat running down Sandison's cheeks into his beard, although he paid it no heed.

"Back then," he all at once spoke in the voice of a man possessed, "this was a paradise of grass. And I bought up homestead claims and mining claims and every other kind of land until every square foot of it was Triple S range. I tell you, there never was a better ranch nor a prettier one." His words cast a spell. What a picture it made in the mind, the green valley filled with red cattle with that sinuous brand on their hips.

The bearded head swung in my direction. His voice dropped ominously.

"Then it got to be the old story. The snake into Eden." The meaty hand swept around again and, past my ineffectual flinch toward the Lady's Special, pointed over my shoulder.

"That thing."

He had taken dead aim at the smelter stack. Even at this distance, the giant chimney dwarfed all of nature around it, clouding that half of the horizon like a permanent storm. Staring at that ashen plume along with Sandison, I felt something more oppressive creep over me than the heat of the day.

With a great grunt he climbed down from his horse, stooped low, and scooped a handful of dirt. Holding the dull-colored stuff up to me, he uttered:

"Here. Have some arsenic."

Choosing to consider that rhetorical, I

cleared my throat and managed to respond.

"Sandy, am I to understand we are camped on a patch of poison?"

"That's what it comes down to," he said, letting the unhealthy soil sift from his fist. Each word bitter, he recited to me that the furnaces of the smelting process released arsenic and sulphur, and the Anaconda stack piped those into the air like a ceaseless spout.

Wiping his hand on his pantleg, he went on: "It kills cattle like picking them off with a rifle. The first year after the smokestack came in, we lost a thousand head. Hell, it wasn't ranching anymore. All we were doing was burning carcasses." He shook his head violently at the memory. "We sued the mining company every way there is. The Anaconda bunch had the big money for eastern lawyers, so they beat us. But that was later." His voice sharpened again. He gestured as if in dismissal toward the smokestack and its almighty smudge. "That isn't what you're here to see. Let's get to it." With cowboy agility, he again swung onto his horse and headed us toward a grove of trees along a slip of a stream not far ahead. Damp as I was with sweat from the unrelenting sun — and just as relentless, Sandison — I welcomed the notion of shade.

The trees, though, revealed themselves to be leafless as we approached. What had been a thicket was now a stand of lifeless trunks and limbs, graying above the soil that had sickened them. In the midst of the witchy trees stood eight or ten huge old cottonwoods, dying more slowly than the rest.

Sandison dismounted and walked his horse over to the nearest great wrinkled trunk. I gingerly did likewise. Under a big overhanging limb, he turned to me with that unsettling royal glint in his eyes again.

"Welcome to the grove of justice, Morgan."

At first I did not take his meaning.

"It was before copper was on everyone's mind," he began. "This valley was just sitting here, best place on the face of the earth to raise cattle. My backers put up most of the money and I built the herd, cows from here to breakfast. Until one branding time when the count was way off. There weren't dead cows lying around from winterkill or some disease, so you didn't need to be a genius to figure out the malady was rustlers." The fixed intensity of that blue gaze was hypnotic as he told it all. "The money men threw a fit, said if it happened again they'd sell the place out from under me. They were town men, they didn't have a fig of a notion about how you have to let the good years carry you through the bad ones in the livestock business. I had to do something to keep the herd count up or lose the ranch." Trickles of sweat from under his hat into his beard retraced that predicament of long ago. "My riders told me they'd seen some of the squatters up in those hills" — he indicated across the valley to coulees that must have held shanties at that time — "acting funny around our stock. And there were always drifters riding through, you could bet they'd about as soon rustle your cattle as look at them. Try tell that to a sheriff who'd rather sit with his boots up on his desk than chase after rustlers with a couple of days' head start, though." His gaze at me never wavered. "Now, you know what my answer to that was, don't you?"

I was afraid I did. The Montana necktie had a reputation to the far ends of the world, ever since frontier times when vigilantes in the untamed gold camps took the law, along with a noose, into their own hands.

"My riders knew how to handle a rope in more ways than one," he was saying in that voice terrible to hear. "Anybody they caught in the vicinity of a cow or calf with a Triple S brand on it had some hard answering to do." The man who had been lord of this valley turned ponderously, broad back to me now, toward the line of sturdy cottonwoods. "We hung them like butchered meat. Right here." Facing around to me again, he lifted those thick hands. "Many a time I tied the noose myself."

The old saying could not have been more right: my blood ran cold.

Had I gambled wrong, in coming with him to this desolate patch of earth? Was I about to be murdered, for knowing too much? The pistol stayed glued to me where it rode in my pocket; I realized, for once and all, that I could not bring myself to use it. Sandison's stare had my fate in it, but I could not read those icy eyes. I tried to speak and couldn't.

He stared at me that way long moments more, then his words came slowly.

"What gets into a man, Morgan, to set himself up as an executioner? I made those dim-witted rustlers pay far too high a price." He shook his head. "Cows are just cows." Turning from me, he gazed at the gray old trees as if looking a long way back. His shoulders slumped. As I watched, the Earl of Hell was deposed, by himself.

After some moments, I found words.

"Section 37 is off the face of the earth."

"That's where I sent them, on a length of rope," Sandison was speaking huskily. "Now you know why I brought you here, eh?"

I thought so, but said nothing, watching the same shrewd expression come over him as when he found a bargain in a rare books catalogue. "You're a learned man," he said in that husky tone, "you know a little something about how to read a life. But there's always more. I know what they say about me behind my back, but they miss half the story." One more time he shook his head. " 'The music of men's lives' isn't as easy to recognize as the average fool thinks, you were right about that. Back then" — he pointed his beard to the cottonwood grove — "I let the money men call the tune on me and did more than any man should, to hold on to the best ranch in Montana. And then poison came out of the air and I lost the Triple S anyway."

Now he looked hard at me, nodding as if making sure to himself. "It takes a collector to know a collector, even if you do stack your treasures in your head instead of out on a shelf. You'll remember this, fair and square, there's that about you. Not like the ones who only gossip, which is almost everybody." He set his face as if into a prevailing wind. "I goddamn well know I

365

could turn Butte into a city of gold, and still the one thing I'll take with me to my grave is the reputation for stringing people up."

Monumental and weary, Samuel Sandison cast a last glance at the hanging tree, then turned away to where our horses stood. Over his shoulder, he said, as if we were back in the library:

"Add it all to your brainbox, Morgan."

12

Night was coming on, with the streetlights of downtown Butte starting to glow golden and the mines of the Hill already lit like the mineral earth's own constellation, when Sandison and I left the train.

He had said next to nothing during our journey back from Section 37. As ever, the beard masked more than just his jawline. Accordingly, there on the depot platform he turned to me and dispensed the day in the shortest manner possible: "That takes care of that." His boot heels resounded on the planks as he traipsed off, leaving me with the parting sentiment: "Don't be late for work in the morning, it's a bad habit."

I stood there for an extended moment, inhaling the chill air, simply to breathe free.

"*Hsst!* Over here, you!"

My nerves shot back up to high alarm, the threat of goons never absent. Fumbling for the pistol in my side pocket, I stopped when I got a full look at the figure speeding toward me from the depot waiting room. "Grace!"

In a sensible woolly wrap against the early October night, she still shivered as she drew up to me and stared after the monumental form of Sandison receding into the dusk. "If you hadn't been on this train, I'd have gone to the police yelling bloody murder. Where on earth did that creature haul you off to?"

"It is not exactly on the map."

Setting off together up the sloping street, I recounted the day to her as best I could, on edge as I was, and she listened the same way as we navigated the noisy neighborhood and reached the boardinghouse. The shared time of the previous night was still with us, but so was too much else and we were uncertain and awkward with each other. It didn't help matters that Venus Alley, a mere block away, was filling the night with lusty laughter and more.

Paused at the door of our lodging, I glanced aside at Grace and could only come up with: "Thank you for watching out for me."

"You seem to need it," she replied with a small smile, shyly pocketing the pearl-handled gun I had handed back to her.

"Besides, I hate to lose a boarder."

"You'll have this one again in the morning." I gestured in the general direction of the library. "For now, though, I'm too wound up to go to bed — there's something waiting for me I must tend to."

"Good night, then, Morrie. Don't let the bad dreams bite," she said soberly.

I switched on the mezzanine lights. The Reading Room below was as dark and hushed as the audience portion of a theater. Up onstage, so to speak, the books waited in titled ranks, and in their reassuring company I moved idly along the laden shelves, running the tips of my fingers over the exquisite spines, taking down an old loved volume every so often and opening it to the stored glory of words. Around me was the wealth of minds down through all of recorded time. The dramatic capacities of Shakespeare, as all-seeing in his foolscap scripts as in the sagacious portrait above the doorway to reading. The gallant confabulations of Cervantes, showing us the universal meaning of quixotic. The Russian army of impossible geniuses, Turgenev, Tolstoy, Dostoevsky, Chekhov. Mark Twain, as fresh on the page as a comet inscribing the dark. Robert Louis Stevenson, master of tales goldenly told. (The twofold nature of Dr. Jekyll and Mr. Hyde seemed a lot more convincing after being around Samuel Sandison.) And my ever-familiar exemplar of classic Latin and daring generalship, Caesar, in tanned leather and impeccable threading. These and the hundreds upon hundreds of others Rabrab and I had evaluated, insofar as mortals can, into the inventory. Valued treasures, in more ways than one.

In such company, you wonder about your own tale in the long book of life. What would they have made of me, these grandmasters of storytelling? Arriving out of nowhere to the richest of hills with the intention of filling my pockets from it, and all this time later, finding that the only thing that had paid off was the railroad, for my own trunk. Thrown together for a second time in life with an appealing widow, and for a second time gaining no ground there, either. Casting my lot with an unpredictable bibliophile who also turned out to be Montana's leading vigilante. No matter how I looked at it, my story lacked conclusion.

Suddenly I knew what to do. Can inspiration come off on the fingers? I rubbed my hands together appreciatively, there among the literary classics. It was as if the risk-taking lifetimes of composition, the reckless romances with language, the tricky business of plots stealing onto pages, all the wiles of Samuel Sandison's glorious books answered to my touch. There was no mistaking their message: sometimes you must set sail on the winds of chance.

Stroking a last row of embossed titles as I went, I turned off the mezzanine lights and made my way out of the darkened library. What I was about to attempt was a gamble, but that was nothing new in human experience. The first thing it required was a messenger who was not Russian Famine. I headed directly to the cigar store where Skinner hung out.

Discordant as it was by nature, the song session the next night came as something of a relief after Section 37. At least, up there onstage I did not have to fear for my neck when one rough-hewn miner or another climbed up with me and sang off-key, although my ears were another matter.

The songwriting efforts unveiled at this tryout were all over the map, in more ways than one. The only thing the musical penchants of the neighborhoods of the Hill had in common was strenuous exercise of the vocal cords. As diplomatically as I could, I touched up rhyme and word rhythm here and there, and the concertina tuned things up a little, but in the end the attempted songs were pretty much the same rough creatures as at the start of the evening.

Well, no one in his right mind could expect to turn the basement auditorium of the Butte Public Library into Tin Pan Alley, I had to tell myself afterward. But Jared and Rab and I were a somber trio when we adjourned to the Purity.

"What do you think, Professor," Jared asked directly over pie and coffee, "is the work song we want hiding in any of those?"

"You heard the same performances I did," I sidestepped. "The groups still have almost a week to work on things, perhaps something" — I almost said *miraculous* — "unforgettable will find its way in." We both looked to Rab for a boost in our spirits.

"I'll stick with my sixth-graders," she passed judgment ruthlessly now that she was back to teaching. "They only get into fistfights at recess." At the height of the song session Jared had needed to jump in and separate a Finn and an Italian who came to blows over a question of tempo.

He conceded that was a case of somewhat too much enthusiasm, but maintained strong feelings of that sort could be a good sign. "The men are fired up against Anaconda, and the right song will catch that," he insisted, as if insistence would do the job. I could see what was coming next as he looked over at me: in his checklist way he would want to know how I was going to handle the big night when two hundred people had to materialize in the library basement without anyone noticing. Omitting to say it was the brainstorm of Griff and Hoop, I brightly volunteered that our salvation was an eisteddfod.

Jared turned his unscathed ear toward me as if that would help with the word. "Run that by me again?"

I did so in as much detail as I could think up. The dubious expression on Jared kept growing until Rab, at her conspiratorial best, poked him insistently. "Mr. Morgan has the knack of doing what can't be done," she said, canny as an abbess. "You either have to let him or think up something better, sweetheart."

That decided him. "Well, hell, if none of us can savvy it, maybe the cops and goons can't either." As we rose to go, though, he gave me the Butte salute, a whap on the shoulder, and warned, "Just remember, Professor, plenty of people are going to want your hide if this doesn't work out right."

Out into the night he and Rab went, with me brooding behind, when the bow-tied impresario at the cash register called after me: "Hey, you with the pie in you, don't run off!"

Just the ending the evening needed, I thought to myself balefully, Jared sticking me with the bill.

That proved not to be the case, however. Hopping down from his stool and coming up close to me, the Purity proprietor dropped his usual repartee. "Haven't I seen you with that messenger kid who goes around like his pants are on fire? What is he, your nephew?"

"Second cousin," I answered negotiably; Russian Famine barely had a shirttail, let alone a shirttail relative, but imaginary kinship might be better than none. "Why?"

"I need someone to run errands and so on," he said as if that ought to be perfectly obvious. "Tell the kid he's got a job after school if he wants it. I'll give him a fair wage."

"He needs more than that," I interjected. "His is the, um, lean side of the family line. He very nearly lives hand to mouth."

The cafeteria owner swayed back from

me, frowning. "What are you, his union?" Observing the rules of the game, he hemmed and hawed for a minute before grandly offering: "Oh, all right, I'll throw in his meals, how's that?"

"Allow me." I squared his bow tie for him; tonight's was royal purple. "All he can eat, I trust that means?"

"Sure. How much can that be, a runt like him?"

In the book of life we are chapters in one another's stories, and with Russian Famine given a place at the feast, so to speak, I felt like an author drawing a scene to a successful close. That was only the first episode to be resolved, however, while more than I wanted to count waited in line.

A crisp expectancy was in the air of Butte those next days and nights. The season turned as if October was a signpost for the weather: the first snow, dazzling and spotless, appeared in the mountain heights above Columbia Gardens, while downtown blocks at midday echoed with the loudspeaker version of anklet baseball — *"Flash! The Redlegs win again, they lead the White Sox in the Series three games to two!"* — and in the dusk, fresh war cries whooped from the Hill as boys played football on barren

375

patches between mine heaps. The change in climate could be measured any number of ways. More than once I noticed women and daughters trooping past the boardinghouse with gunnysacks, and I asked Grace about it. "Coal," she said simply. The thought of it pulled the skin tight around her eyes. "They go down to the tracks and pick up what's spilled from the trains. I did it myself when I was a girl and a strike was coming. Anything to get ready for the worst."

I knew the feeling. As a precautionary measure, I resumed my habit of keeping watch into the shadows for the darker presence of goons; Eel Eyes and Typhoon now had no reason to pack me off to Chicago, but if it ever entered their thick heads that I had turned the library into a choir loft of the miners' union, they were bound to be renewed trouble. Nor were they the only concern. In the back of my mind the Welsh minister kept preaching his "unlawful assembly" sermon (*"Butte's finest, to call them that, will pick you off like ripe apples"*). And there was always Sandison. The man had wrung out his soul for me to see, there beneath the hanging tree, but he still was impossible to predict. Which was I going to encounter at the crucial time, the merely gruff city librarian or the Earl of Hell?

When I at last told him, as I had to, that the Lyre Club would be honoring an old bardic tradition by holding an eisteddfod and braced for a volley from him about the library turning into a madhouse, he merely grunted and said, "What's your next field of knowledge, Morgan, druidic chants?"

All the while, Hoop and Griff assured me at every meal that there was nothing to worry about.

Ready or not, the night of nights arrived to us.

"Remember, Professor, when you step out there, this isn't some lilies-of-the-valley crowd. These men have been through everything Anaconda could do to them and they're about to be on strike for hell knows how long. They're not here to fool around. Don't get carried away, just run the songs through and have them vote, savvy?"

"I am not aware that I ever get carried —"

"Oh, don't forget the hat, Mr. Morgan. I stirred the slips of paper around, so when they draw it'll be perfectly fair. Just don't drop it or spill it or —"

"Actually, Rab, I have handled a hat before, thank you very —"

"Another thing. Don't let Quinlan hog the

stage when he gets up to sing whatever his bunch has come up with. This is serious business, not some Irish wake, got that?"

"Jared, I promise I shall muzzle Quin if necessary. Now do you suppose the two of you could possibly give me a minute to get myself ready for this?"

Not that there was any proven way of doing that, given what awaited me out beyond the stage curtain. The buzzing auditorium was filled with men hardened by the copper in their blood, and beside them, doubtful wives brought along for protective coloration. A couple at a time, they had filtered past Hoop and Griff and other Welsh-speaking venerables out there in front of the library acting as doormen beneath the drooping banner that read, like a much magnified eye chart, EISTEDDFOD! Passersby and other curious types asking about it were answered with such a spate of baffling syllables that they went away as if fleeing from banshees. Thus, only the mine families whom Jared counted on to be the heart of the union during the strike made up this gathering. Unanimity stopped at that, however. The neighborhoods were mapped in this restless audience as they were on the Hill: the Finns in sturdy rows, the Irish in a looser, louder group centered on Quinlan, the Cornish in chapel-like conclave, the Serbs and Italians across an aisle from each other as though the Adriatic lapped between them. Perched on tables at the back of the hall, Griff and Hoop and the Welsh cronies were like a rebel tribe grinning madly at the edge of the plantation.

My mind raced, but in a circle. As thronged as the place was, I kept feeling the absence of Grace. When I had gingerly asked if she might be on hand to lend moral support to the three of us from the boardinghouse, she just looked at me as if I had taken leave of common sense. "Morrie, I very nearly broke out in hives when you went off with Sandison, and I can't risk it again. Besides, somebody should be on the outside if the lot of you get locked up, or worse." Wise woman. I took one last peek past the curtain and drew the deepest breath I could. It was time to face the music, in every sense of that saying.

Stepping out to the front of the stage with a music stand in one hand and the hat held upside down in the other, I cleared my throat and spoke into the general hubbub.

"Good evening. Welcome to an evening of magic."

Naturally that brought hoots to pull a rabbit out of that hat. Down in the front row I saw Jared cover his face with his hand, while Rab mouthed something like *The songs, get to the songs!*

"Ah, but there are more kinds of magic than the furry sort that a stage conjuror plucks up by the ears," I said, carefully setting the hat aside so as not to spill the slips of paper. "The more lasting sort is not really visible. And that is the variety we hope to produce tonight. Something that will sing on and on in us like a fondest memory."

"It better be a doozy, mister," a skeptic in the middle of the crowd yelled out, "to beat what the Wobs have got."

"I take it you refer to that celestial pastry, 'pie in the sky,' " I replied, more cordially than I felt. "You are quite right, that is indeed a clever musical couplet. Yet it is not on the same footing with the classic musical compositions your fellow miners are striving to emulate here."

"Like what?" came back like a shot.

That snared me. A couple of hundred unconvinced faces were waiting for my response, which had better not be a stuttering one.

The lesson of the old tale-tellers whispered itself again: sometimes you must set sail on the wind of chance. I whipped off my suitcoat and tossed it over the music stand.

Rabrab nudged Jared forcefully, recognizing the signs in me. I stepped to the lip of the stage, snapping my sleeve garters like a sideshow barker. "You leave me no choice," I announced, "this is the kind of thing I mean." In music-hall style, I shuffled some soft-shoe and twanged out at the top of my voice:

In a cavern, in a canyon,
Excavating for a mine,
Dwelt a miner, a Forty-niner,
And his daughter Clementine.

As catchy as any song ever written, that ditty caught up this audience to the fullest extent, a roomful of voices lustily joining in with me by the end. After raucous applause and my brief bow, I slipped into my suitcoat again and stepped back in favor of the song contestants. "Just as darling Clementine is unforgettable to us all," I told the readied crowd, "now we shall choose the song that works a similar wonder for the union." Or not. I hoped with everything in me that the efforts of the neighborhoods had improved spectacularly since the last Lyre Club session. There was one way to find out. "The representatives will now come up to draw for order of presentation, please."

The burly half dozen of them crowded around me as I held out the hat with the numbered slips in it. Quin winked at me; the others were as serious as novitiates into some mystical ritual. At my signal, work-callused hands dipped into the hat crown and drew out.

"It be we!" The man at my left happily brandished the slip with a big penciled "1" on it, while the other five studied their lesser positions.

"The luck of the Cornish has prevailed," I announced. "Our Centerville friends will sing first." I retired to the side of the stage, the concertina made its pneumatic presence known, and the song competition was under way.

It was a contest, I realized with a sinking feeling, in which the participants felt bound by no particular rules but their own.

The miners from Cornwall in their practical manner sang from a standard recipe: a verse about the iniquities of the mine owners, then a verse about the travails of working in the mines, followed by a verse about the toll on miners' families, capped by a verse about standing solidly together and defeating the villainous mining overlords.

The Irish entry, as rendered by Quinlan, sounded suspiciously like a borrowing from a drinking song.

The Welsh nomination was so grave and bass in register that only the Welsh could sing it.

And so on down the line. By the time Finntown and the Italian contingent from Meaderville had been heard from, I had to generate a good deal more gusto in my remarks than I really felt. The plainly mandatory smile on Jared and Rab's overenthusiastic clapping told me they had reached the same conclusion; even Hoop and Griff looked a little worried. One by one and all in all, the songs were at that level which causes a person to say, "Oh well, it could have been worse." Which always implies that it could have been much better.

The audience members were muttering among themselves, not a good sign, when I reclaimed center stage after the last song.

"There we have it" — I swung my arms as if pumping enthusiasm into the room — "somewhere among those is the anthem that will carry the union to victory. Now, Jared, if you would come up and conduct the vote, and I'll do the tallying."

As Jared was getting to his feet, I searched through my coat pockets for the tally sheet I had tucked away. When I looked up again, something like a shock wave from the audience met me. A roomwide gulp might be the closest description. Whatever had materialized in back of me, it had caused two hundred people to swallow their Adam's apples and Jared to angle his arms out to protect Rab.

With a sense of doom, I turned around expecting to be face-to-face with Eel Eyes, Typhoon, or some walrus-mustached policeman.

It was worse than that. It was Sandison.

An Aztec god could not have loomed any more ominously than that massive white-bearded figure. For a long, long moment, he just stood there, looking stonily around at the crowd as if counting up the total of trespassers to be dealt with. His sudden appearance from the back of the stage changed the equilibrium of the room, tilted the will in us all. There were men here who had done things beyond reckoning in the mineshaft or on the battlefield, but none with the reputation of having sent other men off the face of the earth with their bare hands.

As for me, I wanted to dissolve into the floorboards.

The crowd began to stir, with Quinlan and other hard-faced miners looking around for the best route to fight their way out through the police, the Anaconda goons, whatever phalanx of enforcement the lord of the library had brought with him.

"Sit down, nitwits," Sandison thundered at them.

They sat.

He caught sight of Rab in the front row and gave her a gaze that said what a pity it was she was associated with riffraff like us. Inevitable as fate, his attention shifted to me.

"Stay where you are, Morgan, you've caused enough trouble." Now he scowled at the silent audience. "Who's the head fool here?"

Jared drew himself up. "I happen to be president of the mineworkers' union, and we've been having a social evening of musical —"

" 'Social,' my hind leg," Sandison overrode him. "A person would have to be deaf not to know that you and your gussied-up inside accomplice" — that initial adjective I found unfair; I was merely wearing my blue serge suit with a dove-gray vest added — "are using the Butte Public Library for a purpose the powers that be say is against the law."

I must say, he summarized the situation beyond dispute. Standing nervously on one foot and then the other as he glowered around, I wished I was elsewhere, such as Tasmania. From the sound of it, the audience was witnessing more of a show than it had anticipated; someone now shouted out from the back in jittery defiance, "Are you going to string us up, or what?"

Shaking his head and beard at Jared and me in turn, Sandison said, with final disgust, "Let's get this over with." He lumbered to the very edge of the stage and thrust a sheet of paper in Jared's face.

Handling it as if it were the warrant that would put the whole crowd of us away, Jared scanned the single page. Then studied it with more deliberation. He sent Sandison a measuring look. Strangely, he had that fixed gleam toward the next objective when he passed the sheet up to me. "Better do what the man wants, Professor. We'll sit tight until you get done."

Apprehensively I read the piece of paper. I saw why Jared had done so twice. Once for the handprinted words, then for the dotted lines of musical notes.

"I shall need help," I announced at once; this was too important for me to flub alone. "Quin, would you come up, please?" Next I singled out the Cornish leader: "And Jack? And, mmm, Griff?"

With no great willingness they joined me

386

onstage and we huddled around the music sheet. The Cornishman's eyebrows drew down in concentration, while Quinlan's lifted as if liking what he saw. Griff ceremoniously cleared his throat. At my signal, the concertina wheezed a note for us. Somewhat ragged at first, our impromptu quartet gained harmony as we sang.

Drill, drill, drill,
That's the music of the Hill.
The Richest Hill on Earth
We work for all it's worth.

Those who mine are all one race,
Born and bred 'neath a tunnel brace;
Down there deep we're all one kind,
All one blood, all of one mind.
I back you and you back me.
All one song in unity.
Drill, drill, drill,
That's the music of the Hill . . .

It was homely, it was distinctly old-fashioned, it was not particularly profound, but most of all, it was infectious. You could jig to it, march to it, swing a pick and chip out ore to it, hum it, whistle it, sing it in your sleep — it was as catchy as "Camptown Races," what more can I say? The atmosphere in the auditorium changed for the better with every line we sang of that lucky combination of unifying words and bouncy tune, Sandison's song working its magic like the proverbial charm. When we were done, the audience came out of its reverent spell and jumped to its feet, clapping and cheering.

Leaping to the stage, Jared seized the moment, raising his arms for attention. "Are we agreed? 'The Song of the Hill,' is it?" Unanimity answered him.

Afterward, as Hoop and Griff and the cronies craftily discharged people into the street in imitation of whatever an eisteddfod is like when it winds down, I tended to last things, such as chairs, with Jared helping. At the back of the auditorium Rab was in one-way conversation with Sandison, enthusing about the evening's outcome while he stood there like a totem.

"Well done, Professor." Grinning keenly, Jared gave me credit I was not sure I entirely deserved. "It's a dandy," he was saying of the song. "It'll help pull us through any strike. The Wobs can't outsing us anymore. They can keep their pie in the sky, we've got hold of the Hill in one sweet damn tune. And the Anaconda bosses will hear it in their sleep before we're done. They might bend us, but they can't break us now," he vowed. He stopped to whack my shoulder in appreciation.

Buoyant with relief, I admitted: "Now I can tell you, I half-expected that pair of goons and forty others to burst in on us tonight."

He tugged his ear thoughtfully. "I guess you haven't heard. Butte has seen the last of those two."

Stunned, I visualized the two of them meeting the fate that had been hinted at for me, at the bottom of a glory hole.

I must have gasped, because Jared lifted his hands in clean denial. "None of it was our doing, and they're still among the living. The word is" — I understood he was alluding to gossip on the Hill — "the Wobblies were pretty badly annoyed about that noose and decided to return the hint. So, when the goons went to turn in the other night, there was a dynamite fuse on each pillow and a note saying next time it would be the dynamite." He grinned in admiration of a maneuver neatly done. "The last anyone saw, the pair of them were piling onto a train with their suitcases."

Alas, then, for Eel Eyes and Typhoon, their part in the story flickered out as Rab surged over to us. "See? I knew the two of you could bring this off." She linked arms with Jared and invited triumphantly, "Come celebrate with us at the Purity, Mr. Morgan."

"You'll manage nicely without me. I have one last thing to do here."

I waved them on their way, and as they went out, Jared did an about-face in the doorway and snapped me a salute, while Rabrab blew me a kiss.

When the auditorium was cleared, I took a final look around and went upstairs in search of Sandison.

His desk lamp was on, an open catalogue of rare books in the pool of light, but the big chair was empty.

When Samuel Sandison was in a room, however, you could feel it. Over at the window, the stained glass muted in the darkness, he was peering steadily at the Hill through a whorl peephole. With the starry host of night lights at the mines, it was a rare Butte quietude to remember. Hearing me come in, he glanced in my direction and away again. "What are you doing here? You know we don't pay overtime."

"I came to say what a wonder 'The Song of the Hill' is, Sandy. Written with a pen of iron and the point of a diamond."

Sandison grunted.

"And cleverly adapted," I said the rest to his back, "from when the unheralded pastoral poet Jonathan Cartwright put it to paper as 'The Song of the Mill' a century ago."

He stood deathly still, long enough that my heartbeats grew loud in my ears. At last the slope-shaped man swung around to me, the dim light making it hard to read the face that had taken other men off the earth. *Clomp, clomp,* the boots advanced toward me, the beard and summit of hair growing whiter as the lord of the library came looming into the lamplight. Just when I began to fear for my neck, he stopped short, an arm-length away. "Morgan," he sighed heavily, "you're the only one in Butte who's enough of an educated fool to know that. Sit down, nuisance."

Relieved, I took to my chair while Sandison squashed into his. "All right, just between us, I helped myself to old Cartwright's work where it seemed to fit."

I could not resist: "Rustled it, might one say?"

Another gusty sigh. "That's fair, I suppose. Who the hell ever knows what you end up doing in this life?" He rested his folded hands on his belly. "Anyhow, Dora touched

391

up the tune a little," he blandly shared the credit and guilt. "She's musical, you know."

"How did you know about the songwriting sessions?"

"Hah. Don't you savvy anything yet about running an outfit? First rule is to keep track of what's going on in the bunkhouse."

"You sided with the union."

He brushed away virtue, redemption, whatever it was, with a rough hand. "Anybody who puts a hornet up Anaconda's nose, I'm with."

"If I may say so, Sandy, you've given the miners one of those anthems authored into the mind beyond forgetting."

"They'll need it, won't they."

For a minute we sat in silence, in tribute to the workers' battle ahead for a fair share of the yield of the Hill. Sandison stirred before I could. Gruff as a grindstone, at least trying to be, he appraised me. "You didn't come by just to say nighty-night. Am I going to see that milk face of yours from now on?"

"I fear you won't, Sandy. I have another chore to tend to, and the library is best left out of it." Goodbye was not easy to say, no matter how I tried to dress it. "I must draw my wages and — what is the ranch phrase? — ride the grub line for a while."

Sandison frowned sadly and reached for the cashbox. "Now I'll have to hire a pack of flunkies to do whatever you've been doing."

We both stood, and shook hands the way people do when they know it is for the last time. "One good thing about you, Morgan," he looked down his beard at me. "You don't stick around long enough for a person to get sick of you."

For the next matter I needed the satchel, which I had brought with me and stowed in the sorting room. A full moon carpeted the library steps with silver as I departed the citadel of books, and there was a promise of frost in the air. Butte slept as much as it ever does. The main activity in the downtown streets was out front of the *Daily Post* building, where the night janitor was dismantling the scoreboard, and I tipped my hat to it as I strode by. Like everything else, baseball was over with the passing of its season.

A few blocks farther on, I turned in at the well-lit cigar store. The regulars telling stories at the counter fell silent and met me with stares, all except the messenger, Skinner, who jerked his head toward the back room.

When we were alone there, Skinner jittered from one foot to the other in agitation. "How'd you know?" he asked sourly. "The World Series stinks. The Sox should of won."

"Rightly or wrongly, Cincinnati did," I chided. With the kindness that can be afforded from picking a winner, I elaborated: "Use your noggin. If you were any of the White Sox being paid Maxwell Street wages, would you play your heart out for Cheap Charlie Comiskey?"

"It beats me," he surrendered, and got down to business. "Like I told you, we had to lay your bet off with the big-city boys to cover it. The bookies back east in Chicago ain't happy with this, but we pay off honest in Butte."

"I was counting on that." I opened the satchel. Sorrowfully, Skinner began dumping in the bundles of cash.

Grace was waiting up.

"I heard." Apronless there in the dining room, she nonetheless appeared to be laboring over something. She tried a smile that she couldn't make stick. "Hoop and Griff came home to spruce up before they spend the night celebrating in a speakeasy. They went out of here singing the thing at the

394

top of their lungs."

"The union has its work song," I concurred, "and its work cut out for it, as always." I halted near one end of the dining table as she had stopped at the other. From her eyes, I could tell that a question was tugging hard at her. "What is it, Grace? You seem on edge."

The catch in her breath audible, she made a flustered motion in my direction. "I wasn't sure you would be back. I don't know why, I just had a feeling — I peeked in your room and saw your satchel was gone."

"I needed it for an errand." Setting the satchel on the table, I opened it as wide as it would go. "Come and see."

Bringing her quizzical expression, she looked inside, and looked again.

"Morrie," she gasped, "did you hold up a bank?"

"Not at all. An honest wager on a sporting event paid off."

Before she could tell me again what she thought of betting, I hastened to add: "It was very nearly a sure thing." Still, it seemed only fair to give myself a bit of credit. "Although perhaps not everyone would have recognized it as the kind of chance that comes along only once in a lifetime." History soon enough confirmed me in that, as several White Sox players were found to have been bribed and made miscues that let the Red Stockings win. So much for the 1919 Anklet Series.

Unable to resist, Grace peeked into the satchel for the third time. "There's an absolute fortune in there!"

"Mmm, an adequate fortune, I'd call it."

"I'm still in the dark." She gestured helplessly at the trove on the table. "To win this much, didn't you have to put up a whopping stake? Where did you get that?"

Her eyes widened with every word as I told her.

"You" — she had trouble finding her voice — "you bet the library books?"

"Sandison's, let us say." I explained that the inventory with the accompanying assessment made a highly impressive asset, and Butte bookies had seen stranger things put up as a stake. "They don't ask too many questions."

Grace still fumbled for adequate words.

"But — then — what if you had lost?"

"Ah, that. Sandison would have told the gamblers in no uncertain terms the books belonged to him and not some minor functionary of the library, I felt quite certain."

With an incredulous laugh Grace sank

into a chair at the table and sat looking up at me as if I had grown wings. "You're rich. How does that feel?"

"Better than most other choices," honesty compelled me to say. I gestured to the satchel. "There's enough to go around. Take what's needed to put the boardinghouse on easy street, why don't you. And the union strike fund will get a share. So will a certain pair of young lovers, as a wedding gift. Then another sum for them to help Russian Famine along in life and keep the copper collar off him." I knew myself well enough to admit: "As for the rest, I'll see how fast it wrinkles."

I paused. The time had come. Sitting down across from Grace, I reached over and took her hand, patting it as she so recently had caressed mine before I set forth with Sam Sandison to Section 37. "There is a complicating circumstance, unhappily." If I knew anything in this world, it was that the Chicago gambling mob was going to be angrily curious about the major betting loss in some outpost of the Rockies. So it had to be said, and pats of the hand did not really soften it: "I must move on."

A goodbye to a good woman costs a piece of the soul, and having already paid once when I departed from Rose in that earlier time, not much was left in me after I spoke this one. The old feeling of leaving love behind came back like a terrible ache; pernicious bachelorhood was no joking matter. With regret I watched Grace's face, so near and yet so far, for the effect of my news. I hoped she was not going to cry, because that affliction is catching. But there was a glisten as her eyes met mine. Her chin came up an inch in the Butte way, and I was bracing myself for a landlady-like farewell when she uttered instead:

"Morrie? I've never seen any of the world except Butte. I — I want to go with you."

Something like a galvanic shock went through me. Could I have heard right? Her tremulous look took the question away. Mutely I gestured to the two vacant spots at the table.

Those she took care of with boarding-house dispatch. "Griff and Hoop could scrape by on their own. They pretty much run the place anyway."

Still wordless, I touched a finger to skin.

"No sign of hives whatsoever," she reported bravely, "yet."

"Ah," I recovered my voice. "This is most serious, Grace. We must examine this matter before we do anything rash. Let us say you board the train with me tomorrow —"

She nodded tensely.

"— in full sight of this town and everyone you have ever known —"

She could not help sending a lip-biting glance toward the wedding photograph of Arthur Faraday, on duty at the sideboard.

"— in which case," I finished, "we should perhaps do it as man and wife."

Grace blinked.

"Or, if you prefer," I spread my hands in offer, "woman and husband."

My proposal took full effect. She covered her mouth with her hand as if a hiccup wanted out. When the hand came away, there was a rosy glow of anticipation on her face, dimple and all. "You mean it?"

"I do. As you shall hear me repeat at an altar, if you so wish."

"Grace *Morgan?*" she tested out with a lilt very close to music. "I'll need to make a clean start on the name."

I gave her a smile that went back to the beginning before this one. "You wouldn't be the first."

ACKNOWLEDGMENTS

My imagined Butte and its Richest Hill and Morrie's beloved library could not have taken shape in these pages without the unflinching help of librarians in the right places: Rich Aarstad, Ellie Arguimbau, Karen Bjork, Jodie Foley, Lory Morrow, Barbara Pepper-Rotness, Brian Shovers, and Zoe Ann Stoltz of the Montana Historical Society; Anne M. Mattioli and Christine Call of the Butte–Silver Bow Public Library; and Sandra Kroupa, Rare Book Curator of the University of Washington Libraries. My heartfelt thanks to them all.

I'm similarly indebted to the cadre of talented souls who vitally aided in one way or another in the making of this book: Liz Darhansoff, Charles Hulin, Marshall J. Nelson, Becky Saletan, Elaine Trevorrow, Marcella Walter, Mark Wyman; and Carol Doig, this lucky thirteenth time.

ABOUT THE AUTHOR

Ivan Doig was born in Montana and has worked as a ranch hand, newspaperman, and magazine editor. The author of twelve previous books, including the bestselling novel *The Whistling Season* and classic memoir *This House of Sky,* he has been a National Book Award finalist and has received the Wallace Stegner Award and a Distinguished Achievement Award from the Western Literature Association, among other honors. He lives in Seattle.

The employees of Thorndike Press hope you have enjoyed this Large Print book. All our Thorndike, Wheeler, and Kennebec Large Print titles are designed for easy reading, and all our books are made to last. Other Thorndike Press Large Print books are available at your library, through selected bookstores, or directly from us.

For information about titles, please call:
(800) 223-1244

or visit our Web site at:
http://gale.cengage.com/thorndike

To share your comments, please write:
Publisher
Thorndike Press
295 Kennedy Memorial Drive
Waterville, ME 04901